TURN A BLIND EYE

BILLY PARKS BURTON

This is a work of fiction, inspired by real events. While certain elements may reflect actual occurrences, all characters, names, and specific details are either products of the author's imagination or have been fictionalized for dramatic purposes. The situations, incidents, and dialogue are entirely fictional and are not intended to depict actual events or to change the entirely fictional nature of the work. In all other respects, any resemblance to actual persons, living or dead, events, or locales is entirely coincidental.

Cover design by Scott Stortz
Page design by Eric Butler

ISBN 978-1-964530-12-3

Published by Butler Books
www.butlerbooks.com

Beginning in grade school, James Gordon "Jim" Bantly, James Leland "Sonny" Ward, and Ronald Davis "Ronnie" Hallmark became my lifelong friends in every sense of the term. I lost all three in rapid succession. But while their passing creates a void that cannot be filled, I am left with warm recollections of their companionship, loyalty, support, counsel, and humor, which enriched my life immeasurably. This book is dedicated to the memory of our friendship.

PROLOGUE

Moisture hung heavy in the night air, and the sky was black as the depths of a cave. The darkness seemed to block even sound; shapes and shadows were indistinct. He was sitting in the front seat of his '37 Dodge, leaning against the door on the driver's side, feet extended across the front seat, smoking a cigarette, and waiting for payday. Tonight would be his best score ever. Tonight would make it all worthwhile.

His vehicle was backed deep into the woods, among scrub oak and black walnut trees, 50 yards from the nearest evidence of civilization, completely obscured by thicket and underbrush. As was his design, he could see anyone or anything approaching from the front, but he couldn't be seen. He had a clear field of vision of the spot he was watching.

He'd been there almost an hour, occasionally taking a long pull on the half-pint of Cabin Still he commonly had in his hip pocket. Because he was about half drunk when he arrived, he really wasn't aware that the man he was waiting on was late. It didn't matter anyway. He had nothing else to do and no place to go. Besides, what he was expecting was well worth the wait. This was the fourth and largest payoff. He wasn't sure how much further he could push it. Off in the distance the diffuse glimmer of a distant river barge's searchlight illuminated the sky intermittently, creating the eerie impression of heat lightning.

He wasn't scared out there, alone at that hour. He had a loaded .38 revolver in the glove compartment and was competent in its use. Hell, he'd used it often enough to intimidate other men. He'd pistol-whipped several guys, and he had a reputation for violent behavior.

Because he'd slouched down in his seat and pulled his hat down over his eyes, he didn't see the other man moving through the trees and brush behind the car. The man wore faded denim coveralls, with the sleeves torn off at the shoulder. He had on a sweat-stained fedora, the brim mostly obscuring his face. His pant legs were shoved down inside a pair of muddy galoshes, unbuckled almost all the way and flared open like the collar of a navy pea coat. There was no wind rustling the large leaves of the catalpa trees.

To keep the inside buckles from becoming entangled, the man walked slightly spraddle-legged. That didn't impede his gait any more than the hat hid his identity. The intruder was well over six feet tall with huge arms and shoulders. His girth strained the fabric of the one-piece garment. His hands were big, thick, and calloused, and they hung casually at his sides. But for his size, his appearance wasn't all that distinguishable from many working men in the area. But two things were generally uncommon: This man wore brass knuckles on his left hand and his right hand clutched a two-foot length of galvanized pipe.

As he approached, he slipped the pipe under his left arm and yanked open the driver's side door with his right.

"What the hell!" The occupant bolted upright in his seat. "What're you doing here? You better get on out of here, I'm expecting someone."

PROLOGUE

"He ain't coming!" the big man said, yanking the occupant from his car and standing him against the rear fender in one effortless motion. His prey tried to protest, but—mercifully—the big man hit him with the pipe so fast and so hard, the victim knew nothing else of the savage beating he was about to receive. The birds and creatures of the night held their breath. There was the sharp crack of a limb breaking in the distance.

When the big man finished administering the retribution he'd come to deliver, he shoved the bloody, brutalized body back onto the front seat of the car and closed the door. He walked past the front of the old building, under the faded wooden sign that declared *Scuffletown Post Office.* He continued out through the trees and down over the bank past rotting deadfall, to the river. Though it was only about three o'clock, the oppressive heat of that early summer morning clung to his face like a steamy barber towel. The odor of dead and decaying organic matter rose from the river. Mosquitoes swarmed and insects buzzed—the beginning of another sultry summer day on a forlorn stretch of western Kentucky's river bottoms.

‡

Scuffletown Bottoms had once been a town. Now it was just a loosely defined area, rarely represented on local maps. Founded in 1800, it got its name from the flatboat people coming down the Ohio River. The Cherokee played stick ball and had wrestling matches right outside the tavern, also used as a trading post. White settlers called it scuffling.

CHAPTER 1

Club 41 was like all of the other bars in town: dim lighting, neon beer sign, hanging cigarette smoke, slot machines around the walls, and more serious gambling pursuits in a different room. A solo female performer was singing *Buttons and Bows* to piano accompaniment. The bartender, his apron tied high and tight under his armpits, set another beer in front of me as I finished my fried chicken.

He extended his hand. "I'm Fred. Don't believe I've seen you in here before." His face was friendly, and his handshake was firm.

"Hoyt Cole, work at the newspaper."

"Nice to meet you."

The smell of fried food drifted from the kitchen, behind the bar. A swinging door with Bommer hinges and a glass porthole allowed servers to move easily between the kitchen and the main service area. There was a three-by-four-foot opening to the left of the door where written food orders were clipped to a rotating carousel.

I crossed my knife and fork over each other and placed them

on the bones on my plate. I shoved it forward toward the back of the bar surface.

"Lively crowd for a Monday night," said the barkeep. The noisy clatter of tables being bused and plates of food being delivered underscored his observation.

I graduated high school in May of '41, and on the eighth of December, I joined the Marine Corps. I served my entire tour in the South Pacific, discharged in 1946. I returned to my hometown in 1949, after graduating from the University of Kentucky with a journalism degree. It was a time of roadhouses, honkytonks, garter belts, and Chesterfield cigarettes in the rural South, before the interstate highway system connected and homogenized the country.

A border state, Kentucky had seemed uncommitted and uncertain during the Civil War, even though 70 percent of the men in uniform fought for Abe Lincoln and the Union Army. A popular opinion among historians is that Kentucky didn't secede from the Union until after the war was over. This is called the "Lost Cause Syndrome" among Southern sympathizers. Even 85 years after the war's end, the South was still economically devastated and racially segregated. In no small measure, the one contributed to the other. From my earliest memories, Kentucky always seemed to struggle for identity, straddling the social and cultural fences. Geographically too far north to be truly Southern, Kentucky was too culturally and economically aligned with the South to be considered Northern.

Like most of the state in the late '40s, the place where I grew up was in transition economically and socially, and the people were still poor and largely uneducated, living mostly hand to mouth with little or no government-supported social underpinnings. The war had ended, service men were returning, the baby boom was beginning, and the G. I. Bill was available. Although low paying, jobs were becoming more plentiful.

Thomas Wolfe wrote *You Can't Go Home Again*, but I did. After I completed my degree courtesy of the Servicemen's Readjustment Act (the G. I. Bill), Uncle George called to tell me there was a job opening at the local newspaper. It paid $45 a week with a room and breakfast in the Kingdon Hotel thrown in. I had no plans to return home; in fact, I had no plans of any kind. But I had no other prospects, so I took it.

I'd started to question that decision. While there had been gambling when I left, it had become systemic and pervasive while I was away, earning Henderson the name "Little Chicago." Back then I was oblivious, full of high school pursuits and self-interest, leaving such concerns to the adults. After surviving campaigns in the South Pacific on Saipan, Tinian, and other atolls, and serving in the cleanup on Nagasaki after the second bomb was dropped, I'd gotten older, more observant, and more cynical.

After almost a decade's absence, I was able to see the town more objectively. Not unlike most other western Kentucky river towns at the time, it was the county seat of the mostly agricultural economy, where the blue-collar citizenry struggled to push and shove its way from under the long shadow of the Great Depression. American entrepreneur, economist, and business theorist Roger Ward Babson had declared Henderson, Kentucky, the community most impacted by it.

One of the working girls took a stool beside me. Her perfume preceded her into the space. A number of other single men at the bar took notice and eyed her with interest. Heavy mascara and lipstick, exposed cleavage and a tight dress left little doubt about her pursuits, at least on that evening. She made no overt offers or suggestions, just subtle innuendos. "Buy me a drink, honey?"

she asked with a wet-lipped smile and laughing eyes. I signaled to the bartender and he served her whatever watered-down drink she and her sisters of the evening were accustomed to imbibing in the joint.

"You're obviously alone. Are you lonely, is something troubling you? I'm a good listener."

"No . . . I just prefer being alone."

"It's not good to be alone."

Experience had taught her, when prospects are abundant, not to waste time in a lengthy sales presentation. Her come-on smile fell and her flashing eyes grew dull. She wiped the sympathetic and intimate pretense she'd mastered from her face like day-old makeup, grabbed her drink, and slipped off the stool, moving in the direction of one of the other men at the bar.

A large, raw-boned man came in and walked casually around the place, engaged by many as he meandered around. He snagged a beer and continued his stroll. I measured him at close to six feet tall and weighing upwards of 230 pounds. His hair was thinning, and closely cropped. He might have been 40.

After a quick trip to the men's room, I returned to my drink and cigarette, left burning in an ashtray on the bar. I saw that the big man had taken the stool the girl had recently vacated. His elbows claimed more than his allotted space, but I ignored it, ordered another beer, and let the night settle in.

Without looking at me he spoke straight ahead. "You new around here, ain't ye?"

"I was raised here, but been gone awhile. Came back about a year ago."

"Nice enough place, just as it is, don't you think?"

I'd begun to question the gambling and corruption, and as my inquiries became more probing, I began to experience serious pushback. I turned to look at the side of his face. He had long sideburns and a double chin. "You trying to tell me something mister? Spit it out!"

He turned to face me and said with a smirk, "Well . . . I *am* a kinda messenger, I guess you might say. Most people here 'bouts like things the way they are. I consider it my duty to warn newcomers about pushing to change things. Challenging the status quo, so to speak."

He nodded for another beer and lit a cigarette. He kept his elbows spread wide on the bar top, attempting to exaggerate his bulk, I suppose. From time to time he'd turn toward me, taking my measure or trying to intimidate me. Realizing he wasn't going to provoke me, he rose to leave. Standing slightly behind me and to the left he leaned in and snarled, "Watch your back, pal!"

"Thanks for the warning," I said. I knew that wasn't the end of it. He wasn't the type to be satisfied with verbal banter, particularly when he came up empty.

I ordered a cup of black coffee and smoked another cigarette. I wanted him to have time to anticipate what he was going to do, create a little apprehension in him. Half an hour later, I paid my tab and left from the rear entrance, where I'd parked my truck. Out over the river, silent lightning flashed and the moon hung white in the night sky. Closer, crickets chirped and the clamor of various night creatures created a low cacophony of sound. Ominous-looking clouds floated in and a dust-filled wind blew across the gravel. Eddies of dried leaves swirled in the night air.

As I approached my truck, near the back of the lot, I heard the crunch of footfalls on the rocky surface. He was thick through the middle with large forearms, exposed by his rolled-up sleeves. He seemed to imagine that his size and demeanor were intimidating, giving him an exaggerated sense of confidence and self-importance.

His first move was to shove me, trying to slam me against my truck. I guess he figured a little rough treatment would be all he'd need to make his point. I saw his reflection in my window and timed his lunge. Sticking both arms out, I pushed off against my truck and swung around to face him, causing him to rush forward and stumble into the fender.

A little surprised, he tried to recover, rushed and awkward. He squared himself around as if the misstep never occurred. Marshaling as much boldness as he could, he said, "Some men learn by being told, others have to be shown."

"You're out of your league, ole buddy."

"You think so?" He telegraphed a roundhouse haymaker toward my head. Guys like him are brawlers, big and clumsy, relying on their size and past successes. His experience had taught him most men don't want to fight. He probably counted on that to give him all the advantage he needed. His size, weight, and power would do the rest.

The Marine Corps recruiter made no claims about education or learning a trade. A marine is trained to kill, be it with a gun, a bayonet, or bare hands. I didn't have to move my head more than a couple inches to avoid his wild swing. As his fist passed my face, his momentum moved his body toward my right shoulder. I hit him with a right cross to the nose, breaking it. I followed with a quick left hook to his jaw, snapping his head back. Blood rushed from his nose and into his mouth.

Stunned and frustrated, he did what all brawlers do. He rushed me, attempted to grab me in a bear hug and wrestle me to the ground. Momentum has its advantages, but so does being quick. It was easy to sidestep his lumbering grasp as he made another stumbling pass at me. I hit him again, this time behind his ear, knocking him further forward. He turned back toward me. He shook his head to clear it and wiped the blood and snot from his face with the back of his hand. He rushed me again. When he did, he planted his right leg to throw all his body weight into me. I stepped to the side and viciously kicked his knee perpendicular to its intended anatomical function. He screamed in agony and fell to the ground. The encounter had lasted no more than 30 to 45 seconds, but he'd walk with a limp for some time. His knee was broken or badly damaged.

I drove away. He'd be found soon enough. I'd leave it to him to concoct a story about how he'd been injured.

CHAPTER 2

With nothing else to do, I left for the office earlier than usual the following morning. The newspaper office was located in the middle of town, on Elm Street. From the Kingdon, I walked east on Second, to the corner of Elm. The drug store where Sally Morgan and I used to meet for fountain cokes before going to the movies on Saturday afternoons stood on the opposite corner of Second, and I lingered a moment before turning onto Elm. I crossed the street at the American Legion building, the only art deco building in town.

As I neared the entrance of the newspaper building, the wonderful aroma of fresh baked bread and pastries emanated from the bakery next door. I mounted the two, age-worn limestone steps, walked between the twin Ionic columns, through the arched entryway and into the business office of the *River City News.* There was something stable and comforting about our local newspaper office. The smells and sounds let me know I was in the right place: the ink, the coffee, and the cigar smoke, along with an occasional whiff of whiskey and cheap perfume; the clickity-clack of a dozen typewriters, the noisy clatter of the linotype machine, and the incessantly ringing phones. There's nothing like the energy of a hometown newspaper!

Hubert Harrison—"Harry"—Headley was the owner, publisher, and editor of the *River City News*. He was an erudite man with a sophisticated appearance. Hailing from an Indiana family of newspapermen, Harry was East Coast educated, and he took his ownership of the paper and his responsibility to the community very seriously. He involved himself in civic affairs, keeping his ear to the ground as to local economic practices, and early on, he formed a board of trade, the precursor to what would later become the Henderson Chamber of Commerce. Harry had purchased the paper out of receivership during the depth of the Depression. Another devastating effect of the Depression was the closing of the cotton mill, putting hundreds of locals out of work. The mill remained shut down and locked up for more than 12 years. No one knows exactly how he did it, but through his East Coast connections and family influence, Headley convinced a Massachusetts firm to reopen the mill, resulting in the immediate rehiring of many of the unemployed workers.

The overhead fans rotated lazily, circulating warm, humid air. Street noise filtered in through open, double-hung windows. I poured myself a cup of coffee and headed back to my desk, hoping I could pick up an early assignment—a car wreck or a late-night bar fight. If there was nothing on the docket, I was going to head over to the police station and see what I could dig up.

"Back on your feet, Cole?"—the brusque greeting from the news editor.

"Morning to you too, Howard."

Howard Hunsaker was in his mid-40s, balding, stoop-shouldered, and ugly. He'd been the news editor for several years, and the title seemed to satisfy his ambitions. He walked over and hiked a bony hip onto the edge of my desk. His high-water pant leg exposed the white, hairless skin above the top of his sock.

"Cops got a dead guy out in the East End. I swear, that's a rough end of town. Why do people live out there? Get your ass on out there and write it up."

I climbed into my truck and headed east on Washington Street toward the Audubon area. The address was a block beyond the railroad tracks, across Atkinson Street. Washington's a relatively narrow street with shotgun homes, closely abutted, on narrow lots. It was a peaceful neighborhood consisting of Negro families and working-class whites, until you reached Julia Street, the line of demarcation for the still working-class, but all-white, East End.

When I found the address, I parked in front, climbed from the cab and glanced over the truck bed, back toward Atkinson Street, scanning the houses on either side. Women in aprons stood on their porches shaking rugs while men mowed grass with steel-wheeled, reel lawn mowers. Children ran, played, and chased each other across unfenced yards. A dog barked at the whistle and rattle of a freight train rumbling by, one block east. Even at that distance, the smoke and cinders irritated my nostrils.

A couple of city patrolmen had the area secured and the neighborhood gawkers at bay. I could see the victim's body, not 20 yards from the curb, still face down on the dirt floor of the single-car garage on the left side of the property. At right, a porch swing rocked lazily in the morning breeze outside the entrance to the house. The early sun spread over the rooftops like a thin mist, imparting an orange glow to the surfaces. The sweet fragrance from roses planted along the side of the house created a striking contrast to the obvious odor of death emanating from the garage floor. The victim's head lay just inside the garage, and his left leg extended straight out toward the street. His other leg was pulled up at an angle. His left shoe needed to be resoled, I noticed.

Next door, a woman in a print dress, hair rolled in bobby pins, pretended to sweep her porch as she cast a curious eye toward the scene. I walked toward her. "I'm with the newspaper. What's going on here?"

She propped her broom against a porch column and put a hand in her apron. "I saw the red lights of the patrol car bouncing off the front window. Came out on the porch to see. They been here about 45 minutes. Looks like something bad's happened. Nice folks. Kinda standoffish though."

The front and side elevation of the property was unfenced, so I left her and walked unimpeded onto the crime scene. As I approached the victim, I heard one of the patrolmen mumble to another, "Either one of them blows would have killed him. Why'd he hit him twice?"

The back of the man's skull had two gaping holes caked with dried blood and matted hair. One was larger than the other, but it did appear either would have been fatal.

"Coal miners can be a mean bunch."

Homer "Guinea" Brackett, a city police detective, was apparently leading the investigation. A guinea, pronounced *gin-nee,* is a hen-like bird that is wild, loud, and good at pest control—a perfect nickname for Detective Brackett. The narrow bridge of his beak-like nose did little to separate his close-set eyes. He was a small, compact man with a brash demeanor and a lethal mean streak. His wife's murder, several years prior, and the last several years of dealing with the town's underbelly, had soured him like clabbered milk. He was dyspeptic, alcoholic, and cantankerous.

"Who is he, Guinea?" I asked.

"Herman Weiskopf, superintendent of the three Coldiron coal mines."

"Whaddaya know so far?"

"He's Herman Weiskopf and he's dead!"

"Astute, Guinea, stellar detective work. Weapon? Motive?"

"Too early, Cole! I just got here, myself. You know as well as I do, the mines are a hard and hazardous place, full of hard and dangerous men. There've been strikes and union trouble for some time, and coalfield violence is not uncommon. I'd guess that's behind it." He turned his head, hawked up overnight phlegm, and spat into the grass.

People murder for any number of reasons or combination of reasons: jealousy, abuse, fear, or revenge. But the reason can generally be narrowed down to one of three: money, sex, or power.

"Stop by the station later, I'll tell you what I find out," he said.

CHAPTER 3

My mother's father was a sharecropper. She grew up in the Hebbardsville area. She had two sisters and five brothers. Each one of the brothers worked in the coal mines at one time or another. Between 1904 and 1945, no fewer than 25 separate coal camps operated in Henderson County, employing as few as 20 in some and up to 300 in others. During this period, more than 50 million tons of coal was extracted from county soil, removed largely by hand, in underground mines, under the harshest of conditions.

The morning sun burned with mid-afternoon intensity. On my own initiative, I headed southeast through rolling farmland, down two-lane blacktop edged with pawpaw and persimmon trees, toward Hebbardsville. I was able to coax my truck up to almost 50 miles per hour on some of the straighter stretches. With air from the side window and hood vent directed toward me, it was a pleasant drive.

The sounds and smells of farmland brought back memories of childhood visits to the small plot of ground my grandpa farmed on shares. Off in the distance, I heard the noisy rattle of an old

John Deere tractor. I passed ponds with cattle standing placidly, belly deep in water they drank from and defecated into. Further on, the blacktop grew narrower and more crooked. Deeper into the country, the trees and weeds intruded right up to the surface of the gravel road, through hillier ground and shabbier property. The farther from town, the poorer became the land, the dwellings, and the people. The ground was less tillable, contributing to more desperate lives. Most families in this area relied on sharecropping or coal mining for a meager existence. They were grappling what living they could from the soil—on the surface or beneath it.

As I approached Coldiron coal mine number three, the smell of burning coal filled my nose and lungs. Coal smoke is not as pleasant as wood smoke. It has a harsher smell, like cigar smoke compared to a pipe mixture. But like tobacco, it was not unpleasant in a small, dilute dose, which is what I got from a distance. I pulled onto the mine property, crossing coal-blackened dirt leading up to the mine shack and tipple.

The three-story tipple, originally constructed of rough-hewn lumber, had taken on a dirty, silver-gray patina with age. It loomed like some damaged and decaying medieval fortress, menacing and foreboding. The dark structure and the coal-dirty men reflected the times and conditions of the area. I parked my truck and walked toward the mine shack. An old dog snarled as I approached. Apparently, that was the extent of his responsibility; he made no move toward me. The door stood open, so I climbed the coal-blackened, wooden steps and walked into the austere and dirty space. It smelled of coal, ashes, dirt, and human stink. The rotten-egg smell of hydrogen sulfide gas wafted up from the bowels of the mine. With time and exposure, it irritates the nostrils, burns the eyes, and wreaks havoc on the lungs, causing breathing difficulties. An inhospitable environment!

Two metal, army-surplus desks were shoved back-to-back in the middle of the room; cane-bottomed chairs stood on opposite sides. A single telephone was mounted on the wall at the junction of the two desks. One of them was occupied by a small man wearing a denim shirt and bib overalls. He reminded me of my mother's brothers: There wasn't an ounce of fat on his body, only bone, sinew, and thinly stretched muscle. A frayed and dirty fedora was pushed back on the crown of his head, and he wore high-top brogans, worn down at the heels.

"I'm Hoyt Cole with the *River City News*. You got a minute to talk with me?"

"You here 'bout Herman's murder, I reckon. The police called about an hour ago . . . ain't been here yet though."

"You mind answering a few questions?"

"I reckon not."

"You Elwood Suggins, the assistant superintendent?"

"Call me Woody."

"You have any idea who might have killed Weiskopf?" I asked.

"He's superintendent over three mines. On any day of the week, there'd be at least one man who'd kill him, if'n he thought he'd get away with it."

"Was he difficult to work for?"

"If expectin' a man to put in a full day's work for a full day's pay is hard, then I reckon you'd call him hard to work for. Unionizin' and union pay ain't changed that none. If you ask me, it's made it worse."

Before unionization, the mine owners controlled all aspects of the coal industry and the associated culture. Owners opposed unionization, believing they had the right of control over their property. They held to the idea that they should be allowed to conduct business without outside intervention. After all, it was their money invested in a risky and dangerous enterprise, and they believed they should be granted complete autonomy over all aspects of operation. Many owners and operators hired armed guards to control the workers and prevent union organizers from accessing their property.

In 1939, John L. Lewis's United Mine Workers of America made a strong push, with considerable success, to unionize all the coal mines of Henderson County. All the larger mines had acquiesced and signed union contracts, though not without the usual fits and starts associated with cultural evolution. There were mine closings affecting hundreds of workers. Strikes, threatened strikes, picket lines, and scab workers often resulted in violent confrontation, part of the upheaval of an economic power shift. Coldiron mines one, two, and three were unionized, unlike a number of the wagon-truck mines in the area—so called because that's how they moved the coal they mined. Mules and wagons.

Suggins had a small mouth, and his face sloped away from his lower lip backward toward his Adam's apple, interrupted only slightly by his receding chin. His eyes were sunken, his cheeks gaunt, his teeth rotted or missing. The right side of his face bulged with a wad of tobacco. He turned and spat a stream of amber into an old coffee can full of ashes.

"Pretty hard way to make a living," I said.

He removed his hat with his left hand, ran the fingers of his right hand through his receding hair, and pulled his hat back on his head, almost in a rehearsed and singular motion.

"Who said livin' was easy? They knew what the job was when they applied for it! You get what you asked for and what you wanted, then complain and balk because it turns out to be exactly what you knew it was. Don't make no sense, does it?"

"You expect you'll be promoted to the superintendent's job?"

"Coldiron Mining Company has three assistant superintendents, one at each mine. Could be any one of us, but more'n likely they'll bring in someone from out of town. Don't want nobody too familiar with the miners 'round here, 'fraid they'll be too soft on 'em."

"Do you think a miner killed him?"

"I got no idea. Wouldn't surprise me none though, if it was." He leaned over and spat into the can again, then wiped the tobacco spittle off his chin.

"Thanks for your time, Mr. Suggins."

"Woody!"

CHAPTER 4

Back at my desk, I began my article on the murder. I recounted what little I knew, calling it "Henderson's Coalfield Murder." The clacking typewriter keys, the chattering police scanners, and the flash and ringing bells of the teletype machines united in a continuous symphony. The acrid smell of cigarette butts extinguished in dirty coffee mugs and the contrasting human odors can be stimulating, once you get used to them. They're evidence of a viable local paper.

Later that afternoon I stopped for a drink at the Gold Coin Tavern, across from my room at the Kingdon Hotel. The entry gave onto an open area with six, four-top tables. A half-wall partition separated the dining area from the bar, which was typical for the era, except for the padded front. Stemware hung upside down from a rack above the bartender's head, the light twinkling on the glass like rhinestones. An assortment of draft beer taps and plastic tubs of garnish were within easy reach. The Gold Coin was newer and a little more upscale than some of the other joints in town, but as in all the others, gambling was an open secret. At the end of the long hall beginning between the bar and the seating area was a door market *Private*, opened by a buzzer under the bar. It accessed a room with slot machines, poker tables, crap tables, and a roulette wheel.

I was sitting at the bar, waiting for my second beer when Detective Brackett walked in. His shirttail was untucked, concealing the snub-nosed .38 strapped at his waist. A snap-brim, white straw hat and sunglasses completed his off-duty attire. He took the stool next to me. When the bartender walked over, Guinea said, "Gimme a highball and put it on Cole's tab." I nodded. Guinea flipped the lid on his Zippo and lit his cigarette, took a deep pull, and exhaled through his nose. "Found the murder weapon in the Weiskopf killing."

I waited.

"It's a spike maul. One of the officers found it in a heavy patch of weeds in an overgrown garden, back of the house."

"Weiskopf was a mine superintendent, could've been his."

Guinea turned to look toward me. "I don't know whose it is, but it's the murder weapon!"

"You sound certain."

He took another drag on his smoke before answering. "Clotted blood, bits of flesh, and matted hair are certain enough for me."

"You got a motive?"

"Not yet, but I'm guessing a miner or someone close to the labor problems, given the weapon used."

"Did his wife have any insight on who might have killed him?"

"Not really. She acted pretty distraught, as you would expect, under the circumstances."

"Neighbors have anything to allow?" I asked.

"Free lunch is over, Cole. If you want anything more, go ask the questions yourself. Newspaper's paying you, not me. Thanks for the drink," he said, crushing his cigarette out. He headed toward the back. A faint buzzing sound released the lock, allowing him entry to that private room.

I paid my tab and walked across the street to my hotel. The sun was setting lower in the western sky, but it still burned hot and bright, shifting to orange and dimming to a deeper gold as it sank to the horizon.

CHAPTER 5

The next morning, Hunsaker called me to his office and shut the door. "We got a tip from the police chief. He says they're raiding several local bars and taverns tonight. Checking to see if there might be gambling going on." He pushed his sleeves up above his wrists and fixed them in place with a pair of black garters. His pants were buckled high above his waistline. He looked like a question mark with his humped shoulders curving above his rounded back.

I looked at him disbelievingly. "You're kidding, right?"

"What? About the raids? Or whether there might be gambling?"

I stared at him.

"Here's a list of the joints being hit and the approximate time of the raid on each. Try to make as many as you can," he said, straight-faced.

"Why'd you select me, Howard? Cause I'm relatively new to the job and perhaps the most naive? I may be young, and I am new, but I'm certainly not naive. The first beach we hit in the Pacific destroyed any naivete I ever had. I won't be a part of a whitewash! Get somebody else!"

"You're a good reporter, Cole. Take the assignment and report on what you see."

I snatched the list from his hand and stormed out of his office. I didn't like being played for a fool. If there had ever been any doubt that the fix was in and the whole community was involved in the charade, this assignment proved it in spades! I didn't like being drawn in and made complicit. I stewed over it most of the day, unable to concentrate on little else. Did Hunsaker think I would just play along like a good little boy? Had he become so indoctrinated that it never occurred to him I might object?

The first place to be raided was Curley's Blackhorse Stable. Curley Sutton's bar was downstairs beneath Dorothy's Gift Shop on North Green Street. I walked down the stairs under the overhanging porch of the gift shop. Curley had authentic saloon-style swinging doors on Bommer hinges leading into his bar. It was about nine o'clock and only one patron was at the bar. The place seemed unusually quiet. The furnishings didn't seem to fit the space—too sparse. Then it hit me! There were no slot machines on the walls, and none in the men's room either. I ordered a beer and sat at the bar, lit a cigarette, and waited.

About 9:30, a couple of city patrolmen sauntered in. I knew them both. One was Buck Vanover, and the other was Snakes Willingham. They wore their seven-pointed visor caps, blue uniforms with badges prominently displayed, handcuffs, gun belts, and night sticks. An impressive show of force! Curley was cleaning glasses behind the bar. Vanover approached the bar and slid a paper across to Curley. "I got a warrant to search the joint, Curley," he said.

"Whacha looking for, boys?" Curley asked.

"We got a report you was allowing gambling and keeping gaming devices."

"Make yaself at home." Curley turned away from the bar and started straightening the half-pints.

"Mind if I follow along with 'em?" I asked.

Curley gestured with his hand for me to proceed. He inserted a nickel into the jukebox and a boisterous rendition of "Honky Tonkin' " filled the otherwise dead air. The patrolmen made a casual stroll behind the bar, through both restrooms, into the back storage room, and out the back service entrance into the dimly lit space behind. Nothing!

Back inside, Vanover said, "Thanks, Curley, see ya again!"

"Night, boys," Curley replied.

I sat back down and finished my beer. "That happen often?" I asked him.

"Nah, just often enough to keep up appearances."

Curley's hair was still black and wavy, but he was sliding into middle-aged decline, displaying a slight belly and heavier jowls.

"What'd you do with the slot machines, Curley?"

"What slot machines?"

The same scenario repeated itself at two other raids. The last one scheduled was on the opposite end of town at the Wagon Wheel bar, across the train tracks on South Green Street. It was later, and there were more people in the joint. When the patrolmen went through their charade, they found a single busted slot machine and a box of gambling chips in the backroom, behind some empty beer cases. They made a pass through the back door and looked around in the lot. Back inside, they told the owner, Lefty Griffin, what they had found, and informed him that he was under arrest. They lugged the broken-down machine out to the trunk of their cruiser, along with the unopened box of chips, stopping to ask me if I wanted to take any pictures for the paper. They made a big production of handcuffing Lefty and leading him out to their vehicle. The patrons hardly looked up. I followed them outside and watched as they drove off, displaying flashing lights and wailing siren.

The night air had cooled some, and there was a slight breeze. Across the lot and in the distance, the leaves in a honey locust grove rustled. Crickets chirped, a lone owl hooted intermittently, and night creatures swarmed and buzzed. All of a sudden, I saw it! A semitrailer was parked fast up against the grove. The shade and the night shadows almost obscured it, but not completely. It was secluded enough that a fleeting pass could miss it. And I *had* missed it! Three previous times the same evening! The faint label on the trailer advertised GTR. There was one parked behind or off to the side of all the other bars and taverns "raided" that night.

Last evening local police officers raided four previously alerted Henderson establishments, seeking evidence of illegal gambling. In three early raids, no gambling devices or activities were present. It was evident the owners had been tipped off. In the last raid, officers found an old, nonfunctioning slot machine and an unopened box of chips. Salted evidence? The owner of the Wagon Wheel bar, Lefty Griffin, was arrested. He'll be back on the streets later today, out on bail.

And second:

Last evening, in four separate and daring raids, Henderson police officers armed with warrants swarmed in and searched local establishments for evidence of gambling, gambling devices, and illegal games of chance. Curley's Blackhorse Stable, Agnew's Tavern, Bushrod's Tavern, and the Wagon Wheel bar were all hit. After a complete and thorough search, the first three raids produced no evidence of illegal gambling or gambling devices. However, in the final raid of the night, at the Wagon Wheel bar, police discovered gambling devices and other evidence of illegal gaming. Lefty Griffin, the owner, was arrested and is detained in the Henderson jail, awaiting arraignment. Mayor Forest Grimshaw praised the actions of Henderson's police department, citing the bold proceedings as evidence that he would continue to ensure that Henderson remained free of gambling and other illicit activities.

I almost retched writing the second account, because I knew it would be the one printed. I placed both reports in a folder and left it on Hunsaker's desk.

The next morning, I retrieved a copy of the *River City News* from a wire rack in the lobby of the Kingdon. I got my coffee and toast in the cafeteria line and went to a table near the door. Below the fold on the front page was the second version of my article. I didn't have to read it. A waitress refilled my coffee, and I smoked a cigarette. I was in no hurry to get to the office.

Out on the street, the morning traffic was beginning to pick up. Stores were opening, their awnings rolled down; clerks, lawyers, and businessmen were walking the sidewalks toward their various stores and offices. The air smelled clean and fresh. The sky was clear and Henderson was bracing for another placid day of contentment and tolerance.

How does an entire community turn a blind eye to obviously perverse goings-on? How are good people drawn into bad pursuits? Did the economic pendulum swing so far in the negative direction that any movement in the opposite direction, no matter how questionable, was welcomed and embraced? Apparently!

I walked east to the corner, crossed the street, and turned left toward the paper office. The usual bang and jangle permeated the building, while the scents emanating from the bakery evoked warm and pleasant memories. *My grandmother's kitchen.* My mother's touch as she tucked me in bed at night. *If that aroma was a place, everyone would go there and never leave.*

"Nice article," someone said as I made my way through the maze of desks toward my own space. I had no more than sat down when Hunsaker called me to his office. He waited in the doorway for me to enter. Then he closed the door. Moving behind his desk, he motioned for me to sit.

I remained standing. "What's on your mind, Howard?"

"You confound me, Hoyt!" He absentmindedly rotated a wood pencil end over end in his hand.

"Confound you? What do you mean?"

"The fact that you wrote two versions of last night's raids tells me a lot about you." He tapped the eraser end of the pencil nervously on his desk top.

I didn't respond. I stared him dead in his eyes, unblinking.

Unable to hold my gaze, he turned away and looked out the window. After a time, he stood and walked over to the window. With his back to me he said, "Don't you have anything to say?"

"Yeah, I do! But you're not going to like it."

He turned to face me. "Let's hear it."

"The fact that you printed the second version tells me a lot about you!"

"Wha, whaddaya mean?" he stammered.

"I don't like being made complicit in something I don't believe in or approve of. I don't care if the whole damn town—the whole of Henderson County—accepts it. I won't be a party to it."

"A party to what?" he demanded, with as much indignation as he could muster.

"Damn you, Howard, don't add insult to injury. You might want to act like those raids weren't a sham, but don't expect me to join in. You and the entire community can turn a blind eye to what's going on . . . but I can't. And furthermore, don't you *ever* give me another assignment like that. I won't take it—even if it costs me my job. Get some other acquiescing son of a bitch to do it. There must be at least *one* around here."

I'm sure he wasn't used to being talked to like that, but I didn't care. He slid a pack of cigarettes out of his shirt pocket, shook one loose and lit it. He exhaled, and spat a piece of tobacco off his tongue, all the time staring straight at me. I didn't break his gaze. "Take the day off, Cole. Tread lightly, son!"

I felt small and useless under the indifferent blue sky outside. I walked over to the courthouse and looked up the owner of GTR. It wasn't easy to find the owner—a River City Transport, Inc., corporate officers Forrest Grimshaw and his wife, Blanche Pruitt Grimshaw. GTR stood for Grimshaw Trailer Rental.

Damn! Looks like the political corruption here goes all the way to the top. I guess I'm not too surprised, remembering what Dad said about Grimshaw when he was first elected.

Armed with this new revelation I walked over to the police station to find Buck Vanover.

"Out on patrol," I was told.

"Where in town might I find him?"

"You might try the Audubon area."

The bright morning sun and early breeze countered my dark feeling. Reminding myself what a pleasure and blessing it was to be *alive,* I shook it off and walked back to the Kingdon to get my truck. I headed out Washington Street toward the East End. The area is officially called Audubon, for the naturalist. But the inhabitants call it the East End. It's a blue-collar enclave, largely owner-occupied, with a hodgepodge economy of small shops and businesses.

In one five-block section, there are five or six grocery stores, four beauty parlors, a shoe-repair business, two drug stores, three churches, three restaurants, a grade school, a jewelry store, a furniture store and a bank branch, a couple hardware stores, a tavern, and a gas station—all within walking distance of most of the homes in the area. Residents are keenly aware they're not Henderson's social elite, and they take pride in that knowledge. If you're from the East End you wear it like a badge of honor, tinged with a bit of ignominious smugness. Interlopers rarely go up against a local. It's just not good judgment.

By the time I found Buck Vanover on Atkinson Street, near the railroad tracks, it was almost midday. I flagged him into the lot of an abandoned warehouse. He remained in his cruiser. "What's up, Cole?" he asked through the open window.

The inside of his cruiser smelled of leather, Cosmoline, cigarette smoke, and Old Spice aftershave. I glanced inside at a shotgun locked in place, next to his communication radio, and squatted down to face him.

"Can you give me any insight into that mock raid the other evening?"

"Mock!" he said defensively.

"Come on, Buck! It couldn't be more obvious. Everyone was tipped off. What you tell me is strictly off the record. I'm just trying to get the real skinny."

"If you don't know, you're likely the only one in town that doesn't." His left elbow rested on the window opening. A burning cigarette in his right hand draped across the steering wheel.

"Humor me."

"You promise not to use my name!"

"I swear!"

He looked out at me, below his open window. "When L. S. Furlong opened the Cosmopolitan Club out on the strip in 1939, beginning his gambling operation, he gave tacit approval for every tavern and nightclub to do the same. Unafraid of the competition, L. S. sold them the slot machines and gaming tables." He paused, to avoid talking over the dispatcher relaying information and instructions.

"I can understand how the Cosmo gets away with it, out there across the river, outside of city limits. But many clubs are inside city limits, and those that aren't are within the purview of the county sheriff." The sun was beginning to beat down on my bare head, and my knees were starting to ache. I stood to stretch them and looked out across the top of his cruiser at the weeds growing through cracked pavement. Some of the asphalt had been ground into gravel and dirt.

"What do you know about Grimshaw, our illustrious mayor?" Buck asked, turning his head and looking through the windshield.

I leaned over to look him on the eye. "Enough that I don't like him, and I don't trust him."

"Smart boy!" He waited while a kid with one pant leg rolled up rode a bike with no chain guard across the lot to avoid the intersection. Across the tracks, neighborhood kids were playing hopscotch and tag. Others were jumping rope and kicking old cans down the street.

"Gambling provides Forrest Grimshaw another source of income. If you want gambling in your establishment, all you have to do is grease the palm of our mayor, on a monthly basis. If you can't, don't, or won't, your business will be a target of the next 'raid.' But in your case, you won't be tipped off, and you'll go to jail and pay a big fine. Most of which will end up in the mayor's pocket." He brought both hands down to his lap and repositioned himself in the seat to look up at me. "Furlong has organized the joints into a tight-knit alliance, able to resist encroachment from the mobs in Chicago and Detroit. That raid the other evening was just for show. Every so often, three or four joints will agree to take their turn in the barrel. They are told ahead of time when its coming. The selected three or four businesses remove all gambling evidence and paraphernalia and store it in a trailer out of sight, behind the properties."

"Such trailers graciously provided by a company solely owned by Grimshaw—for a small fee of course," I interjected.

"Exactly!" Turning his face to the windshield, Buck continued. "Often, like the other evening, they'll seed the hit with an old slot machine or some such evidence, to make a good show. The county sheriff is just as corrupt, but not as greedy. Oh, he'll take a payoff from time to time. A new over and under shotgun, free meals at the Cosmo, free drinks at most of the taverns and bars in the area. Nothing nearly as systematic as Grimshaw. The sheriff gets his real pay as a minority owner of the Cosmo."

A puff of wind blew newspapers, candy wrappers, and a grocery bag across the lot into a drainage ditch along the tracks. A mongrel dog hiked a leg to relieve himself against a telephone pole. I could smell garbage burning in a nearby yard.

"Why do you guys go along with it, Buck?" I asked. "After all, you're sworn to uphold the law."

Facing me again, he sighed. "Some laws are more worth upholding than others."

I dropped back down on my haunches. "Do you get to decide which are and which are not?"

"Have you forgotten how difficult it was for a man to make a living here in the '30s and early '40s? Do you have any idea what a patrolman's wages are? Good or bad, right or wrong, like it or not, gambling has brought a degree of prosperity to Henderson."

"How do you guys benefit, Buck?"

"The bar and tavern owners make it worth our while with small cash handouts from time to time. If we go in and lay our night stick on the bar, they always see fit to slip a little something our way. We don't make a regular habit of it. Struggling as most of us are, it's hard to see the harm in it."

"Thanks, Buck! You haven't told me anything I didn't suspect, but it's good to have it confirmed. Your name will never come up."

"Watch yourself, Hoyt. You might step on the wrong toes. You're paddling upstream, son." That was the third time I'd been warned to tread lightly. I returned to my truck and drove back uptown.

CHAPTER 6

At work the next morning, I went directly to Hunsaker's office. I didn't wait to be summoned. I didn't speak, just stood in his doorway. His shirt collar was loose and his tie sagged, allowing ample room for his prominent Adam's apple to move up and down. A cup of coffee sat at his right, with a cigarette burning in an ashtray to his left. He was typing, deliberately ignoring me.

He continued busying himself with manufactured and superfluous tasks. I waited. It became a game of wills: Would I become discouraged and leave, or would he ultimately have to acknowledge my presence? When I didn't go away, he finally looked up. "Close the door and take a seat, Hoyt."

I sat across from him. He shuffled papers and moved them around, stripped a sheet of paper from the carriage and laid it ritualistically on his desk, continuing to dawdle and delay, self-consciously moving items around in front of him. He seemed nervous. Without looking at me directly, he finally asked, "How would you feel about being assigned to the night shift, four to midnight, for a time?"—as if I had a choice in the matter.

"You're calling the shots, Howard."

I could have protested I suppose, asked for reasons and justification, but in reality, I've always been more of a night person, and most of the dangerous and interesting assignments came in at night. The night shift was less structured and the newsroom more casual during those hours, a real plus. I didn't want to give him the satisfaction of thinking he'd irritated or provoked me, either. I looked him square in his eyes. After a few seconds, he broke eye contact and looked off to his right. "Let's try that for a while."

I rose and walked out of his office without comment. I didn't know if he considered this punishment for the two articles on the bogus raid or just his way of not having to deal with me directly. Regardless, I was OK with it.

‡

Fistfights were so common, I didn't have to search for them. They occurred in almost every bar in town on every night of the week, and more frequently on weekends. Most of them were of no consequence and didn't merit newspaper ink unless they escalated into something more serious.

My first week on the evening shift, there was a stabbing over on Dixon Street out in front of Dorsey's Tavern. As difficult as the economic conditions of the '30s, '40s, and early '50s were on the entire Henderson population, they were much more devastating to the colored citizens. Often the only work available to a Negro man was back-breaking manual labor, part-time, temporary, and menial. Dorsey's was the center of the Negro community's night life. During the week it seemed the entire colored population ebbed and flowed around the intersection where the tavern was located. Depending on the weather, there might be as many people milling around outside as inside. Only the churches were more important in the social life.

On that particular evening, two men got into an altercation over an issue of no real consequence to either of them. When economic privation pushes a man's self-esteem low enough, often the only thing left to him is physical assertion. It doesn't take much. Knives and razors are cheaper and more readily available than pistols and bullets. Stabbings and cuttings were common at the intersection of Dixon and Alvasia.

Bar fights weren't all. Armed robberies were still an issue. Liquor stores and late-night groceries were common targets. Early in the week, a man brandishing a shotgun held up the Pick-and-Pay grocery store up on Fifth and Green, making off with the day's receipts. Amateur crimes like this were rarely solved or prosecuted. Most likely it was just a local man, down on his luck, needing a quick injection of cash. All I could do was nose around and write up an article that was as interesting as possible.

But one night when I was typing and editing, long after my shift had ended, the scanner reported a robbery at the Kraver Klub out on 41A. Owned by two brothers, Kurtis and Kalvin Kraver, the club featured gambling, but it was relatively benign, limited to slot machines, mostly. I dropped what I was doing and raced out there to get a firsthand account before the witnesses went home.

Approaching, I saw the flashing lights of cars from the sheriff's department. There was quite a bit of frenetic activity in and around the place, even though most of the employees had left earlier, as I soon learned. I parked and entered through the front door. Walking through the now empty nightclub, I went to where most of the activity was concentrated, in the business office. A female secretary sat in a chair, the severed ends of rope that had been used to bind her still hanging from the sides. While she wasn't hysterical, she was distraught, and had obviously been crying. The safe was standing agape, all its contents raked out onto the floor, and the office was in total disarray, obviously plundered. Kalvin Kraver was sitting at his desk, hands hanging at his sides.

The Kraver Klub was primarily a dance club; it catered to young people. While not as plush as the Cosmo, it occupied the second tier of local nightclubs. It featured a square red-leather-clad bar, and the ceiling was blue with silver stars and indirect lighting.

"The sons-of-bitches stole over $5,000. Me and Catherine had just finished counting the take when three men busted in holding handguns and demanding cash. Later, a fourth man shoved Emmitt, the night watchman, through the door. He'd been overpowered while patrolling the grounds outside." Kalvin had opened a bottle of whiskey and was drinking straight from the bottle. He poured a couple fingers in a water glass and handed it to his secretary.

"Sip on that, Catherine."

I turned to Catherine. "Did you recognize any of them? Do you think you could identify them?"

She shook her head vehemently, clutching a handkerchief with both hands pressed tightly to her lips. "They all wore masks." Her breath caught and she looked pleadingly at Kalvin.

"And they had hats pulled low on their faces," he filled in. "They spoke in gestures and grunts. They bound me and Emmitt's hands behind us with tape and locked us in that restroom, yonder." He pointed at a door that had been broken open at the jamb. "After they left, Emmitt kicked the door open, and we called the sheriff's office."

As if suddenly emboldened, the secretary began to speak

rapidly in halting phrases. "One of 'em stuck a gun in my back! He made me get my purse. I thought he was going to take my cash too!" She started breathing rapidly, almost panting.

Once again Kalvin filled in for her. "They took her at gunpoint to her car out back and made her drive it around front. They forced her inside and bound her to that chair she's still sitting in. They all left in her car."

I knew they'd be a while cleaning up the mess left by the robbers. I had all I was going to get, so I returned to the office and wrote up the account.

‡

It was widely speculated, and even believed, that the Chicago underworld had always been behind the gambling and corruption in Henderson and that L. S. Furlong did not control them single-handedly. While it wasn't uncommon for elements from other cities to try and encroach on the area, it was never proven that criminal organizations from outside the county ever actually operated in Henderson.

In reality, Furlong controlled all illegal activities. He got a piece of the action from every establishment in town. He bought and paid for local government, the sheriff, the judge, the mayor, and the commissioners. Often, he backed the winning campaigns. The officeholders were all under his thumb. At one point, Furlong learned that men from Chicago, Detroit, and Cincinnati were in the area. He called a meeting and explained their intent and that they'd likely offer an outrageous price for a piece of the action in Henderson. He impressed on all the local owners not to sell to outside interests. Not a single business acquiesced to the exorbitant prices offered, a testament to his power, control, and business acumen.

After the robbery at the Kraver Klub, Slade Thornton's Kain-Tuck Lounge was robbed for almost $9,000 in cash and valuables. Slade declined both comment and prosecution. A few months later the Henderson Gaming Parlor was held up by men armed with submachine guns. Reports later suggested they netted between $40,000 and $50,000. When questioned about the robbery, the sheriff claimed no knowledge of the event. The series of robberies at local nightclubs and gambling establishments was believed to be perpetrated by outsiders intending to create sufficient dissent and distrust among the proprietors to result in sales.

While I was still on the night shift, the Bottoms was also robbed. The perpetrators got away with between $15,000 and $20,000. They also took the personal belongings of two of the employees on duty at the time. When a local man was charged and found guilty, he was only charged with the theft of the wallets of the two employees. The money in the safe was never mentioned at his trial. The two employees denied any knowledge of money in the safe, underscoring the ludicrous denial of gambling in the area. It was an insult, but an insult that seemed to be easily swallowed by all parties.

One Thursday night around nine, a call came in reporting an altercation at Kluckey's Bar, so I headed over. Kluckey's was in a narrow brick building on the corner of Second and Water Streets, just before Second Street continued as a steep ramp into the Ohio River and a black void. The entrance was on the Second Street side. On the corner, an inadequate street lamp created more shadows and hiding spots than illumination. The entire intersection had an ominous feel about it at night.

Kluckey's was frequented by idlers, hard drinkers, and destitute men. It was a hard-ankle joint with a reputation for violence. Knifings, fistfights, and shootings were commonplace, particularly on weekends. It was a place where men who had long since surrendered to the economic ravages of the Depression went for solace and solitude. Kluckey's smelled of cigarette smoke, stale air, and disinfectant. A smoky haze created halos around the neon beer signs and hanging incandescent bulbs. The lighting was so dim the place seemed to be filled with a heavy gray fog, like the last stop on a dead-end street.

Inside, the coroner, a fleshy man in a too-tight seersucker suit, was making a futile attempt to hold together the severed ends of the victim's jugular vein. His heart squeezed out what blood remained in his body, his life draining onto the oily floor. The other patrons hardly took notice. Dulled by alcohol and despair, their concern for others and the goings-on around them was practically nonexistent.

Apparently, the two men involved had arrived together. A heated argument followed several hours of drinking and playing poker. Suddenly, the perpetrator leaped out of his chair, produced a razor, and cut the throat of the victim. A patrolman on the scene told me the victim was Henry Blackwell, an itinerant plasterer and part-time handyman. He had a few previous arrests, mostly for drunk and disorderly conduct, and an assault-and-battery charge pending.

The culprit was Thomas Perkins, a local ne'er-do-well, recently hired as a flagman for a county road crew. His rap sheet was similar, and he'd recently been charged with cutting the throat of a neighbor's dog. Surprisingly, he hung around the tavern as a mesmerized bystander. "Is Hank gonna be OK?" he asked at one point, of no one in particular.

Strands of Blackwell's hair floated on the dark blood pooled around his head. Staring woodenly at the victim, two city patrolmen gently pulled Perkin's hands behind his back, and cuffed him. He was led away almost docilely, looking back over his shoulder at his victim.

Kluckey's was not unlike Dorsey's Tavern. Men of different races, segregated by culture, bias, and prejudice, nevertheless faced the same economic privation. Bill Wilson, cofounder of Alcoholics Anonymous, could have built a viable chapter from the patrons in Kluckey's on any night of the week.

Are fate and free will opposite sides of the same coin? Without free will, we are helpless against the things and events that impact our lives, outside our control. Free will is the choices we make and the actions we take in response. A man can lose his free will, have it taken from him, or he can surrender it. After a time, men without it give out, give in, and give up. It seems every problem is a problem of will. We create our own despair.

CHAPTER 7

The next evening, I drove to Guinea Brackett's neat weatherboard house on the north end of town. The air grew more visible as dusk neared and the light quality gained a richer hue. Night blooming jasmine released fragrance into the air. Guinea's front yard was spacious, recently mowed and trimmed. A narrow gravel drive led to a single-car garage in the back.

He was sitting on the porch, drinking a glass of iced tea.

"Mind if I join you, Guinea?" He had on a sleeveless undershirt, lightweight pleated pants, pulled up to his knees, and sandals. You'd never have guessed his daily persona from his domestic attire.

"Guess not." He motioned to an empty chair. "What's on your mind, Cole?" He fanned himself with a paper funeral-home fan.

I beat around the bush for as long as I could.

Guinea leaned on the left arm of his chair raised his right hip and adjusted the crotch of his pants, growling, "Get to it, Hoyt. You didn't come here to discuss the weather."

"That so-called raid the other evening was a pretense. What's going on?"

He snapped his head around, staring directly at me. "Who says it was a pretense, and why should I talk to you about it?"

"Look, Guinea, I've been gone for years, but this is my hometown. I was raised here. I've got lifelong friends here. Anything you tell me is off the record."

A neighbor woman walked by with her dog on a leash. Pausing briefly in front of his house, she turned and smiled. "Hi, Homer," she said sweetly.

Obviously embarrassed by her affectionate greeting, he frowned and pinched his eyebrows together. "You're right! You've been gone a long time, and we've managed just fine without you. I don't know how." His voice was thick with sarcasm. "But we have."

I stood to pace his porch. "Political corruption is rampant. The town allows open gambling and games of chance in every venue that wants them, from grocery stores and gas stations to restaurants and taverns. Farmers hold cock fights in their barns almost every night of the week. Along with that, there's prostitution, strong-arm tactics, extortion, shootings, and all types of violence."

"Where'd you come by your high-minded moral principles, Cole? I'd think, given what you've seen and been through in the war, you wouldn't be so naive."

I waved my hand dismissively, "Call it what you will. As a law-enforcement officer, I'd think you'd have more than just a little concern."

"If people didn't break some laws now and again, there'd be no need for the likes of me," he said. "Have you forgotten how impoverished and destitute this area was when you were growing up?"

"No, I haven't forgotten!"

"It's better now, don't you think?"

"Yes, it is, but the war economy had a lot to do with it."

He got up and walked to the edge of the porch, gazing up the street at nothing in particular. He flicked a butt into his yard, turned his head and spat. "One hand washes the other. See ya around, Hoyt!" He turned and walked through the screen door, into his house. I was dismissed, left to stare at the door. As I turned to leave, he came back and spoke through the screen. "A little friendly advice? I'd be careful how hard I press this, was I you!!"

Make that four.

Off I went, Don Quixote tilting at windmills!

CHAPTER 8

Out on the street the next morning, I walked west toward the park on the river, the sun at my back and my shadow racing out before me. The air was cool and clean-smelling. Delicate, feather-like clouds floated in the sky.

The sun streamed through the foliage of the oak and maple trees in the park, sparkling off the water like dancing glass. The warm glow flooded the rusted L&N Railroad bridge, turning it a dark bronze. I found a bench and sat facing the river. A stationary barge in the middle was dredging the channel. A man came up from the river carrying a fishing pole and a can of worms. He sat on the other end of the bench.

"Nice day, huh?"

"It is. You live here?" I asked.

"All my life."

The park was once the site of Red Banks, the earliest documented settlement in present-day Henderson, so named because it was located high on bluffs of red earth overlooking the river and its floodplain. The view from the park is one of the best in Henderson: a gentle curve in the river, the flat wooded plains beyond, and the L&N Railroad bridge that spans the Ohio. It was named for John James Audubon, the famous painter of birds. He and his brother-in-law operated a failed grist mill on the site. The mill's foundation is still outlined in the grass by a stone path. One of the millstones still stands.

The man looked to be about 50 years old. His face bore deep crevasses, high cheek bones, and deep-set gray eyes. He wore a striped railroad cap, faded and tattered bib overalls, and a washed-out blue T-shirt. A red handkerchief dangled from his hip pocket, and he smelled of tobacco and the river.

"What's life like around here?" I asked.

He looked at me suspiciously, as if he'd been trapped into a test he hadn't studied for. "What kinda question is that?"

"I'm just curious. I came here recently, and I'm just trying to get the lay of the land."

"Like any place else, I reckon. Better'n some, worse than others. Life comes at you . . . and you live with it. I don't question it." He picked up his pole and can of worms and moved away cautiously, looking back over his shoulder as if fearful I might follow him.

One could characterize his response as that of an uneducated man—one with limited experiences and exposure. "Life comes at you . . . and you live with it." A simple-minded philosophy? Or the response of a defeated man, so beat down by conditions, that he'd lost his fight and the belief that he *could* fight?

How does corruption take hold and permeate a community? It generally starts with packaging something the people desire, feel they've been deprived of, and feel they legitimately have a right to. In this case, the right to make a living. When the presentation is good and the initial results provide what's been waited for and wanted, swallowing the rest of the bait seems painless.

Subsequent negative fallout seems inconvenient but tolerable, at least for a time.

The Black Patch Tobacco Wars had devastated the market for dark tobacco, the primary cash crop in the area. Next, Prohibition was foisted on the country, further damaging an economy reliant on alcohol and its principal ingredient, corn. Then the Depression eliminated financial independence, made beggars of previously hardworking men, destroyed their self-esteem and their dignity.

Men define themselves by what they do, be they carpenters, barbers, bricklayers, store clerks, factory workers, mechanics, electricians, plumbers, or farmers. It matters not so much what each job pays, the importance rests in a man's identity and in a consistent income that supports him and his family. It is difficult to predict and unfair to condemn what measures men may resort to in order to regain a measure of dignity and economic well-being. Deprive one man of those things and you have a sad individual. Deprive 25 percent of the men in a community of them for 10 long years, and you reap social and economic disaster.

People can endure hard times for a while, particularly when they see their efforts to overcome rewarded by even brief periods of success. But after 10 years of unrelenting setbacks, people were willing to accept almost any promised solution. Bootlegging, and later gambling, offered the local remedies. Don't tell a man something is illegal when it's the only means available to feed his family.

We had just fought a war in Europe with a country that had traveled the full length of the continuum between overlooking wrongdoing and persecuting those who called it out, and there I was, only a few years later, observing my hometown not only ignoring, but actually *permitting*, lawlessness. Surly I wasn't the only one disturbed by it. Yet where were the others?

Henderson was rife with bootlegging, gambling, prostitution, murder, shootings, and public graft. Yet the entire community went whistling past the graveyard. This was my home! I could imagine marrying here, raising a family here. How could I disregard seeing what I saw, knowing what I knew? But what could one man do?

I hadn't come home with any purpose beyond gainful employment. *I didn't come with the intent of correcting the ills and righting the wrongs. Why stir the pot? If conditions here are OK with everybody else, what's it to me?* I wasn't the moral arbiter of the community.

You're talking out of both sides of your mouth, Cole.

As the sun climbed higher, the wind picked up. Cumulus clouds began to form, growing quickly as the day heated up, becoming dark, anvil-shaped, and heavy with rain. White caps flared on the churning river. I headed back up the street toward my hotel room. Just as I was crossing Main Street, the sky unleashed the full fury of a late summer thunderstorm. Running beside the buildings and under the lee of storefront awnings, I made it to the lobby of the Kingdon without getting completely drenched.

CHAPTER 9

The barber shop in the Kingdon Hotel was a five-chair enterprise, running away from the entrance, down the right wall. A continuous mirror was situated above the stations, each furnished with a sink and a supply of talcum, combs, scissors, tonics, towels, mugs, razors, strops, and brushes. A row of eight chairs ran down the other wall for waiting patrons, and Stormy Jack's shoeshine stand stood at the end of that row. Jack sat on his stool, facing the barbers.

"Hi, Storms," I said, climbing up.

"Shine, Mista Hoyt?"

"You betcha!"

Four of the barbers' chairs were occupied. One man lay back with a drape covering his upper body from his throat to mid-thighs. A steaming towel was wrapped around his face, covering all but his nose while the barber brushed a mug of soap into a lather. Three other men sat upright, getting haircuts. The fifth station was vacant. The barber sat in his chair reading the day's paper. Conversations about sports, politics, and weather bounced around.

Three ceiling fans rotated slowly above the room. The terrazzo tile floor and high, stamped-metal ceiling produced a slight echo, creating a general buzz of talk, but making it difficult to follow any conversation without careful concentration. This community noise allowed for under-the-breath, semiprivate discussions.

"You heard anything about the murder out on Washington Street?" I asked.

"You mean Mr. Herman Weiskopf?"

"Yeah." I nodded. "Police are leaning toward labor problems at the mines. They say he was killed with a spike maul."

Stormy Jack had brushed my shoes clean and applied polish with his bare hands. Now he used a brush to produce a soft luster in the dried polish. "I don't know, Mista Hoyt, maybe you might wanna consider other prospects."

"Any suggestions?"

"No suh, I don't. . . . Least ways, not now."

John Calhoun Storm, known locally as Stormy Jack, was a Henderson fixture. Previously exceeding 500 pounds in weight, he had traveled for a time with a carnival, billed as the world's fattest man. Summer or winter, he always wore a snap-brim felt fedora, gaberdine trousers, shirt and tie, protected by a large denim apron. All the downtown businessmen used his services. They consulted him and confided in him, making him an invaluable source of scuttlebutt. Men confided in him because he never identified the source of anything he might pass along. He was also astute enough to know to whom he could confide information and to whom he should just listen.

"You Mr. Cleatus Clore's grandson, ain't ya?" he asked.

"I am!"

"Fine old man. Shame him dying like he did. He was just

getting his Kentucky Stag distillery back up and running again when he up and closed it. Next thing I heard, he's dead."

Throughout Prohibition, my grandfather's distillery was a federally-bonded warehouse, used for whiskey storage. Kentucky Stag Bourbon was one of the few legal whiskeys sold by doctor's prescription—for "medicinal use only." In 1933, when the Volstead Act was repealed, my grandfather had to increase production and expand the facility in order to remain viable and competitive in a rapidly expanding market.

"Shame," Jack continued. "He used to sit right where you are now. Good customer. I liked him." He directed his words at my feet, not looking up, as he busied himself snapping and popping his polishing rag back and forth across my shoes, bringing them to a high gloss. When he finished, I climbed down. He charged 10 cents a shoe, but I paid a half-dollar and flipped him a quarter tip.

"Thank ya, Mista Hoyt!"

Almost as an afterthought, Stormy said, "Suh, I understand the vice president of the mining company Mr. Weiskopf worked fer is staying down the street at the Soaper Hotel." I gave him a slight pat on the shoulder as a sign of appreciation and walked out on the sidewalk.

‡

The six-story Soaper Hotel was on the southwest corner of Second and Main Streets, across from a bank on each street. It was newer and nicer than the Kingdon. Late in the day, I left the office and walked down the street to the Soaper. An early afternoon rain had left shallow puddles that jumped and rippled in the wake of passing cars.

I entered the small lobby through the entrance off Second

Street and approached the registration desk, which looked as much like a bank teller's window as anything else. Through the grilled opening, I slid a dollar bill toward the clerk.

"For the name and room number of the vice president of Coldiron mines," I said.

"His name's Maurice Rednour, and he's downstairs in the bar. He's a tall, thin fellow with horn-rimmed glasses and a large Adam's apple; you can't miss him."

Like the lobby, the bar was small but elegant. The walls displayed enlarged photographs of early Henderson landmarks, river barges, and fields of bright tobacco. Padded leather chairs surrounded six or eight low cocktail tables.

Rednour sat alone at one of the tables, drinking a bourbon, neat. A cigar lay smoking in an ashtray. He wore a light gray suit with a lighter gray shirt and solid black tie. He looked up as I approached.

"Mr. Rednour, I'm Hoyt Cole with the *River City News*. Do you mind if I join you and ask a few questions?"

"Not at all" he said. "Have a seat. I'd enjoy the company."

"You up here from Nashville?" I asked.

He nodded.

The bar was toward the back, about 25 feet long. A neon juke box stood in a corner, and a row of slot machines lined the wall perpendicular to the bar.

"I understand Coldiron mines has offered a $500 reward for information leading to the arrest and conviction of Weiskopf's killer."

He sipped his drink and nodded.

"Anything you'd be willing to share with me, either on or off the record?"

"The night before Herman was killed, he picked me up at the

depot and brought me to the hotel. I'd say it was about 10:30. We discussed matters at the mines in the lobby, until about midnight, when we agreed to meet again the next morning at 7:30. We said goodnight, I called for a bellboy to show me to my room, and Herman left.

"I got a call the next morning telling me he'd been killed."

"Was there anything or anyone in particular he was concerned about?"

"We'd been meeting at least once a month, but because of some of the union trouble and labor issues, he asked me to come up early." He retrieved his cigar, knocked the ash off, and relit it. The tip glowed red and hot. "Weiskopf was fairly well-liked—as well-liked as you'd expect a mine superintendent to be in this day and time. There are some wagon-truck owners that didn't like him because he'd worked with the union, trying to make the transition as smooth as possible.

"They expected him to be tougher on the miners, make their way difficult, discourage unionization. They met with him from time to time, trying to put pressure on him, making innuendos and thinly veiled threats. But he was a company man, following company policy, trying to make the best he could out of a bad situation.

"Plus, Herman didn't scare easily," he continued.

"To your knowledge, was there anyone in particular that he *was* afraid of or concerned about?" I asked.

"Everyone in general, no one in particular."

"Do you have any idea who might have killed him, Mr. Rednour?"

"No, Mr. Cole, I don't. Wish I did. That's why I'm still here." He signaled the bartender for another bourbon and offered to buy me a drink.

I ordered a beer. "Can you tell me anything about his home life, his personal life?"

Somehow, he seemed a little uncomfortable with that question. He adjusted himself in his seat and sipped his bourbon. He seemed to gather his composure and organize his response.

"Well, he'd been married about eight years. I understand Herman was her second husband. His mother and dad are currently living in the house." He took a last puff from his cigar and crushed it out in the ashtray. "He's got a good friend, a miner named Clyde Gish, who hangs around their house quite a bit. He's a good piano player. Herman and his wife liked to listen to him play and enjoyed singing along."

"How long do you expect to be in town?" I asked.

"Meeting with a couple federal agents from Evansville tomorrow. I'll probably stay around for a day or two."

"Is there a way for me to reach you after you leave town?" I asked. He gave me his business card. I shook his hand, thanked him for his time and the drink, and headed back upstairs and outside.

CHAPTER 10

The next morning, I went to see Detective Brackett. I met him as he was going up the steps into the station. "Gotta minute, Guinea?"

"Sure! Let me go check in, and we'll get a cup of coffee at Ruby's."

He returned about 15 minutes later. The wind and traffic swirled street debris, and the occasional breeze snapped and popped the flags flying from a corner of city hall. Ohio Valley humidity was approaching its midday peak, causing women's hairdos to wilt and men to perspire through their shirts. Shimmering heat waves were already rising off the concrete sidewalks as we walked to the café.

A waitress brought us coffee as soon as we took a seat in our booth. "Any new developments in the Weiskopf murder?" I asked.

"We spoke with his father. The spike maul belongs to Herman. He kept it in the coal shed to bust up coal."

"Several days before he died, Herman mentioned to a neighbor that the maul was missing from his coal shed," I told him.

Guinea shook his head, sucked his teeth. "Be hard for the old man to know who it belonged to." He paused, considering. "One spike maul looks like every other. And there've been several recent robberies of mining tools."

"Did Herman's father tell you anything about the night before he found Herman's body?"

"He said they were all home that night. Herman's wife Selma had been sick for several days, though not in bed. He said he thought Clyde Gish came by a little after six. He was a close friend of Herman's, works at one of the mines."

Guinea stirred an excessive amount of sugar into his coffee and turned it almost white with cream. "Clyde was playing the piano for Herman and his wife to sing with. The old man said around 9:00, Herman left to meet the train. About 20 minutes to 10, he and his wife went to bed, and Clyde left. A few minutes later, Selma went to bed."

I told him about my meeting with Rednour. "That time frame fits what Mr. Rednour told me."

"The old man told me that for some reason, he'd been worried about Herman all night. He said he got up twice during the night to see if he'd come in. He said he made sure the door was unlocked for him, and left a light burning.

"At five the next morning, Herman still wasn't home. He woke Selma and told her. She said she'd call the hotel, and told him to check the garage to see if Herman's car was there.

"It was still dark outside. The old man stumbled over the body and realized immediately that Herman was dead."

"Whaddaya know about Clyde Gish?"

"Nothing much," Guinea admitted.

I turned in my seat and crossed my legs. "Neighbors say he hangs around the house a lot, even when Herman's not home. How's that strike you?"

He turned to me and raised an eyebrow. "Thanks, detective."

‡

After work, I walked down to Wolff's for supper. It was still early; the crowd was sparse. I sat in a booth by myself and ordered a beer, a bowl of bean soup, and a hot ham on rye with brown mustard. Wolff's is well-known for the best bean soup in town. I had barely taken the first sip of my beer when the waitress slid the soup and sandwich in front of me.

I sat alone, enjoying my meal. I didn't really consider myself a loner, but I wasn't troubled by periods of solitude. I don't think I'm antisocial, but I'm not a glad-hander or backslapper, either. I enjoy company, but I don't seek it.

"Hey, Hoyt! How you doing, boy?"

I hadn't seen Bobby Workins's dad since I graduated high school. He used to come down to the football field and watch us practice. Always encouraged us as we ran wind sprints.

"Fine Mr. Workins. How're you, sir?" Mr. Workins had worked at my grandfather's distillery for a time. Circumstance, fate, and coincidence—do they work in concert?

"Glad to have you back in town, Hoyt. It's been a while, hasn't it?"

"Have a seat, Mr. Workins, if you've got a minute."

He slid on to the bench across from me.

"What can you tell me about our illustrious mayor?"

"Why do you ask?"

"Just trying to get the lay of the land here. I've been gone a long time. I'm getting the sense there's more than a little political corruption going on. You been here all these years. I don't want to jump to the wrong conclusions. Just curious, I guess. Reporter's background information you might say."

"Well, son . . . You don't become mayor of Henderson 'cause it pays such a large salary."

"He was mayor when I left in '41. It appears he's become quite wealthy."

"You're right about that," he said.

"How do you get rich on a mayor's salary?"

"If he's anything Hoyt, he's no fool. Grimshaw is shrewd and conniving. He borrowed strategies from the Gilded Age."

"Whaddaya mean?"

"Let's say a business man needed a permit to expand his building or physical plant. In order to obtain it, he'd have to deliver a prescribed amount of cash, in person and in private. Hand it over directly to the mayor himself. Same thing if a homeowner needed electricity run to a new garage he'd built."

"Why would anyone go along with a scheme like that?"

"Oh, you didn't *have* to! You could go through normal channels and wait. And wait you would, as Grimshaw controlled the municipal machinery and determined when and if the work would ever get done. He figured, depending on how bad the applicant needed or wanted the work to be done, eventually he'd come to him for assistance. Commonly, the longer he waited, the more it cost."

"Sounds like corruption to me!"

"Call it what you will, Hoyt," he said as he slid out of the booth. "Good to see you, glad you're back in town."

CHAPTER 11

It was another oppressive summer night. Few stars were visible in the pewter-gray sky. A sliver of moon hung high in the overhead expanse, and a warm, damp breeze blew off the river. As I crossed the bridge, a lone barge plowed its cargo of coal beneath it, through the murky waters of the Ohio River.

I passed between the lights and busy parking lot of the Cosmopolitan Club, at left, and the darkened Dade Park Race Track across the road. Live thoroughbred racing had been held on the park's 1 1/8-mile dirt and sand track from July through Labor Day, every summer since it opened in 1922. A few dim lights on the back side were the only evidence of activity that night. The back side of a horse track is unlike anyplace else; there the gypsy-like people live their lives not just day by day, but hour by hour.

While the sophisticated and hugely popular big bands of the '40s had a venue in clubs like the Cosmo, the poorer, rural populace was gravitating to country music, made hugely popular by Hiram "Hank" Williams, a whiskey-drinking, woman-chasing, skinny white boy out of Montgomery, Alabama, who was taking

Nashville and the Grand Ole Opry by storm. Hank's success encouraged every skinny son of Southern dirt-farming sharecroppers who could scrape enough together to buy a $7.00 Sears and Roebuck guitar to try to pick and sing his way out of poverty.

Their aversion to hard work and their desire to escape the plight their birthright and birthplace dictated also played a part. Anyone who could master a three-chord progression, beat drums, play a fiddle, or sing through his nose, formed a small group and played the roadhouses and honkytonks lining the dirt roads and two-lane blacktops in western Kentucky and southern Indiana. Pearly Martin numbered himself among them.

Otis Earl Martin was born in 1920 near Smith Mills, Kentucky, a small farming community in the southern part of the county. His father was a cheat, a petty thief, and a mostly out-of-work, violent alcoholic. A ne'er-do-well. Once a pretty girl, Otis's mother died when he was eleven. People said she died of abuse, malnutrition, and despair, leaving Otis as the nearest target for his father. The boy was an easy and frequent target for bullies, too. He found every reason possible to avoid school. Without much formal education, he was still well taught and a quick learner. He adopted his father's lying, cheating, stealing, and drinking. By 13, he had mastered the skills that would inform and guide him for the rest of his life. A rapid growth spurt made him a full five feet, ten inches and 175 pounds by 15—physically a man—but he still wore his insecurities like stale body odor. Over time he'd developed a protective facade which he hid behind. He wore boldness as a shield, affecting false courage and arrogance like a suit of armor.

Otis Earl had one congenial characteristic. He had unusually straight and brilliantly white teeth. He smiled often to cover his fear, pain, and shame, earning him the nickname *Pearly*. He quickly learned the effect his white-toothed smile had on the girls in and around Smith Mills—and not only the girls. Because of his new physique and beautiful smile, he became attractive to many of the married women in the area.

One in particular seemed more attentive than others. On afternoons, while her husband was still at work, she sat on her porch with Pearly as he shared his dreams, fears and ambition.

She became more than a comfort to him, gradually leading him from her front porch swing to her couch. And on one memorable afternoon, to her bed. Beyond the sexual awakening, that episode established in his 15-year-old psyche the idea that married women were willing participants and acceptable conquests, a concept that held sway over him the remainder of his life.

‡

Another quarter of a mile north, I turned off the highway and drove a few hundred yards down the old river road that meandered through cropland toward Evansville's downtown. Deep on the right, back in a tree-shrouded clearing crouched the Bottoms, a down-at-the-heels operation that catered to, entertained, and fleeced a less discriminating clientele, another of L. S. Furlong's enterprises. Its patrons were not welcome—nor would they have felt comfortable—at the Cosmo. The place was accessible most of the year, except when spring rains forced the river out of its banks into the low-lying fields and bottomland. It was the epitome of the terms *roadhouse* and *honkytonk.*

Near the road, a mobile, backlit display announced *Leon Remington and the Shotgun Cowboys, featuring Pearly Martin.* The gravel lot was already full, so I parked my truck behind the building and went inside.

The smell of cropland leached in through the wide-open doors at the front and back. Dim incandescent bulbs and neon beer signs provided sufficient lighting to navigate the interior. Moths were drawn to the light, and mosquitoes from the moist, soggy riverbed feasted on the alcohol-numbed patrons. Open steel-framed windows near the ceiling provided air circulation and ventilation. In spite of this, cigarette smoke hung heavily from the ceiling. The place smelled of smoke, beer, hormones, body odor, and perfume. Unlike the Cosmo, single and unescorted women were not only allowed, they were welcomed.

I ordered a beer from the bartender, Woodrow Burdette. His was a name I'd heard while growing up. Woodrow was balding and getting thick through the middle, but he'd been a pretty good minor league baseball player whose exploits were often bragged about in the barber shop where I got my hair cut as a boy.

"You old man Cole's boy ain't ya, son? Heard you were back in town." He spoke with a peckerwood nasal twang. "Good to see you. Been a while, ain't it?"

"A while, I guess," I tipped my head toward the room. "Looks like a pretty good crowd."

"Anytime Pearly Martin is playing here it's a good crowd! He sounds just like Hank Williams. All the women go apeshit."

"He's not as skinny as Hank Williams," I observed.

Country music leans heavily on emotion. It's about drinkin' and cheatin', loneliness, pain, and heartache. But it can also be upbeat and raucous. Cheap booze flowed freely. On the dance floor, couples were jitterbugging suggestively. Slot machines occupied every vacant area along each wall and in the restrooms, like every other place around. The Bottoms had a rowdy atmosphere with hardworking, economically deprived individuals trying to buy temporary respite from the mundane drudgery of their desperate lives.

The bandstand was a plywood platform eight inches above the dance floor. Leon Remington, the bandleader, was up there singing what had become the Cowboys' theme song: "Shotgun Boogie." Leon cut an imposing figure in his western hat, particularly compared to the rest of the band. He was a big man with broad shoulders, large forearms, and a thick waist. Leon played lead guitar and sometimes sang. The Cowboys had a fiddle, a steel guitar, an upright bass, and Pearly Martin on rhythm guitar and vocals. They all wore western shirts, with ivory buttons and piping. Cowboy boots and hats completed the popular look.

I don't know why, but I asked, "What kind of guy is this Martin fella?"

He tugged at his ear and leaned into me. "Don't loan him money and keep your wife or girlfriend away from him."

"You speaking from personal experience?"

"I loaned him 30 bucks six months ago. Ain't seen hide ner hair of it since. Keeps tellin' me he'll pay me next week. Lyin' don't bother him none neither! He's from down around Smith Mills. Daddy wasn't worth the powder and lead took to blow his ass off."

I smelled the unmistakable fragrance of Evening in Paris as the bare arm of a woman brushed against mine. She wore heavy lipstick and rouge, and her hair was styled in a Victory Roll in an attempt to lengthen her rather round face.

"Pardon me, honey, I'm Selma. I know you?"

"I doubt it, I've been gone for a while."

She looked into my eyes and squared her shoulders to emphasize the cleavage exposed by her low-cut, red dress. She held an empty highball glass and tipped it toward me, winking suggestively.

"Would you like a drink?"

"Sure!" She tossed her hair back over her bare shoulder. Woodrow set it on the bar in front of me, and I passed it to her. "Thanks, honey!" She turned, placed both elbows on the bar and leaned back against it, just as Pearly Martin stepped up to the microphone and began singing "Cold, Cold, Heart." I had to admit, he sounded a lot like Hank Williams.

"I can tell you, my heart wouldn't be cold, if I was with him," she said, to no one in particular. She pushed off the bar, grabbed her drink, and hip-rolled her way toward three other women at a nearby table. She seated herself, crossed her legs, and dangled one of her white pumps off her toes.

I lit a cigarette and ordered another beer. "Didn't take her long to get back in action," the bartender said.

"Who is she?" I asked.

"That's Selma Weiskopf, Herman's widow."

"The man killed recently out on Washington Street?"

"Yup!"

My! My! Unbelievable.

Why do people—women and *men—become starstruck? Perhaps it's because celebrities are viewed in a contrived environment, where nothing but their physical presence, talent, and attractiveness are evident. Even out here in this run-down roadhouse, their "glamorous" existence and personae replace the real and often negative images we have of ourselves and our lives. Does the mere presence of a spotlight transform them in our eyes? Maybe. But there's also the animal magnetism many entertainers exude. If the women's response to Pearly's performance was any indication, he was possessed of it in spades.*

As the night wore on, the playlist slipped from boisterous to sad and lonely. The patrons were more inebriated, and the mood was sultry. Hormone levels rose and inhibitions fell. When the band took their second break, I went to the men's room, washed my hands, and headed out to my truck. As I was pulling out, my headlights caught a brief glimpse of a woman in a red dress, holding a pair of white heels and climbing into the back seat of a vacant car with Pearly Martin.

CHAPTER 12

Like a woman, water can be life-giving, calming, beautiful, seductive, and treacherous.

The Ohio River defines the northern border of Kentucky, from the eastern mountains, across the Knobs, the Bluegrass and Pennyroyal regions, into the Western Coal Fields and the Jackson Purchase. In the summer the river soaks the region with damp and steam, mildly reminiscent of the jungles of the South Pacific. The resultant pastiness seems to bind the people to each other, as well as to the land itself. Living here demands a certain persistence. It's not for the timorous or the weak of spirit.

The river and Kentucky's people are inseparable. The one defines the other. One of the definitions for the word *Kentucky* is from the Iroquois word "ken-tah-ten," meaning, among other things, "the river of blood." Mostly taken for granted and often ignored, in the early months when even the dams can't contain her, the river overflows into bottomland, signaling the arrival of spring. She divides cultures, dialects, and attitudes. She's been polluted and recovered. She's been dammed, but not tamed. Not quite wider than a mile, except at the Smithland Dam, she's no Moon River.

While appearing slow and lazy on the surface, she can be deceitful and lethal. One summer, the river claimed the lives of 14 locals—from drunkenness, outboard motor accidents, fishing mishaps, swimming accidents, ferry accidents, foolishness, and carelessness. Earlier that same summer, a private plane had nosedived into it at 150 mph.

A morning fog hung heavy over the bottomland, rolling in off the river to the surface of Main Street. An early morning walk through it was eerie, akin to wading ankle-deep in the clouds. A breeze blew the curtains into my open window. I sat on the side of my bed, watching the light play over my knuckles and the veins in my hands. Outside the morning sky grew darker. The wind picked up and blew over the lamp on the table near the window. Shadows and light chased each other around the room like two boys playing tag.

Are we really possessed of free will? Or are we manipulated by unseen forces in conflict with everything we believe to be true? Go to work, do your job, keep your head down and move on.

I went downstairs, picked up a paper and went into the cafeteria for breakfast. Uncle George was sitting at a table by himself, finishing off his coffee and smoking a cigarette. I moved over to his table. "Morning, Uncle George."

"Have a seat, Hoyt. Glad to see you."

Uncle George was approaching 60. His mousy-gray hair was neatly trimmed and smartly parted. He had high cheekbones, a sharp nose, narrow lips, and a swarthy complexion. That morning, I broached a topic I hadn't planned to discuss with him. I still don't know what made me do it.

"If you've got time, there's something I'd like to explore with you."

His clear and intelligent eyes peered at me through rimless bifocals. "Sure, go ahead."

"I've thanked you for apprising me of the job at the *River City News*, but I never told you about my fear about coming back here. It had nothing to do with the job. I was overcome by apprehension related to my childhood."

"No, you didn't. What was so troubling for you?"

"When I was a small boy, I remember fear and uncertainty having to do with my grandfather, Cletus Clore. There was a lot of caution and secrecy for a time. I felt confined and cloistered. It was never explained to me, and I wasn't old enough or bold enough to ask what was going on. I felt I was in some unknown danger, and it caused me lots of sleepless nights. As I grew older, it faded from my memory—until you invited me to come back home and take the job at the newspaper. Strange, don't you think?"

"That was a while back, Hoyt," he said cautiously.

"You remember anything about my grandfather?"

"I do. Cleatus terminated an ill-advised deal he'd made with Mayor Grimshaw. Almost immediately, he received an anonymous letter, threatening your life and damage to the distillery. Your family was concerned for your safety for a period of time. Shortly thereafter, your grandfather closed the distillery and nothing more came of it. Long time ago, Hoyt."

"What was the 'ill-advised' deal?" I asked.

"Your grandfather needed to increase production and expand the facility to remain competitive in a rapidly expanding market. That required permits and city approval.

"Rather than his usual ploy of a single cash payment, for permits and expanded utility supply, Grimshaw seized upon a plan to tap into a continuous stream of your grandfather's income. In exchange for the town's permission and support for the planned expansion, Grimshaw coerced Cletus into underreporting sales, in order to cheat the government out of excise tax revenue, with his honor personally pocketing the difference.

"A man of principal and integrity, your grandfather was troubled by the arrangement from the outset. As his business grew, the skim became excessive. The stress and strain, along with his distaste for Grimshaw and his deal with the devil, bothered him to the extent that he refused to participate any longer. Cletus sent Grimshaw a certified letter advising him he was no longer going to participate in the scam.

"In poor health, and by that time a widower, your grandfather closed the distillery late in the fall of 1935, rather than be intimidated further. It was a remarkable feat of courage and economic sacrifice. He had a stroke and died 11 months later, at age 78.

"Your grandfather was a good and respected man who allowed himself to be used and manipulated by a powerful and greedy man."

"I never knew that. Thank you for telling me."

Changing the subject, he said, "I was going to leave you a message at the desk." He looked at me over his glasses. "It seems, in addition to the $5,000 life insurance policy Coldiron Mining Company had on Weiskopf's life, there was another personal policy for $25,000. His wife, Selma, is the sole beneficiary."

"How'd you find that out?"

"One of my nephews is a partner in a local insurance agency. He called me last night."

"How come the police don't know about this?"

"I guess they haven't asked."

"What do you make of it?"

"Well, of a sudden Herman is worth a lot more dead than he was alive." He rose to leave. "It certainly provides a credible motive."

"Thanks, Uncle George," I said to his back, as he walked away.

After dropping off a cup of coffee to Stormy Jack, I headed to the police station. Detective Brackett was talking to the dispatcher when I entered. "Gotta a minute, Guinea?"

"Yeah, I'll meet you outside."

I walked down the five limestone steps to the sidewalk and leaned on the closest parking meter, looking down First Street past store fronts and parked cars to the park along the river. The sky was a pale and transparent blue that blended into the clouds on the horizon and faded to white against the trees across the river.

Sheriff's deputies and patrolmen came and went. Detective Brackett stepped out to meet me. His forehead was furrowed and the inside corners of his brows leaned toward the bridge of his nose. "What's on your mind, Hoyt?"

"Are you aware that in addition to the $5,000 policy the mining company had on Weiskopf, there is a personal life insurance policy for an additional $25,000? Selma is the sole beneficiary."

"No! How do *you* know that?

"Check with the local insurance offices; you'll find the one generating the check."

"Think I'll send a couple patrolmen to search Clyde Gish's room while he's at work. Thanks, Hoyt—appreciate your help." He hurried back into the station.

Later he told me the search revealed very little. The shoes in the room were about the size of the footprints found at the murder scene, but they were clean. Clean clothes were found, none with bloodstains.

CHAPTER 13

It was after midnight, and Pearly Martin was driving his '37 Dodge east, up Highway 60 from Union County, back to Henderson. He'd just left the farmhouse of a woman he'd picked up at a bar in Morganfield. The air was still and the sky a dark purple. With the windows down, wind and road noise roared into his car, filling the cab with farm smells and night sounds. A deep yellow moon hung low, just above the tree line, imparting an orange rim light along their tops.

The smell of hickory-smoked pork filled his nostrils 100 yards before he reached Peak Brothers Bar-B-Q, and trailed after him at least that far. Self-satisfied, Pearly enjoyed the aroma, the cool of the evening, and the afterglow of illicit sex. A shiny black '49 Buick pulled slowly from the shadows of the restaurant and eased cautiously up onto the blacktop, falling in behind him, unnoticed. The driver lagged behind about 200 yards, keeping the make and model unidentifiable in the dark. Pearly drove on, oblivious.

Dry lightning flashed silently and menacingly in the northern sky. He had never questioned life or his place in it. He never blamed anyone or took any responsibility for his role. From his perspective, things were as they'd always been. He felt free to do as he pleased without accountability. While outside forces had preyed on Pearly most of his life, he had the capacity, or failing, of living almost exclusively in the moment. He didn't plan or consider. There were no *what-if's* for Pearly. He merely acted or reacted, all predicated on his wants and desires or on the obstacles presented. He was mostly unmindful of conditions beyond his immediate interests.

The Buick closed the gap by 100 yards.

It never occurred to Pearly that people he considered well-off might not have started out that way. They might have worked and sacrificed to gain their position in society. Likewise, people like him were like they were and would remain that way. Nothing they could do about it, nothing wrong with it . . . just the way things were. He had no thoughts of improvement or change. With little education and no mooring in principles, he was virtually amoral. Untroubled. Do or take what you can get away with.

Pearly's first awareness of the car trailing him was when the Buick's big chrome grill was illuminated in his rearview mirror by the headlights of an oncoming car. Slowly, the Buick moved closer and closer until the grill's image was obscured by the back of Pearly's own car. Now and again, the Buick bumped his car and shoved it forward, like a schoolyard bully taunting, intimidating, picking a fight. Pearly felt the hair lifting on his forearms and the back of his neck.

The threatening presence brought back the fear and shame he'd experienced from childhood abuse. His palms began to sweat and feel clammy on the wheel, his knuckles white from the pressure of his grip. His breath became labored, and he could smell his own stink. He felt the sweat beading on his upper lip.

He reached for the pistol in the glove box and laid it in the seat by his side.

At the outskirts of town, the Buick suddenly slowed and turned left onto a road leading over to the south end of Main Street and the country club. Pearly relaxed, and the tension drained from him. Late-night traffic was light, and he drove through the drizzle in town at a leisurely pace, full of satisfaction. Street lights shimmered on the surface of the shining blacktop. The incident on the highway faded from his mind. Pearly continued up Green Street, turned left onto Eighth Street, and drove one block west to his apartment on the corner of Elm. He carried the pistol with him when he left the car.

The Eighth Street Apartments were low-rent units in a building that had been an elementary school. His was one of three basement units, and the only one occupied. As he descended the stairs, his eyes looked out the ground-level window. For a moment, he thought he was looking into the toothy grin of a giant chrome grill. He discounted it as an illusion and walked on down the hall to his unit. The expected dark confines were dimly lit by the floor lamp behind his easy chair. Strange, he didn't remember leaving it on.

He laid the gun on a table in the sitting room, near the door leading into the kitchen. He went to the bathroom, relieved himself, flushed the commode, and washed his hands. When he returned to the living area, he was startled by a man sitting in his chair. Pearly instinctively reached for the pistol. Almost imperceptibly, the man rose, snatched the gun from his hand, and reseated himself in one effortless movement.

He wasn't a big man. Compact, efficient, and professional. His hair was parted in the middle, his eyes deep-set, his ears small and thick, swollen with broken cartilage. He wore a heavily starched white shirt and a necktie held in place by a diamond stickpin! He casually crossed his legs and unloaded Pearly's pistol nonchalantly, without looking at him, as if he weren't there. His hands were small and steady.

"Sit down, Pearly!"

Pearly backed up to a chair, feeling it with the back of his legs, and gingerly sat, looking straight into the man's face. "Who the hell are you, and how'd you get in here?"—displaying all the bluster he could summon.

"Shut up, Pearly! If you do as I instruct, you will never see me again. If you don't, I'll come back and kill you." His eyes were dead; there was no emotion in his face. He said these things calmly and matter-of-factly, raising his face to look at Pearly for the first time.

This wasn't an empty threat. This man wasn't playing games. Pearly could feel his heart racing, his bravado gone. He tried to calm his rapid breathing and racing heart. When he spoke, his voice came in a raspy whisper.

"Whadda you want me to do?"

The man stood and moved toward the door. "Leave his daughter alone!" he said over his shoulder as he left, closing the door softly behind him.

"Whose daughter?" he tried to scream, but all that came out was an unintelligible, eerie, moan. Still sitting motionless, Pearly felt a pleasant warmth cross his lap and spread into the crotch of his trousers as his bladder released its contents.

‡

The experience changed Pearly. He gave up smoking, drinking, gambling, and women. He was scared, more than ever in his life. He was committed!

His resolution lasted a full 72 hours.

The following Friday night, while playing at a club in Rockport, Indiana, his resolve vanished completely. All memory of the man in the Buick disappeared like cigarette smoke in a ceiling fan. Tempted by the flirtatious eyes, smiles, and suggestive body motions of a woman at a table up front, Pearly ordered two whiskeys and followed her out to the parking lot, into the backseat of her car.

At the end of the evening, as he approached the bridge into Owensboro, sitting in the intersection of a country road and the highway, Pearly thought he glimpsed three chrome VentiPorts on the fender of a long black car.

CHAPTER 14

Off Saturday evening, I showered, shaved, and dressed. I put on pleated trousers and a tan, open-collared shirt turned down over the collar of my sport coat. I laced up a pair of brown and white wing-tipped spectators—together, a serviceman's typical civilian attire.

I headed across the bridge toward the Cosmopolitan Club. I was hungry for a steak dinner. Regardless of all else, it was a fine supper club. The music of big bands and cheap drinks were additional enticement. I joined the benign, but guilty, supporters of the problem I was railing against. Shunning valet parking, I drove my truck toward the back of the lot and walked the 50 yards or so to the entrance. There were as many cars with Indiana plates as local. Mine was the only truck.

Arriving couples were generally dressed to the nines, talking and laughing, walking lightly. The sky was clear, a wispy silver with dramatic stabs of orange streaking across in random patterns, the kind of sky that catches your vision and holds it for much longer than ordinary. The defuse glow of the slowly setting sun splashed across the tops of cars in the lot. A light evening breeze carried the smell of diluvial bottomland and river detritus.

The Cosmopolitan Club had a dance floor that could accommodate 220 couples and a grand stage that had hosted Duke Ellington, Cab Calloway, the Ink Spots, Gene Krupa, Woody Herman, the Mills Brothers, and the like. It offered $3.00 sirloin strip, 25 cent beer, and 35 cent highballs. I saw nothing larger or finer in San Diego while training there. It was an upscale establishment with a strict dress code. Unescorted women were not allowed entrance. There was no cover charge at the door, but patrons were expected to spend a minimum of $2.00. That night, Henry Busse and his orchestra were featured.

The ballroom, bar, and restaurant were on the opulent first floor. Upstairs there was a lavish, illegal casino, with its own bar, spacious restrooms, and numerous slot machines and gaming tables, including roulette, craps, and poker. Stylishly dressed waitresses circulated, wearing nothing provocative or suggestive. The casino employees were all smartly dressed; men wore ties, white Eisenhower jackets, and black slacks. Several rather large and imposing young men prowled the floor to provide assistance and ensure proper behavior.

I was stopped at the door by the maître d'. "Sorry sir, only couples are allowed entrance."

I slipped him a dollar, presented my press credentials and asked for his consideration.

"What's your name, sir?"

I told him and he walked off. After a brief wait, he returned.

"Here's a guest pass, sir. Please clip it to the pocket of your jacket. You'll have to remain on the first floor."

"Much obliged."

A server escorted me to a small table near the back and close to the bar. He presented me with a menu, took my drink order, and removed the extra glass and linen-wrapped silverware from the white tablecloth before hurrying off to other duties.

It was still early, not even 8:00. At least 50 couples were already seated in the dining area, but the room easily held twice that number. The acoustics were excellent. The room was gay and lively, but even with dozens of conversations, clinking glasses, plates, and silverware, it remained elegantly subdued. A small trio played tasteful dinner music, adding to the sophisticated atmosphere. It was almost impossible to believe that this upscale establishment existed—thrived!—in a Kentucky river town of fewer than 15,000 people. Someone plucked from other environs and dropped here could easily imagine he was in New York, Chicago, or Los Angeles.

The server returned with my Manhattan and a crystal glass of water. I lit a cigarette with the matches provided—gold-embossed lettering on a scarlet ground proclaiming *Cosmopolitan Club* in elegant script—and nursed my drink, gazing at the room. Most of the couples were in their mid-30s, at a guess, but more than a few couples were in their 50s and older, doctors, lawyers, and businessmen, with their wives and clients.

I gave the menu a cursory pass, focusing on the steaks. A 14-ounce T-bone with baked potato, salad, and drink was $5.95. I made my selection, folded the menu, and laid it aside.

Right at eight o'clock, Mayor Grimshaw and his entourage arrived, receiving the anticipated bowing and scraping from the entire staff. The party was escorted to a table for eight near the dance floor, with great ceremony. The mayor glad-handed and spoke to at least one person at almost every table on the way. The city attorney, the chief of police, the county sheriff, and their wives were with him. I'd been told by employees of the Cosmo that Grimshaw's table was always comped by the house. Virtually all legal authorities in the city and county, if not bought and paid for, were certainly effectively placated.

The Cosmopolitan Club was across the Ohio River, outside of the city's jurisdiction. The club was technically in the county, but the sheriff took very little interest in what happened there. The Indiana state line was only a few hundred yards north, but the area was still in Kentucky and of no concern to Evansville or the Indiana state police. It was a virtual legal no-mans-land—a brilliant and strategic location for owner L. S. Furlong.

When the waiter returned, I ordered another Manhattan and gave him my dinner order. I stretched my legs out under the table, leaned back in my chair, listened to the music, smoked a cigarette, and savored my drink. I began to relax and enjoy the evening. I was lost in thought when she came around the table and stood behind the chair across from me.

"Hi, Hoyt. I heard you were back in town. It's good to see you."

My mouth dropped open. Caught completely off guard, I leaped to my feet so quickly, I nearly knocked my chair over. I reached to catch it with one hand and extended the other to her at the same time. My knees were weak. "Hi, Sally," I stammered.

"Don't I deserve more than a handshake? Can't I have a hug?"

I stepped toward her and gave her an obviously awkward hug. "Where's your husband?"

"Upstairs at the crap tables. I saw you here when we came in. I slipped off to come down and say *hi*."

Sally Morgan told me she loved me in the fall of our junior year in high school. The first girl ever to say those words to me. I was young, impressionable, and emotionally needy. I believed her. Perhaps she meant it—at the time. She was high school cute, vivacious, intelligent, popular and confident. We went steady for two years. A cheerleader, she was at all my ballgames. We went to sock hops, proms, and movies, and hung out at the soda shop with all our friends. We double-dated, parked and petted. It was the most idyllic time of my life. I was in love!

I realized later that it was a rare episode that could never last. In a melancholy mood, after my discharge and while still at UK, I did one of the stupidest things I've done in my adult life. I sent Sally a letter in care of the bank where she worked. I tried as subtly as possible to convey that I still loved her without actually writing the words. I asked nothing of her and proposed no actions on the part of either of us, leaving it open-ended.

I received no response. Adolescent crushes do not require equal and reciprocal participation. There was no consideration of what might have been, not for me.

"Dance with me Hoyt . . . just once more?" The orchestra had taken the bandstand and was playing "Moonlight Serenade." Before I could object, she took my hand and walked me between the tables to the dance floor. We fell into a comfortable embrace. She moved her cheek close to mine and whispered, "I got your letter."

Startled, I pulled away and looked at her. "I'm sorry Sally! That was a mistake, I apologize."

"Don't be," she said, pulling me back close to her.

I was relieved when the song ended and we walked back to my table. Still standing and not knowing what else to say, I asked, "Would you like a drink, Sally?"

"I've got to get back. I still love you, Hoyt." On tiptoes, she turned my face to hers and kissed me. A soft and tender kiss. A kiss full of meaning and emotion. Then she turned and walked away. I don't know how long I remained standing there, looking toward the wide staircase leading upstairs to the casino.

"Your dinner, sir" the waiter said, placing it on the table. "Can I get you anything else?"

"Bring me a glass of Pinot Noir, if you will, please."

The steak was perfectly cooked: medium rare, tender, and delicious. When I finished the meal and the wine, I ordered another Manhattan.

I had not expected to see her. I hadn't wanted to see her. I didn't want to think of her. In the brief 24 months of our junior and senior years, she burned a brand on my immature psyche that is sensitive still, when brushed by remembrance. Those old feelings for her return to me from time to time, only slightly dulled by the years passed. They remain vivid and deliciously bittersweet. It was that wonderfully painful kind of first love that makes you feel forever young and alive with 10,000 tomorrows endlessly laid out in front of you.

After graduation, our romance cooled, like most high school romances—at least from Sally's perspective. But not from mine. I was in love with her. She enrolled in Centre College in the fall, and I joined the marines on December eighth, after Pearl Harbor. She promised to write, but really never did. Oh, I received a couple current-events letters informing me of campus life and her studies, but never anything personal. It was obvious that, at least for her, our relationship had been relegated to the past. A couple years later, she married Robert Bryce Craig. Robert joined an established local law firm, and they made their home here, in the south end of town.

The fragrance in her hair lingered, and the warmth of her body brought back familiar longings. Alcohol and emotions can often be a toxic mix. Anger can build slowly, like a storm, silently becoming more and more intense. Then of a sudden it erupts and causes unexpected and sometimes unintended consequences.

First I became angry with Sally for walking back into my life. Then I became angry at her for dropping me. And then I was angry at myself for allowing my feelings for her to reemerge. And the more I drank, the more the anger intensified, and the more it seemed justified. Raw nerves and emotion took over. Like a brewing storm, it had to find release. I receded into a dark and brooding place, alone, in a room full of people, invisible to them all. I felt I was walking down a path that had no end. I signaled for my check, paid and tipped the server, and rose to leave.

My shoulder unintentionally knocked Forest Grimshaw aside as he was leaving with his party. Embarrassed and incredulous, he bristled and said, "Pay attention, there, pal!"

My anger boiled over, and Grimshaw offered an outlet. *Here's the bastard who threatened my life as a child, ruined my grandfather's business—and ultimately, ended his life.*

"Pardon me, Mr. Mayor," I said. "Do you remember Cletus Clore?"

"Why yes, yes, I do remember Cletus. Why do you ask?"

I moved in as close to his face as possible and said, "I'm his grandson, you son of a bitch!"

‡

"Mr. Cole! Mr. Cole!" A voice from somewhere in the distance kept calling my name.

Pushing and shoving shoulders, marines with their packs and weapons in the landing craft with me as we neared the beach . . . The engine, the ocean, the exploding shells, and the violent shaking . . . And the screaming in my ear? Who was screaming my name? The incessant, endless screaming! Finally, I was able to fight my way up and out of the deep pit of fear that had enveloped me. I was soaked with sweat! I looked into the eyes of . . . Freddie? The bellhop? Why was he in the Higgins boat with me? Incongruous images surrounded him: body parts, human corpses, decaying flesh, human excrement.

"Mr. Cole! Mr. Cole! Are you all right?"

"What's going on, Freddie?"

"You were screaming so loud, other guests reported it. I came up to investigate. I beat on your door, but couldn't raise you. I let myself in to see if you were okay. I'm sorry, Mr. Cole."

Still in a fog, I said, "That's OK, Freddie. Where are we?"

"Why, we're in your room at the Kingdon Hotel, Mr. Cole."

"Sure, Freddie. Yeah, I'm fine. Thanks, Freddie! Thanks, a lot. I'll see ya downstairs in a bit."

"OK, Mr. Cole," he said as he left my room.

The war comes back to me from time to time, like it does to all combatants. For me, those times are rare and brief. For most of us, our minds, aided by the passage of enough time, allow memories, even the most horrific memories, to be pushed back so far that after a while, they don't return. Oh, you can recall them if you choose. But you don't want to. You let them out too often, they remain out, and they drive you mad. That's why few veterans ever talk about their war experiences.

War is hell! is the grossest simplification imaginable. It's beyond any conceivable hell, to the nth degree. There are times you would trade the briefest moments in combat for an eternity in hell, if such a trade were offered. You always have the uncomfortable and distasteful awareness that you're never the same afterward. And you never will be.

I was finally fully awake and still sitting on the side of my bed, and the events of the previous evening came flooding back to me. Sunlight streaking through the slats of the blinds made parallel lines across the floor, each pointing condemning fingers directly at me. I began to feel shame and embarrassment—not about *what* I said. What I said needed saying. Just not then. Not there, and not in that context. I had fired a flashy roman candle. I should have waited for the opportunity when a mortar round would have been more meaningful and effective.

In certain situations, anger can turn to violence. Violence can save your life in a kill or be killed instance. When the results are assessed, violent actions are sometimes labeled courage. The Marine Corps awarded me the Silver Star and the Navy Cross for courageous actions on two occasions. Find me a recipient of such awards that feels deserving. Most, like me, feel fraudulent at worst, and just lucky at best. Paraphrasing G. K. Chesterton, courage is a contradiction in terms, a paradox. It's a desire to live that is so strong, you are willing to risk your own death to ensure it.

Along with the anger there is always a large measure of gut-gripping, paralyzing fear. Sometimes, anger can light the fuse that turns the fear to violence, the result of which is later called valor. But when anger flairs to paltry actions and remarks, there's nothing courageous about it. In exchange for the momentarily venting of your spleen, you expose yourself as weak. Last evening, I was left to do nothing but stand and glare at Grimshaw's back as he walked away, not sure if he had even heard me.

CHAPTER 15

Sunday afternoon I was sent to cover a local baseball game. The league of teams from Henderson, Union, and Webster counties was comprised of pretty good former high school athletes who had enjoyed a modicum of success and praise. As young men, fathers, and laborers, they were just not ready to give up the experience. And, to be fair, most just liked to play baseball. They got business and civic groups to pony up enough money for uniforms and some equipment. There was no remuneration for the players. Admission to the games went to cover equipment and field maintenance. The men bought their own cleats and gloves. They drove themselves to the out-of-town games and mostly played on Sunday afternoons. They sometimes played a night game in a community with a lighted field. The games were a good way to while away an hour or two on a summer afternoon and an opportunity to interact with the local citizenry. From time to time, you'd see some pretty good baseball.

Henderson's Park Field, so named because it was an extension of Atkinson Park, was accessed by a dusty road off North Elm Street. Like most baseball venues of the era, it was a no-frills structure. It had about 10 rows of bleachers, running 20 or 30 feet in length, covered by a sloped tin roof. The dugouts were just one-row, covered structures, strategically placed down the first-base and third-base lines. The infield was dusty clay, kept level enough to protect against serious leg injury, and the outfield showed scattered clumps of crabgrass and weeds. As an enhancement, Park Field was lighted.

During the seventh inning that afternoon, I climbed down the bleachers and went to the concession stand, where I found Maurice Rednour waiting in line. After he purchased his sodas and hot dogs, I asked if he had a moment to speak with me.

"Sure."

I motioned toward the fence along the first-base line and started to move in that direction. I placed a foot in an opening in the wire fence, leaned on the topmost strand, and looked out over the field. "Any breaks in the murder of your superintendent?"

"You probably already know they found the murder weapon.

"The company hired a private detective firm out of Evansville to assist in the investigation. You must know that they set up an office in the Kingdon Hotel. Someone running from the scene left tracks leading to the back of the property and down the alley to the street, where they vanished. One of the first patrolmen to arrive covered the prints with a wash tub and later made a plaster cast. The shoes were a rather small size."

"Have they determined a motive?" I asked.

"Robbery is apparently out. They searched Herman's clothing, and beside the small items a man might be expected to carry, the search revealed $11.00 and a watch."

"Many of the townspeople hold to the belief the murder marks another chapter in the long history of labor warfare throughout the region," I interjected.

"There is another possible motive they're following. Herman was scheduled to appear as a witness in a bootlegging case. There are some tough characters in that racket around here. It's possible someone in that business killed him to keep him quiet. Also, Clyde Gish named a few miners that had made threats against Herman."

"What're your thoughts, Mr. Rednour?"

"It could be one of any number of possibilities, none of which I can rule out at this point. That's why I'm still here. I'm satisfied we'll identify the motive, and that should lead to the killer. I'm going to head back to my hotel. See you again, Hoyt."

"Thanks, Mr. Rednour. I appreciate your time."

As I was on my way back to my seat, an old friend approached and began to talk about the Weiskopf murder. After some back-and-forth, he offered the following: "I heard Weiskopf's wife was having an affair with a man calls himself *Carl Duncan*." He said the name skeptically.

"Really? How do you know that?"

"Local scuttlebutt. Wouldn't be the first time for her," he said.

Carl Duncan? Who the hell?

I went back to the office and wrote my account of the ballgame. The Henderson Merchants defeated the Corydon Lions, three to two.

CHAPTER 16

The next morning, after eating breakfast in Ardith's café, I got an extra cup of coffee, with lots of sugar and cream, in a to-go cup, and carried it into the barber shop. With growing trust in our friendship, Jack had begun to drop most of his affected "niggra" vernacular and verbiage. At least in private. I enjoyed our daily visits.

"Morning, Storms," I said, handing him the coffee and climbing onto his chair. Jack smelled of the witch hazel he used after a shave.

"Thank ya, Mista Hoyt." He looked at my feet. "Them shoes don't need no shine."

"Dust 'em off for me John—just want to talk with you."

"Yessuh?" Stormy sat on his stool, leg spread, his apron making a tent across his knees.

"Got anything I might find useful?"

He passed his brushes perfunctorily over the toes, sides, and backs of my shoes and sat back down on his stool in front of me. "Whatcha interested in, Mista Hoyt?"

"Looking for anything on the Weiskopf murder." On a hunch,

I asked, "You ever heard mention of a man named Carl Duncan, here 'bouts?"

He paused, as if pondering my question, but I knew he was just putting the proper amount of time between my question and what he intended to say. He took the lid off his coffee, blew on it, stirred it with his finger, and licked it off. He gazed in the direction of the front of the shop and spoke toward the front window, as if I weren't there.

"Can't rightly say I have, Mr. Hoyt. Let me see what can I find out."

Stormy Jack exuded an aura of calm and personal contentment. A man satisfied with, and accepting of, his lot in life. Qualities to be respected and admired. Born a mere 30 years after the Civil War, John Calhoun Storm had first-person knowledge and experience of the full impact of the Jim Crow South.

It is a common misconception that all white Southerners owned slaves. In fact, of the roughly 8 million people in the antebellum South, only 4.5 percent owned slaves. White Southern society consisted of three classes: the planters, the middle class, and the poor whites. The poor whites—often called white trash—were at the bottom of the Southern social and economic pecking order. They were generally considered lazy, largely due to the diseases that ravaged their numbers. Because of their living conditions, they were victims of hookworm, malaria, and pellagra, all of which produced intense lethargy. They occupied the least desirable land and worked as tenants, dependent on, and indebted to, the wealthy landowners for ground and equipment, sometimes even groceries. They owned no slaves.

Prior to the war, even white trash could always feel that they were better than colored people. The times, mores, and culture all ensured this. The total ruin of the war made it obvious that a man of this class was not superior to anyone, not even a former slave. The simplest and vilest way for a human being to elevate himself is to put down those around him. And that was exactly what these men had been doing ever since. They doubled down on their prejudice and abuse. The social, cultural, institutional, and human injustice had been perpetuated for 85 years after the passage of Lincoln's Emancipation Proclamation (the 13th Amendment) and the end of the Civil War.

John C. Storm was fully aware that generations of racism, taught and learned, had reduced the Negro to almost subhuman status in the minds of many, making the injustice acceptable to them. Fear of reprisal may have been another strong motivator for continued oppression. How vicious and vengeful would they have been, had the roles been reversed, and the opportunity for payback arose? John seemed to bear no outward animus toward his condition or the people responsible for it, even though he had suffered from some of the worst. There was a peace about him, perhaps *the peace that passes all understanding*. He was one of the most admirable men I ever knew.

I stepped down from his stand, put a dollar bill in his hand, patted him on the shoulder, and walked out.

CHAPTER 17

The following morning, I was shocked to find a message from H. H. Headley waiting for me at the front desk. It was very formal: He asked if I would come in early to discuss a special assignment. While my shift didn't start until 4:00, I was curious. *It must be something important for Headley to send a personal message.* I headed to the office.

The morning air was unseasonably pleasant and free of humidity. A slight breeze was blowing up from the river. The sky was clear, and the early sun bathed the city streets with a warm yellow glow, invigorating the populace. At the newspaper office, there was a flurry of hasty business activity. My early entry was greeted by jeers and catcalls. I smiled knowingly, nodded, and waved in acknowledgment. I went to the receptionist and told her I had a message to see Mr. Headley.

"Uh-oh. A call to the throne or onto the carpet. Which is it, Hoyt?" She was smiling.

"No idea," I said. "Thought you might tell me, Marge."

"Don't know," she said. "I'll let him know you're here." She picked up her phone to buzz his office. "Hoyt Cole here to see you, sir."

Within seconds, she said, "Go on back, Hoyt. He'll see you right now."

I knocked on his door, opened it a crack, and stuck my head in. "Mr. Headley?"

A worn, but ornate rug extended from under his desk to three or four feet in front of it. Two comfortable, upholstered chairs were situated on the portion exposed. His desk was larger and more imposing than others in the building and cluttered with the typical paraphernalia: phone, typewriter, desk calendar, pen and pencil set, ashtray, and the ubiquitous in-and-out trays. His chair was a leather, wingback variety, on casters.

Come on in, Hoyt." Headley wore his age with pride, conveying authority and assurance. "Have a seat, son."

I eased down in the chair closest to the door and considered the man's Errol Flynn–type mustache above his cleft chin and prominent jaw line. His black hair was parted slightly off center, and he wore a lightweight seersucker suit, a 1930s penny collar shirt, and a tie in a half-Windsor knot.

"Thanks for coming in so promptly, Hoyt," he began.

"Yes, sir!"

While not showy, Headley's office reflected his position as owner of a local daily newspaper. Framed diplomas, citations, and certificates were displayed on the walls, as were pictures of Headley with local, state, and national dignitaries. A pleasant breeze blew in through the open windows.

"What's your relationship with our mayor?" he asked, catching me entirely off guard.

Trying not to stutter and stammer, I sat forward in my chair, both elbows on the arms, hands clasped in front of me, leaning toward him, trying to buy as much time as possible. *Is this where I get my ass handed to me?*

"Not personal, sir. Nor, professional either, I suppose. Only been in his presence once."—as evasive and still truthful as possible . . .

"Well, you must have made a good impression. His honor is having a soiree next Sunday afternoon from five to seven and requested that I send you to cover it. A somewhat unusual request, as our society editor usually covers these events."

"Never been to any such gathering."

"Nothing to it. Just show up, maybe around 5:30, and mingle with the crowd. Take note of the dignitaries present, smile, listen, and be cordial. Interact when engaged. Don't initiate contact. Help yourself to food and drink in modest amounts. Describe the food and drink offerings, the presentation, the decorations, and the theme, if there is one. Be straightforward, and not hurried in your reporting. The mayor likes to bask in his glory. Be gracious, but not fawning. This'll be a walk in the park for you, Hoyt."

"I'll do my best, sir." I said, standing to leave. *I'll be on his turf and at his mercy.*

"You're doing a good job, here Hoyt. I'm glad to have you on staff. Good luck, Sunday." He stood and extended his hand.

I've been in tighter jams. This time I won't be under the influence of too much alcohol.

I let myself out, closing the door as discreetly as possible, and headed out before anyone had a chance to question me about the meeting.

"Bye Marge, see you later today," I said as I passed her desk.

"See ya, Hoyt. Oh, I almost forgot. Sally Craig stopped by to see you yesterday afternoon."

"She leave a message?"

"No, she just asked if you were in. Cute little thing, isn't she?"

CHAPTER 18

My father had a lifelong friend named Carla Broadbent he'd gone to school with—a reliable and credible source for local information. She agreed to meet me after work at the Right Quick Café, across from the law office where she worked. I arrived first and selected a booth off to the side. The bartender was bent over the sinks, transferring glasses from wash water to rinse water to sanitizing water, and setting them on the drain to dry. Servers carried trays of food from the kitchen into the dining area; the smell of fried meat was pervasive.

When Carla arrived, her presence radiated a symphony of fragrance, evoking my boyhood among gentle, Southern women: the delicate aroma of a woman at Sunday worship, drifting above the subtle bass notes of line-dried sheets. I sensed immediately she was genuine, strong, and steadfast. Widowed and in her late 60s, Mrs. Broadbent was still very attractive; she carried herself erect and with confidence.

After we finished our meal, the waitress cleared the table. Over a second cup of coffee, I broached my inquiry. "I'm sure you're aware of Herman Weiskopf's murder, having been raised in the East End."

Looking intently at me, she nodded slightly.

"You have any idea who may have killed him or why?"

The "happy hour" crowd began to filter in and take seats at the bar and nearby tables. The place was filling up fast. Carla removed a compact from her purse and checked her lipstick and makeup, touching her nose and cheeks lightly with the powder puff.

"Narrow it down for me Hoyt." She continued to inspect her face in the small mirror. "What are you looking for?"

I sat back in the booth and crossed my legs. "OK, let's start with his personal life. What do you know about him and his wife, Selma?"

"Well, Herman was sent here about 12 years ago to oversee the three Coldiron mines. I think he came from the coalfields of Pennsylvania. As far as I know, he's done his job as well as possible, given the unstable labor conditions in the mines. Never any controversy, never any legal problems, a solid citizen by all accounts."

"And his wife?" I asked. The rumor about Selma having an affair seemed believable, given her recent carousing in a place like the Bottoms so soon after Herman's murder. I wondered if Carla had heard it.

Carla raised an eyebrow, looked at me and then looked down and to her right. "Selma's a Griffin, out from Niagara: dirt poor all her life, and certainly not satisfied with her plight. Everyone knew she was ambitious to a fault, using any means possible to scratch and claw her way out of poverty.

"An attractive girl, she used what she had to get ahead. You might say she was generous with her charms." Carla took a breath. "She married an ole boy from the Hebbardsville area who had been recently promoted to assistant superintendent of one of the three Coldiron mines. His job was good enough to allow him to rent a house and move her into town. But when Herman Weiskopf was sent here to oversee all three of the mines, Selma immediately set her cap for him."

The waitress stopped by to refresh our water and leave the check.

"Herman was no match for her feminine wiles, and before long he fell under her spell. After about a year, she divorced her husband and married Herman."

"I'm told they'd been married about eight years. Has the marriage been relatively stable?" I asked.

"Let me put it this way: Herman was a nice guy, very trusting, and maybe even naive. Have you heard of Clyde Gish?"

"His name has come up during the investigation."

"Well, I'm not going to speak on anything I have no real knowledge of, but I'd investigate that relationship closely. Draw your own conclusions."

She slid out of our booth and rose to her feet. "Keep this in mind, Hoyt. Selma hasn't lost her ambition or the drive to improve her social status. I'm sure she has another conquest lined up."

I stood to join her. "You've been most helpful Mrs. Broadbent. Thank you for joining me for dinner, not to mention for your knowledge and local perspective."

"You're welcome, Hoyt, and call me Carla. Your daddy and I were old friends, raised down the street from each other. He and my late husband were close friends, as well."

I paid the check and walked her outside to her car.

Could Clyde Gish be the mysterious Carl Duncan?

CHAPTER 19

The following day, I went out to pick up a pack of cigarettes. What breeze there had been had abated, and the humidity from the river increased, decreasing everyone's comfort. Still, I decided to continue to the police station to see if I could talk to Detective Brackett.

The dispatcher told me Brackett was out but should be back momentarily, if I wanted to wait. Anticipating where he might be, I crossed the street to Ruby's. Pushing through the door, I smelled fresh donuts, and coffee warming on the hotplates. The waitress was just serving Brackett toast and coffee.

"Morning, detective, mind if I join you?"

"Free country."

Without asking, the waitress poured me a cup of coffee.

"I talked to Rednour the other afternoon. He said there were a couple new leads in the Weiskopf murder."

"Oh, really?"

"Yeah. Rednour said Herman was scheduled to testify in a bootlegging case. 'There's some tough characters in that racket,' he said. He thought maybe somebody killed Wieskopf to keep him quiet. He also told me that Clyde Gish had named a few miners who had made threats. Said he gave you guys their names."

"The bootlegging angle led nowhere," Brackett said. "Weiskopf's testimony was only to corroborate a timeline in a minor aspect of the investigation. Nothing that would have led to murder."

"What about the threats from the miners Gish named?" I asked. "Lots of people believe the murder's labor related."

"That Evansville agency set up offices and started questioning miners day one. Surprised you haven't noticed, staying in the Kingdon and all. The most consistent testimony is that Weiskopf was pretty well-liked. Sure, there was some bitching from time to time, but the consensus is he was a good boss. Better'n most.

"I personally questioned the three Gish named. Just guys shooting their mouths off. Coalfield bluster." Brackett cleared his throat. "Gish likes to inflate his own importance."

"People keep bringing up Gish's relationship with Herman's wife," I probed. "Word has it he was a frequent visitor in the Weiskopf home, often when Herman wasn't there. Supposedly, he's driven her to town from time to time. Neighbors have reported seeing Selma and Clyde, setting together in the swing on the front porch, even dancing together," I went on. "Pretty cozy, don't you think, Guinea?"

Brackett lit a cigarette and blew the smoke toward the ceiling. "Credible suspicions Cole. The story has grown to the point investigators are giving it closer scrutiny. It's a pretty serious charge to make, particularly against a sick woman who has just lost her husband."

She wasn't sick enough to prevent her escapade with Pearly Martin.

I relayed the episode at the Bottoms to Guinea. He didn't respond. I decided not to tell him about my friend revealing she was supposedly having an affair with the shadowy Carl Duncan.

"Nobody has actually seen anything that's wrong at face value. Setting in the porch swing, dancing, and riding in a car together, visits to a home where he was unquestionably welcomed by the husband. All done out in the open, for all to see. Nothing clandestine. None of these constituted a romance—at least in the eyes of the investigators," Brackett allowed.

"I suppose. Even the people giving me the information concede Clyde and Herman were close friends right up to the last."

"We're working on it, Hoyt. I'll keep you in the loop, and you do the same."

We paid our tabs and walked out together. He crossed the street to the station, and I headed back toward my office.

CHAPTER 20

The next afternoon, I went in early. Reporters and typists were banging out copy for the afternoon edition. Phones rang, people stripped paper from typewriter carriages—all the noises of a busy office. I walked directly to Hunsaker's office.

He looked up and motioned me in. "You're here early, Hoyt. What's on your mind?"

"If you don't have anything assigned to me when my shift begins, I'd like to go out to interview Clyde Gish."

"Who's he?"

"His name keeps coming up in the Weiskopf investigation. Apparently, he works at the mines and was a close friend of Herman's. He was at his house the night before the murder. It seems he's been there quite often, even when Herman wasn't. I'm told he boarded with the Weiskopfs, before Herman's parents moved in. None of the investigators seem to have much interest in him."

"That oughta tell you something, Hoyt."

"He might reveal an angle no one's thought of," I told him. "There's still no clear motive."

"Go ahead then, see what you come up with. But get on back here as soon as you can." I pushed out past another reporter, who'd been waiting for the opportunity to speak with him.

I had been told that Gish was working at Coldiron mine number two that week, out near Robards Station. The area covered about three square miles on a low parcel of land between the watershed of Canoe Creek and Grand Creek, and was home to about 400 people. The mine was another mile or so beyond the center of the community. I drove past herds of cattle grazing contentedly on fields of lespedeza, on down a narrow, crooked road edged with gum trees and post oak scrub, and pocked with holes from the relentless pounding of the coal trucks. Birds perched on utility wires against a mottled sky the color of dirty linen. Turning onto the property, I faced the identical coal-stained black dirt, the persistent acrid smell and the same silver-gray wooden tipple I'd seen at mine number three.

When I inquired after Gish, I was directed to a man operating an electric locomotive, a few hundred yards off. I parked my truck and walked out through coal slag and dirty weeds. The miners possessed the same hangdog posture and ghost-like stare I'd seen before. They wore the same coal-stained overalls, brogan shoes, and mining caps with carbide lights. Their faces were smudged with coal dust, heavily concentrated around the nose and mouth. Desperate men, the living personification of the adage *root hog or die!*, they looked considerably older than they probably were. With every passing hour, they left segments of their lives in a dirty, black hole.

The heat from the sun cast a shimmering gleam across the desolate landscape. The air was hot and dry, and a dark, sooty vapor rose up in protest to my strides through the underbrush. My nostrils picked up the pungent, toxic reek. As I neared, a man walked from the other side of the electrified black engine. Catching sight of me, he nodded and threw up his hand in greeting. He seemed unusually small; I allowed it was due to his juxtaposition with the giant engine. But as I drew closer, I realized it wasn't an illusion. He was a small man, with unusually small feet.

He was an incongruous figure in such a setting. Unlike the rest of the men on the property, he wore a derby hat with a rolled brim pushed back on the crown of his head. He had on a suit coat, albeit worn and dirty, over a soiled white shirt with a frayed collar and a black leather bow tie. His dungarees were turned up at the bottom in tall cuffs. He seemed possessed of a certain self-importance.

"You Clyde Gish?" I asked.

He turned a round face and high forehead in my direction. "That's me." He spoke with a country brogue.

"I'm Hoyt Cole with the *River City News*. You got time to talk to me a bit?"

"Why not?"

Another man approached and engaged Clyde regarding an issue back at the mine shack.

After the man left, I began again. "I understand you were close friends with Herman Weiskopf."

"I was. Fine man! Prince of a fella. Shame what happened to him."

"You got any thoughts on who killed him or why?"

He propped one foot on the hub of a wheel, stretching somewhat to get his foot that high. He leaned forward with an arm crossed on the elevated knee. He nodded his head toward the black monster.

"In addition to operating this beast, Herman relied on me to keep him apprised of any talk or shirking by the miners."

"So, you're a kinda 'labor spy?' "

"I don't particularly like that term, but yeah, I guess you could say that."

"So, you're a man that would know about any trouble brewing?"

"You bet! I could tell you plenty."

"Really? Tell me"

"There never was a better fellow than Herman! But just the same, some people didn't like him. There have been plenty of threats made, and I know who made them." He emphasized the *I* by cocking his head, throwing his shoulders back, and expanding his chest. A real banty rooster. He placed his foot back on the ground and tilted his hat forward on his brow.

Looking at him for a time, I asked, "You gonna tell me?"

He moved his hand over his chin and straightened his bow tie. "I told the police and them investigators from across the river. I've already said enough, and I gotta get back to work."

"Thanks, Clyde 'preciate your time."

He turned abruptly and walked away, as if he feared he'd already said too much.

I walked back toward my truck.

Clyde Gish exuded the typical "small-man syndrome," full of bluster and cockiness, trying to project confidence as compensation for his small stature. Men so affected apparently never realized that height was not an accomplishment. Instead, they seemed to believe that if they'd only tried harder, they could have been taller.

I felt wary of Gish. On the surface, he seemed harmless enough, yet somehow, he didn't seem truthful or trustworthy. I didn't think I'd want to go into battle with him. Often, when I formed a negative first-impression of a man, I was wrong, I knew.

I didn't think I was wrong about Clyde Gish.

CHAPTER 21

I dreaded the assignment. I wasn't reared in society with *soirées*. We had homemade ice cream and cold, sliced watermelon in the yard with neighbors and family members. I wasn't an officer in the marines. I never set foot inside the Officers' Club. It never occurs to folks of modest means to put their social standing on public display. But it's done all the time in well-to-do circles.

In all honesty though, the real reason for my dread had nothing to do with social awkwardness. I knew I'd be confronted. I knew I'd be provoked. I recognized a trap; I'd been set up before. Oh, I knew Grimshaw didn't arrange the affair for the sole purpose of belittling Hoyt Cole. But it *did* provide him the opportunity. I had no one to blame but myself. I set the trap and baited it with my own stupidity and lack of emotional control.

Summer Sunday afternoons in Henderson were mostly uneventful. Family picnics and baseball games in the park were common. Visits to grandparents and rides in the country occupied lots of families. But even the most economically devastated communities have their upper crust, and they like to show themselves to be such.

Mayor Forrest Grishaw's home was a three-story brick structure, five blocks east of Main Street, located among a number of elegant older homes belonging to former tobacco barons, distillery owners, and wholesale grocery magnates. Behind a huge setback, 150 feet from Center Street, three tiers of steps, spaced about 20 feet apart, led to a tall, arched-limestone porch entrance, maybe 6 feet above the lawn. The third floor was flanked by a hexagonal turret on the right and a dramatic limestone gable on the left.

I parked a block away, on Ingram Street, and walked to the house. The air smelled of freshly mown grass and the earthy aroma of the azaleas and rhododendrons embracing the porch. Japanese lanterns festooned mature and blooming crepe myrtles framing the right side of the home and the giant oak and magnolia trees beyond them. Birds splashed in a birdbath and flew in and out of trees. The lot sloped gently toward Ingram Street on the side, providing a beautifully landscaped, tree-shaded space where 50 to 60 guests enjoyed a gathering in full swing. A generous buffet was set up for easy access from either side, and three separate bars were strategically situated, manned by men in starched white jackets, black pants, and ties. A three-piece string combo played unobtrusively, off in the distance.

The weather was pleasant, the air cooling as the sun began its slow descent into the river, to the west. It was a subdued gathering, with an older crowd, smug and confident in their success and station. Everyone was trying hard not to appear impressed. The mayor was nowhere in view; but the local dignitaries were there, and I assumed those that I didn't recognize were prominent business owners. The men were dressed in suits or sport coats with ties. The ladies hung on their arms, their throats and wrists sparkling with jewelry. Obvious by his absence was L. S. Furlong.

The afternoon softened, and the mayor and his wife appeared

descending the porch steps, followed by a state representative and his wife. Guests closed in, greeting them. Servers carried trays of champagne and tropical drinks, and stylishly clad waitresses circulated with food offerings.

Feeling totally out of place, I remained at a distance, obscured by the shade of the giant trees. I tried to be as inconspicuous as possible, slowly moving about, keeping my back to as many as possible so as not to be noticeably approachable. I confined my libation to a single glass of orange juice and vanilla ice cream ladled from a large crystal bowl. Very refreshing. As the afternoon wore on, I decided my fears of confrontation were unfounded. I had enough information to write an acceptable account of the event; there was no need to remain any longer.

I moved toward the Ingram Street side. The murmur of the partygoers faded as I crossed the lawn. The shadows had lengthened, and a mild breeze blew from the river. I scented the faint aroma of daylilies and four o'clocks on the evening air. The light was waning, becoming an orange glimmer along the river, to the west. I had escaped!

"Mr. Cole . . . a word, please?"

Grimshaw!

I stopped and turned slowly around. He was alone. Grimshaw was average sized and slightly balding. He wore rimless bifocals perched on a bulbous nose above a self-satisfied smile, but his approach was conciliatory.

"Please thank Harry for sending you to cover this little gathering."

I didn't respond.

"Our last meeting was less than cordial, don't you agree? In fact, I thought you were a little rude," he said, still smiling, but now smugly.

I didn't respond.

"Perhaps you aren't aware, but your grandfather welched on a business arrangement between the two of us."

I restrained my vitriol and said, "Grimshaw, I'm on your property, as an invited guest. If not a guest, an emissary or messenger. I'm also here in the employ of a man I respect, doing a job I like. I won't be provoked. Good day to you, sir." I turned to walk away.

I felt his hand on my shoulder, in an attempt to stop me. I turned quickly and stepped backward, away from his grip, causing him to stumble forward awkwardly. He obviously resented my refusal to react, but my size, demeanor, and facial expression must have troubled him. I saw fear in his eyes. He was unsure of what his next move should be. His face flushed and puffed like an overfilled toy balloon.

"In another 10 feet, I'll be out of your yard," I said. "Let's both agree, this didn't turn out liked you'd hoped and leave it at that." Again, I turned and walked away. He stood huffing and sputtering, isolated at the edge of his property.

I drove back to town and wrote my account of the event, careful to name all the bigwigs, to describe the food and drink, and to provide as glowing an account of the gathering as possible, concealing, with some difficulty, my personal animus.

I hoped it would make our society editor proud.

‡

Still wired from my altercation with Grimshaw, I drove out Zion Road to the Checkerboard, a county restaurant and watering hole frequented by farmers and coal miners. I seated myself at a high-top table for two. The chalkboard menu announced the evening special: meatloaf, mashed potatoes, and peas, with a roll.

When the waitress came by, that's what I ordered, along with a glass of iced tea. Within a brief period, the food was placed in front of me, sizzling hot. I knifed open my dinner roll and buttered it. Fragrant steam and the smell of yeast filled my nose. Down-home cooking at its finest!

Busboys busied themselves clearing tables, as servers circulated through the space taking orders. The noise of dishes, glasses, and silverware rattling together, along with the sound of chairs being scooted and moved into place across the wooden floor, filled the room as I enjoyed my meal. I savored each mouthful, reflecting on some of my mother's meals when I was a boy. Fully satisfied, I placed my knife and fork on my plate and pushed it to the middle of the table. I wiped my mouth with the paper napkin and leaned back against my chair, emitting a contented sigh. I signaled my server and ordered a cup of black coffee, lit a cigarette and continued to rest and digest my food. As pleasant as the meal was, I still couldn't shake Grimshaw from my mind.

Finally, I paid my check, retrieved a toothpick from the counter dispenser and walked out to my truck. It was the shank of the evening. The humidity refused to die, and the clouds bore a slight sheen of moisture from the river. The wind felt warm on my face, and the taste of dust was in the air.

I opened the door of my truck. The cabin reeked from the cow paddy in the center of the front seat. It was crusted over on top, but still green, slick, and slimy. Someone had made considerable effort to deliver it intact from the pasture. There was a note taped to my steering wheel: "Stay out of the coal fields. We can handle things ourself."

Damn it!

I went around to the passenger side, away from the entrance, sat on the running board and waited, knowing whoever was guilty would come out soon to enjoy my reaction. In no more than five minutes, two men came out of the café, laughing and shoulder-shoving.

One was medium height, thick through the shoulders and gut. He had on an open-collared shirt, worn over a pair of pleated slacks, loafers, and white socks. His dark hair was cut high and tight, parted on one side and hanging long over the eye opposite the part. The other was smaller in weight and height, but more muscular. He wore his hair in a G. I. cut. He wore a black T-shirt tucked into a pair of dirty dungarees. A pack of cigarettes was rolled into the sleeve of his shirt. One was lit and burning in his right hand.

Obviously proud of their feat, one said, "Wonder where he went? I'd love to have seen the look on his face when he opened the cab door. *Colletch* boy, coming back home! Don't need nobody snooping around the coal fields. He wouldn't last 24 hours in the mines."

Blowhards like these two relish vocal jousting, anticipating that their size and intimidating words are enough to cow anyone confronted by their swagger and bluster. I stood and walked around the front of my truck to meet them.

Laughing and nudging his friend, one said, "What's a matter, paperboy? Cow shit in your truck?"

Likely these ole boys had lived a hardscrabble existence, hand to mouth for the last several years. No real trade, no marketable skills, no true identity. With little else going for them, guys like these often resort to establishing themselves physically, creating a distinction. They target the weak and vulnerable, establishing if only to themselves, that they have some value: They're tough!

I approached the bigger, the one closer to me, both hands at my sides. I slammed my cupped right hand hard into his crotch, grabbed his package and squeezed like I was going to tear it off and hand it to him. At the same time, I grabbed his shirt front with my left hand and headbutted the bridge of his nose, crushing the bone. Bullies, loud-mouths, and would-be tough guys are not accustomed to their own pain, particularly when it is administered unexpectedly. Blood and snot rushed from his nose and mouth. He screamed and dropped to his knees, one hand clutching his bloody face, the other clamped tightly between his upper thighs. "You busted my nose! Hell man, why'd you do that? We was just playing a little joke."

"Not funny," I said, walking toward the second man.

He immediately threw up both hands, palms forward indicating surrender, as he backed away. I continued toward him until he backed into the side of another parked car.

"Look man, it was Jim Ed there that done it. I just walked out with him to see your reaction."

"What'd you think of it?" I asked.

Before he could respond, I pushed off the ground with my feet and drove my body weight through my right fist into his gut. The blow bent him over and forward, accommodating my left cross to his jaw. He dropped to his knees, facing his still moaning and groaning buddy.

"Now, both of you take off your shirts!"

They glanced at each other questioningly, but without hesitation and by mutual consent, they began to remove their shirts. I retrieved some cardboard from behind my front seat and scooped the cow patty from the front cushion, flinging it on the ground between them.

"Gimme those shirts!"

I took one and wiped the residue from my seat cushion and folded the other over it to sit on. Standing between them, I said

"Now look, a few days from now when you've recovered a bit and are feeling better, you may decide to gather a few more of your good ole boys and exact retribution on this *paperboy*. Just know this: Regardless how it turns out, good or bad, and regardless of who else is involved, I'll come after you! And next time, I won't be as gentle." I left them coughing, wheezing, and spitting blood onto the gravel of the parking lot.

I took no satisfaction in the encounter, but if I hadn't responded as I did, I would have been the target of every hard-ankle ole boy in the county. Reason, psychology, and discussion would have been viewed as weakness, and wasted on those guys. May as well address it sooner, rather than later.

CHAPTER 22

In the early '50s, a new entertainment media phenomenon came to the tristate area. Television station WEHT, a fledgling CBS affiliate, was the first, with tower and station atop Marywood Hill in Henderson. Later that year, WFIE opened, and early the next year, WTVW, both located in Evansville, Indiana. The original building in Henderson was a small, Quonset-hut kind of thing with narrow halls and a gravel parking lot.

Early on, local programming prevailed. News, weather, and sports, with a smattering of children's programs were common fare. "River City Hay Ride," featuring Leon Remmington and his Shotgun Cowboys, starring Pearly Martin, became an immediate local hit. It was a live transmission, unpolished and rudimentary. But local fascination with the new entertainment medium overshadowed any lack of technical polish.

This venue expanded Pearly's already considerable popularity exponentially. Television exposure allowed him unfettered access to women. He took full advantage of it, on any and every occasion possible. Married or single, young or not so young. His appetite was limitless, and there was no shortage of women welcoming his advances. Station employees reported that it wasn't uncommon for Pearly to bring a different woman to the show every night. He'd take them through the station, introducing them to the staff and explaining the operations in an obvious attempt to impress them. From all accounts, it worked. He was a star!

Pearly mostly lived hand to mouth, even though he dressed and spent money like he had plenty. It's not how much we earn, but how much we spend that determines our financial well-being. Pearly had no trouble outspending his earnings. He womanized, lied, and cheated. He had affairs with several women at the same time. It didn't bother him at all if they were married. If they offered, he accepted. He borrowed money from friends and coworkers with no intent to ever pay it back. He just kept making excuses until most creditors got tired and gave up, writing off the debt.

Fans were anxious to buy him drinks and cigarettes and to do favors for him. He took advantage of them all. He drank heavy and gambled hard, on anything and everything, always believing he was going to make a big score. He ran up as large a tab as local bookies would allow, before one by one they cut him off. Some even threatened him physically.

‡

Pearly always felt safer in the dark. The charcoal haze of the evening sky melted into black, like a curtain dropping, hiding all the things he feared and disliked about himself. He backed his car deep into the wooded park, toward the river, in a thicket of black walnut trees. Small animals scampered about the undergrowth, and yapping squirrels leaped from branch to branch. Occasionally a cool breeze wafted up from the river, carrying a moist plume of water vapor through the open windows of his car. The calming sound of the flowing water and the muted, discordant murmurings of night insects brought him a sense of contentment.

Ahead of him were a couple of enclosed picnic shelters, each with a solitary, dim bulb lighting the entrance. Obscured from the view of others, he could see anyone approaching. He was relishing a postcoital cigarette with another man's wife when he heard the low resonance of an engine, well before he saw the illumination of the low-beam parking lights. As the car neared, the driver parked in front of the farthest shelter. A blond young man got out and cautiously looked around before going inside.

Pearly took a bottle of Cabin Still from his glove box, unscrewed the cap and took a long pull, handing the bottle to the woman. She took a quick swallow and handed it back to him. Not 10 minutes later, a second car parked beside the first, and a second, older, man headed inside the shelter, but not before first unscrewing the light bulb at the entrance, fully exposing his face in the yellow glow—a homosexual tryst, a not altogether uncommon occurrence on the river at night.

"My God! That's Ed Triplett," the woman said. "My brother used to work for him, before Triplett fired him. My brother is still pissed about it. He'd love to have something he could use against Triplett."

They waited for some time, not sure who or what might be revealed. After a few minutes, a third car approached the shelter. It never came to a complete stop, but the driver passed slowly, apparently examining the parked vehicles—perhaps checking license plates. Pearly noted the car's Indiana plates. They remained hidden there, staring fixedly at the shelter without speaking, waiting to see what else might transpire.

After a time, the third car looped around the drive through the park and returned. This time, the driver parked a distance away and approached the shelter on foot. He peered cautiously through a side window, crouching low and taking care not to be seen from the inside. Even in the dim light, they could tell the man was smartly dressed, well groomed, and no common laborer.

Pearly turned to the woman. "You know that guy?"

"No! Never seen him. Nice-looking though."

The man finally returned to his car and drove away, only to return a third time. He killed his lights well before coming into view and parked in a shaded area out of view of the shelters. Pearly and the woman sat transfixed. They couldn't leave and expose themselves to the mysterious man. What were they witnessing? A potential blackmail setup? A love triangle? Might there be a violent confrontation? Even a double murder?

Another 30 minutes elapsed. The first young man watchfully exited the shelter and departed. A full 15 minutes passed before Ed Triplett came out and drove away. The third man remained.

CHAPTER 23

Saturday afternoon, I met an old friend at the Gold Coin for a late lunch. I passed the vacant hostess stand, the chalkboard announcing the day's specials, and a busboy clearing empty tables on my way to the bar. A man and his wife sat at one table, and four young women dressed in pastel sundresses occupied another. They'd obviously been there a while. The table was cluttered with their napkins, wine and cocktail glasses, and ashtrays full of lipstick-smeared cigarette butts. They were in high spirits, and obviously full of spirits. They were giggling and talking over each other in loud voices with animated gestures. I recognized the two facing my direction, but did not know them.

Guy Prentice was waiting in the second booth in the bar. I slid into the seat across from him, facing the back. Guy was a year older than me, but we had played ball together in school. He was short and solidly built with a slightly receding hairline, even in high school. He was gregarious, friendly, and well-liked, one of my best friends back home. Guy had gone to Murray State College on a baseball scholarship. He'd married a girl from Calloway County the summer before his senior year when they realized she was pregnant. After graduation, he moved his young family back home and went to work for his father's farm implement business. I don't know how he avoided the draft.

Guy and I visited and talked, ordered and ate, reminisced and caught up. After about 30 minutes, a couple of the boozy women passed our booth on the way to the ladies' room. One lurched as she walked and leaned on her companion. I didn't recognize either of them; I barely registered them passing. I was watching the group at the bar: the bartender was shaking a frosty chrome canister while chatting up the men seated there. One of them was unconsciously swiveling his stool back and forth, making hand gestures for emphasis.

"Wasn't that Sally Morgan?" Guy asked.

"What?"

"The one having trouble walking."

"I didn't see her face."

It was Sally. When they came out, she was having some difficulty. Approaching our booth, Sally recognized me.

"Why, Hoyt Cole," she slurred.

"Hi, Sally."

"This is Jeannie, er uh, Gina. Gina Statler. Her husband works at the bank." Sally's eyes were droopy.

"Hi guys," Gina said, somewhat apologetically.

"You go on Jeannie, uh Gina. I'm gonna visit here with Hoyt a moment."

"We're leaving, Sally."

"You go on. Hoyt'll take me home." Shoving me over with her hip, Sally seated herself next to me.

Gina rolled her eyes and walked away.

"Hi! I'm Sally," she said to Guy.

"Hi Sally, I know who you are," he replied politely.

"Of course you do." She giggled.

Sensing my discomfort and the awkwardness of the situation, Guy said, "I'm gonna run, Hoyt, it was good to see you. Call me again, sometime." He got up and left.

"Buy me a drink, Hoyt?"

"I'll buy you some coffee."

"Oh, pooh, you're no fun." She nudged me with her hip, tipping her head to tap my shoulder.

"You girls have been here a while, and having a good time, but don't you think you better get on home, maybe take a nap?"

"Okay, Hoyt." She put her head on my shoulder and nuzzled my neck, tickling it with her hair. "Take Sally home . . . put me to bed." The heat in her gaze made her intentions clear.

"I can't do that Sally, and you don't mean that."

"Why not, don't you love me?" She sat up, glared at me and extended her lower lip in a pout.

I had dreamed of her for years—while I was in the marines, and yes, even after, from time to time.

"Don't do this! You made a choice long ago. You're a married woman, and you've had too much to drink. What kind of man would I be to take advantage of that?"

While I was still at UK, on learning that I was from Henderson, a girl I was dating asked me if I knew a Bob Craig. She said one of her sorority sisters had met him in a bar the prior weekend. He was in Lexington with some buddies attending a ballgame. He told her friend he was single, so she went out with him the following evening. "Nice guy," she'd said.

"I'll call you a cab and wait with you until it arrives, give the driver directions to your house, and pay the fare, but I can't take you home."

"I don't see why *you* can't take me home. Don't you have your truck?"

I grasped both her shoulders and turned her to face me. "I'm not about to drive Bob Craig's obviously inebriated wife to his house, late on a Saturday afternoon, and escort her to his front door for all the neighborhood women to see and gossip about. My reputation can stand it, but think what they'd say about you. You don't want to live with that, and I won't be the cause of it!"

She folded her arms on the table top, laid her head down, and started to sob. After a time, I laid my arm on her shoulder to comfort her. She immediately turned and melted into my arms, continuing to sob. She cried and sniffled like an injured child, uncontrollably! I held her, gently kissed the top of her head, and tried to assuage whatever was troubling her—aside from being drunk. I reached for my handkerchief, gently pushed her away, and dried her eyes.

I motioned the bartender over and ordered a cup of black coffee. He brought it immediately.

"Drink this, Sally."

She shook her head and turned aside. By this time a couple of the men at the bar had surreptitiously turned and glanced in our direction. Henderson's too small for there not to have been someone there who knew who she was.

"Please . . . for me?"

She took a tentative sip, recoiling from the bitter taste.

"Go on, it's not that bad. Here, let me add some sugar."

With more coaxing, she drank almost half the cup.

"Oh God, Hoyt! What have I done?"

You chose him, not me!

"You've had too much to drink, that's all. You'll feel better tomorrow. This'll all fade into a distant memory."

And he cheats on you.

"That's not what I mean. What have I done to our lives, mine and yours? I'm so sorry, Hoyt. Can you forgive me?"

"Nothing to forgive, Sally. We're both adults. We've both made choices. Life comes at us . . . and we live with it." *My God! Did I really say that?*

I stepped to the counter and asked the barkeep to call a cab and to let me know when it arrived. When he signaled, I helped Sally out of the booth and walked her outside, paid the driver, and sent her home to her unfaithful creep of a husband.

But not before leaning in to kiss her lightly on the cheek.

My feelings for her lingered softly in my mind throughout the following day. I wasn't sure I could stand running into Sally again. Bittersweet, poignant, nostalgic—none of those words adequately expressed the feelings she evoked.

CHAPTER 24

As I stepped out onto the street, an old friend sidled up to me. His cap was pulled low, mostly concealing his eyes, and his hands were shoved deep into his pants pockets, his chin pressed down on his chest.

"Tommy Joe, is that you? How ya doing?" Tommy Joe Hall was a boyhood friend. We played pickup basketball at the YMCA. His father had a farm in the county—pretty successful, by all accounts. They weren't wealthy but had a good living.

"Uh . . . you got a minute, Hoyt?" he asked shamefaced, hardly looking me in the eyes. This was entirely out of character. He was never brash or cocky, but proud, confident, and self-assured. Now he exuded doubt and defeat.

"Sure, Tommy Joe, what's going on? What can I do for you?"

"I'm sorry to bother you. . . . Er, uh . . . You reckon you can loan me five dollars?

"Why, sure. Let's get off the street; walk with me across to the Kingdon, we'll go in, have a seat and visit." Tommy Joe lagged a half step behind me, his shoulders slumped, his chest caved in—trying to be as inconspicuous as possible.

Inside, I led him over to a couple chairs off in a secluded corner. I reached into my pocket and retrieved a five-dollar bill and slipped it to him. "Sit down Tommy, tell me what's going on."

"It's a long story, Hoyt."

"I got time, but you don't have to tell me if you don't want to."

"Everybody here 'bouts knows it anyway. You'd find out sooner or later, I reckon." He paused as the bellhop stopped at his chair to empty an ash tray and straighten magazines on the table between us.

"I got married a few years back, and I went to working for Dad on the farm. We had a kid pretty soon after and things were goin' along OK. Then Dad lost the farm about three years ago. Only job I could find was at the furniture factory. Job don't pay much, 90 cents an hour. We just had our second baby. My wife's milk dried up, and she can't nurse. Right now, I don't have money enough to buy formula. I'm sorry, Hoyt."

"How'd he lose the farm?"

Damn! That farm's been in their family for years.

A taxi pulled up out front and the passenger walked through the entrance to the registration desk, set his suitcase down, and reached into his hip pocket for his wallet.

"Well, it *was* a little tight, two families living off 100 acres, so Dad decided to expand our operation, increase production, and make more money.

"Farming's changed, Hoyt. You can farm 1,000 acres with the same equipment it takes to farm 100. Dad decided we could farm other men's ground and increase our income. So we contracted with a couple other farms about our size. We put in the crops and harvested them on halves and did well, taking on an additional farm or two each season. Then it got to the point we needed some new equipment, a new combine and a two-row cultivator.

Dad had borrowed money to build a second small house on the farm for me and my wife. The bank wouldn't loan him any more money."

Tommy Joe sat up in his chair, leaned forward with both elbows on the arms, hands clasped in front of him. He turned his head side to side and lowered his voice. "That's when Dad decided he'd try his luck at the gambling tables. Each week, he'd take a few hundred and try his luck. And I have to say, he did really well for several weeks, running the original sum up to over $3,500. That's when he made a fatal mistake."

A maid began to clean the carpet strip at the entrance. Glancing toward the distraction, Tommy Joe raised his voice over the drone of the vacuum. "Dad decided to take the full amount to the Cosmo and bet it all, hoping to make enough to buy the new equipment we needed. He lost it all, Hoyt. Desperate and afraid, he signed markers for more chips, hoping to win it back. Needless to say, he didn't. He ended up owing about $7,000 before they cut him off. Furlong took our farm in exchange for Dad's gambling debt."

Son of a bitch! That bastard!

Relating that story had further shamed and embarrassed him.

"I'm sorry, Tommy. That's a tragic story. You don't have to pay me back. Consider it a gift, from one old friend to another. If I can help you along from time to time . . . come see me. Hold your head up; you've nothing to be ashamed of." He grabbed my hand in both his and pumped it in sincere gratitude. He got up and hurried out on to the sidewalk.

Tommy Joe's story made it very difficult for me to remain on the sidelines, a silent, uninvolved critic. I'd lectured Hunsaker about not wanting to be complicit. I kept thinking how everyone in town seemed perfectly accepting of the crime and lawlessness going on. No public outcry, no editorial condemnation from the paper I worked for. By my own count, there were at least 38 gambling establishments besides Furlong's Cosmo and the Bottoms, most of them on the North 41 strip. How does a town of 15,000 turn a collective blind eye to such activities and obvious political corruption? Tommy Joe's story brought it pretty close to home.

Am I being complicit by doing nothing? Does my silence demonstrate acceptance?

Is there such a thing as evil? Real, pure, 100 percent evil, universally recognized and undeniable by all people? Or is it a moving target, a sliding scale, dependent on circumstances and the people involved? *After all, the old man went to the casino of his own volition. What a dumbass thing to do!*

Is it merely a matter of semantics? "Yeah, that's bad, but it's not really *evil*! Is it merely the absence of good?" Define *good*. Is God a symbol of goodness? G. K. Chesterton says, no; goodness is a symbol of God.

Is evil like pornography—*I can't define it, but I recognize it when I see it?* I'm in over my head! I've led myself in a circuitous argument.

None of us are guiltless in the evil around us. Since the Fall we've all been participants, to some degree. We are guilty, either by direct action, or by excusing, justifying, or ignoring the misdeeds around us—evil by omission or commission.

Directly across from Furlong's Cosmopolitan Club, Dade Park has hosted pari-mutuel wagering on horse racing and harness racing since 1922—permitted by the Kentucky State Constitution. *Is gambling evil, in and of itself? Or is it merely criminal because there are laws prohibiting it?* Is it evil to break the law? Are all laws just? *I'm chasing my tail.* Perhaps I needed to clarify my terms and simplify my pursuits. *I need better insight and perspective.* I had to talk to Dr. Bass, a Henderson native with degrees in history, economics, and philosophy, and recently retired from the University of Kentucky faculty. He'd moved back to town and into the family home.

The more I thought about Tommy Joe's circumstances the madder I got! I had to do something! I didn't know what, but I couldn't just remain on the sidelines.

CHAPTER 25

Two weeks after the Weiskopf killing, community unrest was escalating. The conversation about the crime took an ominous turn, with people murmuring variants of a threat: "When they arrest the killer, there won't be any need of a trial." Tensions continued to mount, and the overworked officers on the case feared there'd be a lynching.

Friday morning, Hobert Watson, a plainclothesman on the force, took an early morning phone call. The excited caller on the other end, an employee of a local laundry, asked to see a detective at once. The laundry was nearby, and Watson hurried over. The manager handed him a set of men's underwear.

"Look at these stains," he said, pointing to the garment. "I could be wrong, but I'm almost certain they're blood. One of the drivers brought it in last night, but we didn't unbundle it 'til this morning."

"Who does it belong to?"

"Clyde Gish."

The garment was rushed to a lab for analysis. The stains were confirmed to be human blood, several days old. By this time,

Detective Brackett had been called in. While the evidence was compelling, Guinea cautioned Watson against making a premature arrest. "Let's tie up any loose ends."

They called Herman's widow in for interrogation, armed with this new evidence and the information about the life insurance policy. After more than two hours of questioning and confrontation with the evidence, and in the presence of the two detectives and the Coldiron attorney, Selma Weiskopf made a sensational statement: "Clyde forced his attentions on me and threatened Herman. I was terrified!" Selma claimed she had lived in mortal fear of her husband's *best friend*. The more she talked the more incredible her story became. Over a period of several weeks, she said, Gish had proposed several plans that would enable her to collect the insurance money and marry him—plans as wide ranging as poisoning Herman's coffee or bootleg whiskey and shooting him with a pistol.

The final plan had taken shape on the Tuesday night preceding the killing. Gish would lie in wait in the coal shed until Herman came home. At some point in the evening, Selma was to claim she heard a disturbance in the shed, and send Herman out to investigate. But Selma claimed that she refused to send her husband to his death. According to her statement, Gish acted on his own. The following evening, when Herman returned home from his meeting at the hotel, Gish was waiting behind the garage. When Weiskopf was exiting the structure, Gish struck him down with two blows to the back of his head.

If Clyde Gish knew he faced arrest, he showed no signs of it at work on Friday. The attorney for the Coldiron Mining Company called and asked him to come by the hotel. "We got some points we think you might be able to help us with," he said.

Clyde entered the hotel early and started up the stairs to the third-floor headquarters. Detectives Brackett and Watkins followed and entered an adjoining room. When Clyde arrived, the attorney asked him if he was carrying a gun.

"Why no!" Clyde responded, apparently surprised. Brackett and Watson then entered the room and arrested him. While he didn't resist arrest, Clyde denied the charges vehemently.

The detectives were concerned with the rapidly forming mob; it was reported that a site had been selected for a lynching. Gish was therefore taken out a back door. Half a dozen heavily armed guards in two automobiles escorted the arresting officers in a rush up the river, 30 miles east to the jail in Owensboro. It was immediately evident that there was no safety in Owensboro: vigilantes from other mining towns were joining the mob from Henderson. Gish was promptly transported by train to Louisville, another 125 miles east.

Clyde remained unconcerned, laughing and joking with reporters while in jail and labeling Selma Weiskopf's story a lie. A clever ruse by a Henderson deputy brought the case to a dramatic climax. None of the footprints at the crime scene could be positively identified, but Clyde didn't know that. The deputy visited Clyde's cell, where he sat silent, looking at him for a long moment.

"I got some news for you, Clyde. You and I wear the same kind of shoes. The ordinary shoe has only six nails in the heel, but ours have eight. The footprints found in the alley behind Herman's house showed the imprint of eight nails. We matched them with your shoes."

Clyde took a long pull on his cigarette, looked at the ceiling for a time and said, "Well, I guess you've got me; may as well tell everything." Clyde admitted his advances toward Herman's wife, but said she hadn't resisted them. He told of the various schemes devised to kill Herman, but blamed her as the motivating force. "I never had a better friend than Herman Weiskopf. She kept nagging at me. Eventually, I killed him."

CHAPTER 26

Later that week, Dr. Flavius Bass agreed to meet me in the spacious lobby of the Kingdon Hotel. A couple of the chairs there were strategically situated in a corner for privacy and conversation. We would be unobserved there, adjacent to the bustle of daily hotel lobby activities.

I watched Dr. Bass find his way into the lobby. His head was large and his feet, nose, and ears didn't seem to match. He appeared to be created from incongruous parts, each unrelated to the other. His crumpled, snap-brim fedora sat at an oblique angle, and while the individual elements of his clothing were of good quality, it was apparent that no thought was given to coordination or style. His narrow hips allowed his trousers to slip below his ample stomach, creating concentric pools of fabric surrounding his ankles and concealing his shoes from the bottom of the laces up.

His mind appeared to occupy a different plane. Had I failed to call his name, I think he'd have walked past me, perhaps down the hall and right out the back door.

I stood. "Dr. Bass!"

He stopped abruptly and turned in my direction.

"Hoyt Cole, Dr. Bass. Thanks for agreeing to meet me."

"Ah, yes, of course . . . Mr. Cole." Then, quizzically, "How do I know you?"

"Well, we're both Henderson natives, and I took a philosophy class from you a couple years ago."

"Certainly, certainly, I remember you now."

I didn't know if he did, or if he was just being polite. I invited him to sit in one of the two chairs I'd staked out and briefly explained how and why I had come back to town. As succinctly as I could, I related my concerns about the illegal activities I'd observed. I wondered why I was so completely out of step with the laissez-faire attitude of the majority of the citizenry, and told him so.

"Dr. Bass, it is difficult to effectively articulate such a complex set of issues. It may be too complex to address in a single session, here in the middle of the hotel lobby."

"Not at all, Hoyt. You demonstrate a legitimate moral alarm and obvious apprehensions for your home town."

"Thank you, sir."

He gazed about the lobby, appearing to study the runners carrying messages through it, to and from the Western Union office just outside. After taking in the activity for a time, he gradually turned to me and began on point, as if his mind had never stopped considering what I'd said. He crossed his legs, removed his hat, and hung it on his shoe.

"Ours is a rather complex situation, and not a recent one. There are numerous factors in play, and few justifications. I'll give you the best explanation I can and offer my insight, perhaps telling you more than you bargained for. First, I think it is important for me to state, and for you to know: *You are not the only one concerned about the current state of affairs.*"

"That's good to know, sir, because I see very little evidence to the contrary."

"In such matters, there often must be a tipping point, an occurrence of sufficient magnitude to raise the collective ire and stimulate action. We haven't yet reached that point." He fidgeted with his hat while thinking. "Gambling has existed here and been dealt with in various ways since the early 1800s. There have been indictments for horse racing on Sundays. A gambler was lynched in the mid-1820s because his neighbor felt he was a bit too lucky, too often." He paused to watch a bellhop push a luggage cart toward the elevator.

"Horse racing on the city streets wasn't outlawed until 1840," he continued. "And gambling was a very serious problem early in this century. There were 32 arrests for gambling in 1907, when the city marshal vowed to close every gambling house in town. There were sufficient laws in place to justify the effort.

"I don't know if gambling, in and of itself is sinful, or even bad. The problem here is, it's against the law, which makes it wrong *here and now.* There is no gambling problem in Nevada; gambling has been legal there since 1931. Same activity, different conditions. Can it be evil or sinful in one place and not another? I'll leave that debate to theologians."

He leaned forward, shifting his weight to his left hip to remove a handkerchief from his pocket and blow his nose, then folded the cloth and returned it to his pocket. "Gambling is illegal here, and therefore a real problem. Tolerance of one illegal activity often prepares the way for tolerance of other illegal activities."

He fell silent while one of the maids pushed a service cart across the lobby toward the first-floor guest rooms. The smell of clean linen and pine-scented disinfectant trailed behind. Another crossed the room to where we sat, stopping to sift the butts from a sand-filled ash stand, using a kitchen strainer. When she'd gone, he began again.

"Prohibition also contributed to current attitudes. While a noble idea, the universally unpopular and virtually unenforceable Volstead Act was so outrageous that nearly everyone felt justified in violating it, creating a pervasive atmosphere of doubt and distrust in all authority. The collapse of the economy, prolonged and aggravated by FDR's failed economic policies further entrenched that distrust. For more than a decade, men struggled to eke out the meagerest living. They lost concern for whether an endeavor was legal or illegal. By the time conditions improved, the attitudes and behaviors had become so engrained they continued.

"Political corruption is the third leg of the stool supporting the present conditions here, and it's also dependent on a degree of tolerance by society. If the powers that be are willing to look the other way, for a price, all forms of criminal behavior are possible.

"All the things I've enumerated have worked in concert over time to create the present conditions. You'll have to deal with all of them."

"How can anything change?" I asked.

"Tipping point, Hoyt. Tipping point. February 14, 1929 in Chicago: the Saint Valentine's Day Massacre, the event that tipped the scales against Capone and his cronies. It took two more years to send him to prison, but the massacre turned the tide of public opinion. Sooner or later, there'll be a tipping point here."

"Thank you, Dr. Bass. I appreciate your time and your historical perspective. It was good to see you again."

We shook hands and he wandered off.

Wow! Fascinating man! A little eccentric, but fascinating.

Tommy Joe Hall's story was my own, personal tipping point. I didn't know what impact I could have, but I knew I could no longer remain complacent, regardless of what anyone else did or didn't do.

CHAPTER 27

Not long after my meeting with Dr. Bass, Hunsaker sent me to cover a shooting at the Bottoms. There were several cars in the lot when I got there. Boots scuffled over the gravel in the lot—a cluster of people moving in and out of the building. Several sheriff vehicles were present, and deputies stood about, interviewing witnesses. The wind whispered through weeds and wild grass near the edge of the property.

I finally was able to corner a deputy. "What's going on here?"

He moved cautiously away from me, hoping I'd be discouraged and walk away. I followed him doggedly. "May as well tell me. I'm going to find out sooner or later."

He stopped abruptly. Looking back and forth over both shoulders, he almost whispered, "Lloyd Furlong shot and killed Melvin Browder. Claimed it was self-defense."

Even though employees and deputies came and went, I was not allowed inside the nightclub. I later learned that Sheriff Agnew was in a lengthy private conference with Furlong, apparently crafting the most plausible explanation for the shooting. Finally, Furlong and the sheriff came out. Agnew hustled Furlong toward his car. "I'm taking Lloyd into custody until this thing gets sorted out," he said.

As things unfolded, it appeared to me that Agnew was Furlong's pet lawman. According to corporate papers, he owned a minority interest in the Cosmo. He'd kept Furlong's Uncle Amos Barker out of jail after he shot a colored man at the Bottoms, earlier that year. Barker admitted hitting the man in the head with a pistol, but an X-ray found bullet fragments in his brain. The particulars surrounding the current shooting got fuzzier and fuzzier as time elapsed, but Melvin Browder was also shot in the head. The bullet that killed him entered through his upper lip and exited via the top of his head, almost in the center. It could have been deflected by his false teeth, which were found next to his body, fractured and lying in two pieces.

Furlong was released later that day.

My writeup presented the bare facts: L. S. Furlong, owner of the Bottoms nightclub on Old Waterworks Road shot and killed Melvin Browder, an employee at that establishment about two o'clock that morning. The coroner stated that Browder was still alive when he arrived, but he was struggling to breathe. Browder was dead on arrival to the hospital. Witnesses at the scene, all employees of the Bottoms, substantiated Furlong's claim of self-defense. No charges were filed. A coroner's inquest was scheduled for the following week.

‡

L. S. Furlong freely admitted that he fired the bullet that killed Melvin Browder but insisted that he'd done it in self-defense. That was the official version and the one accepted by the coroner's jury, as well as by the grand jury investigating Browder's death.

I was told that Furlong and Browder's association had begun several years earlier, when Browder owned a grocery store. He had provided Furlong a large and continuous source of sugar in five-pound bags, as bulk sales of large amounts of sugar waved a red flag to federal revenuers. The two became friends, and when Browder's grocery failed, Furlong put him to work bartending at the Bottoms.

Legally and officially, the matter seemed closed. However, the issue just couldn't be set aside all that easily. Almost immediately, conflicting accounts began to surface and spread throughout the community, igniting a firestorm of gossip and speculation as to what had really happened. One report was that Browder had won a considerable amount of money at blackjack and when he went to collect, the cashier refused to pay him. Furlong was called into the fracas. Browder, who reportedly had been drinking and quarreling, assaulted Furlong with a pistol. Furlong defended himself by shooting Browder. This account seemed contrived at best. The gambling tables were accustomed to paying off when a patron won, employee or not. No logical explanation was offered as to why they would refuse to pay him.

Another account was equally implausible. Apparently, Furlong and his staff had after-hours parties at the Bottoms. One of the waiters was a good tap dancer. L. S. liked to fire his pistol at his feet while he was dancing—just full of high spirits and having fun. Supposedly, one of the bullets hit an exposed nailhead, ricocheted off the floor, and stuck Browder, killing him.

Perhaps these were the versions Furlong and Sheriff Agnew were discussing during their closed-door skull session. In the end, they must have determined that the best thing to say was that Browder drew a gun on Furlong, and L. S. shot him.

Browder's family wasn't satisfied with the official version.

His widow filed a wrongful death suit in US District Court in Evansville, seeking $50,000. The court awarded her $35,000. Furlong's lawyers filed a motion to set the verdict aside, arguing that the award was excessive and based on insufficient evidence. The motion was denied, and the case wound up in the Seventh Circuit Court of Appeals.

The appellate court eventually reversed the federal court and ordered it to disregard the jury's verdict and find for Furlong. In many ways it was a rational decision. All the witnesses agreed an angry Browder had shot at Furlong. Of course, they all worked for Furlong. These unsettling circumstances began to slowly turn the tide of public sentiment against Furlong. For the first time in years, his activities came into question and under scrutiny.

It seemed Browder's killing was the tipping point.

CHAPTER 28

I'd been putting it off, but I knew I was going to Forrest Grimshaw's office to confront him. His was the only operating tobacco warehouse remaining in Henderson. Two impressive wood-framed, iron-clad warehouse buildings faced each other on the south side of Hancock Street, near Main. A gravel alley off Hancock Street served as a driveway between them.

I made an appointment with Grimshaw on my own time. That Saturday afternoon, willows rustled in the breeze down by the river. A father and small boy sat contentedly in the shade, mostly ignoring their fishing lines. The sun danced golden off the current. A big perch rolled over and slapped the surface with a broad tail. A sudden gust of wind from across the river seemed to push me up the steps and into one of Grimshaw's buildings.

Both were open warehouses with large, open louvers along the exterior walls. Concrete loading docks at the front of each building allowed loading and unloading. A smaller two-story brick office building faced the river. It was abutted on the south side by a one-story garage. I let myself in through an unlocked door labeled *Office*. There was no one behind the reception desk, but I spied a door standing ajar off to the left, down the adjacent hallway.

"Grimshaw?" I waited before calling again, louder this time. After a time, Grimshaw appeared in the doorway and moved to greet me.

"Hello, Mr. Cole, come in and have a seat." He gestured toward the open door, and I followed him into the room.

He rolled up his sleeves and loosened the knot in his wide, colorful tie as he settled into his chair. "To what do I owe the pleasure?"

"With all due respects, mayor, this is not a pleasure for me, and I doubt you'll consider it a pleasure when we're done. You accused my grandfather of 'welching' on an agreement between the two of you. I'm here to defend against that accusation and your characterization of an honorable man. Please note, sir: I'm here on my own time, representing no one but myself."

"Understood, Mr. Cole," he pushed the bifocals up his bulbous nose. "Those events were years back. Do you really feel it necessary to address them now?"

"I do!"

"Then by all means." He nodded and made a gesture, rather condescending, I thought. "Please proceed." He leaned back in his chair.

"By terminating his deal with you, my grandfather was trying to spit the bit and relieve himself of a distasteful bargain he made in a weak moment. A bargain, if not with the devil, then certainly with a close emissary. He gave you proper notification of his intent to put an end to the arrangement."

"Harsh words!" he said. "However, your horse-racing reference is most colorful."

"Your response was to threaten my life and his home and distilling facilities."

"Quite a strong accusation, Mr. Cole, an accusation for which you have no proof!"

"We both know it's true." I allowed the statement to hang on the air before continuing.

"You've become quite wealthy and wield considerable power. Have you ever made a single dollar by your own efforts? Your record suggests the source of your wealth is exacting payment for favors, for city services, and from skimming other men's wealth through extortion—as you did with my grandfather. You brought economic pressure to bear on the previous owner of this warehouse, leaving him no choice but to sell, then bought it for pennies on the dollar."

"Business, Mr. Cole," he said, tenting his fingertips. His elbows rested on the arms of his chair, which swiveled back and forth, slightly.

"I don't know when you became corrupt, but you are. I don't know when this community acquiesced, but it did. I don't know why this community continues to tolerate your corruption, but it does. But know this: your reign will be terminated. That's not a threat, just a statement of fact. No matter how long it takes, fiefdoms such as yours always come to an ignoble end. And I intend to do everything in my power to bring it about. That, sir, *is* a threat!"

"Eloquently stated, Mr. Cole. Quite a speech. However, I don't take threats lightly. Likewise, I don't scare easily. You may have chosen the wrong adversary in the wrong battle."

"You don't have anything I want or need."

He stood from behind his desk and walked around it toward me, "No, but you have a job, don't you?" He smirked, obviously pleased with himself. "You work for a man with whom I have a business association and a close acquaintance."

I stood to face him. "You're a blackguard!"

"A what?" he asked.

"Look it up." I stood, turned my back to him and walked out.

Outside, the sky was overcast and the humidity hung undisturbed by a breath of fresh air. I could feel my heart pounding and knew my face was red with anger.

Well done, Cole! You vented your spleen. To what end? Was that satisfaction enough for you? It's likely all you're going to get. Was it worth it?

I climbed into my truck and drove to South Main Street. Housewives went to the grocery, children attended school. Business was conducted, ballgames played, and traffic moved up and down the streets. Drowsy neighborhood tranquility concealed the sordid underbelly of my hometown. I felt claustrophobic in the narrow confines of my life, my hometown, my truck cab!

I drove to the river.

The water flowed on, effortless and unimpeded. Somehow, this calmed me. It underscored my insignificance and put this one individual's worries into perspective. The lawlessness and violence in my hometown notwithstanding, I was keenly aware of the issues developing on the national scene—perhaps a lingering effect of military service. Not much more than five years after the end of World War II, many were already predicting another world war. Journalist Walter Lippman said we were engaged in a "cold war," the ideological struggle between capitalism in the West and communism in the East—the US vs. the USSR, with other nations jockeying to pick a side. We were already engaged in armed conflict again in what was euphemistically being called a police action in Korea—which many viewed as a proxy war between the US and Russia.

Man can't keep the ten, most direct and unambiguous laws God gave him. Ten! Hell, we couldn't keep the one, simple, first law: Don't eat of the fruit from the tree of knowledge of good and evil. If we couldn't keep one, we had no hope of keeping ten. And if we couldn't keep a mere ten, simple laws, how futile was it to continue to enact more? Were all laws destined to be broken? One person cannot break a law without consequence, but an entire society can, in concert, break almost any law with impunity, or so it seemed to me that day.

Our use of the atomic bomb against Japan awoke the threat of nuclear annihilation—a threat mankind would have to live with forever. A genie that could never be put back in the bottle. The political and cultural struggles going on in town didn't amount to a hoot in hell when compared to the potential for the total extermination of life on earth. The main and most important difference? We could *do* something about the conditions in Henderson. We could only sit by, watch, and wait for the issues on the world stage to unfold.

CHAPTER 29

It was two o'clock in the morning. Overwhelmed with self-loathing and shame, Eddie G. crept around on his hands and knees over tree roots, dirt, and leaves, through animal scat, bat guano, and clumps of fur, under the dance pavilion in Atkinson Park, to pay for his indiscretions: $2,500 this time.

The structure sat at the crest of a hill, the ground sloping upward toward the crown and back down again. A long flight of steps led to the front entrance; behind it, the hillside descended between trees and through undergrowth to a service road. The pavilion was a popular place for teenagers to dance with wet hair and red eyes after swimming at the pool in the afternoon sun. It was also the location of this last drop.

The note he found in the back seat of his car told him he would find a single concrete block under the back side of the building, third piling from the left. He was instructed to hide the money under it. As before, he was to come alone, leave immediately, and not return. He would be watched, the note promised.

Eddie found the block and hid the bag of cash beneath it. Whoever it *was* was getting greedier. When six weeks had passed between the second and third demands for money, he'd dared to hope it was over; now he knew otherwise. It would never stop. He'd left $500 at a secure location near the boat docks on the river, $1,000 on a gravestone at the back of Cash Creek Cemetery. The price of silence kept increasing. Eddie wouldn't be able to conceal larger amounts. How much would he have to pay? How could he extract himself from the consequences of his abhorrent desires and poor judgment? Eddie began to weep, overcome with despair. There was no way out. He was helpless against his blackmailer.

Now out from under the building, Eddie walked stoop-shouldered, emitting an eerie, uncontrolled moan. He wrapped his arms around his body tightly. Back in his car, he shook uncontrollably, unable to insert the key into the ignition. Finally, with gasping breath and tears streaming down his cheeks, he was able to start his car and drive away.

The sex drive is the natural method to ensure procreation. It was intended by God. Why had such an ugly trick been played on him? From his earliest memory, he had known that he was different, though he wasn't sure how. As he matured and his difference began to manifest itself in desire, it terrified and overwhelmed him. All of his friends' jokes, comments, and actions underscored the difference he felt but could not explain.

He was able to suppress his longings—most of the time. He dared not reveal them or give any indication of how or what he was feeling. He knew it was wrong. Everybody said so! He affected the posture and mannerisms necessary to conceal it. He grew handsome, strong, and masculine in appearance, making him naturally attractive to girls. He liked girls. He felt comfortable in their company. He availed himself of their charms.

He resisted his other yearnings. God, how he resisted! How much energy and effort had he expended in battling those damning urges? He could keep them at bay for long periods of time, feeling almost *normal*. His wife was beautiful, and he loved his son, his namesake. His business was successful, his future promising.

The moonlight cast long shadows across the narrow lane leading out of the park. Mature trees stood sentinel on all sides, silent witness to his actions. He could not be exposed. He couldn't do that to Beatie and his son. He couldn't allow his parents to share his shame. He had to devise a plan to prevent impending disaster. He drove through the overhanging foliage, a never-ending tunnel of darkness, back to the desolate public streets of town, sneaking back to his home and into his wife's bed.

CHAPTER 30

As soon as I entered the office on Monday morning, the receptionist handed me a note. I waited until I reached my desk to read it. Once again, I was being summoned. I got a cup of coffee and knocked on the door jamb, as the door was standing ajar.

"You want to see me, Mr. Headley?"

"Come in, Hoyt. Close the door and take a seat."

"Thank you, sir."

Without any pleasantries, he said, "I understand you paid a visit to our mayor this weekend."

This is it! I thought.

After a lengthy pause, he said, "No response, Hoyt?"

"That sounded like a declarative statement, sir, requiring no response. If, however, you're asking a question, I suspect you know the answer."

"Very well, Hoyt. Let's do it this way. After your visit to the mayor this past Saturday afternoon, his honor called me to strongly suggest I dismiss you from our staff."

He paused, waiting for my reaction. Bile filled my mouth, and

I'm sure my face reddened. "Fire me, or don't fire me. That's your call. I went there on my own time to address a personal matter."

"While he wields considerable power in town, I assure you, it doesn't extend to what I do with my employees."

When Headley first came to Henderson, locals bragged, "We'll run that Yankee out of town in six weeks!" That had proved much harder than imagined. As time passed, the town began to embrace him as a real asset and to recognize their original notion as a bad idea.

"I would, however, like to hear your reasons for confronting and threatening him—according to his account."

I stood and walked around my chair to the front window of his office, trying to contain the rage building in my chest. I turned back to face him. "As I said, it was a personal matter, Mr. Headley, on my own time."

"Come on, Hoyt! Work with me here. I want to hear your side of the story."

Sensing his sincerity, I bit off my anger, breathed deeply and calmed myself. I returned to my seat and sat down. Leaning forward, I began. "It goes back a ways." I told him about my grandfather's ill-advised agreement with the mayor after Prohibition, his termination of the agreement, and about Mayor Grimshaw's response. I told him about my grandfather's decision to close his distillery.

"In truth sir, I don't know all the particulars of the agreement he entered into with Grimshaw. But Grimshaw threatened him when he ended it." I included my drunken confrontation with the mayor at the Cosmo and related how he'd attempted to provoke me at his home. "What I said was that sooner or later, his reign of corruption would come to an end, and that I would do all in my limited power to expedite that."

A loud siren interrupted my train of thought. I paused momentarily to recover.

"I'll be glad to resign, sir. If that'll make it easier for you."

His fingertips formed a tent under his chin, as he listened. He stared over my shoulder and out the window, seemingly in thought. After a time, he said, "He's a real asshole!" After a lengthy pause, he finally said, "You're not being fired, and I won't accept your resignation.

"Just a couple points for your future consideration. Even though you visited him on your own time, you are associated with this paper and your actions, by extension, get connected to the paper. It may not be fair, but that's the way it is. Likewise, as a newspaper man, your personal matters, when prosecuted in public, also become linked with the paper. I tell you this not to tie your hands, or restrict your freedoms, just to give you pause."

His phone rang. Irritated, he lifted the receiver. "Please take a message, Marge."

He took a breath and looked at me. "I don't want to give you the impression I'm checking up on you, based on what else I'm about to discuss. I don't have to tell you this is a small town. People are anxious to talk about other people's activities. . . . It's evident you have strong feelings and concerns about the degree of lawlessness present here."

"Yes, I do! I would think, as editor of the local newspaper, you would also."

"You seem to be under the erroneous impression that you're the only one in town aware of and concerned about the lawlessness here. Forgive me son, but that's presumptuous on your part, and rather naive. It's also far from the truth."

Emboldened, I said, "Pardon me, sir, but since you brought it up, I find it strange and a bit unsettling that this paper has never written a piece on the subject. You control all editorial content, yet you've never written a single word calling attention to the gambling and resultant illegal activities."

"Hoyt, you've been back here only a brief period of time. Matters such as these sometimes require the long view." He stood, walked around his desk and sat in the chair beside me. He moved it slightly to better face me.

"There have been several attempts to address these issues, all of which have failed—for several reasons. Most of them were poorly planned and hastily executed. The most prevalent reason for failure is they were not kept secret enough. The illegal elements have tentacles deep in the community. There are a number of things in the works that can aid a proper and thoroughly executed, broad-based attack. I have my reasons for not addressing the situation in the paper, reasons I won't divulge to you, at least not just now.

"You weren't offered the job on this paper just because you're local and have a degree in journalism—not to discount either of those reasons. Your tenure here has revealed you to be the man we hoped you would be. No one else on our staff has your passion, nor your writing talent." He rose again and walked toward the front window. He stood with both hands behind his back gazing out. He paused for a long moment, as if in deliberation.

Finally turning around, he returned to his desk. "G. L. Butler, along with several other individuals, have been working in concert with other concerned citizens for months—years, in some cases. Their end goal is to rid this community of the political corruption and gambling. We are at the point where we need newspaper condemnation, but it can't come from this local paper. And believe me we have our reasons.

"I have a proposition for you. You will continue your customary reporting duties here at *River City News*. But I have arranged with the *Evansville Courier & Press*, as well as the *Louisville Courier-Journal*, to loan you to their editorial staff. No one on this paper, except you and I, will know of this assignment. No one on either of the other two papers will know who you are or where you're headquartered.

"You will use the byline *Noah Logan*. You can write anything you feel will have an impact on the citizens here, regarding gambling and corruption. Obviously, all proper editorial protocol must be followed. If so, these two papers will print what you write. Both papers have wide circulation, not only here, but throughout western Kentucky.

"Don't respond now. I want you to give it proper deliberation. I'd ask you not to ever discuss this arrangement with anyone, regardless of whether you accept or decline my offer. Take as much time as you need and let me know when you decide."

"One thing, sir. Should I agree to your proposal, how would I submit my articles?"

"You'd give them to me. I'll see they reach the right person for publication. And don't worry, I won't edit or censor them in any manner. Of course, I can't be responsible for how the other papers may edit your pieces. We'll both be at their discretion in that regard."

"Thank you, sir. I appreciate your confidence. I'll let you know soon."

He stood and extended his hand across his desk. "Thanks Hoyt! Keep up your good work."

I walked back to my desk, unable to concentrate on anything else. It's one thing to run around bitching with no responsibility or accountability. I had been offered a professional opportunity—

along with a tremendous responsibility. He had, in effect, called my bluff. Now, the onus would be on me. I could no longer make baseless claims.

Anything I might write had to be supported by facts, not feelings or innuendo. I knew I was going to accept the assignment, but I wasn't going to do it hastily. I needed to formulate a plan.

CHAPTER 31

You had to know of the alley's existence in order to find it. *There it is.* I turned left off Second Street, heading south toward First. The entrance was between two buildings, so narrow I'd never noticed it before. I slipped between the backs of brick buildings, careful not to bump the old lichen-crusted walls and spill the cup of coffee I carried. *It's not like Jack to miss work.* The pathway was so narrow, the pavement remained moist because the sunlight rarely penetrated to warm it. *Man, I hope he's OK!*

I passed rust-pitted garbage bins. A cat scampered from behind a stack of water-stained crates. Empty liquor bottles, broken glass, and soggy cigarette butts littered my way. I pressed on, passing through the narrow, musty canyon. A few feet off the alley there was a small frame house behind the Puckett home on Water Street. *Completely unknown to the vast majority of Henderson residents, I bet!*

I rapped lightly on the screen door and called. "Storms?"

"Yessuh? That you, Hoyt? Come on in."

I opened the door and walked into a dimly lit room that served the dual purpose of bedroom and sitting room. His bed was against the left wall, under the only window in the room. Jack sat on the side of the bed in a sleeveless undershirt and boxer shorts. His bulk appeared even more massive in that state of undress. His feet were swollen and his face was ashen. He was breathing heavily. A small electric fan was blowing air in his direction.

"Since you weren't in the shop this morning, I brought your coffee to you," I said. "Hope it's not cold."

"Thank you, Hoyt," he said between breaths.

"What's going on, Jack?" I looked around at the sparse furnishings: his bed, an oversized wooden rocking chair, and an ancient chifforobe standing on a bare wood floor.

He bent over, both elbows on his knees, his gaze on the floor. "Oh, it's nothing, Hoyt. I have one of these spells ever now and again. Most times, I can work through them, go on to work, but this morning . . . I don't know," he said, shaking his head.

"You don't look good, Jack. You got a doctor?"

"From time to time, when I get down like this, Lloyd will send Doc Williams by to look in on me."

"Lloyd?"

"L. S. Furlong. He helps me out quite a bit. Most here 'bouts don't know it, but we been friends since we was boys. He brought me back here when I left the carnival. He got this place for me, pays the rent every month. Pays the utilities, too. I never get a bill. Last year he put in that phone yonder by the bed." He motioned over his shoulder with a slight head gesture.

I walked over and sat on the foot of his bed. A slight breeze rustled the muslin curtains on the window.

"Nobody ever calls, but I can call him if I really need to. Just getting older, Hoyt. Had high blood pressure a long time now. Take a water pill ever day. Now, they tell me I got the sugar diabetes. Can't do much about that, I reckon. I try to stay 'way from sugar, but it's hard."

"Can I do anything for you while I'm here?"

"Wouldn't mind a cool glass of water. In the kitchen, yonder, in the ice box . . . if you don't care."

I went through the door into the small kitchen behind his bedroom. A little wooden table and two cane-bottom chairs stood in the middle of the room. A small bowl of artificial fruit sat forlornly in the middle of the bare table. I retrieved a glass from the cabinet over the porcelain sink, which hung at an angle from the wall, exposed drainpipes beneath. The rim of the drain was rusting where the porcelain had worn away. To my right, a door opened onto a cramped bathroom: tub, commode, and sink.

I poured a glass of water from the pitcher I found in the ancient wooden icebox before returning to this bedroom to hand him the water. There was a small, framed picture of a beautiful young colored girl on the nightstand by his bed.

"Thanks for coming by Hoyt, and for the water." He paused and drew a deep breath. "I'll likely be back to work tomorrow."

"I'm gonna leave this card for you, Jack. It's got my phone number on it. You call if you need me. If I'm not in my room, leave a message with the hotel operator, she'll get it to me. You can call the number of the newspaper, as well. That number is on the card, also."

"Much obliged, Hoyt! You a good friend." He pressed both hands into the mattress on either side of his hips, struggling to stand.

I placed my hand on his shoulder and patted it lightly. "Keep your seat, John. I'll see you again."

His arms and shoulders relaxed as he allowed his weight to settle back down.

‡

Furlong was born in Shawneetown, Illinois, in 1899, three years after John Calhoun Storm. His mother and John's worked in the same whorehouse. Both were fatherless, dirt poor, and abused by the countless men in their mother's lives. Early on, John, being older, tried as best he could to protect Lloyd from the mean streets and back alleys of Shawneetown. But by age 15, L. S. had grown into a large, athletic boy, well on his way to the full six feet he would ultimately reach. Their roles gradually reversed, with L. S. looking out for John, who was called Jack by then. In the desperate environment in which they grew up, L. S. had one distinct advantage that John would never have: L. S. was white.

In 1919, Congress ratified the Volstead Act, prohibiting the production and sale of alcohol. This well-intended piece of legislation ushered in a period of lawlessness and crime that was impossible to predict. Sensing opportunity, and with the encouragement and protection of some of his mother's clientele, Lloyd Furlong became a "bootlegger"—a nickname first applied to smugglers during the reign of King George III. It derived from their custom of hiding packages of valuables in the legs of their large sea boots when dodging the king's coast guard. Apparently, the word came into general use in the Midwest in the 1880s, when it denoted the practice of concealing flasks of illicit liquor in boot tops for trade with Native Americans.

While all the temperance league instigators were patting themselves on their collective backs and taking great delight in their legislative accomplishments, others immediately realized the opportunity for vast wealth—individuals as diverse as Joseph

P. Kennedy and L. S. Furlong, whose enterprise grew so rapidly, the local stills couldn't produce enough product to supply his demand.

When trafficking in an illegal commodity, one must often enter into an illegal society. Furlong's demand became so large that he had to seek merchandise elsewhere, necessitating trips to Chicago and relationships with some of the city's most unsavory characters. His return trips took him south through Evansville, Indiana, and across the Ohio River into Henderson. Recognizing the uniqueness of the three-to-five square-mile area, across the Ohio River from Henderson but still in Kentucky, and maybe 500 yards from the Indiana state line, L. S. decided to move his bootlegging enterprise to Kentucky in the spring of 1930.

A specific advantage to the location lay in the fact that it was much more economically devastated by the Depression than the rest of the country. Furlong found a number of businesses willing to serve as retail outlets for his product in Henderson. Corn was in plentiful supply, and out-of-work tenant farmers were more than willing to set up stills for production.

Even though Prohibition was repealed three years later, a lucrative market for moonshine and illegal booze remained. The major distilleries, long shut down, couldn't get back in production overnight. And they were hampered by the tax levied on legitimate distilleries, putting them at a pricing disadvantage.

With all the elements in place, L. S. paid a visit to the mayor at his office in Grimshaw's Loose Leaf Tobacco Warehouse, a business he'd acquired through nefarious means during the Black Patch Tobacco Wars. Rumor had it that Mayor Grimshaw was not averse to cash persuasion. The modest $2,000 yearly salary meant that being mayor was essentially a part-time job. Previous mayors had all held other jobs, resulting in less than efficient and progressive leadership, but a reduced opportunity for graft and corruption. Grimshaw operated the office full time.

Furlong explained what he had planned for the area. "How much will it cost me to be left unencumbered by the local constabulary?" he asked.

Up to that point, the most Grimshaw was able to fleece out of any one business shake-down scheme was $50 a month. Leaning back in his chair, he responded, "Well, for an operation such as you describe, I'd say $100 a month will be sufficient . . . to start."

Furlong paused a long time, staring straight at Grimshaw. Finally, he said, "Mayor, I've done business with Capone's cronies in Chicago. I'm sure you're aware they give no consideration to what local law enforcement does or doesn't do. However, as you also know, it results in violence, murder, and mayhem. I have the contacts and influence to bring that type of business support to your little town. Now, I don't want that, and I'm sure you don't, either. Here's my response to your $100 a month bribe."

Grimshaw sat upright in his chair and affected as much outrage as he could muster. "Now, see here Furlong, bribe is a nasty word. I prefer to call it the cost of doing business."

"Call it what you will," replied Furlong. "I'll pay you $250 a month. Never, *ever* a dime more! Don't entertain the idea you can, at some point in time, leverage me for more. My contacts in Chicago remain and are always available. If you accept my proposal, it is to remain in effect for as long as I'm in business here."

"Well now, I'm gonna need time to think that over," Grimshaw said.

"Your time is up! Good day to you, sir." Furlong rose to leave.

Grimshaw leaped from his chair. "Hold on there, Mr. Furlong. You drive a hard bargain, but under the circumstances . . . I can accept it." He extended his right hand.

"One other thing," Grimshaw went on. "I suspect most of your stills are in the county. What kind of arrangements have you made with the sheriff?"

"You concern yourself with your own fiefdom. I'll deal with the sheriff."

That meeting put in place conditions that prevailed for years to come. Furlong's bootlegging enterprise, and the deal he made with the mayor, made him a wealthy man. He began to buy up farmland in southwestern Henderson County, around Geneva and Smith Mills. By the end of the 1930s he had amassed a sizable fortune. Always on the lookout for new business opportunities, he decided to build an upscale supper club and gambling casino in the area on the north side of the bridge, just shy of the Indiana state line.

Before the end of 1939, he had erected a 14,000 square-foot facility at the cost of $120,000, a tremendous sum at the time. With its art deco design and stucco facade, his Club Cosmopolitan was unlike anything of its kind between Chicago and Miami. The dining, dancing, and gambling enterprise occupied a lawless area known locally as no-man's-land. In a stroke of genius—because he didn't trust Mayor Grimshaw—Furlong made the sheriff of Henderson County a minority stockholder, ensuring his gambling activities would be left alone.

‡

No one in town knew that John Calhoun Storm was the childhood friend of Lloyd Stanly Furlong. No one except for me.

The Henderson of my youth was racist, like all of the South. Racism was ubiquitous, universally accepted, and went unchallenged in the classroom and the pulpit. It never occurred to me to question it. No one did.

That is until I fought side by side with colored troops in the Pacific—all good fighting men, as good as any in uniform. When you're dependent on another man in battle, the color of his skin never enters your mind. The Marine Corps didn't accept or recruit colored troops until June, 1942. Those men fought on Saipan, Tinian, Guam, and Iwo Jima. At the end of the war, they were no longer "colored" marines. They were US Marines, no qualifier. In July of '48, President Truman integrated all the US Armed Forces by executive order. While long overdue, it didn't translate to the population at large.

My friendship with those marines, and now with John Storm, made it difficult for me to understand why they continued to be treated like second-class citizens. I'd come to believe the blame lay at the feet of Southern white man, aided and abetted by the Ku Klux Klan and the southern Democratic Party. The Democratic Party can't be blamed for the *creation* of racism in the South. It was indigenous, ubiquitous, and inbred. However, over the years, because of its early prominence in the South, the Democratic Party became at first an unwitting tool, and later a willing participant, in the enforcement of Jim Crow laws and pervasive racism—in the South, initially, and later throughout the entire country. How long this would continue before our country admitted to these wrongs and made legitimate efforts to right them was anybody's guess. Maybe a charismatic, colored man would emerge. Perhaps a church minister—a tipping point, so to speak. For the time being, John Calhoun Storm and others of his race had to live with terrible conditions. As with the gambling and corruption, it seemed all I could do was rail against them, to no avail.

An old adage came back to me: *Some good in the worst of us and some bad in the best of us*. Damned if it wasn't almost impossible for me to reconcile the two sides of L. S. Furlong—a man whose actions had so damaged an entire community, on the one hand, with the man who had demonstrated care and compassion for John Storm, on the other. I didn't want to reconcile it: I wanted to keep my dislike for Furlong alive and well fueled. But Stormy Jack had elevated L. S. Furlong in my opinion that morning, all the same.

Not that my opinion mattered much to Furlong, one way or the other.

CHAPTER 32

Later that evening I stopped in at Club 101, located two blocks north of city limits at the intersection of 14th and Green Streets. The place was alive with Breckinridge soldiers, their noise competing with barking squirrels animating parking lot trees dripping with moisture from a recent shower.

Army Camp Breckinridge was 45 minutes down Highway 60, in Union County. The young men stationed there, away from home for the first time, were full of piss and vinegar and raging hormones. Naturally, they sought thrills and entertainment in the closest available outlets. The joints, taverns, and nightclubs along the strip welcomed their coin.

Many of them were obviously underage, as evidenced not only by their youthful appearance, but by their behavior and lack of good judgment and emotional restraint. Immature 18-year-olds are sadly ill-equipped to navigate the adult world. Their bodies are physically mature, leading them to conclude they're fully formed adults, but it will be years before they think like them. Local establishments made no effort to determine if patrons were of legal age to purchase and consume alcohol. When two or three of these boys got a few beers in them, anything could happen, and usually did.

On this particular night, the jukebox was playing "I'm Movin' On," by Ernest Tubb. Soldiers were pulling the arms of the slot machines stationed around the walls. They were loud and full of beer and high spirits, but mostly harmless, just having a good time. Pearly Martin was nursing a double shot of whiskey with a beer back at the bar, obviously not his first. He was sitting next to a working man wearing heavy boots. I left a stool vacant between them and the one I took and ordered burgers, fries, and a beer. When my order came, I smeared mustard on my burgers, pounded ketchup onto my fries, and ordered another beer.

"Gimme an order of chicken livers, a double shot of Cabin Still, and a beer," Pearly yelled. It seemed the Shotgun Cowboys weren't playing that night, and he was carousing. The bartender set the drinks in front of him. He tossed back the whiskey in one swallow and chugged half the beer. "Whewee!" Pearly gasped, wiping his mouth on his shirtsleeve. "That hit my stomach like fireworks on the Fourth of July!"

When the bartender brought the chicken livers, Pearly took a bite, spat it back onto the plate, and threw his fork across the bar. "How long have they been in the deep-fryer? There's no taste left! The life's been cooked out of 'em! Take that shit home and feed it to your hogs!"

"Sorry, Pearly," the bartender said, removing the plate. "Can I get you anything else?"

"A fried bologna sandwich," he hollered. "And where's my drink? Bring me another damn drink!"

One of the young soldiers was further along than the rest, mostly feeling gregarious and friendly. He approached the bar to get another beer, squeezing between Pearly and the man next to him, bumping Pearly's elbow just as he was lifting his glass to his mouth and spilling most of the contents down the front of his shirt. Pearly leaped from his barstool, pulled a revolver from under his shirt, and hit the kid across the back of the head, knocking him forward and busting his mouth on the edge of the bar. The man next to Pearly immediately jumped up and out of the way.

Pearly drew the pistol back to hit the boy again. I rose from my stool, stepped forward and blocked the arc of Pearly's swing with my left hand, and ripped the gun from his hand with my right.

Pearly looked at me with a shocked expression. He sneered, eyes narrowed, and said, "Butt out, buddy!"

"That's enough, Pearly," I told him. "Head down to the end of the bar. I'll buy you another double."

A couple of other soldiers helped the boy back to his table and tried to clean the blood off his mouth and face. The others froze, silent, and watched each other, uncertain what to do next. By this time, the bartender was standing behind the bar directly in front of the fracas. I ejected the shells and handed the empty revolver to the bartender.

"Keep it until Pearly decides to leave. Walk him out to his car and give it back to him."

I handed the bartender a five-dollar bill and told him to cover Pearly's drinks until it was gone, then walked outside and tossed the cartridges into the woods behind the building. Pearly might be talented, but he had very little else to recommend him.

‡

When I got to work the next morning, there was a large man waiting for me. I paused at a coworker's desk. "Who's that? Did you catch his name?"

"Marge asked, but he wouldn't give it. Said he'd only talk to you. He was waiting outside before the doors were opened."

From where I stood, I only saw the back of a broad-shouldered man, seated in the chair in front of my desk. Walking around him to my desk, I said, "I'm Hoyt Cole. You wanted to see me?"

The man had deep-set dark eyes hooded by heavy brows. He was clean shaven, but the dark shadow on his face indicated a heavy beard. He stood and extended a meaty, calloused hand. "I'm Walter T. Browder. Is there a place we can talk privately?"

I studied his face. He had an anxious demeanor, like a tightly wound coil. "My desk is not private, as you can see, and this space is all I have."

"The only reason I'm here is Uncle George told me to talk to you—not the newspaper."

Looking around the space for possible places to talk, I said, "We can go outside to my truck."

Browder stood from his chair. I gauged his height to be right at six feet, and looked to weight about 200 pounds, no fat. He was rather intimidating. He appeared angry, even though he didn't act like he was. *Maybe just concentrating and focused.*

Outside, the sky was clear and the air was crisp. Fall was nearing. The sun was bright with no clouds and no humidity, a beautiful morning. The lot was almost full. When we climbed into my truck, I noticed the faint aroma of oil and grease, even though he and his clothes were clean. I invited him to roll down his window.

"I'd rather not. I don't want what I have to say to be overheard."

"Mr. Browder, you're being quite secretive. If you hadn't mentioned Uncle George, I doubt I'd continue this conversation."

"What I have to tell you *is* secret! I don't want what I have to reveal to fall into the wrong hands."

Recently discharged from the army, Walter Thomas Browder was the only son of Melvin Browder—whom L. S. Furlong had killed. Reared in the East End, Walter T. was reluctant to approach anyone outside the confines of Audubon. He'd visited Uncle George because of the high regard people there had for him.

"Furlong was never even charged with the crime!" He bounced his right leg nervously and raked his hand through a head full of black hair. "If it's the last thing I do, I'll bring him down. Furlong and his entire enterprise."

He fell silent, brooding. The midtown sounds intruded into my truck cab, despite the closed windows. Tires screeched as cars turned corners, doors slammed, horns honked impatiently, people yelled to each other in friendly acknowledgment.

"Uncle George said I can trust you. He said you had a great concern for the situation here."

"Situation?" I was still in the dark about what this was all about.

"Political corruption, gambling, and crime. It's all been accepted fact in Henderson for years," he said. "But in the past few months, a group of concerned citizens and a few honest officials submitted evidence to a grand jury."

"I'm listening, Mr. Browder."

"Call me Walter T.," he said. "It was thrown out on a technicality."

Was the evidence poorly presented, or were public officials too frightened—or too well paid—to confront what everyone in town knew was going on?

"I haven't given up. I began a one-man campaign to destroy Furlong. Along with a trusted friend, my wife and I visited every gambling spot in the county. We gathered considerable evidence in just a few short weeks. We recorded the names of the places we visited, the dates of our visits, and we cataloged details about the gambling machines, including their serial numbers. We've listed the names of city and county officials participating in the activities, all recorded in this loose-leaf notebook." He tapped on it for emphasis.

"I've worked too hard obtaining these records to see Furlong get off scot-free."

He handed me the notebook. I gave it a cursory pass. As I thumbed through it, it became evident he had lots of incriminating evidence. This was more than just a bitter man, motivated by hatred. It appeared he had enough valid and convincing evidence to gain indictments, if handled properly by the right people.

"Impressive, Walter T., and admirable. How do you plan to proceed?"

He turned to face me. "That's why I'm talking to you, Mr. Cole. I hope you can help me."

All sorts of objections and roadblocks crossed my mind. *In or out Cole! You can't stand on the periphery any longer.*

"Personally, I can do very little, I'm afraid. One thing I can assure you of is my confidentiality. I promise you, what you've said is safe with me. Will you give me a chance to think about it? Perhaps I can connect you with some people here that you can trust. And equally important, people who have the know-how, connections, and commitment to move this forward. If you trust me, I'll do all in my power to help you," I told him.

"I appreciate that, Mr. Cole, that's what I'm looking for."

"One last thing I feel must be made clear between us. I certainly understand your personal animosity toward L. S. Furlong, and in your shoes, I'm sure I'd feel the same. But you need to know, from my perspective, what you have uncovered and detailed is much more far-reaching than your personal vendetta. If we can accomplish the big picture, your personal pursuits will be satisfied. But the more important objective must be the goal."

"I understand, Mr. Cole. Fair enough."

"How can I reach you?"

"Don't call me. My house phone is on a party line, and I don't want anyone listening in. Come to my repair shop out on Pringle Street. If I'm not in the shop, I live in the house next door."

"I'll get back to you as soon as possible."

We shook hands. He exited my truck and walked off.

I sat for a time, enjoying the delightful aroma from the bakery next door and contemplating the enormity of what he'd accomplished.

You're in it now, Cole! I thought. *How do I proceed?*

Until recently, I'd just complained about the goings-on in my home town. Given permission to write about it and armed with the information Browder had accumulated, I felt a tremendous weight of responsibility. Was I up to it? *I could blow this wide open, or I could kill it in its tracks, depending how I handle it.* I'd been responsible for other men's lives. I'd never been responsible for the fate of an entire community.

Easy, Cole! I thought. *Don't puff up too much. You're a minor player on a local stage. Go at this one small step at a time. You can't defeat or complete this on your own. You're gonna need help. Lots of help!*

I'd heard that the commonwealth attorney, Nathan W. Norsworthy, was honest. Would he stick his neck out for this? I had also learned that there were several, disconnected factions working independently, albeit ineffectually, to correct the present situation. *How to bring them all together? How to accomplish a common goal?* Perhaps with the proper impetus and encouragement, we could marshal a small cadre of citizens into effective action.

I need to talk to Uncle George.

CHAPTER 33

Gish's trial lasted only a few days. I attended part of each. Clyde presented a rather pathetic figure, his hands and feet in irons, further accenting his diminutive stature. When the bailiff ushered him into the court room, he shuffled in short steps on tiny feet and looked around with a comic smile on his face, as if looking for a familiar face. His bluster and cockiness were gone. I couldn't believe that Clyde Gish was the target of Selma's next step up the financial and social ladder. He just didn't possess the requisite wherewithal. Clyde would be a step *down*. Did Selma play on Clyde's affection and use him as an unwitting dupe to rid her of her husband, thereby eliminating a huge roadblock in her pursuit of a more appealing target?

The old courthouse, built atop a hill on the corner of First and Main Streets in 1813, had cracked, fifteen-foot ceilings, exposed lath, and eight-foot oak doors. The judge's bench, considerably elevated above the witness stand and jury box, enhanced his importance. The bench seating for the public resembled worn church pews. A low barrier separated the public from the prosecutor and the defense.

Gish pleaded not guilty. His attorneys entered his sworn affidavit, repudiating the confession and denying that he knew what crime he had been arrested for. Detective Browder and the first patrolmen on the scene testified, along with the deputy sheriff that tricked Clyde into confessing. Selma's emotional testimony blamed Clyde for the plot and execution of the murder. The jury deliberated 23 hours before returning a guilty verdict. The judge sentenced Clyde Gish to life in prison. He followed the bailiff from the courtroom docilely, seemingly resigned to his fate.

While it was a victory for the local investigators, the trial left some points unexplained. Gish's account of the night of the crime was ambiguous and convoluted, leaving more questions than answers. If he'd had been coached on his testimony, it was done poorly. Or maybe he just wasn't smart enough to follow the narrative laid out for him. According to him, on the night of the murder, he had waited on the street corner until Herman came by in the car. He was carrying an umbrella loaned him by Mrs. Weiskopf. Entering the car, he laid the umbrella in the back seat and rode to the garage with Weiskopf. When he started to get out, he reached back for the umbrella, but his hand closed, instead, on a maul.

It was his own maul, he said, one that he had put in the car several days earlier, when Herman asked him to take it to the mine. As they got out of the car, he held the maul behind him and then struck as Weiskopf turned his back. Then he went back through the garden, threw the maul away and went straight home to bed.

Officers never accepted the story of the ride in the automobile and the maul in the back seat. Instead, they believed Gish had gone home after leaving the Weiskopf house. Then he returned to lie in wait in the garage, hidden behind a second car parked there. Then when Herman returned from his meeting at the hotel and turned off the car lights, Gish stepped out of the shadows and struck him down with the practiced arm of a coal miner. Ownership of the maul remained shrouded in the mystery of conflicting claims.

CHAPTER 34

The sun was a dirty orange from the dust and dirt blowing off the road and out of the fields. At the bottom of the bluff, dead fish lay tangled in river snags jutting from the water, their bloated bellies gleaming ghost white on the surface. Everett Lightfoot was just closing the doors to his garage, wiping his hands on a rag and heading toward his house when Eddie G. pulled up. Everett nodded, threw up his hand and managed a slight smile. He waved Eddie toward the house.

Lightfoot was 59 years old. He had lived his life largely by his own choosing. He was dependent on no man and beholding to none. A hard life had cut deep crevices into his face. He walked with a slight stoop, the power in his arms and shoulders evident in his easy movements. Eddie dreaded seeing him, but he knew his uncle was the only man he could ask for help. The blackmailer's latest demand—$5,000—had come only about a month after the previous payoff. It was an amount Eddie knew he couldn't keep secret. He certainly couldn't hide that amount in a petty cash withdrawal.

It wasn't that Eddie was afraid to reveal his secret—they

shared the secret. But he knew his uncle would be disappointed in him for getting caught in an indiscretion. He had warned him of the danger from his first awakening.

The interior of the house was spartan, but clean and neat. No clutter. Lightfoot pulled one of two wooden chairs from around the kitchen table, motioned Eddie toward it, as he seated himself across in the other. Eddie haltingly recounted his circumstance, resisting the urge to rush. He spoke slowly and deliberately, pausing for long intervals, trying to control his breathing. He struggled to retain his composure.

Lightfoot sat calm and resolute, nonjudgmental. He fixed a hooded gaze below Eddie's chin, intense, but expressionless. Eddie fought the fierce urge to bolt and run, too ashamed to finish. He paused for a long moment, staring out the kitchen window across the overgrown backyard, toward the wooded fence line. Lightfoot rose and retrieved an open bottle of Old Forester bourbon, along with two small glasses. He pulled the cork-tipped cap, and poured three fingers into each glass. He picked up one and slid the other toward Eddie, who took a swig before telling about the past letters and how much he'd paid the blackmailer to date. He recounted the circumstances of each payoff.

"This could ruin me! I can't let Beatie and my boy suffer for what I've done." Eyes downcast, he said matter-of-factly, "I got nobody to blame but myself."

The sun was setting and dark shadows filled the space. Lightfoot pulled a lucifer match from his pocket, struck it in a long pull under the kitchen table. It flared to life, and he lit the oil lamp in the middle of the table. The sulfur stench from the match lingered. Lightfoot remained still and stoic. He stared straight ahead; the only evidence of emotion was the tight clenching and unclenching of his jaw.

They sat silent for a time: Lightfoot, rough-hewn, solitary, unsophisticated, and physical; Eddie G., polished, handsome, gregarious, and social. Two very different men in all aspects of their lives—except one. Eddie G. folded his hands, gripped them between his knees, and dropped his head. "I'm sorry, Uncle."

"Hold your head up, Eddie!" A breeze blew through the open window. "You must not be ashamed of who you are. Even though people see it otherwise. You and I—we're how God made us. I'm satisfied he loves us as much as he loves every other soul on this earth. This cannot be allowed to ruin your life! You got too much going for you. You got a successful business and a bright future. I won't see it ended!

"You'll make no more payments. Go home and put this out of your mind. I'll handle it from here on out. Where and when is the next payment to be made?"

"I didn't come here for you to fix this. I'm just looking for advice and direction."

Lightfoot's eyes were set and his face flushed. "Past time for advice and direction, son. Go home. This is over for you. Where and when?"

The table lamp illuminated the side of his face imparting a sliver hue to the gray whiskers along his jawline. His gaze was intense, but somehow reassuring. A mixture of tremendous relief and terrible fear filled Eddie G. Triplett. Experience had taught him not to challenge his uncle when he was resolute. There'd be no dissuading him. Lightfoot didn't deal in delicate shadings. He was a man of direct action, never weighing the consequences.

"Two o'clock in the morning, two weeks from today, under an overturned wheelbarrow on the porch of the abandoned Scuffletown Post Office," Eddie told him. He stood to leave, not knowing what else to say. He knew his uncle wouldn't allow expressions of gratitude.

When he reached the door, Lightfoot called out. Eddie turned to face him. With two long strides, Everett grabbed Eddie in his arms and hugged him tightly. "Bye, Eddie!" he said, releasing him.

The setting sun bled into the purple of the evening sky. The grass was browning up, and falling leaves formed drifts of muted color in the roadside ditches. Eddie was never afraid of Everett, but he feared what he was capable of. His shame and consternation were overpowering. "I should never have come here!" He drove back to town, squinting into the setting sun. Once more, tears rolled down his cheeks.

CHAPTER 35

I arrived late the next morning. I'd barely seated myself, when Marge called me. "There's a Major Maglone here to see you."

What the hell is going on?

I walked to the front to greet my new visitor. There was no mistaking him. He appeared to be in his late 40s, of medium height and weight, and he wore the standard summer officer's uniform of cotton khaki with the spit-and-polish of career military.

I extended my hand, "Major Maglone? I'm Hoyt Cole. You're here to see me?"

"Yes, I am. Do you have a place we can talk?"

"We can talk at my desk, but I'm afraid it's not real private."

"That'll do," he said.

I led him back to my desk and motioned him to the chair in front of it. If it's possible to *sit* at attention, the major appeared to do so. His back was erect, his chin level with the floor, bright blue eyes straight ahead.

"I'm here on behalf of General Matthew F. Harwood, commanding officer of US Army Camp Breckinridge."

"Nice to meet you, but are you sure you have the right person?"

"I was instructed to speak with Mr. Hoyt Cole at the *River City News*. That's you, is it not?"

"It is, sir. What is it you're here to speak to me about?"

"I won't insult your intelligence by outlining the illegal activities that have been going on for the past several years. As you know, Camp Breckinridge houses over 30,000 service men, a high percentage of them under the age of 21.

"These underage boys are being sold wine, beer, and whiskey illegally. They squander their pay in the myriad gambling establishments and risk their health, and perhaps the security of the nation, in these dives and honkytonks."

I realized I was sitting upright in my chair, feet square on the floor. Relaxing, I placed both elbows on my desk, folded my arms in front of me and leaned forward slightly to listen to the message he'd been charged with delivering.

"In addition to alcohol, women of easy virtue and questionable health are readily available to teenage soldiers, provided they have the money."

"I am aware of the gambling and associated vice in Henderson. Forgive me sir, but it seems the US Army would have more control over the men than anyone else. I understand that Breckinridge issues up to 10,000 passes each week. I mean no disrespect—why don't you make Henderson and the strip off-limits to all enlisted men? Patrol the area with MPs?"

"We don't have that many MPs, Mr. Cole, and it serves no good purpose to put a bunch of boys on base confinement. We'd be trading one set of problems for another. I am here to place General Matthew F. Harwood on public record as opposing the illegal activities here. He speaks on behalf of the underage enlisted men, their parents, and the US military personnel stationed at Camp Breckinridge." He rose briskly, extended his hand and said, "Good day to you, sir." He turned smartly and strode back through the office and out onto the street, mission accomplished, no wasted time, words, or motions.

Obviously, it was not by accident that he had come to speak with me. If I wasn't being set up, I felt I was certainly being *propped* up. In less than a day and a half, I had been presented with two compelling reasons to take action.

‡

Ironically, that same evening, there was a serious altercation out on the strip, involving a Breckinridge soldier.

By the time I arrived on the scene, an ambulance crew was loading a blood-stained roll-cot into the rear hatch. They closed the door and sped toward the Henderson hospital, siren blaring and lights flashing. Red and blue lights flashed from the sheriff cruisers on the scene, but the patrons had largely dispersed.

A Deputy Nichols gave me the scoop. "Apparently, it all started at the crap table. A soldier name of Scaretti, Scavelli maybe—can't pronounce them foreign names—was having a big night at the table. He'd amassed almost $1,000 in winnings. When he lost the dice, his luck began to change, and he lost it all. He bought $20 more in chips and tried to catch up, playing the Big 6/Big 8, the ultimate sucker bet. He lost that as well.

"He'd been drinking all evening, and by then he was drunk and belligerent. His buddies had left him alone at the table. The bouncers escorted him outside and into the parking lot. He stumbled around out there, cussin' and mouthin' at everybody coming and going. Most just ignored him, but he wouldn't be ignored.

When Harlan Jenkins and his date walked by, the soldier yelled, 'Nice ass!'

"Jenkins gave him the finger and continued walking toward the entrance. That's when the soldier pulled a switchblade and stabbed at Jenkins, but he was so drunk, he stumbled and cut jut the back of Harlan's jacket. Harlan pulled a .38 and fired twice. That's pretty much it."

"You gonna arrest Jenkins?"

"What for? Self-defense?"

"Anyone see it happen?"

"Yeah, two other couples confirmed Harlan's account."

I went inside to see if any of his buddies were still there, but apparently, they left as soon as they found out he was shot. I hung around for a time. I questioned some players who'd been at the crap table with him and spoke to the two men who threw him out. I questioned Jenkins and his date and the couples that witnessed the altercation. Their stories were consistent with the deputy's account. Jenkins appeared unharmed and unfazed. The only damage to his person was a six-inch gash down the left sleeve of his jacket. Jenkins was lucky!

I drove to the hospital, where the emergency-room staff told me that Scavelli was alive and expected to survive. When Jenkins turned to fire, the motion likely moved the gun slightly. One bullet hit Scavelli in his right shoulder exiting through the back, and the other missed entirely.

Three soldiers had stopped by the hospital to check on their pal. They sat side by side, solemn and dejected, all the testosterone drained from them. Those three young guys, away from home, alone, and scared, looked like anything but well-trained fighting men.

A nurse told me that after the soldier came out of recovery, he would be transported to Breckinridge. Jenkins had elected not to file charges. Scavelli was lucky!

That was just one of many clashes involving Breckinridge soldiers in Henderson nightclubs, albeit likely the most serious.

CHAPTER 36

Shortly after my meeting with Walter T. Browder, I was eating breakfast in the hotel restaurant when I spotted G. L. Butler getting a cup of coffee. I beckoned for him to join me at my table. He was dressed in what could almost be considered his uniform: blue serge, three-piece suit, starched white shirt, and solid black tie.

I stood to greet him. "Morning, Uncle George."

"Morning, Hoyt."

I made small talk—weather, politics, and so on.

"What's on your mind, Hoyt? Something's troubling you."

I leaned forward and put both elbows on the table, sipping my coffee. "I've obtained some very credible and potentially explosive information. I don't know where to go with it."

He sipped his coffee and lit a cigarette. The smoke encircled his head and was pulled upward by the ceiling fans. "Information regarding . . ?"

"The local gambling syndication."

"How credible?" He turned to his left, opening himself to the table and crossing his legs.

"Extremely!" I looked around the room. Businessmen were drinking coffee and eating breakfast. Others were sliding their trays into the return window. "I understand from you and others, there have been genuine and sincere efforts to eliminate this scourge in the past, all of which have failed, for various reasons. And while some have been poorly planned and hastily executed, the primary reason is the leadership and organization of the criminal elements here. Working in concert with the pervasive political corruption, they are formidable." I sat back. "Is that a fair assessment? I asked.

"Fair, I'd say, Hoyt."

"I don't have the knowledge, contacts, or influence to execute this myself. No one man does. I'm hoping you know a group or organization that is trustworthy, dedicated, and capable of maintaining confidentiality over a period of time. One to whom I can share this information. Dedication, commitment, and confidentiality are essential."

He leaned back in his chair, passed his hand over his chin, and looked out the window at the street. Finally, he turned to me, folded both hands across his chest and said, "If I had the kind of information you seem to possess, I'd take it first to Reverend David Dahlke, the pastor of the Christian Church and president of the ministerial association. Visit him privately, preferably at home. Outline what you have and your expectations. Impress upon him that confidentiality is paramount. He'll tell you honestly if he can help. Start there. I have his home phone number, and you can tell him I told you to call."

He pulled a spiral Blue Horse note pad from his coat, tore off a single sheet, and wrote a name and phone number on it, using a pencil obviously sharpened by his pocket knife. Sliding it across the table to me he said, "Give him a call."

We sat silent for a time, smoking and looking out to the street. It was too early to know where this would lead, but things were beginning to take shape. *I dealt with uncertainty, every time I went into combat, but there were tried and true rules of engagement, even though you mostly couldn't rely on them, once the shooting started. I have no rules of engagement for the path upon which I'm embarking.*

"Good luck, Hoyt," he said as he rose to leave. I stood and extended my hand. "Thanks, Uncle George."

‡

I called the number from my desk at the office. Mrs. Dahlke told me that her husband was at the church office and gave me that phone number. Dahlke answered the phone himself. I told him who I was and how I had obtained his name and number. He agreed to meet me privately, at his office, that evening at seven. I told him I'd be bringing another person. Strangely, he didn't ask the purpose of the meeting.

I needed to speak with Walter T. Browder, so I headed for the East End, enjoying the brisk morning air and billowy puffs of white clouds floating high in the sky along the way. I passed one of the three neighborhood churches, crossed railroad tracks, and drove uphill to Pringle Street. Browder's garage sat at the corner on the left, a barnlike structure made of concrete blocks, with two wide doors thrown open to a crowded workspace. Browder was changing a tire on one of the vehicles inside.

"Got a minute, Walter T.?"

"Sure." He was dressed in one-piece coveralls, and his hulking frame and brooding dark eyes were foreboding. He had a nervous uncertainty about him, suspicious and unwelcoming. I knew that Walter T. suffered from narcolepsy, a sleep disorder causing uncontrollable daytime drowsiness. The only available treatment was Dexedrine, a powerful central nervous system stimulant. Common side effects of long-term use were anxiety, agitation, mistrust, and even combativeness. That fit Walter to a T.

"I've found someone I believe we can trust—someone I'm satisfied will maintain confidentiality. He's willing to meet with us this evening."

"You gonna tell me who it is?" he asked, somewhat skeptically.

"Reverend David Dahlke."

He paused for the briefest time, wiped his hands on a greasy rag, and pushed his hair back out of his eyes. "OK!" he said, extending his hand.

"I'll pick you up at 6:30," I told him.

He nodded.

‡

I stopped for lunch at Metzger's Tavern, on the corner of Powell and Julia Streets. That intersection was the invisible border between the colored community and the all-white East End. Metzger's was a unique amalgamation—a shabbier version of Wolf's Tavern and an established East End watering hole, with a small grocery at the front where locals could purchase milk, butter, eggs, bread, cigarettes, soft drinks, and candy bars, along with their half-pints.

Neighborhood Negroes were served from the back door. While accepting of commerce, from any source, Metzger's adhered to prevailing social standards. A colored man could buy a half-pint at the back door, but he couldn't have a beer at the bar. Metzger's served hamburgers, hot dogs, chili, bean soup, beer, and whiskey. I ordered a hamburger and bowl of bean soup with a beer. Almost immediately, the beer—bottle only, no glass—was shoved in front of me. The cooks and waitstaff were all males. *White* males. Men in brogans, bib overalls, and various other combinations of dirty work clothes sat further down the bar. Heavy cigarette smoke hung on the air throughout: an authentic blue-collar bar.

My bowl of soup slid in front of me shortly after I ordered, along with my hamburger, served unceremoniously on a piece of glassine paper. Men raised in Audubon who had risen above the level of laborer gravitated back to their roots and were accepted warmly by staff and patrons alike. Lawyers and bankers in coats and ties mingled comfortably with factory workers, carpenters, and bricklayers. The common thread: they were all raised in the East End. All the credibility needed.

A single restroom served the entire place. Metzger's was a stag bar. It's not that women weren't allowed. Better judgment prevailed, and they just didn't come in. Oh, they'd often stop up front for milk, bread, and maybe a Coke, but that was the extent of their foray into the confines.

Metzger's was a warm and friendly place, provided you weren't looking for ambiance, fine dining, or racial tolerance. Generations of East End men had come of age at Metzger's. I paid my tab, returned to my truck and drove back to the office.

CHAPTER 37

The Good Humor Man was selling ice-cream novelties to neighborhood children from his bicycle-powered freezer when I went to pick up Walter T. Six or eight kids gathered around him, pushing, shoving, and giggling. They were waiting their turns to make a selection and give him their nickels, anxious to get a rare, after-supper treat.

Walter T. was waiting on the porch of his house, next to the garage. He wore a thin jacket over an open-collared, denim shirt tucked into a pair of pleated khaki slacks, atop a pair of brown oxford shoes. While washed, cleaned, and presentable, he looked unfamiliar with and uncomfortable in his attire.

Incandescent lights illuminated the windows of the houses we passed. Starlings and spatzies voiced protests to the summer temperatures, and the evening air bore the heat of the day. The water maple trees' leaves drooped as if they, too, were exhausted by it. Shadows began to lengthen, as light faded from the sky.

"This is your project, Walter T.," I told him. "I'm going to make the introductions and let you take it from there. You tell Dahlke as much or as little as you feel like revealing. What transpires after that, I'll leave between you and the reverend."

"Fair enough," he said, trying to suppress his excitement.

I parked in front of the Christian Church, situated fast up against the sidewalk on the corner of Washington and Green Streets. The small church had no off-street parking. We got out in front of a little frame structure, abutted to the church proper and sitting back from the sidewalk about 15 feet. A light shone from the front window, and Walter T. was banging at the entrance before I got out of my truck. I walked around to join him on the porch.

When Dahlke opened the door, Browder charged in like a fullback rushing a scrimmage line. Rev. David Dahlke was a balding, rather fleshy, middle-aged man. He wore a white shirt with the collar open and tie loosened at the neck. Even though he seemed taken aback by Browder's suddenness and his imposing size, the corners of his mouth formed the slightest indication of a smile. "Come in, gentlemen," he said pleasantly.

Dahlke's desk was littered with sheets of paper and open books, including the Bible—no doubt sermon sources. A sheet of typing paper protruded from the carriage of his typewriter. Once we were seated, I took the initiative, trying to smooth over Walter's abruptness and perhaps set the reverend more at ease. I introduced myself and thanked him for consenting to meet with us on such a short notice. "The gentleman with me is Walter T. Browder. He goes by 'Walter T.' He has information I hope you'll find enlightening and ultimately useful. If so, we both hope you'll want to help us."

Not used to formality, Walter T. was unable to contain his enthusiasm and leaped immediately to our reason for being there with no reserved back-and-forth testing to see if Dahlke was trustworthy. "Reverend, I have something I think you'll be interested in," he blurted as he reached inside his cotton jacket to extract the notebook. Ignoring my previous introduction, he said, "My name's Walter T. Browder. Call me Walter T. I'm looking for someone seriously interested in cleaning up this town. I heard you might be. Them gamblers control this town from cock fights to politicians!"

Browder began to recount what his little notebook contained and how he had amassed it. "In this notebook, I've got records of the visits, my wife and I, along with a friend, have been making to every gambling joint in Henderson County. Here, see for yourself!" He passed the notebook to Dahlke as he stopped to catch his breath.

Dahlke's face was a mixture of bewilderment and curiosity. His eyes were bright and attentive, displaying a slight twinkle of humor through frameless bifocals. He scanned the notebook, carefully and deliberately, rising to pace the small space and reading as he moved.

Walter T. fidgeted restlessly in his chair, waiting for Dahlke to finish reading—obviously anxious for his reaction and response.

The notebook was full of specific and incriminating evidence. Walter T. had documented every visit, along with the dates. He had recorded how many gambling devices were present, their brands and serial numbers. In locations where public officials were present, he named them. He listed the names of the individuals flipping chuck-a-luck, manning roulette wheels, and dealing blackjack.

The strong aroma of scorched coffee came from the hot plate behind Dahlke's desk, but he kept reading. "The gambling devices were no doubt purchased from the Chicago mob," he murmured, "but I suspect the money to purchase them originated right here in Henderson."

Unable to contain his excitement, Dahlke exclaimed, "Walter T. this is amazing! How in the world did you obtain such detailed information, and why?" Previously, rumors and speculation regarding the pervasive gambling in Henderson County and the blindness of politicians were just that: rumor and speculation. "Mr. Browder, you've got the goods! The hard evidence to prove what we all know to be true."

"Furlong killed my daddy while I was still in the army." Walter became increasingly agitated. His cheeks were flushed when he blurted out: "He killed my dad in cold blood! Furlong was never even arrested. When I returned home, I discovered no one here would say anything against him. That's why I'm after him and his whole damn operation!"

Walter T. stood and paced the small space, waving his arms for emphasis, "I ain't got the connections or influence to do what needs to be done. I heard you and the ministerial association have been trying to find a way to address the gambling and corruption here. That's why me and my wife and my friend went around to all the joints and gathered the information in that-there notebook."

Seated back at his desk, Dahlke pushed his spectacles up on his forehead, "This is remarkable. I'll say you got it. I'm not sure how to proceed, or what to do with the information you have. If you'll trust me with the notebook for a few days, I'd like to discuss it with J. Rhodes Cunningham, a lawyer friend of mine. I believe he may know how best to protect and properly utilize this data."

"Can we trust him?" Browder asked.

"I assure you Walter T., he's not only trustworthy, but honest. He and I've been talking for a while now about how to clean up the county."

"Keep the notebook," Browder said. "I trust you to care for it.

Any case we might have hinges on what's in that notebook, don't you agree?"

"Absolutely!" Dahlke stood and moved from behind his desk, "I'll contact you as soon as I've discussed this with Cunningham."

"Get in touch with Mr. Cole, here. He knows how to reach me."

I handed the preacher my business card. We shook hands and departed. It was full dark by that time. Street lights were on, and the air was cooler. I was surprised at how trusting Walter T. had been, and how easily he surrendered the information he'd worked so hard to gather.

Back in my truck, Browder couldn't contain himself. "By God! Cole! I believe we can make this work, don't you?"

"I sure hope so," I said. "What you have is certainly hard to refute. It's just got to be kept secret and presented properly and timely. It's up to you and Dahlke and whoever else you get involved. I'll help in any way I can, but I can't take an active role. You deserve the credit if this works."

"By God, Cole! By God!"

He was silent all the way back to his house. I'm sure his mind was racing. When we pulled up in front, he grabbed my hand in a vice-like grip and pumped it vigorously several times.

"Thanks, Cole! I'll stay in touch." He leaped from my truck and ran to his front door. I have to say, I was also, if not excited, at least guardedly hopeful. Projects like this often end up with too many participants and too many moving parts. At the same time, handled properly, it just might work.

I wanted to talk to Stormy Jack. I'd never spoken to him about my dislike of the gambling syndicate and the role his oldest friend played in it. And with my visit from Major Maglone and Browder's project, I felt I had sufficient information to write a credible newspaper article.

CHAPTER 38

I rarely parked in front of my hotel, but on one particular afternoon, I pulled into a slot on Second Street. Exiting, I glanced toward the river and saw Maurice Rednour getting into a taxi in front of the Soaper Hotel. For reasons I can't explain, I decided to follow. Staying way back, hopefully undetected, I followed him all the way to the Gateway Motel out on the strip. I pulled into the gas station across the road. *What business could Rednour have out here at the Gateway?*

The motel had about 50 individual units, each with an attached garage, in a contiguous horseshoe arrangement around an office and restaurant—a very nice, upscale facility. It had become the stopping point on the first leg for Chicago travelers on the way to Miami. I watched the taxi stop in front of unit 22. Rednour got out, pulled a key from his pocket, and entered without stopping at the office. Moments later, he raised the garage door from the inside. No more than half an hour later, another cab arrived and pulled completely inside the garage; a female exited the cab and entered the door leading into the motel room. The dark interior of the garage obscured her identity.

After a time, I felt conspicuous parked on the gas station property, so I went in and bought a package of cheese crackers and a Coke and went back to the truck. The sound of highway traffic filled the cab. The afternoon heat of the summer sun made waiting uncomfortable.

A couple hours later, a cab pulled directly into the garage at unit 22, but another vehicle pulled onto the service apron, blocking my view. I jumped from my truck in time to see the woman ride away from the motel. A few minutes later, another cab picked up Rednour.

I left my truck parked and crossed the highway on foot, spotting a woman wearing a tan cotton dress and a starched headband coming out of unit 18. She was pushing a service cart: a housekeeper.

"Pardon me miss, is this your regular shift?" I asked as I approached.

"Yeah, why?"

"I'm with a private detective agency in Evansville, investigating suspicious activity in unit 22. Do you mind answering a few questions?"

"Look, I just started here last week. The head of housekeeping is in unit 25, go talk to her."

"What's her name?"

"Sudie Barnes."

"Thanks!"

The door to 25 was ajar, so I tapped lightly and pushed it open. It was a centrally located workspace for housekeeping carts and cleaning supplies. A similarly attired, middle-aged woman sat behind a small desk.

"Mrs. Barnes?"

"Yeah!"

I gave her the same line I'd used on the younger woman. "Do you mind answering a few questions? It could help me wrap up an investigation."

"Whaddaya wanna know?" she asked around the cigarette hanging from her mouth.

"I know unit 22 is being used as a love nest for an extramarital affair with a local woman. Can you tell me how long the man's had the unit?"

"First of all, he doesn't use it often. We don't have to clean it more than once a month, maybe less. But to answer your question, I'd say about six months or so."

"Do they always arrive and depart in separate taxis?"

"Only way I've ever seem 'em come and go."

"Do you know the woman?"

She hesitated. "Well, maybe . . . why?"

"What's her name?" I pressed.

"Now look mister, I'm a live-and-let-live woman. Lotta indiscretions go on around here these days. It's none of my business, and I need this job."

"I understand completely." I pulled out a $10 bill and tore it in half. I handed half of it to her. "We're pretty sure of her name, but we need to corroborate it from another source." I extended the remainder of the bill toward her. "Your name won't be used."

She looked at me, then at the other half of the bill. Glancing through the open door to see if we were being observed, she said, "You swear, mister?"

I nodded.

"Selma Weiskopf." She snatched the other half of the bill from my hand and shoved it deep into her apron pocket, grabbed a service cart, and rushed out the door.

"Thank you, Mrs. Barnes. You've been a big help."

I walked to the motel office, and laid a $5 bill on the counter with my hand covering half of it. "How long has Maurice Rednour held unit 22?"

"Who?" He eyed the five spot.

"Maurice Rednour."

"I don't know no Rednour. That room belongs to Carl Duncan. He's held it for more'n six months or so. Pays by the month."

Son of a bitch! That opens up all sorts of considerations in Herman Weiskopf's murder.

I drove directly to the police station. An oscillating fan was intermittently disturbing a pile of papers on Brackett's desk when I walked into his office.

"Rednour's been keeping a unit at the Gateway Motel, under the name of Carl Duncan. I watched a liaison play out there, just this afternoon. A few minutes after Rednour arrived, a second taxi delivered a woman to the same unit. A motel employee identified the woman as Selma Weiskopf."

"So, he's having an affair with Selma Weiskopf. He's probably not the first." He adjusted his tie at his throat.

"Guinea, she's the wife of his murdered mine superintendent. You don't think that's at least a little suspicious?"

He shoved his chair back from his desk and peered out his window, onto the street.

"Dammit Cole! Why are you telling me this now? Clyde Gish has been found guilty and sentenced. The case is closed, put to bed. We don't want any extenuating circumstances that might result in an appeal or a mistrial." He turned to face me. "I'm not touching it, Cole."

"Look Guinea, Gish probably did the actual killing. But if Rednour knew of the plan, he's at the very least an accessory in a capital murder.

"What role did Rednour play in this sordid drama? Was he merely Selma's lover, viewing her as a local convenience, unaware of her devious plans? Was Clyde a hapless tool and witless victim of an ambitious woman's conniving nature? Did she have designs on Rednour? Was he as naive and ill-fated as Clyde Gish, stupidly playing into Selma's masterplan? Or did he *know*? Did he manipulate weaker people in order to steal his employee's wife?"

"All right Cole! We'll look into it. Leave the investigation to us." Detective Brackett stood and hurriedly walked me to the door, anxious for me to be out of his sight. I got the feeling nothing more would be done with the information I'd just imparted to an arm of local law enforcement. The case was closed.

Leave well enough alone—the unofficial motto of my hometown!

CHAPTER 39

Stormy Jack had been back at work for a few weeks. Every morning, I took him coffee and visited with him for a while, as had become my custom. And each day I was aware of changes: He moved a little slower, more gingerly; his breath was more labored; his ankles were swelling, and his shirt collar hung looser around his neck. His face was ashen—a grayish-purple hue showed through his dark skin; his hands were not as firm and steady on the brushes. In the watery pools of the old man's eyes there was a kindness and tolerance that can't be manufactured or faked.

John Calhoun Storm had become my friend. He was in his mid- to late-50s, and predisposed to heart trouble, high blood pressure, and diabetes. They were ravaging his body. There was no way of knowing how much damage the stress of living in the Jim Crow South exacted on the life and body of a colored man. I was concerned for his welfare, but the social mores of our time prevented us from publicly assuming the role of equals. And he was a proud man. I was careful to avoid appearing condescending.

"How're you feeling this morning, John?" I asked, using his given name.

"Poorly, Hoyt."

"What can I do for you?"

"Jest set here with me for a time," he replied.

So I did—him on his stool and me in the chair next to him, each sipping our coffee. Cooler temperatures seemed to put a spring in the step of passersby. Businessmen and women, clerks, lawyers, and bankers passed by the front window. Cars passed in the street. Bus brakes squeaked and taxis honked. The rising sun cast long shadows toward the river. I sat a while longer. We had no need for conversation. After a while, I turned to him, lifted my empty cup toward him, and nodded. He, in turn, tipped his cup toward me and managed a weak smile. I rose, momentarily resting my hand on his shoulder as I walked out. "See ya tomorrow, Storms."

"Bye, Mista Hoyt."

I understand why the race disparity arose, and why it persisted. But there is no way I can defend it. The antebellum South was an agrarian economy, largely successful because of cheap labor. The Civil War destroyed that economy and devastated the entire Southern culture. Sherman's March to the Sea laid waste to all aspects of an established way of life. The plantations and the planter class were justifiably eliminated. But the rest of the South bore the brunt of his scorched earth campaign.

Before the war, the South consisted mainly of yeoman farmers—small landowners who lived in modest houses and cabins. They were subsistence farmers, growing the crops and raising the livestock they needed to survive. Most did not own slaves, but they supported the slave-based economy, knowing that they'd be unable to compete with wealthier farmers for land and labor should the slaves be freed.

While the smallest in number, the planter class controlled

most of the wealth. They represented one to two percent of the population. The majority of white Southerners did not own slaves and were not wealthy. The economy created great wealth for a few—a very few! The remaining white Southerners—who ranged from middle- and lower-middle-class to the frankly poor—were the ones most impacted by the total economic collapse and devastation.

In terms of economic reality, the Confederacy was doomed when the first shots were fired on Fort Sumter. The South had never developed or attracted a qualified labor force. Immigrants remained in the North or moved out West. There were no manufacturing and industrial jobs to supplant the losses from the war, and most financial institutions were in the North, effectively isolating the South from industrial investment. As a consequence, the majority of Southern whites went from a modest means of earning a living and feeding a family at best, to a situation of total ruin and devastation.

After the ratification of the 13th Amendment, which abolished slavery in the United States, the Jim Crow laws began to take root throughout the South. Colored codes were strict local and state laws that detailed when, where, and how formerly enslaved people could work, and for how much compensation, and they served as a legal way to put Negro citizens into indentured servitude, to take voting rights away from them, to control where they lived and how they traveled, and to seize children for labor purposes.

CHAPTER 40

It was hard to get motivated on Wednesdays. Most weeks, though, some mundane, commonplace event occurred to shake the entire staff out of the pervasive boredom in the newsroom. The last day of August, a Wednesday, was no exception, except the event was anything but commonplace. Two local boys discovered a body out in the Scuffletown bottoms.

I headed east on Highway 60, out of town. We'd had sufficient rain to ensure a good yield, and I looked out at fields of corn and beans in full flourish, awaiting harvest. The sun shone through gaps in the clouds, creating alternating patterns of light and dark across the tops of the lush, green growth. At the Spottsville Bridge, loaded coal trucks tore at the road's thin layer of asphalt and created traffic congestion. The smell of wildflowers and the dust off the fields rode the breeze through my open windows. A coal barge shoved its cargo up the Green River toward its confluence with the Ohio.

On the other side of the bridge, I passed isolated and run-down dwellings and yards littered with rusted, obsolete farm equipment, overgrown with weeds. Sheriff's department cars had pulled off the road, and deputies gathered in and around what had been the community's post office.

I parked and walked toward the woods behind the old building. A damp, fetid odor rose from the river. Sheriff Fletcher Agnew was moving in my direction, his lemon-squeezer ranger's hat perched on his head and his badge prominently displayed on his left breast.

"What's going on, Sheriff?"

His uniform was smartly tailored and neatly pressed, but the left side of his face bulged with a huge wad of chewing tobacco. He deftly switched it to the right, spat a stream of amber into the weeds. "There's a body in the front seat of that car yonder," he said, indicating the direction with a twitch of his head. The sun glanced off his aviator sunglasses. "It's been beaten so bad, no one here can identify him. Take a look, if you'd like. Check your gag reflex and try not to puke on your shoes. Maybe you know who he is."

I pushed through the undergrowth obscuring the crime scene. A two-door Dodge was backed deep into the brush. Through the open driver's side door, I could see the beaten, bloody, and brutalized body of a man. I'd seen my share of bodies in every state of distortion and horrific disfigurement during my military service. Most of those gruesome combat deaths were administered from a distance, impersonal and random, the consequence of the pandemonium of battle. The common denominator was the shocked expression on the face of the victims, if there was any face remaining. This man's eyes stared blankly toward the headliner in the car, his nose contorted at a grotesque angle. His mouth was just a gash. His blood was dried black, and the distorted body was bruised and purple, and drawn into a fetal position. An obviously broken leg lay at an improbable angle.

This was not a random, detached, and anonymous killing. The perpetrator had obviously been enraged.

I surveyed the scene. The rear fender on the driver's side was smeared and splattered with dried blood, indicating where the savagery had begun. Moving counterclockwise around the vehicle, I located a wallet in the weeds, near the exhaust pipe. I whistled loudly and motioned for the sheriff. The wallet contained two fives and a single, along with the driver's license. Otis Earl Martin.

Pearly Martin had been murdered.

"Who reported this, Sheriff?"

"Bertha Collins, a grass widow living up the road a piece. Her two boys were playing nearby and found the body."

"Got any idea who may have done this?"

Deep vertical creases separated his eyebrows, suggesting careful thought. Looking off in the distance, he jiggled his index finger in his right ear canal and pulled his shorts from between his butt cheeks with his left hand. "Nope."

"Mind if I talk to Mrs. Collins?" I asked.

He nodded and pointed up the road in the direction of her house. "About a quarter mile up 'atta way on the right. Nothing else around it, can't miss it."

I got back in my truck and headed in the direction indicated, dodging pot holes. Gravel from the deteriorating asphalt kicked up and struck the bottom of my truck, sounding like maracas. Mrs. Collins lived in a run-down, shotgun house leached of color, about 100 feet off the road. A dozen or more chickens clucked, pecked, and strutted around the weed-infested yard, and a cinder path led to a sagging porch beneath a rusted tin roof. A puff of cotton was pinned to the door—a rural ploy intended to deny flies and mosquitoes entry.

She was a large, tired-looking woman with a put-upon expression on her face. The material of her faded print dress was so wash-worn it was past any realistic life expectancy.

"Mrs. Collins, I'm Hoyt Cole with the *River City News*. Sheriff Agnew said I could talk to you about the killing up the road."

"My boys came running from the woods, breathless and excited, claiming they'd found a dead man. They took me down the road to the scene. I came back home and called the sheriff."

"Did you recognize the body?"

"It don't look like nobody from around here."

"Much obliged." I got back in my truck and headed for the office.

My story printed above the fold—a front page headline, the first for me. Pearly's murder set the whole town to talking, wondering, and speculating. The local television station requested permission to use my article as information in their six and ten o'clock news broadcasts. Pearly's killing was the biggest local story of its kind since the end of the war.

Few communities have local television celebrities—certainly, communities of our size. In those that do, rarely are they murdered. The sheriff's department and the local police were immediately under pressure to find the killer.

CHAPTER 41

In 1949, the American Municipal Association, representing more than 10,000 cities nationwide, petitioned the federal government to combat the growing influence of organized crime. First-term senator Estes Kefauver of Tennessee drafted a resolution to create a special committee to investigate the issue. The Commerce and Judiciary Committees battled to control the investigation, and following a protracted debate, Vice President Alben Barkley, from Kentucky, cast the tie-breaking vote to establish a special committee.

Senate Resolution 202 provided the Special Committee on Organized Crime in Interstate Commerce, commonly known as the Kefauver Committee, with $150,000 to study interstate crime. Politically ambitious, Kefauver sought the Democratic Party's nomination for president. He won several primaries by strong margins, but the political bosses instead nominated Adlai Stevenson.

The five-member committee was set to expire at the end of February 1951, but the public inundated Congress with letters demanding that the inquiry continue. The Senate responded, extending support for the investigation to September 1, 1951. During the course of the 15-month investigation, the committee met in 14 major US cities and interviewed hundreds of witnesses in open and executive session. Their focus was on major cities. Because of its proximity to Cincinnati, the gambling in northern Kentucky towns such as Covington, Newport, Florence, and Ft. Mitchell received the only scrutiny in our state. This left Henderson out completely.

‡

When the Kefauver Committee failed to investigate the illegal gambling in our area, Henderson's many concerned citizens felt cheated, knowing that a federal vice cleanup here would have exposed the local gambling lords and political corruption, along with possible federal income-tax evasion. I wrote an op-ed piece for submission under my new byline, enumerating the shocking conditions: the gaming devices openly displayed in retail establishments from the smallest mom-and-pop café to the poshest super clubs; open prostitution in just about every bar, tavern, and roadhouse in the county; and the condemnation of Camp Breckinridge's commanding officer. I detailed my visits to the Cosmopolitan Club, the Bottoms, the Halfway Club, the River City Tavern, and several other local clubs and honkytonks. Many, if not most, of the patrons were teenage soldiers who freely admitted they were under 21 years of age. I summarized personal interviews with 50 or more citizens who felt the gambling bosses had become so powerful that they controlled local elections. It was widely believed that state officials from the governor to the local chief of police had closed their eyes to these facts, and I said so. Just about every business that offered gambling held a state license to sell alcoholic beverages. Every one of these places violated state law each time they opened their doors.

I placed the article in a manila envelope and slid it under Mr. Headley's office door. Two days later, the complete article, word for word, appeared in the *Evansville Courier* and the *Evansville Press*, under the byline of Noah Logan. One week later, the article appeared in the *Louisville Courier-Journal*, Western Kentucky Edition, with only slight editorial modifications—again, byline Noah Logan.

The morning after the article appeared in the Louisville paper, I made my daily stop at Stormy Jack's shoeshine stand, coffee in hand.

"Morning, John."

"Morning, Hoyt."

He took the coffee cup, lifted it slightly in a perfunctory toast and nodded his thanks. He seated himself on the stool in front of his bench. "You been reading them articles 'bout gambling here 'bouts," he asked, looking at me askance.

"Yeah, I read 'em. Same article in different papers," I said.

"That Logan feller, you ever heard of him, you being in the newspaper bidness and all?"

"No, I don't know him."

"Sure seems to know a lot about the goin's on around here, don't he?" He trained a sly grin on me. He removed the lid from his coffee and blew on it.

"That's what investigative reporters do, John." I was trying hard to maintain a mask of marginal interest, ignorance, and innocence.

"Well, whoever he is, his article should shake things up around here."

"Could, I suppose. Gotta run, John, see ya tomorrow."

"See ya tomorrow."

John Calhoun Storm, was not naive, nor easily fooled. But he *was* loyal. Another of his traits I respected.

CHAPTER 42

Over the past few months, I'd seen a lot of the underbelly of this community. Some of it, like the upscale Cosmo, was considered respectable—*illegal,* but respectable. Some, like Kluckey's on Second and Water Streets, were just sad and pathetic, catering to people who were sad and pathetic. Most places filled a space somewhere along the scale between the two extremes. Some were modest and underfunded attempts to emulate the Cosmo. Some were well managed and profitable. Some were operated hand to mouth by men that liked the idea of owning a bar or tavern. None of these, as a stand-alone entity, could have really damaged the reputation or moral fiber of an entire community. But together they presented an accumulation of vice that constituted a serious local issue.

Of the dozens of bars, taverns, and nightclubs, the most notorious, by far, was the Kain-Tuck Lounge. The owner, Slade Thornton, was big, tough, and mean. He prided himself on running the roughest joint in the area. Located on the south end of town, up the road and across from the high school football stadium, the Kain-Tuck was a 3,500 square-foot, frame building with a gable roof. The place was loud, rowdy, and profane, free of any semblance of social decorum. Rude and indecent behavior was the norm at the Kain-Tuck, and prostitutes plied their trade openly, there. It served minors and drunks. Camp Breckinridge had placed it off-limits to all military personnel. The Kain-Tuck didn't attract the A-list of Henderson society.

Since I'd visited every other gambling house in the area, I decided to pay it a visit. I waited until what I thought would be the height of activity: ten o'clock, Friday night. I could hear the loud music 200–300 yards away. While you don't go to such a place looking for trouble, you'd better go prepared for it.

The place sat about 100 feet off the road. Cars were parked haphazardly, crowding the gravel lot in front and around one side of the building toward the back. I pulled my truck around to the rear and backed in, front forward, and left my USMC issued, semi-automatic M 1911 Colt .45 in the glove box. A swarm of insects surrounded the uncovered bulb dimly illuminating the back door. It gave way easily when I twisted the knob, and I pushed through it to a narrow corridor leading past restrooms and supply items to the door into the main room. My entrance seemed to go unnoticed.

The evening was at full throttle. The front half of the place held crap and blackjack tables, roulette wheels, poker tables, and slot machines. The back half was devoted to a bar, a dance floor, and a small band stand, where a three-piece combo—piano, upright bass, and saxophone—was making more noise than music. Women in provocative dress danced barefoot and hustled watered-down drinks from the male patrons. The purple haze and murky lighting limited clear visibility to just a few feet. Three ominous-looking men armed with shotguns patrolled a six-foot wide catwalk that ran around the perimeter. The place had all the hallmarks of a Depression-era roadhouse.

I ordered a beer and started to move around the room, taking in all the goings-on. The crowd around the gambling tables was two to three deep, depending on the level of winnings and excitement at each station. The smell of tobacco, booze, cheap perfume, and body odor was sufficient to offend the nasal sensors of a hyena. There was the usual jostling, pushing, and shoving. It took a while to navigate completely through the action.

Back at the bar, I ordered another beer. I felt crowding on my right by an oversized hulk. Attempting to slide to my left, I was aware of another man fast up against my left side. Turning to face the bar again, I straightened and spread my shoulders and widened my elbows in an attempt to gain purchase of some maneuverable space. Before I could step from between them, a third man moved in against my back.

"You boys on a mission?" I asked.

"You're the 'paperboy' ain't you?" the big one on my right said.

"I work for the local newspaper, if that's what you mean."

"We don't like what's being written about the entertainment business here," the guy on my left chimed in.

"In that case, complain to the Evansville and Louisville papers."

The guy behind me began to press something rigid into my right kidney.

"You're here. We're complaining to you!"

I'd learned in situations such as this you are either going to act, or be forced to *react*. My best results have always come from acting. I shoved back hard and fast against the man behind me, pivoted to my left, slashing my right elbow into the face and mouth of the guy to my left. I headbutted the man behind me, kneed him hard in the groin and when he bent forward, I broke my beer bottle over his head. I shoved the jagged remains of the glass bottle into the face of the man originally on my right and twisted, causing as much damage as possible in a brief period—all this in two or three seconds. Surprise is critical when outnumbered.

A man accustomed to killing and mayhem often has no recall of the events he is involved in after a degree of rage takes over. He reverts from a brain-controlled, thinking man to a reactive, spinal animal. My vision flared white-hot before gradually fading to black. Incongruous images faded in and out. Mortar shells exploded amid .50 caliber machine-gun fire. Dirt, leaves, and limbs ricocheted off the jungle floor. Men were running and diving, leaping and falling. The rain poured down, and the Higgins boats rose and fell in the ocean chop. The smell of vomit and feces filled my nostrils. I was drinking Mai Tais in a Honolulu bar to the sound of ukulele music when MPs burst through the door.

I awoke face up in the front seat of my truck. The sun was blazing through my windshield and into my eyes, forcing them to flutter open. My head was throbbing, and every limb and bone felt broken. I wasn't sure I'd ever move again. Finally, I managed to pull myself up and look into the rearview mirror. Both my eyes were swollen to purple slits, my nose was twice its normal size and my mouth merely a black slit of dried blood. I had no recollection of the previous evening, once the fight got going.

A terrible cacophonous noise pushed my aching head to a pounding crescendo. Through my swollen eyelids, I determined it to be a man hammering trash from a 30-gallon metal trash can into an outdoor garbage bin. To get his attention, I managed to reach my horn and honk weakly. He dropped the trash can and ran to my truck.

A small man with a flat nose and wide-set eyes looked through the windshield at me.

"My God, Hoyt! Is that you?" I dimly registered his crumpled ball cap, plaid shirt, and soiled bib-apron. "My God, Hoyt! You look like hell. I can't believe you're alive."

He came around to the side of my truck and opened the door.

"Who are you? Where am I?"

"It's Termite, Hoyt. Termite Hawkins. I was equipment manager in high school. You know, for football and basketball. It's Termite, Hoyt!"

"Where am I?"

"You're out on South Green Street, behind the Kain-Tuck Lounge. Don't you remember?"

"What are you doing here?" I asked through thick mental fog. "The stadium's across the road."

"I work here, Hoyt. Do odd jobs, clean up and such. Anything Slade needs me to do. Been here a while."

"The Kain-Tuck?"

"You tore hell out of the place, that's for damn sure!" he said. "Don't you remember?"

"Not much. What happened? Who beat me up?"

"Who? Hell! It took five of 'em to subdue you. After you clocked the three that braced you at the bar, you picked up the steel pipe the guy was poking in your back and damn near killed them. I never seen so much blood. Teeth, hair, blood, and snot everywhere. It happened so damn fast, I never seen anything like it. All three of 'em are in the hospital. Slade was finally able to hit you with a spring-handled, lead-loaded sap—with five men holding you for him. Even then he had to hit your three times. I don't know how you're still alive.

"Never seen anything like it. God Almighty, Hoyt!"

The next day, Sunday, I woke up in my hotel room. Apparently, I had passed out again, and Termite called Karl Kockritz, who took me home and sent deputies to get my truck. Karl and I had known each other all our lives. We grew up in the same blue-collar neighborhood and attended the same grade school, played high school sports together, double-dated, and graduated the same year. When the war broke out, we joined the marines together, but Karl couldn't pass the physical because of congenital asthma. He cleaned my cuts and bandaged my wounds. He left me four morphine tablets. I took one and slept until mid-morning.

Every part of my body ached. A vicious headache suggested I had a concussion. I thought I could go to work Monday morning, but I was wrong; I missed two days. It wasn't until Wednesday morning that I felt well enough to go in. No one approached me or questioned me about my appearance. I suppose news of the previous Friday night had preceded me. That little episode proved nothing, and it didn't alter a thing on the road to closing down gambling and corruption. I believe it *did* reveal that the gambling elements were feeling pressure. On the other hand, it may have been just an excuse to give vent to cruelty.

CHAPTER 43

Through conversations with Browder and Reverend Dahlke, I was able to stay apprised of the progress associated with Walter T.'s notebook. Shortly after our introductory meeting, Nathan W. Norsworthy, commonwealth attorney, met privately with Dahlke. Ironically, Norsworthy asked Dahlke, as president of the ministerial association, if he couldn't get a few men to go around to joints to take notes on what they saw—the number of slot machines, gambling tables, dice games, etc.—to capture the names of city and county officials that might be present, all the things Browder had already collected in his notebook. Uncertain of his motives, the reverend demurred. "Haven't you tried that before?'

"Yes, but we've got to try again, we've got to keep at it!" Norsworthy replied.

Dahlke told him he'd discuss it with the ministerial association.

Later he met with his trusted attorney friend, J. Rhodes Cunningham. He shared the contents of Browder's notebook and explained Browder's motives. Dahlke sought Cunningham's input and directions on how to proceed. Sitting behind his desk as he thumbed through Walter T.'s notebook, Cunningham said,

"While I trust Norsworthy completely, there might be a better way. The last time we presented an anti-gambling complaint to a grand jury, it got waylaid somewhere in the process. Have you ever heard of Louis Jeffries?"

Dahlke told him he had not.

"He was a candidate for state attorney general a while back. I mention him because he's honest to a fault and was one of the attorneys that broke up the gambling in northern Kentucky, at least for a while."

"How do you think he fits in to what we're trying to do here?" Dahlke asked.

"I think you and Browder should make an appointment with him. Go visit him in his home and show him what you've got." Cunningham pointed at Browder's notebook. "Seek his advice. Ask him to help you plan a strategy," he said. "You'll need to proceed cautiously and remain secretive until you're prepared to proceed with a well-devised plan."

Acting on Cunningham's advice, Dahlke and Browder drove the almost 400 miles to northern Kentucky on Labor Day, the day Jeffries suggested.

Jeffries began immediately. "I have an idea why you gentlemen drove up here. I've read the article about the gambling and corruption in Henderson. Apparently, nothing has changed since the last grand jury investigation. It's a shame you have so many crooked elected officials!"

"The ministerial association and other concerned parties have been trying to get something done for some time now," Reverend Dahlke began. "Often, we're more discouraged than encouraged. But a few days ago, Walter T. here, brought me his notebook with the information he's accumulated." He handed Jeffries the notebook. "J. Rhodes Cunningham suggested you might have some ideas on how we should proceed."

Jeffries took the notebook, put his glasses on, and began to read it, giving it his full attention, rather than just a cursory scan.

"By God, gentlemen, this is fantastic. You've got all you need to convict the SOBs—the gamblers and the corrupt politicians, especially the sheriff and the mayor. Here's the first thing you need to do." He pointed to Dahlke. "Get yourself a good typist and make out an affidavit for each visit by each person noted here and present it to Judge Davenport in open court. I emphasize *in open court*!"

Jeffries explained that they couldn't present the evidence directly to a grand jury. Grand juries operate behind closed doors, and the proceedings and deliberations are shielded from public scrutiny. "Once evidence is placed in the hands of the grand jury it is, for all intents and purposes, lost to the public." This could tilt the scales in favor of the guilty in a community where criminal elements hold sway over a majority of the citizens. The grand jury could simply quash a legitimate criminal complaint, and no one could challenge it. But if the material was presented in open court, it could be published by newspapers as allegations.

"Make sure your commonwealth attorney is in on this. Then just sit back and watch the fur fly. Since the governor is running for reelection, you might ask him to hold an ouster hearing on the sheriff."

"How are these affidavits going to accomplish what the previous grand jury investigation did not?" Dahlke asked.

"They won't if you don't get the public on your side." Jeffries recommended that they organize a citizens' group representing a cross section of the community to raise public interest and outrage. "Gather God-fearing people—laypeople, professionals, and preachers. Get just plain folks, farmers, laborers, along with the women in the community. You need as many as you can get." It wouldn't be easy to create a climate for change, but it was essential—and it was essential to keep everything quiet until they were ready to act. "You'll need some legal oversight to ensure it's done properly. Your buddy Cunningham can do that. Keep it on the QT until you've got all your ducks in a row."

Jeffries gave them some forms that could be used to prepare the affidavits properly. He particularly emphasized creating an affidavit for each visit, by each person, for each gambling place. He stressed again the importance of presenting them in open court and insisting they be given to the judge and not the commonwealth attorney. That was also critical!

On the trip back home, Dahlke shared ideas about how to raise money for legal fees and other expenses. He began to formulate ideas about publicity and organizing an active citizens group.

Over the next few days, Dahlke and Cunningham raised almost $1,000 for expenses and legal fees. They enlisted the aid of a typist they could trust, and she began to type up the affidavits in the manner prescribed by Jeffries. They obtained reprint rights for the Noah Logan article and began to circulate it among the individuals known to be sympathetic to their cause.

Even though I was pleased with the results of my Noah Logan article, I was still appalled that my employer and the local newspaper had yet to make mention of the situation. One local effect of the Noah Logan articles came through the obvious impact on the governor seeking reelection in November: The state Democratic administration prevailed on Henderson County gamblers to shut down until after the elections.

Dahlke contacted me and took me into his confidence, likely

because I'd made the initial introduction of Browder and his notebook. He wanted to know if I knew the elusive Noah Logan.

"If we're successful in our presentation of these affidavits to the judge in open court, is there any way Logan could get them published that same day?" he asked.

"That's kinda dicey, preacher. I need to think about that." I paused, trying to think it through, "Let me see what I can do. I'll need copies of all the affidavits in advance, so the press can be ready to roll, if all goes as planned."

He gladly provided individual copies of all 57 affidavits.

With no other way to effect what needed to be done, I made an appointment to talk to Harry Headley. I had no other way of getting the Evansville paper involved. Revealing Dahlke's plans to anyone felt tremendously risky. After all, secrecy was the critical element, if they were to have a chance of success.

Seated in his office, I began. "Mr. Headley, I have 57 affidavits regarding gambling in Henderson County. I'd like them submitted to the *Evansville Courier & Press* as allegations in an article by Noah Logan. But they must be held secretly, in abeyance against the day they are presented in open court."

He asked no questions and assured me he would see that everything was handled properly to our best advantage. I'd really stuck my neck out. If this was botched or mishandled, it could blow the entire efforts to hell and gone. If Headley was in cahoots with Furlong and the gamblers, I had orchestrated the failure of the most promising assault yet!

CHAPTER 44

After church on Sunday, I picked up two barbecued mutton dinners from Hare's Bar-B-Q on Green Street, and headed to Stormy Jack's house. I wanted him in his home and as comfortable as possible. I knocked on his door about 12:30.

"C'mon in," I heard him call.

"Hey, John! I got us a couple mutton dinners. Hope you're hungry." The tinfoil covering the paper plates served to keep the food hot, but couldn't contain the combined aroma of pickles, onions, barbecue sauce, and hickory smoke.

"Oh, man, that's great! I got some cold iced tea in my ice box. Let's set in there at the kitchen table. I'll get the knives and forks out. Set down, Hoyt. Thanks so much. I love mutton!"

We spread it all out, poured sweet tea into ice-filled glasses, and sat down across from each other. John returned thanks, saying a blessing for our food and our friendship. We ate in silence—not an awkward silence, but the knowing silence between two friends with no need to make idle conversation. John ate with the gusto of a man who enjoyed food. He frequently smacked his lips and made appreciative humming sounds, smiling and shaking his head.

Barbecue is mainly a Southern way of cooking meat. It is regionally distinct, varying slightly from one area to another. The principal variant is the sauce or "dip." Some use more vinegar, some more tomato sauce. In our state it's mainly a western Kentucky dish. Mutton has a distinct taste, bordering on gamey to some palates. You either like it or you don't. We liked it.

"Boy, Hoyt, that was delicious," he said. He wiped his mouth with the back of his hand and shoved his plate into the middle of the table.

After we cleared the table and washed up the dishes we moved into his bedroom–living room to visit. He sat in the oversize wooden rocking chair, and I sat on the foot of his bed. After a time, I said, "We've never talked about this, John. What are your thoughts about the gambling and lawlessness here in Henderson?"

Rolling his shirt sleeves up on his forearms, he rocked himself gently. "I don't gamble, Hoyt."

"I know that, but surely you know about it and have an opinion on the subject."

"A colored man don't get asked his opinion on such matters—you know that."

Looking out his front door I said, "I'm asking, John."

"I know it goes on. I know it's been tolerated here for some time, now. I know lots of people benefit from it. And I know there have been, and still are, movements to shut it down."

I crossed my legs, leaned forward, and placed both elbows on my knee. "That's what you know. How do you feel about it? What's your opinion?"

His brow furrowed a bit. "Because something is available, doesn't obligate a man to partake of it. Sometime, a thing, an act, a service, gets labeled wrong or sinful, not because it is wrong or sinful, in and of itself. It gets labeled like that because of the sinful nature of the men involved. When men can't control theyselves, they often enact laws to protect theyselves from they own sinfulness." He shuffled his feet, trying to improve circulation.

"I've always known you were a philosopher, John. But you'd make a pretty good courtroom lawyer."

"Whaddaya mean?" His slight smile betrayed his slyness.

"You're quite skillful at avoiding a direct response," I said, grinning.

He lowered his head, slapped his knee and chuckled.

"I'm beating around the bush. Let me get to the point." I returned both feet to the floor and sat up straight, hands rubbing their corresponding knees. "I'm involved with some people in a pursuit that, if successful, could put an end to gambling and all associated activities here in Henderson County."

"Yessuh," he said. "Why are you telling me?"

Leaning back again, I crossed my ankles. "If successful, it could put an end to your old friend Furlong's enterprise. I'm not looking for your endorsement, but I don't want to make you mad at me or lose your friendship over it."

He looked directly at me for a long moment. He rubbed his hand over the beard stubble on his face. Then he looked at the floor and out his window. I feared he was going to ask me to leave.

"You're right! Lloyd is my old friend. I'm indebted to him on lots of levels, for lots of reasons, over lots of years. But I'm not responsible for him. We started from a place most peoples don't even know exists. We did what we had to do to get by. He in his manner, me in mine. We've both done things only God can forgive us for. But we've been grown men for a long time. We have both assumed responsibility for our own actions. He never asked me, but I'm satisfied Lloyd didn't expect this to last forever. And if I know him, and I do, I'm equally satisfied he's made arrangements for the time when all this comes to an end.

"Now, that's one thing, Hoyt," he said.

"Yes sir?"

"The other is me and you." He labored to stand and walked slowly to his front door, peered outside for a moment, and turned to face me. His chair continued to rock from the momentum his rising created.

"You visited in a colored man's home when he was too sick to come to work. Most peoples in this town don't know where I live. You've brought food and shared a meal with a colored man. You drank from my glasses, and ate with my knife and fork. You've demonstrated a friendship that most peoples only talk about. You've come here to inform me of something you're involved in, out of concern for me and my friendship. You're the only white man, other than Lloyd, that refers to me by my Christian name. You don't have to worry about me and you, Hoyt. I thank you for your concern, but we're good, son."

"Thank you, John."

"You do what you feel is right, Hoyt. Nobody can fault you for that—leastways, not me." He sat back down.

I stayed with him for another hour or so, just talking and visiting. He spoke of his childhood in Shawneetown—guardedly, careful not to reveal too much. Even through all the obvious hardship, he found humor, and recounted instances that made him smile and sometimes, even laugh. I enjoyed his stories. Poverty, abuse, and privation know no race or color, but I doubt few came up any harder than John Calhoun Storm. Still, there was not the slightest hint of self-pity about him—just *another* of the things I admired about him.

CHAPTER 45

The very next morning, I was told of a body floating near the bank of the Green River at Ranger's Landing. I grabbed my pad and pencil and headed out the front door. It was the kind of morning that seemed to carry over from the previous day, providing no respite from the summer swelter. Cattle sought early morning shade, and hogs wallowed in the mud of farm ponds.

In Henderson County, if the Ohio River is a US highway, the Green River is a country road—narrower, deeper, and muddier. Local belief holds there are places in the Green where the bottom can't be reached. Its 384 miles provide an important transportation artery for the coal industry. During the Civil War, Confederate General John Hunt Morgan raided southern Indiana and Ohio through the Green River country.

I took the last road off the highway before it ended at Hambleton's ferry and drove until I spotted a cruiser blocking the lane to the Marshall cabin. I parked and started on foot. The sky was still and streaked with cotton-candy clouds. I'd seen similar morning skies in the jungles of the South Pacific. In itself it wasn't ominous; the surroundings and what you knew might await colored your feelings about it.

Mosquitoes buzzed and frogs croaked in the shadow of Leyland Cypress trees that mostly obscured the sun. Bright shafts of light filtered through the canopy, sprinkling the ground like salt crystals. Starlings and barn swallows squawked and clattered. The fetid odor of decaying and primordial river life, combined with the oppressive humidity, underscored the desolation of the site. The cabin sat in a small clearing, surrounded by a thick grove of trees and underbrush. A narrow path led down to the river bank. Nearer the river, a misty fog hung low beneath the trees. The bank was littered with deadfall, long since stripped of foliage and leeched bone-gray, rotted by time and worms.

There was a dead man floating face up a few feet from the sloping bank, hair splayed around the lifeless head and gaping mouth. The eyes were wide open in a fixed stare. The body appeared foreshortened and caved in around a dark hole in the middle. A human corpse is never pretty, but one caused by violence has a distinctively desecrated appearance. No matter how many I've seen, I can't imagine ever becoming immune to it. Turtles and small fish had begun to feed on the body. Had it not been secured to a tree by a length of rope, the corpse might not have been found for weeks, if at all. Whoever did this intended the body to be found.

The coroner and his assistant untied the rope and pulled the body toward the bank. Because of the remote location and the early hour, there were no locals milling around, only a couple of sheriff's deputies, the coroner, and another man with him. One of the deputies was Karl Kockritz. I made my way over to him.

"Whaddaya think, Karl?"

He shrugged. "Looks like a murder to me."

"Who is he?"

"Coroner hasn't positively identified him, but it looks like Ed Triplett. You remember him? He was a few years ahead of us in high school, good athlete, popular—a real ladies' man."

Even as a teenager, Eddie'd been a good-looking guy. After graduation he married Beatrice Worth, the most beautiful and shapeliest girl in school. With a loan from his dad, he started a tool-and-die business.

"Hey Karl, look at this!" another deputy yelled. He came up carrying what at first looked like a 12–14 inch piece of muddy tree limb. On closer inspection, I saw that it was a 12-inch, double-barreled gun with a pistol grip.

"Coroner found it just off the bank, in the mud near the body," the deputy said. "No doubt the weapon used."

"A sawed-off shotgun. Looks like a 16- or 20-gauge," Karl commented.

When he laid it in the grass, I knew right away it wasn't a sawed-off shotgun. While it broke down like a shotgun, this particular 20-gauge wasn't modified. It was manufactured with a short, double barrel, a wooden stock, and a pistol grip. It had two triggers, so you could fire one or both. It was made by the Ithaca Gun Company: an Automobile Riot Gun.

"Karl, when you interview his wife, let me know what you find," I said. "I'm headed back to the office."

He nodded, then pushed past a slight deputy leaning against the fender of one of the cars, without a word of acknowledgment, to get to where the others were wrestling the body out of the water and onto the bank. I drove back to town, but not to my office. My mind was racing. Eddie G. had been successful right from the start, with contracts for small plastic parts for the Chrysler plant across the river in Evansville. When the war came and Chrysler converted to war matériel, his business really took off. Locals thought he was on his way to substantial wealth. However, constant union problems in Evansville threatened closure of the Chrysler plant, along with the Servel Refrigeration plant. Either or both would have been devastating to Eddie's business.

The apparent murder of a prominent local business man with a weapon owned by a man he *and I* both knew well! I didn't like the implications; there had to be an explanation.

‡

The offices of Tom's Grocery Stores were in the Kingdon Hotel, at the back of the first floor. Parking was in back, as was the entry. I pushed through the half-glass door with "Tom's Stores, Inc." hand-lettered on the pane. I asked the receptionist if I could speak to Uncle George.

"He's got someone with him now, but I'll tell him you're here. Have a seat."

I sat in one of four wooden chairs lining the wall in the waiting area. A few slowly rotating ceiling fans were strategically placed above an open and functional, but unadorned, space, crowded with similarly functional desks, chairs, typewriters, filing cabinets, and adding machines. A few private offices surrounded the common work area. One was completely walled off, but the other three were walled halfway up with glass to the ceiling, allowing for partial exposure of the interiors.

The entire time, an unsettling thought gnawed at my mind: I knew only one man in the entire county who had a weapon like the one found at the scene. He kept it under the front seat of his car.

George Luther Butler supervised some 30 of Tom's 70-plus neighborhood grocery stores throughout western Kentucky, southern Indiana, and southern Illinois. In addition to his duties overseeing the operation of the stores, he was in charge of consolidating and converting the smaller neighborhood stores to the modern "Master Market"—stores that were much larger, mostly self-service, and even air-conditioned.

"Uncle" George had been with the chain for more than 30 years. He was an avuncular local insider—not in the sense of influencer or string-puller, but insider in the sense of "in the know." He knew who to see, who to use, who to trust, who to hire, and from whom to seek advice. Most importantly, he knew who to avoid, regardless of the task you might be contemplating.

He had several nephews; during the Depression, he put them all to work with the grocery chain. A butcher by trade, he taught them all to break down a side of beef and become butchers as well, a way to make a living. When the war broke out and economic conditions improved, many of them became store managers or assistant managers. When George became supervisor, he was always greeted as *Uncle George* when he visited their stores. The sobriquet stuck, and he became Uncle George in every store in the chain.

When I was about 12 years old, during the Great Depression, he gave me a part-time job stocking shelves and sweeping floors. Late one night, a local man, his face partially covered with a handkerchief tied cowboy-style over his lower face, carried a gun into the store Uncle George managed on Clay Street. Recognizing the man, he said, "Put the gun down, Pete."

"My family's starving, George, I gotta get some money."

"Come on with me." He turned his back to the gunman and headed toward the rear of the store, behind the meat counter.

Uncle George filled a large cardboard box with meat scraps, end pieces of baloney, chicken necks, and pig's feet. He calmly filled a paper bag with "about-to-spoil" vegetables, a half dozen potatoes, and two, one-pound bags of navy beans. Last, he put a Hershey bar at the top of the bag.

"Take that home, Pete. Come see me again if you have to." The man grabbed the food like a drowning man clutching a life preserver and ran from the store. "Tough times, Hoyt," was all he said.

While on that occasion it was at gunpoint, Uncle George often made the same gesture to families fending off starvation in the neighborhood. If he, himself, was stealing, it didn't bother him, and no one told. Difficult times often necessitate hard decisions. There are times when human kindness holds sway over what's legal or illegal.

Uncle George came to the door of his office and motioned for me to come in. Extending his hand, he greeted me warmly. "Good to see you Hoyt, what can I do for you?"

I walked into his office and waited for him to sit down. Papers were strewn across his desk and a trail of spooled paper extended to the floor from the adding machine to his right.

"Thanks for seeing me Uncle George. Are you aware Eddie G. has been killed?"

"What?!" He lurched forward in his chair, planting both elbows firmly on the top of his desk, his relaxed demeanor suddenly gone. "When did this happen?" He reached for the cigarette burning in his ashtray.

"Overnight, I'd guess. The body was found just this morning."

"Where was he?" he wanted to know. "How did it happen? Who did it?"

"His body was found at his uncle's cabin out at Ranger's Landing. He was tied to a tree and shot through the chest."

"Oh, God, Hoyt!" The color drained from his face. He reached into his hip pocket for a handkerchief, pushed up his glasses, and pinched the bridge of his nose, obviously distraught. He wiped first one eye, then the other, then blew his nose. The starched white shirt and neatly pressed blue suit seemed to wilt around him.

"They found the weapon. It was double-barreled, a 20-gauge resembling a sawed-off shotgun." I waited for him to respond, but he kept his head in his hands, apparently still processing what he'd been told. "It was your Ithaca Riot Gun, Uncle George."

"What?"

"Your 20-gauge Ithaca Riot Gun was found at the scene—apparently the murder weapon."

He was silent for a long time.

"I'm sorry Uncle George, but I have to ask. Do you have any idea how your weapon ended up at the scene of a killing?"

"Oh my God, Hoyt! This is tragic!" He pulled his hand down over his face. "I loaned it to him," he murmured. "Two or three months ago." He was still in a daze.

"Did he say why he wanted to borrow it?"

"He said he was scared someone was trying to kill him. He feared for his life."

"Since most of his business production is for the Chrysler plant, maybe union trouble across the river was starting to impinge on this side. Perhaps some of his workers were starting to make noises about unionizing. I know he was strongly opposed to it."

"Hoyt, you know as well as I do, with all that's going on around here these days, there could be any number of reasons for him to feel threatened. Maybe he had run up a gambling debt. I know he and Beatie frequented the Cosmo."

"Are you the only one at the scene who recognized my gun?"

"Yes, sir."

"Thanks for letting me know. I better get over to the sheriff's office and let 'em know it's mine. If they find out through other channels, it could raise suspicions.

"Oh!" He seemed to suddenly remember: "Beatie knew he borrowed the gun. She was with him."

I left him at his desk, a distressed look on his face. I had always known George Butler to be an honorable man. He was also the man that recommended me for the job at the *River City News.* Could he be involved in a murder?

‡

Back at my desk, I began to draft the account of Eddie Glenn Triplett's death. All information available currently suggested murder. What was he involved in that got him killed? Did he have enemies? Business competitors perhaps? If so, who were they? Was labor strife a factor? Was he involved with another man's wife? Did he have a gambling problem?

The phone on my desk began to ring. It was Kockritz. "Meet me at Wolff's. I'll tell you what I found out."

Located on the corner of First and Green Streets, virtually in the center of town, Wolff's held the second-oldest liquor license in the state. It was in a two-story brick structure with the owner's residence above it. Like almost every other bar, it housed a few slot machines. Bugs Moran, a Chicago mobster infamous for his involvement in the St. Valentine's Day Massacre, was arrested while hiding out only a few blocks from the location in 1946.

Wolff's is a tavern in the strictest sense of the word. The fare is limited, simple, and cheap. Patrons frequent Wolff's for beer and whiskey, not fine dining. The bar is one continuous, warmly polished wood board, with a brass foot rail and spittoons. Patrons stand at the bar—no stools.

I caught Karl's reflection in the huge, oval mirror behind the bar, framed by bottles of liquor and a smattering of cheap wines. Spotting me at the same time, he took a pickled pig's foot from a glass jar, picked up the beer he was nursing, and motioned toward an empty booth. I ordered a highball before joining him. The aroma of fried food drifted from the small kitchen, along with the clash of pots and pans. A Bennie Goodman tune played on the jukebox.

"Apparently, Eddie didn't come home at all last night. He has a monthly high-stakes poker game at his uncle's cabin with local friends and business acquaintances from Evansville. It's always a late night, so Beatie didn't stay up. But when she woke in the morning and he wasn't home, she immediately called our office and gave the location of the cabin—it has no phone service." He took a swig of his beer.

"She said Eddie always stayed after the game ended to clean up: empty the ashtrays and wash and dry the glasses, put all the furniture back in the proper places. We questioned her as thoroughly as appropriate under such circumstances. She wouldn't talk at all until her mother-in-law came to get their boy. She acknowledged Eddie had been different the past few weeks—remote, disengaged, despondent, even fearful. He refused to discuss what was bothering him. She said he'd never been like that before, but she didn't press him. We asked if she thought it had anything to do with trouble at work, either financial or labor related. She said she was not aware of any trouble at his company."

"I'm sure you asked the names of the poker players?"

"Yeah, but she was a little vague. While there are regulars, there are also two or three alternates. She's not sure who sits in on any particular night. She did mention the names of a man or two. We're talking to them now.

"I asked about personal money issues," Karl went on. "Had he amassed any gambling debt? She denied any financial problems, personal or business." Karl looked at me askance. "Mr. Butler came by to identify his riot gun."

I ignored the implication. "Did you return it to him?".

"You know better than that, Hoyt. We'll have to keep it until the investigation is complete."

"Did Beatie know about the gun?" I asked. "Uncle George said she was with Eddie when he came to borrow it"

"She was vague about that, too. Didn't seem to recall the weapon when I described it to her," Karl replied. "I didn't press her on it and didn't know whose it was at the time. Mr. Butler came by later. Whoever killed him made sure the job was complete—pulled the second trigger, emptied both barrels!"

We finished our drinks, and left through separate doors. Could Eddie have been cheating in the poker game? Was he too much of a big winner to sit well with one of the players? Did one man lose more than he could afford and stay around to get his money back?

I walked back to the office to finish the writeup.

> Edward Glenn Triplett, prominent local business man, found dead this morning at a cabin at Ranger's Landing. The body was tied to a tree at the river's edge and shot through the chest. Owner and sole proprietor of Triplett's Tool and Die Company, Eddie is survived by his wife of eight years and a three-year-old son. When he failed to come home from a card game last night, his wife called the sheriff's office and identified the location of the cabin where

the gathering was held. Foul play is suspected. The sheriff's office requests that anyone having information that might be pertinent to the investigation contact them. Currently there are no leads.

I listed other survivors and told of funeral arrangements.

A man's life—in 14 lines and less than 60 words, somewhere in an obscure newspaper column. Somehow, I felt more should be said. Our existence, precious and unique, is something we have absolutely no role in creating. It takes years to fully understand its brevity, fragility, and insignificance, relative to all time and all creation. RIP Eddie G.!

CHAPTER 46

When I went downstairs for breakfast the next morning, Carla Broadbent was waiting in the lobby. She rushed over to me. "You got time to talk?"

"Sure," I said. "I'm going into the cafeteria to have some breakfast, come join me."

"I've already eaten, but I'll come along."

I hurriedly retrieved my toast and coffee and joined her at a table off in a corner. "I read your article about Eddie G. Triplett. I have some information that might be useful. I don't want to get involved with the police, but you use it as you see fit."

"Go ahead, Mrs. Broadbent."

"I have a nephew by marriage. He's my late husband's sister's son." She paused, seeming to want to put some distance between herself and the nephew. "He's a very nice man." She paused again. "He never married." Another longer pause, indicating I should know and understand what she was trying to tell me, but I did not. "He . . . prefers men . . . if you know what I mean."

"That's nothing to be ashamed of, Mrs. Broadbent. What's that got to do with the possible murder of Eddie G.?"

"My nephew frequents a bar in Evansville. It's not a stag bar, as in "men only" but *only men* go there, if you get my meaning."

"Yes ma'am?" I questioned.

"My nephew says Eddie G. Triplett was in there often. He generally had his *friend* with him. I'm told they'd been *friends* for some time."

"Should I need to, can I speak with your nephew?"

"Oh no! He'd kill me if he knew I was telling you this."

"What's the name of the bar?"

"It's called Pal's, on Fulton Avenue. I've got to get to the office, Hoyt. Call me if you need anything more."

She stood and hurried away, not waiting for me to thank her, or say goodbye.

I'm not sure what Eddie G. being homosexual—if in fact he was—has to do with him being murdered. Carla Broadbent's not a busybody or gossip. I'm sure she had a valid reason for imparting that information to me. Did she know more than she revealed, leaving me to pursue her lead? I'll follow up with Deputy Kockritz to see if there's any new information.

Triplett's body was tied to a tree. Could that be indicative of a ritualistic killing? Was there a jealous lover? Carla's revelation had led me to consider things I'd never thought of before. We humans lead convoluted and duplicitous lives.

‡

Howard sent me to cover a late-afternoon meeting of the county fiscal court. An assignment equivalent to a surgeon removing a hemorrhoid: boring, mundane, and shitty!

These assignments are like the rain, they fall on every reporter from time to time. They generate absolutely no direct revenue, but the public has a right to know, and believe it or not, they want to read about it. The exercise of a free press, a critical element of a free society.

It was hard to concentrate on the task at hand. Walking through the corridors of justice I wondered how so many attempts to indict the wrongdoers here had been quashed. Even mundane proceedings leave a serious and somber impression—at least on me. Likewise, Carla Broadbent's revelation about Eddie G.'s secret homosexuality continued to aggravate and tug at my thoughts. What other secrets might Eddie G. have been harboring?

Afterward, I checked my messages at the hotel. Uncle George had called inviting me to come by his house after supper, about 6:30. Uncle George lived in the 1400 block of Powell Street, next to a furniture store and across the street from Tom's number nine grocery store.

I parked my truck in front of his house and walked through the gate of the white picket fence. He was sitting on the porch; a smoking Lucky Strike was burning between the first two fingers of his right hand, both stained yellow with nicotine. The red cocker spaniel next to his chair raised her head to investigate. With no signal from her master and sensing no threat herself, she laid it back down on top of crossed paws and closed her eyes.

"Come in, Hoyt. Take a seat."

"Thanks, Uncle George, nice evening, huh?" I sat in one of three other metal chairs situated around his circular porch.

He held a funeral-home fan in his left hand, cooling himself and shooing away a pesky fly from time to time. "What's on your mind, Hoyt?"

"You have any thoughts on who may have killed Eddie G. and why he may have been killed?" I gazed up Powell Street at the gas station on the corner. A boy was airing up the tires of his bicycle.

The man across the street was mowing his small front lawn with a solid steel, reel-type, hand-pushed lawn mower.

"Yes! I haven't stopped having thoughts about it since you first told me." He stared off down the street and tapped his right hand on the arm of his chair knocking the ashes off his cigarette.

"I know you're friends with his daddy. You talk to him about it?"

"Not beyond offering my sympathies and the usual words of comfort you try to express at such times. A man should never have to bury a child. Words of comfort don't change anything. Brief is better. Too early for me to question him on who or why."

"You've known Eddie G. since he was a boy. Over the years, has there been anything unusual about him that might shed light on his killing?"

"Good kid, growing up. Quiet and mild mannered, always pleasant and polite to adults. Way he was raised. When he got older, up in high school, he matured into a strong, good-looking young man. All the girls sought him out and boys gravitated to him. He seemed to like and be liked by all his peers."

"Uncle George, do you think it's possible he could have been having an extramarital affair?"

"Always possible, Hoyt. But I have no reason to think that. Do you have information to suggest or support that line of questioning?"

"No sir. Not really."

He looked at me over the top of his glasses. He wore only a sleeveless undershirt and suspenders over the pleated trousers of his blue suit. Without the normal cover of his white shirt and suit coat, he presented as a much frailer-looking man. Somehow, the man I'd known most of my life suddenly looked older.

Turning the tables, he asked "What's your interest in the *why* of this? No disrespect, son, but aren't you paid to *report* what happens, not *investigate* what happens?"

"You're absolutely right, Uncle George. But there's just so *much* goin' on here. A lot of it appears to be illegal, and everyone seems accepting of it. I'm beginning to wonder if it's all not somehow related.

"Maybe if I'd stayed on here the past 10 years, I'd be like everybody else. But I didn't, and I'm not. Believe me, Uncle George, I'm no knight in shiny armor, but I don't like what I see, and I'm hard-pressed to just accept it. I'm not a 'go along, to get along' kinda guy."

"I never thought you were, Hoyt. I'm not faulting your interest or inquiry. In fact, I hope you'll stay with it and see where it leads you." He paused again, looking off down the street. While the sun was setting, it was still mostly daylight. An azure sky blanketed a peaceful blue-collar neighborhood.

"Tell you what. Eddie has an uncle that he's been close to all his life. A bachelor—never been married. Eddie spent a lot of time with him as a boy. He's a blacksmith, metal worker, engine mechanic, and recluse, the black-sheep brother on his mother's side. He lives out at Bluff City. Just ask anyone out there for Everett Lightfoot. But tread lightly, Hoyt, he's not to be trifled with. Strange man . . . some call him peculiar."

"Thanks, Uncle George, I'll be going along."

He stood and shook my hand. "You're a good man, Hoyt. I'm proud of you. Good luck and call on me anytime."

Dusk was settling, and the first few lightning bugs of the evening were casually floating around in his yard. I went through his gate to my truck. A waxing gibbous moon hung mid-sky over the river. At about 2/3 illumination, it lit a narrow but shimmering white path across the water to the ramp at the end of Second Street.

CHAPTER 47

I arrived early for the service of Otis Earl "Pearly" Martin and took a seat at the back of the chapel. A few rows up front were designated for family. A crowd eventually filled the funeral home to overflowing, 2/3 of them women. More than 200 people crammed into the chapel, and at least that many were standing around outside. While quiet and respectful, the gathering had something of a circus atmosphere.

Funerals hold a curious fascination for people, and they always have. Every culture back to the dawn of man has had some form of ritual for the dead. Many of them are religious in nature, and they vary greatly from place to place and from one religion to another, with traditions from the macabre to celebratory. It is hard to estimate how many were present that day as mere curiosity seekers. I'm satisfied many were there because of Pearly's fame and to satisfy a morbid fascination with the ferocity of the crime.

Over the prior 50 years, many impressive funerals had been held in large cosmopolitan cities like New York, Chicago, and Los Angeles. They paid respects to mostly nonpolitical personalities—movie stars, in particular. They can seem larger than life, due to closeup shots that increase the audience's emotional involvement with the character on the screen, often resulting in confusion between the actors and their roles. That was certainly the case with Rudolph Valentino, back in the '20s.

The intimacy of a television bringing these images into the home has done the same for lesser, local personalities. While Henderson was not New York, and the celebrity and fame of Pearly Martin in no way compared to Rudolph Valentino's, it's not too great a stretch to suggest that Pearly's death and funeral had as big an impact locally as Valentino's did on the national scene.

A gospel quartet opened the service with a hymn entitled "In the Garden." Leon Remington and members of his group were in attendance, but strangely they were not part of the service. I later learned that the pall bearers were men Pearly had worked with in Evansville. The officiant, the pastor of a local church, had no personal relationship with or knowledge of the deceased, beyond what he had recently learned of Pearly's reputation, putting him at a decided disadvantage in his attempts to put a positive spin on the proceedings. The minister spoke of the violence perpetrated against his person and reminded everyone of God's forgiveness. He avoided speaking of Pearly's character or his past. When the service ended, members of the family filed past the casket for one last look at the body, while organ music filled the chapel. Young girls sobbed openly and older women wept silently into handkerchiefs.

Outside the sky was gray and the atmosphere thick and heavy with moisture. The color was beginning to fade from the trees. Leaves swirled and collected in the gutter. The procession to the grave site appeared to be over a mile long. A number of cars had arrived ahead of the procession, jamming the parking area and surrounding streets.

After a final prayer, funeral-home personnel urged people to disperse to allow the cemetery workers to inter the casket. Relatives and friends began to move toward their cars. Suddenly, gasps and loud voices erupted as a lone women leaped from one of the parked cars and raced toward the open grave. Only the quick reaction of a cemetery worker prevented her from diving headfirst into the crypt. She screamed hysterically. "He loved me! I know he loved me!" Other attendants had to help restrain her. They led her forcibly back to her car where the minister tried to console her.

When the shocked gathering of relatives and friends finally regained composure, they moved toward their cars. A light rain began to fall, and groundskeepers lowered the casket into the earth. Most of those present were unpretentious, working-class people who accepted death as commonplace and universal. They wore their resignation to life and their role in it like their worn clothes. Several clusters of two to three women lingered, offering each other solace in their individual and shared grief.

I remained after the last vehicle was out of sight. The grave was filled, creating a small mound which the attendants covered with flowers. Upon completion of the task, they threw their shovels into the back of their service truck, loaded in, and drove out of sight. The fragrance of flowers mingled with the odor of damp earth, a unique and inharmonious smell. Every life, no matter how it begins, ends in a hole in the ground. Rich or poor, white or Black, famous, infamous, known, or unknown, the occupant is left there alone for the rest of eternity.

Rest in peace, Pearly Martin.

‡

Over the following weeks, the investigation into the murder produced a lot of rumors, leads, suspects, and speculation, all of them credible, at least at first, because of Martin's reprehensible character and actions.

Armchair detectives speculated that Leon Remington was a likely suspect. His teenage daughter had recently left town, and from their perspective, there couldn't be but one reason she'd do that. She had been known to hang around the nightclubs and the TV station where Pearly and her daddy performed. Adding two and two and leaping to ten, that made Leon a likely candidate. Where could you find a more justifiable motive? Lots of assumptions are required of course, but easily made in such a heated environment.

I decided I should try to interview Leon Remington. The sun was low and burning bright when I drove out to his home and guitar shop, a few miles out of town in the Zion community. I passed an oil rig pumping lazily by the roadside; the aroma of raw petroleum hung heavily on the air. Leon's house sat 50 yards or so off the road, among a number of mature oak trees providing a shady canopy. His shop was in a wooden structure, about the size of a garage.

The door opened immediately to my knock. Up close, Remington was much bigger than he appeared on stage, hulking and powerful. He wore a one-piece union suit in gray, striped denim. The sleeves were cut off at the shoulders.

"Yeah?"

His face was full and beefy, but blank, revealing nothing and concealing everything. He looked older without his cowboy hat—his hair was thin to balding.

"I'm Hoyt Cole, Mr. Remington. I work for the *River City News*. Can I come in?"

He looked around me, suspiciously searching the area outside. "How'd you know where I live?" he asked.

"Just asked around. Lots of folks in town know where you live. Can I come in?"

"Yeah, I reckon. Come on in." He stepped back into his shop.

The place was neat and well lighted. It smelled of spruce, cedar, maple, and mahogany mingled with varnish, glue, and lacquer. Guitars in various stages of completion were hung from the walls and placed strategically around on work benches. A small basket of kindling and a bucket of coal stood within easy reach of a vented Warm Morning stove in the corner.

"Mr. Remington, I'm sure you're aware of the rumors and speculations surrounding Pearly Martin's murder. Would you care to comment.?"

"Pearly's dead. Somebody killed him," he said tersely.

"You have any idea who did it?" I asked.

"Kinda like a large Sunday buffet, Mr. Cole. Too many choices. Hard to make your selection."

"Did you kill him?"

"Is that what you came out her to ask me?"

"Yes, among other things," I said.

"Well, if I did, do you honestly believe I'd acknowledge it to you?"

"Unlikely."

"Then why ask?'

"The job of a newspaperman."

A roll of fret wire, commonly called *nickel silver,* hung from a wood peg on the wall. Hand planes, chisels, coping saws, a band saw, drills, and sanders were clearly visible and obviously well-used. Strangely out of place were a half dozen, two-foot lengths of galvanized pipe, leaned into a corner against one wall. A book lay splayed open on a worn pillow in the seat of a wooden rocker off to the side, the front and back cover visible. I was able to make out the words *polygraph exams* in the title.

"Speculation in town believes you had a more than credible motive," I said.

"Yeah? And what would that be?" he asked. "Hold on! Don't answer that. I know what you're driving at, and my daughter's circumstances are private and off-limits in further discussions of Pearly Martin.

"I will tell you this. Had Pearly Martin ever trifled with my daughter, wife, or any other member of my family, I would have killed him, and he knew it," he said, eyes narrowing and face reddening.

"Did you threaten him?"

"Didn't have to."

"What's that mean?"

"Look, Cole. I've known Otis Martin all his life, know where he came from and how he was raised. I knew his character, or lack of it, when I hired him. I needed a lead singer, and he was as good as any around here. All I cared about was, would he be there for rehearsal and show dates, and he always was.

"Equally important, he knew me and he knew not to fuck with me, my family, or any of my band members—and he never did!" He leaned over to pat a disinterested, old coon dog on the floor. "Pearly never touched my daughter, and I didn't kill him!"

He paused and seemed to calm himself. His face relaxed. "Look Cole, I don't know why I'm telling you this. My wife and I certainly don't want it known, and I'm gonna ask you, on your honor, to keep it to yourself. But perhaps if you know the truth, you can diffuse some of the rumors and speculation.

"We adopted our daughter. And right or wrong, we never told

her, hoping against hope I guess, that she'd never find out the truth. She just recently learned of it. Against our objections, she immediately went to work trying to find her real mother. Broke my wife's heart. It seemed like what we'd done for her, all the love we'd given her, was out the window. Well, a month or so ago, she found her. She's not where everyone thinks she is. She's in Hopkinsville, staying with her birth mother."

His size diminished. He gruff exterior vanished, and I was looking at a father with a broken heart. I truly had no response!

"Now, you interested in buying a guitar? Otherwise, we got nothing more to discuss," he said. Remington had developed a reputation for making high quality, hand-built acoustic guitars. He'd been sought out by country singers in Nashville and performers in the Grand Ole Opry. I'd heard his guitars came close to the quality of the Martin D-45, the holy grail of acoustic.

"I guess not, Leon. Thanks for your time." As I exited, I turned to him. "She'll be back, Leon. I'm sure she'll be back."

Outside, the wind rustled the leaves of the oak trees. I paused for a moment enjoying the sights and smells of rural Henderson County. Across the road, the field corn grew straight and tall, dry stalks rattling and tassels floating easy on the afternoon breeze. The air smelled of farmland and livestock and carried crop dust and chemicals. The western sky reflected gold and lavender, darkening toward purple.

I got back in my truck and headed back into town, listening for the whine of automobile tires and the screech of rubber, as aggressive drivers took the curves in the narrow road too fast. While the ride out was not entirely a wasted effort, I really had nothing to report or write about. I tried not to speculate or intentionally create suspicion when I wrote. I didn't know if Leon

Remington was telling the truth or not, but he was convincing. I'd have to leave him to another time.

Most police officers and investigative reporters come to realize that the clues to a crime's solution are always there. It's just a matter of prodding and poking, pushing and shoving until enough is uncovered to lead to a credible conclusion. I'd begun to doubt that this would be the case in the murder of Pearly Martin.

CHAPTER 48

After the funeral, police officers returned to the riddle of Pearly's murder. The investigation led police on circuitous paths, ending in one dead end after another. He'd lived a careless and undisciplined life, with no apparent thought or worry about the consequences of his actions.

And he'd assumed no responsibility for the pain and suffering in his wake. Some of it was petty: borrowing money he never intended to pay back; borrowing another man's tools or equipment and then hocking or selling them for liquor or to pay gambling debt; welching on gambling losses. Then there were more serious offenses such as sleeping with underage girls and married women. He'd offended any number of people, any one of whom might have felt justified in killing him, for any number of reasons.

Martin was widely acknowledged to be a ladies' man. No one denied he had cuckolded many a husband in and around Henderson. Jealousy was believed to be the most likely motive in the unsolved murder. Law enforcement followed up on the two dozen "love letters" found in Pearly's house, many of them from married women. There were two threatening letters from outraged husbands. It was an exhaustive pursuit and follow-up that led nowhere.

Leon Remington, bandleader of the Shotgun Cowboys and Pearly's employer, came under strong suspicion when his underage daughter left town. It was widely believed that she was pregnant—why else would she have left? People speculated that Pearly might have been the father. Remington received threats and intimidating calls at his home. Many accused him directly, others just hung up when they heard his voice.

The pressure on Remington became so great that he gave notice to WEHT TV, ending the Shotgun Cowboys' obligation to the local program, and disbanded his group. He took a job delivering gas for a local Sinclair Oil dealership. When not delivering gas, he remained reclusively at home and in his guitar shop. The pressures only increased; rumormongers insisted that only a guilty man would end a lucrative TV deal. In desperation, he finally begged the local sheriff to administer a lie-detector test. Leon passed it, and the police ruled him out.

Investigators might be faulted for lack of results, but certainly not lack of effort. To their credit, they chased every clue; they often bragged about the hot leads they were pursuing. They questioned a Corydon man who brought an armload of bloody clothes into a local laundromat, a few days after the body was discovered. When questioned, he claimed one of his cows had ripped her leg open on an exposed piece of tin at a watering tank. He said he'd bloodied his clothes tending to the animal—an explanation confirmed by witnesses on his farm.

They interviewed almost everyone who had known Pearly. They questioned coworkers at the Chrysler plant in Evansville. They questioned men, women, and teenage girls. They spoke to nightclub owners and employees where he and the Shotgun Cowboys had played. They questioned the men and husbands, current and former girlfriends. They questioned bandmates. They collected a massive body of notes, names, interviews, and presumed evidence.

In every circumstance they reviewed, there was some disreputable action on Pearly's part, some more egregious than others. He left a trail of offenses so long it was almost impossible to corral them all. He was a liar, a cheat, a thief, and an adulterer. Other than his singing voice, he had few redeeming qualities.

At one point a man was overheard bragging in an Evansville bar that he was "the last man to see Pearly Martin alive." Evansville police brought him in for questioning that led them to believe that he knew who had beaten Pearly to death. Their optimism vanished the next day when this prime suspect failed to show up for his polygraph. Evansville police made no effort to chase him down. The lead and the man had both vanished.

In spite of these discouraging results, the local police offered the case to a grand jury, hinting that heretofore unreported evidence was in hand. The grand jury did not return a single indictment. Instead, it released a derisive statement suggesting they had been lied to by witnesses. The official statement read, "The Grand Jury feels satisfied that some of the witnesses who appeared before it were well acquainted with the details of Martin's beating and death, but that their testimony has not been truthful."

Authorities in Evansville abandoned their investigation and offered no more statements or opinions. The Henderson police chief continued to assure everyone that the investigation was ongoing, but admitted leads and information were drying up. Had he not been a local celebrity, I doubt the death of another man so ill-esteemed would have garnered anywhere near the investigative man power that was spent trying to find Pearly's killer.

The investigation revealed Martin's true character—or lack of it. As the probe dragged on, the community began to speculate that more prominent citizens, for reasons as yet unknown, might have been involved. Folks conjectured that the authorities had felt it might be expedient to pursue the case to a dead end, the implication being that, like everything else in town, a fix was in place. People began to suspect that Pearly was likely killed for a valid reason and no good would be served by exposing his killer.

Did Pearly, at some point cheat or cuckold the wrong man—a man with the power, money, contacts, and influence to arrange his murder? Was it a murder-for-hire? Did a victim—or victims—of Pearly's wanton disregard for others bring in a killer from Chicago or Detroit who could disappear afterward? No one could say.

CHAPTER 49

The neon sign flashed *Pal's Steak House and Bar.* I went in around 5:30, for Happy Hour. Located on Fulton Avenue, a couple blocks beyond the railroad tracks, the space was subdued and unpretentious—neat, clean, and understated, with no attempt at theme or ambiance. Innocuous. While being homosexual was not illegal per se, certain *acts* were, and homosexual haunts were often the target of police raids.

As expected, the patrons were mostly male, though there were a couple of tables with out-of-place single women and one occupied by a man and woman. Most of the stations were tables for two, where male couples huddled closely together. Trying not to display the awkwardness I felt, I took a seat at the bar. The bartender offered a dinner menu. "Dinner or just drinking?"

Like the space, he was inoffensive and forgettable. I judged him to be in his mid-40s to early 50s. He was well groomed and clean shaven. He wore a black tie and white shirt under a waist-length, starched white serving jacket. He presented himself as a utilitarian functionary, making no social or political statement.

"Give me a draft, and let me look at the menu."

He slid a menu in front of me and pulled me a frosty mug of draft beer.

The first steak offered was an 8-ounce filet mignon named "The Queen," leaving no doubt as to the targeted clientele. Similar suggestive names labeled the other menu items—like "Big Boy," a 16-ounce T-bone. I ordered a hamburger and fries.

A three-piece combo filtered in and set up in a corner. There was a small dance floor, off to the side. I lit a cigarette and nursed my beer. At the moment, I was the only single party in the place. The bartender moved down to my end of the bar. "Don't believe I've ever seen you in here before."

"First time. I'm investigating the murder of Edward G. Triplett. What can you tell me that might be helpful?"

"Sorry mister, I don't know anyone by that name."

"You sure? I'm told he came in here from time to time, nice-looking guy, middle-aged, owns a tool-and-die business. From Henderson."

"Oh, you mean *Glenn* Triplett. Yeah! I heard about it. Shame what happened to him."

"You have any idea who might have killed him or wanted him dead?"

"No, not really. I've always found him to be a nice guy—at least when he was in here. A gentleman, nothing flashy or flamboyant."

"I'm told he has a friend he meets here. Can you tell me his name? Anything about him?"

The bartender moved away to serve a new patron who'd taken a seat at the bar. In a few minutes the man picked up his drink and moved to a table by himself.

The bartender returned. "This a good gig, mister, mainly

because of the generous tips. Intended to ensure discretion. Tell ya what: You stick around for a while. If he comes in, I'll point him out to you."

The trio began with some '40s swing. As they moved into more danceable music, men rose together and moved to the dance floor, falling into familiar embraces. About 7:30, a single man in his late 30s walked in. Catching my eye, the bartender nodded. The man carried himself with self-assurance. If his suit wasn't bespoke, it was finely tailored. He was dressed to the nines, his shoes buffed to a warm luster; his hair was styled and trimmed, his nails manicured and polished. An incongruous bruise under his right eye, fading to yellow and purple, was the only thing marring his appearance—a real shiner. That and the one-inch cut in his right eyebrow. Curious, as he certainly didn't appear to be a brawler.

He nodded politely to some of the men in the room and casually moved to the table occupied by the man previously at the bar. After seating himself, he reached out and surreptitiously touched the other man on the wrist. I watched him reach for his left pinky repeatedly, as if to grip a ring that was not there—perhaps a favorite he had lost.

I folded a $20 bill around my business card and laid it beneath the ashtray before heading to the men's room. When I returned, the money and my card were gone. In their place was a note: *David Howard—Maxims.* Maxims was an upscale men's clothing store in downtown Evansville.

I paid my tab, tapped my head with two fingers in a slight salute to the bartender. "Thanks!" I walked out into the heat of the evening.

Maybe I'd shop for a new sport coat.

CHAPTER 50

I waded through soggy autumn leaves to the Gold Coin Tavern. There was a certain heaviness to the sky, and bright storefronts and street lights seemed to fight the lengthening shadows.

I walked through the Gold Coin to the bar area and took a booth. A middle-aged waitress brought a menu, and I checked the evening specials while waiting for my beer. When she returned, I ordered the special: two pork chops, mashed potatoes, and gravy with stewed tomatoes and corn bread. I asked for a cup of coffee.

I pushed back into the corner and stretched both legs out over the remainder of the seat. I was deep in thought, rehashing the events of the day and my experience at Pal's Steak House when someone called my name.

"Hoyt!—Hoyt Cole!" Standing off to my right, between my booth and the bar stools, was Virginia "Ginny" Blackwell. Ginny had been Sally's close friend since high school. She'd married Gary Busby, the son of a local car dealer.

"You must have been a thousand miles away," she said.

"Sorry Ginny. Yeah, I guess I was." Dropping my legs to the

floor, I turned and sat forward in my seat. "How are you? Where's Gary?"

"He's at our table up front. I was on my way back from the ladies' room. "You're sitting so deep in the booth I didn't see you when I went by the first time." She tucked her purse under her arm.

"Good to see you, Ginny, tell Gary *hi*."

She stepped closer to my booth and leaned forward a bit so I could hear what she said to me, very softly. "Did you know Sally had a miscarriage? She's in the hospital."

"No, I hadn't heard, I trust she's OK?"

"Physically she's doing OK. Emotionally—not so much. She was only four months along. Their marriage has been shaky. I think she was hoping a baby would help. You should go see her, Hoyt. It would mean a lot to her."

"No, I shouldn't, Ginny." I shook my head. "The last thing she needs at a time like this is a visit from an old boyfriend. She needs love and emotional support from her husband."

"What if I told you he can't provide it?"

That doesn't surprise me!

"She asked to see you . . . I know you still love her, Hoyt."

"I hope you'll understand, Ginny. I don't want to be rude, but how I feel or don't feel about Sally is personal and none of your business. I won't discuss it with you or anyone else."

Looking at her watch, she slid into the booth seat across from me and took a cigarette from her purse. I lit it for her.

"You men!" She squinted as the smoke curled around her face. "How blind and thick-headed can you be? She never stopped loving you, Hoyt."

I took a sip of my beer, looking down the glass into her eyes. "She married Bob."

She placed her purse on the seat, beside her. Leaning forward, she placed both elbows on the table. "She always regretted breaking up with you. She knows she was too young and impetuous to marry Bob Craig." Taking a pull on her cigarette, she blew the smoke upward above her head, and she picked a cut of tobacco off her tongue. She tapped the cigarette on the ashtray and placed it in one of the indentations.

"She told me about seeing you at the Cosmo and reflected on it for days after. And that encounter at the Gold Coin, while embarrassing, left her with a warm glow she still talks about. Go to her, Hoyt!"

"Sorry Ginny, but no!"

Ginny sighed exasperatedly. "I just thought you'd want to know. I'll tell Sally I ran into you. Bye."

"Bye, Ginny." I leaned back in the booth and crossed my ankles under the table.

Damn! Why'd she tell me that? People don't realize how they can torment another person. Did Sally really ask to see me? I wonder. I try not to think about her. It's too painful. How can I push back the emotions when they come rushing at me, uninvited?

I hadn't thought of Sally in weeks. Ginny dumps her news and all my feelings for Sally Morgan come flooding back. *All I'm left with is emptiness, the painful awareness of what I don't have! Aw Sally! Why couldn't you have waited?*

Being alone doesn't bother me. Aristotle said, "The ideal man is his own best friend and takes delight in privacy." But loneliness . . . *What the hell's he know about loneliness?*

That's bullshit, Cole. I was filled with a desperate sense of total isolation. *You've built a defensive facade to help you live without her! OK! So What? Do I mope around wearing a long face, constantly filled with self-pity?*

The waitress brought my dinner and a cup of coffee. I ate in silence, finished my meal with a bourbon neat, paid my tab, and walked out into the night, back to my room. Alone.

‡

But I couldn't get her off my mind. Damn you, Ginny! And your *thought you'd want to know.*

Memories of Sally, and our time together, evoked warm feelings. They made me feel good about myself, about us, and about a particular period of our lives. I confess, when those memories returned, they were welcome. I enjoyed them . . . for a time. A *brief* time! But I was able to let them recede into the past, so I tried not to bring them back. They were too painful! I couldn't prevent someone else or some unplanned event from resurrecting them.

What can you do about dreams? How do you prevent yourself from dreaming about an old love? I had resigned myself to loving Sally, probably for the rest of my life. Resigned to relishing that brief, idyllic moment in our lives that could never be retrieved or duplicated.

I can live with that. I have lived with that. I will live with that.

I didn't know if her recently expressed love was real, or just an unhappy Sally being needy. If she was unhappy with Bob Craig, how soon might she become unhappy with me? *I won't risk being hurt again!* At the same time, I was planning something that contradicted rational thought, something I'd likely regret. *Like praying for forgiveness for a sin you know you're going to repeat.*

An otherwise rational person with a practical and common-sense approach to life, was I deluding myself, dismissing my actions as merely compassion and concern for an old friend going through a difficult time? *Hey! I'd do that for anybody.* Or was

I trying to erase the years and experience the pleasure of being with her again, her miscarriage providing a perfect opportunity. *Or excuse?*

On my lunch hour, I bought a dozen, long-stem red roses and headed over there. The entire way, a red-hot core in the back of my consciousness told me, *you're about to make a fool of yourself, Cole!* But I drove through it, ignored it.

Henderson Methodist Hospital was a sprawling, single-story structure opened in 1946. I parked and went through double doors into the reception area. The volunteer at the desk gave me her room number on the OB ward. The florescent lights imparted a cold and sterile atmosphere. My footsteps on the shiny tile floors seemed uncommonly loud, echoing off the corridor walls, insuring everybody on the wing heard me coming.

I passed a nurse pushing a diagnostic cart down the hall to a patient's room, moving silently on soft-soled shoes. *Did she look at me with suspicion? Did she know what I was up to?* I felt like a man on a secret mission who was being exposed every step of the way. My resolve was melting.

Continuing down the corridor, I followed the numbers until I stopped outside Sally's room. The door stood slightly ajar. I heard voices that were not discernible. They were low and muffled. Was one a male voice? Was it the doctor—or was it Bob Craig, Sally's husband? I leaned closer to the opening. *Am I eavesdropping on a private moment?*

There I stood, roses in my arms, feeling like a spurned suitor begging for a second chance. Shame and embarrassment overwhelmed me. I remained there, silent and motionless, paralyzed—by fear or anticipation? I realized I wasn't breathing as I stared at the number on her door. I suddenly turned and almost ran from the ward. I rushed back onto the corridor leading to the receptionist and the exit. I stopped in the middle of the hallway and tried to catch my breath. I stood like a trapped animal, looking around for safe haven. *Did anyone see me?*

Still breathing hard, I proceeded toward the exit. On my way out, I stopped at the gift shop and thrust the roses into the arms of a saleslady dusting shelves. "Give these to the next man shopping for his wife or girlfriend."

In my truck, I sat for the longest time, thankful for escaping humiliation and derision at best and entanglement with a married woman at worse.

Loving Sally, even for the rest of my life, doesn't preclude me loving someone else, does it?

CHAPTER 51

Right after breakfast, I walked to the sheriff's office to see if I could catch Deputy Kockritz, but he was already out on patrol. Outside again, I walked down the hill to the park and sat on the wall surrounding the 26-foot high "Rebecca" fountain, installed in 1892. Transylvania Park, called Central Park by locals, was touted as the oldest municipal park west of the Allegheny Mountains. Crystalline water fell splashing from the jug under Rebecca's arm, and from the mouths of dolphins surrounding her pedestal, into the pool below—a pleasant, calming sound. The cool breeze in the shade of mature trees provided a comfortable temperature for rest and reflection.

All murder investigations probably seemed curious and convoluted at first, presenting far more questions than answers, like the investigation into the murder of Edward Glenn Triplett—particularly in light of what Carla Broadbent had suggested. *Who killed Ed Triplett and why? Did he win too much of another man's money in his monthly poker game? Could he have been caught cheating? Was Triplett really homosexual? Could there be a jealous male lover? Had he amassed a large gambling debt he was unwilling or unable to pay? Was he killed as a warning to other gamblers? Who were the players in his monthly card game?*

"Mr. Cole?"

I hadn't noticed that someone had sat down next to me, on the wall. I turned to face a pleasant and androgynous individual in a deputy sheriff's uniform, with "Katterjohn, B. J." on the nametag pinned over the left breast pocket. The individual was about five feet two, weighing no more than 115 pounds. Short black hair was combed back behind the smooth, hairless face, over the ears, and touching the collar of the uniform.

"I'm Deputy Billie Jean Katterjohn, Mr. Cole. I was at the Marshall cabin the morning Eddie Triplett's body was found." The timbre and lilt of the voice revealed that the deputy was female. She wore no lipstick or other makeup.

"I'm sorry deputy, I don't remember seeing you there."

"Understandable," she said. "I'm tolerated, but seldom utilized."

Unsure what to say, I repositioned myself on the stone wall and looked off down Main Street.

"They moved Mr. Triplett's car to the impound lot down by the stadium that morning. It's been there ever since, never searched or fingerprinted."

I waited, not responding. She was obviously wanting to impart something she probably shouldn't.

"Yesterday, on my day off, but in uniform, I went to the lot and examined the contents of his car." She reached into the back pocket of her pants and retrieved a folded piece of paper. "I found this over the driver's side visor." She extended a folded sheet of paper toward me. "That's a copy."

Looking her in the eye, I took the paper from her hand, and unfolded it. It was hand-printed on three-hole loose-leaf notebook paper.

This is my only option. I see no other solution. They're threatening to say things about me that aren't true! I'm sorry to leave you this way.

I love you, Beatie. Please forgive me.

"A suicide note?" I asked.

"My guess."

"What did you do with the original? Was it signed?"

"It's in an envelope in Deputy Kockritz's mail slot. Not signed."

Curious. Was it forged? "Why give a copy to me?"

"I'm unwanted. Unwelcome and unused by the department." She stood, took a few steps away from me, turned back and said, "Look, I have a degree in forensics and criminal justice from Eastern Kentucky State College in Richmond." She placed both hands on her hips and jutted her chin slightly forward for emphasis. "When they posted the job, I took the civil-service exam and scored higher than anyone ever has. Because of my scores, they hired me without ever interviewing me or meeting me." She returned to the wall and seated herself, looking off blankly into the park and the street beyond. "Even though they hired me, they don't have to utilize me—and they don't."

Without responding, I nodded my head, trying to convey understanding and compassion for the frustration she was obviously feeling.

"I don't know what will become of the note, but I want someone other than myself to know about it. I know you've got your ear to the ground on local issues. If it's followed up on, you'll know soon enough. If not, you'll know that too. I'm trusting you not to reveal where it came from."

"Be hard for me to use information I'm not supposed to have." I folded the note and tucked it into my shirt pocket. "Thanks, deputy. Regardless how you're viewed by your peers, this is good police work." I pulled one of my cards from my pocket and handed it to her. "Call me if you'd like."

She stood and walked back up the hill into the courthouse.

‡

It was barely mid-morning. Acting on a hunch, I decided to drive to Triplett's Tool and Die Company, located out on the south end of town. The building was concrete block, painted beige—maybe 12,000–15,000 square feet—with gravel parking. There was a deep, two-bay loading dock toward the back on the left side.

I slid my press credentials to the female receptionist in the small lobby through an eight-inch round hole in her glass-enclosed workspace. "Could I speak to the vice president or manager? Whoever's in charge."

She scrutinized my card through cat-eye glasses, seeming to read every word before removing her glasses and leaving them suspended from a beaded chain around her neck. She fancied herself a gate-keeper and took the job seriously. When she finally looked up, she said coolly, "Please have a seat Mr. Cole. Someone will be with you shortly."

Is it just me, or have you ever noticed how a portrait of a person you know to be dead somehow looks different than it does when you know the person to still be alive? A portrait of Edward Glenn Triplett hung prominently in the lobby. He was a strikingly handsome man; I couldn't help but stare.

A few minutes later, the plant supervisor opened a door into the lobby and approached me. He looked to be about 35. He wore his dark hair in a flattop cut above a blue shirt and patterned tie. His face was square, with heavy eyebrows and deep-set eyes.

"Mr. Cole, I'm Claude Brown. What can I do for you?"

"I'd like to speak with you privately for a few minutes, if you've got the time," I said.

"We're pretty busy, but I can spare a few minutes. Come on back to my office." He led me through the door into the plant proper. We walked past machinery, assembly lines, and shipping lanes to his office.

He closed the door, took a seat behind his desk and motioned to a chair for me.

"I'm sure you're here about Eddie's murder," he said. "It's difficult for me to talk about. We were great friends. This is the only job I've ever had. Started here right out of high school. I was among the first people hired."

"A great shock and a great loss to the entire community, Mr. Brown. Please accept my sincere sympathies."

"Thank you."

"You have any thoughts on why he was killed, or who may have done it?"

"No! And frankly I've had little time to think on it. It has thrown things into such disarray, it's been nothing but assholes and elbows around here. Everybody taking on duties and responsibilities they haven't had, in addition to what they customarily do. Eddie made all of the important decisions. The police have explored several angles and questioned me and the other employees at length."

"What about a succession plan, Claude?"

"Huh? Whaddaya mean?"

"Who's in line to run the plant? Did he designate anyone to take over the day-to-day operations of the company in the event of his untimely demise?"

"Not that I know of. Honestly, I haven't thought about it. Just been showing up and doing my job ever day, like everbody else.

"I guess, when it comes down to it, his widow and the company lawyer will have to make them decisions."

"Do you suppose they might sell the company?"

"You know as much about that as I do."

I then asked a question I had no reason to. Sometimes, unexpected questions evoke surprising but helpful responses. "Do you think he could have killed himself?"

He dropped his face an inch or two, moved his head from side to side in an apparent attempt to gain clarity, and ran his hand front to back over his head.

"Wow! Mr. Cole, you pose some shocking questions.'

"Do you know if he's taken out or paid out any unusual sums of money lately?" I asked.

"I wouldn't know that. My role is operations. The company is a sole proprietorship. Eddie spends what he wants to spend."

"Surely, a company of this size has a bookkeeper or a comptroller?"

"We do, in fact. Jimmy Adams, but he's off sick today."

"You reckon I could talk with him when he returns to work?"

"Don't see why not."

"Thanks for your time, Claude."

Back in the parking lot, I sat staring at the side of the building, trying to make sense of a situation that made no sense.

It was almost straight-up noon when I pulled back on to the highway and headed back to town. As I was driving past the football stadium, Hank Williams came on the radio singing, "I Can't Help It if I'm Still in Love with You."

I switched it off.

CHAPTER 52

Other than stop for a pack of cigarettes, I rarely went into Dunaway's Drug Store. Maybe I was feeling nostalgic. Dunaway's was a favorite hangout during my high school days. Cosmetics were presented in glass cases running down the left wall, like always. The patent medicines and nostrums were on two rows of shelves down the middle of the store, leading back to the prescription department where the pharmacist moved back and forth behind the counter in his white coat. Up front, down the right side of the store, there was a soda fountain and lunch counter. I took a stool at the short end of the counter with my back to the window and ordered a chicken-salad sandwich and a milkshake.

My lunch was as good as I remembered, and as filling, transporting me back to the many days I'd spent at this counter. The buttered toast warming on the grill, the cherry and vanilla aroma of carbonated drinks, the whir of a milkshake machine—all the pleasant scents and sounds that masked the medicinal smells of a drugstore and carried me back. I was lost in a waking dream. I'd been paying no attention to the clientele coming and going through the front door and was unaware of the woman who had seated herself on the stool next to mine.

"I saw you through the window. How you doing, Hoyt?"

Reality suddenly merged with the emotions my memories had revived. I moved closer as I turned to face her, my breath caught in my throat. My heart rate raced, and I moistened my lips self-consciously. I took in the bright tropical print of the short-sleeved dress Sally wore. The vibrant colors added to my surprise and confusion seeing her there, where we had so often been together, before. Everything she wore was perfectly coordinated: her matching pumps, nails, and lipstick. Her hair was smartly styled, her makeup flawless, and her smile genuine. Her fresh, clean fragrance reminded me of the tender moments we'd spent together so long ago.

I'm sure my smile was uncomfortable and my mannerisms awkward. "Hi, Sally," I babbled, finally. "Good to see you."

She looked me in the eye, holding my gaze for a long moment. "Thanks for coming by the hospital. I wish you'd stopped in."

I turned to face the counter. I saw the flush rising up from my throat into my cheeks reflected in the mirror. My face and ears were red. I shuffled my feet and cleared my throat. I was a fumbling, bumbling, self-conscious teenager again.

I couldn't look at her. "How'd you know I was there?" I whispered.

"I told the nurse I was expecting you and what you looked like. She saw you standing outside my door with the roses. She followed you and saw you leave the flowers with the clerk. Later, when I was alone, she brought them to me."

"It was a mistake, Sally. Like that letter I wrote you. I'm sorry."

"No, Hoyt! I wanted you there, I *needed* you there! Don't you realize that?"

Lost for words, I reached out and squeezed her hand.

She stood, brushed my cheek, and left.

What a gut punch. What do I do now?

I moved my sweaty hand over the opposite forearm. I was trembling. I took in a deep breath, and held it as long as possible, letting it out slowly. I closed my eyes, tilted my head back, and drummed my fingers on the counter. If she was trying to set a torch to my desire for her, she had succeeded. *Is she expecting me to make the next move?* Fear and uncertainty enveloped me. Ordinarily a man of action, I sat immobilized.

CHAPTER 53

Following up on Uncle George's suggestion to visit Eddie G.'s uncle, I traveled east on Highway 60 to Spottsville and turned south at the bridge. Outside of Spottsville, the narrow, winding road traveled a steep bluff along the Green River. Trees and vegetation grew right up to the edge of the treacherous path to Bluff City, a small mining town high above the river. *Bluff* was accurate; *City* was a misnomer, and even town would have been a stretch. Settlement would have been much more accurate.

Residents lived there because it was isolated and the property was cheap, either to purchase or to rent. It was unsuitable for crops; mining and living off the river were the only options for most people. There was no center of town in Bluff City. You neared it, and you were out of the hodgepodge of clapboard houses, deteriorating shacks, and rusting trailers sitting on their rims, almost in the same moment. Old rubber tires, long flat and dry-rotted, were scattered about, and trash fires smoldered in rusted 50-gallon barrels.

I stopped at the first activity I saw: people standing by a mailbox at the side of the road. I asked for Everett Lightfoot's place.

A shirtless man in bib overalls turned to me. One strap hung loose down his back; the unhinged side of the bib drooped limply over his chest. "Up the road a piece, on the right, can't miss it," he said amiably.

About 300 yards past the last vestige of civilization, a barnlike structure stood on a hill at right, rusted farm equipment, two or three cars on blocks, and a small, run-down house beside it. The weatherboarding had a silver-gray patina, worn and raw from years of neglect. There was a well, and a wooden outhouse some yards behind the house.

I pulled off the pavement and headed up a rutted dirt road to the top of the hill. The garage had sagging double doors, hanging loose on their hinges. Both were swung open for total access and visibility. A man in coveralls was bent over the engine of a '38 four-door Ford, elevated on a floor jack. A large, short-haired brindle lay off to one side.

"You Mr. Lightfoot?" I asked.

The mongrel stood, bared his teeth and emitted a low, menacing growl. It had the face and chest of a pit bull, but was taller and bigger—maybe a Great Dane mix. The man glared at me over his shoulder.

I looked around at the stationary and mobile work benches, acetylene tanks, masks, and welding tools in his shop. There were wooden tool boxes around the perimeter and lots of hand tools, pipes, and wrenches scattered around. "I'm Hoyt Cole from the *River City News*."

"Got no time for you." He spoke straight into the engine. The dog continued his low growl and barked once for emphasis.

"I'm trying to determine who killed your nephew. Uncle George said you might be willing to talk to me."

He paused and slowly pulled his head and shoulders out of

the engine bay, retrieved a rag from his rear pocket and turned to face me. He wiped the grease from his hands. "George sent you, I'll listen."

"I understand you and Mr. Triplett were close," I began.

"He spent a lot of time out here with me when he was a boy. Only one of my sister's boys had anything to do with me. He had a mechanical aptitude and was smart. I taught him what I could." His voice trailed off, and he looked off into the distance. "We had other interests in common," he said finally.

"You have any idea who might have killed him, Mr. Lightfoot?"

"No!" He rubbed the underside of his chin with the knuckles of his right hand. "Wouldn't do for me to find out, either."

"I've been given some information recently that suggests he may have killed himself."

"Yeah? What kind of information?"

"A note found in his car," I told him. "Is it possible he was being blackmailed?"

He put both hands on his hips, stretched his neck, turned his head to the tree line off to the side of his property, and spat on the ground. "Possible, I suppose."

His eyes seemed to lose interest in me, his mind on an idle thought somewhere on the back side of his consciousness. He turned his back to me and walked back into his garage. Formal farewells were apparently not part of Everett Lightfoot's social protocol.

I headed back toward town. Something he'd said troubled me. Or was it *how* he said what he said? I couldn't put my finger on it. Somehow, I felt Everett Lightfoot knew more than he let on.

CHAPTER 54

The next afternoon I caught Deputy Kockritz exiting the courthouse out the back door, on Elm Street. There was a church on the corner across the street, a calming presence on the busy midtown intersection. We stood on the sidewalk near the park, and I asked him about the attendees at Eddie's poker game.

He told me there was a local banker, two purchasing agents from Evansville companies, an old friend named Bob Edwards, and a man named David Howard, also from Evansville. "None of the others knew the Howard fella; he wasn't a regular in the monthly gatherings. All were questioned, but nothing came of it."

Peering deep into the park I probed a different topic. "Did you ever fire Uncle George's 20-gauge pistol?"

"Yeah, why do you ask?"

"Did you fire both barrels at once?"

"No reason to."

"Whaddaya reckon would happen if a man unaccustomed to firearms were to point the gun out in front of him, like you would a regular pistol, and fire both barrels?"

"If it didn't break his arm, it'd probably kick back and bust his face. You know that as well as I do."

"Just wanted your opinion. Any other developments in the case?" I was giving him a chance to tell me about the note found in Eddie's car—hoping he would.

"We're following up on all the leads, Hoyt," he said tersely. He turned and walked away. Over his shoulder he continued, "Why don't you just leave it to us. We'll handle it."

I don't like the way this is unfolding, I thought.

Maybe Karl was just playing it close to the vest, not wanting to reveal critical information until it was fully investigated. I'd give him that, I supposed.

‡

Up the street at the Western Auto Store, I passed a display of Schwinn bicycles, some lawn mowers, hoses, lawn sprayers, and sprinklers.

"Come in, Hoyt," Bob said in greeting. He'd bought the store from the original owner, a few years back. "What're ya in the market for today?"

"Not really shopping, Bob. You got time to talk a few minutes?"

"Sure," he said. "It's a little slow right now, anyway." He turned toward an employee and called out to her. "Gladys, come get me if something comes up you can't handle. I'll be in the back visiting with Hoyt."

I nodded to Gladys. "How ya doing, Glad, good to see you." She smiled and continued straightening the merchandise.

Toward the back, I passed a key cutting machine and a rounder of blanks. I followed him through a curtained opening into the back room where an old rolltop desk sat on the bare, concrete floor. The space smelled of pine-scented cleaning supplies, potting soil, and fertilizer. Bob sat in the swivel chair at the desk and motioned to the straight-back wooden chair next to it.

"Have a seat Hoyt, what's on your mind?"

"I know the sheriff's office has questioned you, but what can you tell me about the poker game the night before Eddie G.'s body was found?"

"Well, it was like every other poker night at the cabin in many ways, except that night I was the big winner. Went home almost $75.00 to the good." Pausing and rubbing his chin distractedly, he continued. "On the other hand, it *was* a little different."

"How so?"

"There was a new man none of us knew—David Howard. Nice enough guy, I reckon . . . kind of a fancy dresser. While he and Eddie apparently knew each other and seemed to have some history, it was obvious Eddie wasn't expecting him."

Bob sat forward in his chair and piled some invoices together, tapping them on his desk to create a neat stack. Laying them aside, he continued. "In fact, now that I think back on it, Eddie seemed shocked to see him—awkward and uncomfortable. We'd already played a few hands when he showed up. He asked Eddie if he could be dealt in. Eddie hesitated, but finally said, 'Sure, take a seat.' He told him the game and the stakes, and introduced him to each of us."

Still talking, Bob rose and went to the corner to adjust some mops and brooms that had fallen into disarray. "The man played a couple hands, appearing uninterested. In fact, he seemed more focused on a black onyx ring he wore on his left little finger. He kept straightening it and adjusting it. He and Eddie kept exchanging glances. It was real uncomfortable.

"After a brief time, the man excused himself. Said he needed some fresh air and went outside—probably gone 30 to 45 minutes. That really seemed to distract Eddie. He constantly peered out the closest window and toward the door. A good poker player, Eddie's head obviously wasn't in the game. He easily lost the next several hands."

Bob returned to his desk, picked up a pencil and parked it behind his ear. "When the man finally came back in, he played a couple more hands, then announced he needed to get back to Evansville. Since he'd lost every hand he played, some of us hated to see him go. He left without saying thanks or goodbye."

"What time did he leave, Bob?"

"About 9:30 be my guess."

"Anything else stand out about that night?"

"Not really, as I said, only thing unusual was I was the winner." He flashed a slight grin.

"Did you happen to notice how this Howard fellow came and went—what kind of car he was driving?"

"No, Hoyt, I didn't. He came after the game had started and left before the rest of us."

"What time did the game breakup?"

"Around eleven. That's the official ending time. We never start a hand after 11:00. Gives most of us time to get home by midnight. That way our wives know when to expect us and let us keep coming back."

CHAPTER 55

Anger can be suppressed. I'm not sure it can be defused. Dormant like a disease, it can lie buried and in remission for periods of time, left to percolate, undetected by its host. When certain conditions occur, pent-up rage too long restrained is suddenly released.

I had no legitimate reason to go back to the Kain-Tuck, but Saturday night, I followed the front end of my truck all the way down Green Street until of a sudden, there it was. I told myself I'd just turn around in the lot and head back to my hotel.

A man can justify most any decision: *Hey, I'm here . . . may as well have a beer.* The gravel lot returned a leaden reflection as the sun settled behind the trees. Moisture seemed to seep from the evening clouds. Nightclub sounds spilled through the open doors: clinking glasses, indistinguishable voices, loud music, and the mechanical sound of slot-machine arms. I went inside.

I had one beer, then another. The bartender slid a third in front of me, without me asking. I took a long pull and turned my back to the bar, surveying the room. My eyes made a cursory pass around the space and turned back to the bar, but my mind flashed a sight I hadn't caught, initially. I turned back to confirm what I'd seen. At a table in a far corner, Bob Craig was being more than affectionate with a woman who wasn't Sally.

Turn around Cole! Mind your own business. Better still, put down the beer and leave. All good thoughts and valid considerations—which I ignored. After a time, the woman rose, perhaps to go to the ladies' room.

I grabbed my beer, walked over, and took the chair she'd vacated. Craig was obviously drunk because at first my presence didn't resonate with him.

"How ya doing, Bob?"

Through heavily-lidded eyes, he finally focused enough to recognize me. "What're you doing here, Cole?" he slurred.

The woman returned and stood beside the table tapping her foot. I handed her a dollar bill. "Go back and powder your nose, honey. You missed a spot. She placed a hand on one hip and looked at me disgustedly, waiting for Bob to intervene.

"Beat it lady! That's not a suggestion!" She twirled around and stalked toward the bar.

"Go home, Bob!

"Go to hell, Cole!"

"Like I told your girlfriend, that's not a suggestion." I grabbed him under his arm and hauled him outside to the parking lot. I walked, drug, and shoved him over to the car I believed to be his. I should have realized it wouldn't be that easy.

"This guy botherin' you Mr. Craig?" One of Slade's bouncers moved across the parking lot toward us.

"Get out of here, Bob! Go home!"

Lightning flickered silently in the distance. I watched as he started his car and drove off. I felt the bouncer at my side. His hand grasped my shoulder to spin me around.

"This is a private matter, buddy, go back inside," I told him. By this time, bar patrons had filtered out to watch the action. Emboldened by the audience, he shoved me in the chest. "Anybody gets thrown out of here, I'll be the one doing it," he said, attempting to shove me a second time.

Long-suppressed rage erupted from me. I grabbed his left arm in my right hand and hooked his elbow with my left, bending his arm behind him and up toward his shoulder blade. I planted both feet and used all his weight to create momentum. I swung him around and slammed his face into the side of the nearest parked car, then pulled him around to face me and hooked him in the mouth with my left, watching his lips split open against his teeth. I hit him in the stomach with my right, bending him over, allowing me to grab his belt in the back of his pants with one hand and the back of his shirt collar with the other. Again spinning, I smashed his head into the headlight of the same car, crushing his face into a bloody mess. His knees buckled and he crumpled to the ground. He was finished—but I wasn't.

He was curled into the fetal position, and I kicked him in the head and kidneys repeatedly. My arms were spread wide from my body creating the balance necessary to continue the onslaught. As I drew my foot back to kick him again, the onlookers' protests finally penetrated my consciousness. Their terrified faces shone under the soft glow of the parking lot light. With my foot at the back of its arc, I planted it behind me, pivoted away, and walked through a corridor of apprehensive faces, none willing to look me in the eye.

Hushed murmurs trailed after me as I walked toward my truck. The cool night air brought the smell of deadfall rotting on the riverbank. I sat transfixed behind the wheel, slowly coming to the full realization of what I'd done. I'd used the bouncer to release my anger toward Bob Craig. He'd become an unwitting recipient of a vicious attack he didn't fully deserve.

I sat in my truck, staring woodenly into the night. Gawkers filed cautiously by, trying to get a glimpse of the malevolent creature inside. I felt like a caged animal on display. Those who have never succumbed to perpetrating viciousness on another human haven't experienced the shameful adrenaline rush and sense of supremacy that overwhelms you. I realized the animalistic creature I had descended from was still alive, inside me.

Lightning flickered over the river like a shorted electrical circuit. Dried corn stalks rattled in the wind. Gusts glued rain-sodden leaves against my windshield. Thunderheads rumbled in the west, and a heavy rain peppered the roof of my truck. It wasn't happenstance that had led me back to the Kain-Tuck; I was looking for a trigger to unleash all the rage I had stifled. I had to extract myself from Sally Morgan Craig's hold on my life. She was not mine. I had no claim on her. I had no responsibility for the failings in her marriage.

The fecund smell of the river permeated the cab. The humidity was heavy and oppressive. My skin burned, and my hair was dripping with sweat. My jaw clenched and my hands balled into fists. The moon disappeared into the night clouds, and the evening air felt hot and wet against my face.

CHAPTER 56

I was running late the next morning. I grabbed a couple cups of coffee and hurried into the barber shop to see Stormy Jack. It was immediately evident that he wasn't there. I knew his closing routine: he placed his brushes in a certain order on the base of the stand, folded his shoeshine rags neatly, and left them in their proper places. Everything was as he'd left it the night before.

Without asking anyone about him, I rushed outside and headed down the street to the alley where he lived. The early morning air was crisp, but the sky was clear, and the sun was shining warmly—until I reached the alley, where the shade blocked the sun and the dampness of the previous evening imparted a musty odor to the narrow corridor. At his door, I didn't knock. I pulled the screen back and went in.

"John," I called. He was still in his bed, covers up to his chin. His eyes were closed and his breathing shallow. At first, I thought he'd just overslept.

"John?" I said, quieter this time.

He opened his eyes and managed a slight smile. "Hoyt?"

"You OK, John?"

"Poorly, Hoyt . . . feeling poorly."

His complexion was sallow and his eyes watery. He shivered, and his teeth chattered, even as beads of sweat dotted his forehead and upper lip. His bulk seemed diminished under the blanket.

"What do you need, John? What can I do for you?'

"Jest wait . . . with me, Hoyt," he whispered from somewhere deep in the back of his throat.

I pulled up a cane-bottomed chair and sat by his bed. After a time, he pulled his hand from under the bed covers and extended it to me. I took his hand and held it. Light filtered through the window, extending in a broken pattern across the floor. His hand was thick and heavy. He seemed to doze, and his breathing became shallower, with longer intervals between breaths. John Calhoun Storm was dying.

In other, similar, circumstances, my tendencies would be to *do something*! To act! But as the peace of a satisfied life, a well-lived life, fell over his face, that same peace enfolded me. I felt the very best thing I could do was exactly what I was doing.

I sat with him. I held his hand . . . and I waited.

You can't measure the depth of a friendship by time, by proximity, by frequent contact, by shared experiences, or by any other dimension. Friendships don't have to be equal or always reciprocal. Sometime people grow in friendship out of mutual respect. I don't want to define or measure my friendship with John. It can't be quantified.

After about 20 minutes, he breathed no more. His grip loosened, and his hand slipped from mine.

I was in the Pacific when my father died. I'm told he died peacefully, as well. The young physician who attended him the last few months of his life stood by his bedside with my mother and wept openly. I imagined the distinct smell of saddle soap and shoe polish floating into the room on the breeze through his bedroom window.

I glanced toward the end of Jack's bed and realized his swollen feet and ankles were completely uncovered. The soles were leathery and heavily calloused, no doubt from supporting the massive weight of his body, yet no load at all, compared to the weight his soul no doubt carried throughout his life.

My eyes welled and tears spilled over. I'd seen lots of men die. All in, during, or after violent confrontations. I've never experienced a more peaceful passing. I was filled with love for a man I'd known for only a brief time. I felt my life had been richly blessed for having known him.

"Rest in peace, my friend!"

I reached for his bedside phone and called the number he'd penciled on a half-sheet of notebook paper, lying by his bed.

While I'd vilified him in thoughts and writings, I'd never met L. S. Furlong or even spoken to him. He answered the phone himself.

"Mr. Furlong, I'm Hoyt Cole. I'm here with John Storm. He just passed away."

"I'll be right there." He didn't ask for an explanation or for the circumstances. He just hung up the phone.

I returned to the cane-bottom chair and sat by his bed.

Furlong was there in less than 20 minutes. I stood when he entered.

He was tall, well groomed, and well dressed. He had on a three-piece suit, understated tie, and wing-tipped shoes. He gave the impression of being erudite, even though I suspected he wasn't formally educated. He appeared more the lawyer or banker than a bootlegger, gambling impresario, and underworld character.

"Were you with him when he passed?" he asked.

"Yes."

"Thank you."

He went to the bedside, reached for John's hand, and sat in the chair I'd recently vacated. He held it and patted it gently several times. After a time, he leaned forward and whispered something into John's ear.

Straightening up he said, "Goodbye my friend. I'll see you soon." He placed John's hand gently back on his bed and stood for a long moment, becoming part of a poignant moment.

"I'll take care of all the arrangements, Mr. Cole. I'd like you to write his obituary. He held you in high regard. Thank you for your kindness to a good and gentle man. I appreciate it." He began to sing, a cappella, "How Great Thou Art." He sang the entire first verse in a beautiful baritone voice. I stood dumbfounded at this unexpected gesture.

"His favorite hymn," he said.

I was caught completely off guard by this impromptu display and uncertain how to respond. My cynical side wondered if it wasn't a theatrical ploy, designed to create a favorable impression of himself in my eyes. Or was it a true and sincere demonstration of affection for an old friend? Not knowing why he'd care how I felt about him, one way or the other, I was inclined to give him the benefit of the doubt.

"Who's the girl in the picture Mr. Furlong?"

"That's his daughter, Claudette. She was murdered in Biloxi when she was 17."

My mind raced through all kinds of questions, but I didn't ask them. "You knew him well, didn't you?"

"I loved him, and I shall miss him," he said. "He saved me on more than one occasion when we were boys."

I turned and walked out into the alley, out of John's home for the last time.

‡

Back at my desk I wrote the obituary for John Calhoun Storm.

Born in Shawneetown, Illinois, in 1894, John Calhoun Storm died peacefully yesterday morning at his home in the alley behind Water Street.

Known almost exclusively as Stormy Jack, John operated a shoeshine stand in the barber shop of the Kingdon Hotel for more than 25 years. When pressed into service, he also aided downtown merchants as elevator operator from time to time. He also raised and lowered the awnings on the front of several downtown businesses.

As a young man, John traveled across the country with a carnival. He was billed as "the heaviest man in the world," carrying as much as 500 pounds on his five-foot, two-inch frame. He started losing weight in the 1920s, dropping down to his current weight.

As a consequence, he moved to Henderson and set up his shoeshine business. He first operated outside on the corner of Second and Main Streets, before moving to his permanent location inside the Kingdon Hotel barbershop.

John was a Henderson fixture and local icon, known by everyone. He was liked and respected by all. He was affable, sincere, truthful, and trustworthy. All downtown business and professional men used his services.

He had no relatives.

Funeral arrangements are being handled by Douglas Funeral Home. Services will be tomorrow at the First Missionary Baptist Church, the Reverend LeRoy MacFarland presiding.

I was the only white man in attendance at his funeral.

CHAPTER 57

Mid-afternoon, I moved the almost-empty mug of cold coffee to the side and picked up the phone ringing on my desk. "Call for you Hoyt," the receptionist said. I was drafting an article about an anticipated property tax increase and having trouble fashioning the conflict.

Irritated, I said, "Who is it, Marge?"

"Don't know, it's a woman."

"OK." She put the call through.

"Yeah?" I said around the pencil between my teeth.

"I've got to see you!"

It was difficult to hear over the noise of police scanners and general newsroom conversations and clatter. "What? Who is this?"

"I need help, Hoyt. You've got to help me!" There was more urgency in her voice than I remembered hearing—ever.

"Sally?" My irritation dissolved. "Where are you?

"At work. I gotta see you, Hoyt!"

"Calm down, Sally. Tell me what's wrong."

"I can't talk at work. Meet me at the library, in the stacks at the back of the archive department. There's rarely anyone there.

Please come!" The line went dead before I could protest. I immediately called the bank and asked for her, but I was told that she'd just left.

The Sally I knew wasn't prone to histrionics. Perhaps she really was in trouble. Perhaps she *did* need help. *My* help. I was uncertain about what I *should* do, but I knew what I was going to do. I leaped from my seat and rushed for the door, banging my hip on a table on the way. I jumped in my truck and headed toward the Henderson Public Library. I was reacting, rather than acting out of real purpose. *What's she expecting of me?* I tried to control the sense of urgency her words had created. I tried to focus. *How?* I realized I was racing through town and forced myself to slow the truck. *I don't know what the hell I'm walking into.* I was headed to her, nonetheless.

I took the limestone steps two at a time, ran between the two center Ionic columns, yanked the front door open and passed through. I shook both my hands at my sides, trying to calm myself. I took a moment to slow my breathing under the 40-foot domed ceiling in the entry. Larger-than-life portraits of historic Kentucky dignitaries hung on the walls, among them, John James Audubon and Henry Clay.

I climbed to the second-floor archive department and passed the desk in the middle of a large, deserted room. At first there appeared to be no one in the space. Quietly, I proceeded down rows of musty-smelling historical tomes. At the end of a long row, in the corner against the exterior wall, I spotted her. The high walls dwarfed her, and she appeared lost and frail. When she spotted me, she stood tentatively for a long moment, then ran toward me, leaping into my arms. Uncomfortable, I gently pushed her from me and held her at arm's length while looking around to see if we were being observed.

"What in the world, Sally? What's wrong?"

"Oh Hoyt, I can't take it any longer!" She was crying, holding a tissue to her eyes.

"What?"

"The abuse. Bob's abuse."

"Is he hitting you?" I felt the anger rising in me, my protective instincts kicking in.

"It's not physical, it's mental, psychological. Since I lost the baby, his drinking has gotten worse. When he's had enough, he's angry and mean. He blames me for the loss of our son. Oh Hoyt, he says the vilest things!" She dropped her chin, wiped her eyes, and blew her nose.

"How long has this been going on?"

"He's always been a mean drunk, but he didn't used to drink so much so often. The more he drinks, the more he makes me feel worthless and ashamed of who I am. It's horrible, Hoyt. I just can't take it!" Again, she grabbed me and pulled herself into my embrace. The emotional dam broke and she began sobbing uncontrollably.

I hadn't forgotten him cheating on her in Lexington when I was a student, and the recent episode at the Kain-Tuck Lounge was still fresh in my mind. I wanted to find Bob Craig, rip him apart, and leave him on the ground, spitting teeth and blood.

I held her in my arms for a long time, stroked her hair, and wiped her tears. When she gained some composure, we separated slightly. She stood on tiptoe, put her hand behind my head, and bent my head and face down into her, moist, open-mouthed kiss. The passion was electric and very mutual. We kissed and groped each other like the teenagers we had been.

But this was too public a place. I took her hand and led her out of the stacks. "Let's go for a ride." We moved through the library as fast as we could without drawing attention to ourselves. I didn't want to let the intensity dissipate. I put her in my truck, walked around to the driver's side, and got in. She sat demurely close to the passenger door, perhaps realizing that we were on public display in the middle of town.

I started my truck and turned north, toward the strip. I drove up the highway and turned into Audubon Park. During our time together, we had walked the trails, swum in the lake, and sunbathed on the beach together. I followed the narrow, winding road through the park, back to an area away from the lakefront. Parking, I exited my truck and went around to open her door. She took my hand as I helped her out.

We headed down the same trail we'd walked so many times before, hand in hand. The setting was peaceful and bucolic; we'd gone back in time. We were two young people, forever in love.

"Oh, Hoyt, you always know exactly what to do and how to treat me. What a perfect place to come." She stopped and looked up at me. "I made a terrible mistake. I was too young to see what I had in you! Ever since that night at the Cosmo, I knew I'd never stopped loving you."

"So, what do we do now?" We were approaching the end of the trail, figuratively and literally.

"I want to go back to the fall of 1941." She fell into my arms and kissed me again, gently and warmly at first, but as she held the kiss, our mouths opened, and the passion that had overtaken us at the library erupted again, deeper, hotter, and more intense. We pressed our bodies together, fondled and felt each other intimately.

"Take me somewhere, Hoyt, please! I want to be alone with you. I want you to make love to me. I need to feel loved!"

Ordinarily rational and analytical, I was neither. Full of love and lust I grabbed her hand and led her back to my truck. She slid next to me, nuzzling my neck and chest; her left hand was behind my neck, her right hand on my thigh.

I drove north toward the bridge. I was taking her to Evansville, where we wouldn't be seen. I drove as fast as I could without being dangerous—or stopped by the highway patrol.

The leaves along the river bank were dappled with late-afternoon sunlight, the sky the color of bleached linen. I was headed to a motel on Kentucky Avenue, just inside Evansville city limits.

But as I pulled onto Kentucky Avenue, my truck seemed to be slowing. An opaque vapor seemed to cloud my vision and my conscience. For some time, I'd had the feeling that there was someone or something imposing a will on me other than my own. Usually, I was only aware of it in retrospect, when I reflected on foolish actions I had almost taken, but didn't. But this time, I was aware of it *before the fact*! There was no denying it. It was real and powerful. We were headed down a road with no exit. When our passions were spent, what would be left? I didn't want my love for Sally turned into bitter regret—for either of us.

Sally seemed calmer now, pensive even. Her caresses were lighter, and she straightened in the seat and looked straight ahead. I pulled into the motel parking lot, slowly circled the building, and passed trash bins and employees' cars parked there. I neared the highway again, and we sat there silently, both of us staring straight ahead. Finally, I pulled onto the highway, into traffic, and headed south.

We didn't speak the entire way back to Henderson. She had removed her hand from the back of my neck and slid further away from me. She glanced out the passenger-side window from time to time. Road noise and the truck's engine were the only sound in the cab. A light rain began to fall as we approached

Henderson. I pulled into a vacant parking slot in front of the bank and turned the ignition off. I turned to face her.

"I love you! I know now, I always will. Men get a pass in these circumstances. But Hester Prynne's accusers are always waiting to pin a red letter on the woman. Go home, Sally. As long as you're married, I'll be your devoted friend, but I can't be your lover—though God knows I want to."

After what seemed like an eternity, she leaned over and kissed my cheek. She got out of my truck, and slowly walked back into the bank without looking back.

CHAPTER 58

I was trapped between two dimensions. I couldn't separate the woman Sally was from the girl she had been. Had I just driven a stake through my last chance to have the woman I'd loved for years? Should moral principles outweigh personal happiness?

The next morning, I walked to the office of Matt Musgrave, a colleague of Bob Craig's. Matt was middle-aged and a recovering alcoholic. At the bottom rung, with no way out but up, he had embraced the 12 steps, got sober, and resurrected his life and his practice. Since his recovery, he had devoted a large portion of his personal time to helping others into the steps and a lifetime of sobriety, chosen daily.

Fortunately, he was in and willing to see me. Without revealing the personal side of our recent experience, I related to him Sally's difficulty with Bob's drinking and asked if there was any way he might be able to help.

"Delicate matter, Hoyt. The individual generally has to want to be helped. If his marriage has any value and he can be made to see he's losing it . . . maybe. If we can get enough friends and family involved, perhaps we can stage an intervention. I'll see what I can do."

‡

Afterward, I went to the office. A message waited on my desk from a Jimmy Adams—a name I didn't recognize. I dialed the number on the paper.

"Triplett Tool and Die Company," a female voice reported. Suddenly, I recalled the name: Jimmy Adams was the company comptroller.

"I'm Hoyt Cole. I have a message to call Jimmy Adams."

"One moment, please."

As soon as I was connected, Adams blurted without preamble: "Mr. Cole, I need to talk to you."

"Go ahead, Jimmy."

"Somewhere away from here." His voice was low and urgent.

"You name it, Jimmy."

"Can you meet me at the South Y Tavern?"

"I'll be there in 20 minutes." I was already grabbing my keys.

Green Street is a state highway leading south, out of town, through a mix of homes and businesses that become more industrial as you leave Henderson behind. The South Y Tavern sits in the middle of the "Y" created by Highway 41-A splitting off to the left from Highway 60. It's a small frame building, likely an old home converted into a business, long ago. It has a front gable and a porch entry. Inside, it's little more than a beer joint. Hamburgers and hot dogs are served to absorb the alcohol. Wooden floors, wooden tables, and ladderback chairs serve as furnishings. A short bar with six stools is located along the left wall, with cigarettes and half-pints on display. Jimmy Adams was sitting at a table as far back as the small space would allow.

Even though I'd never met him, he was easy to identify: small, pale complexion, horn-rimmed glasses—and nervous. It had to be him.

"Jimmy?"

"Thanks for coming, Mr. Cole." His pupils were dilated to let in more light in that dark corner.

"What's on your mind?"

"You asked Claude about unaccounted for expenditures?" He pushed his glasses up his nose and pulled at his ear.

"I raised the question," I said.

"I've found some . . . irregularities." Adams fiddled with the knot in his tie.

"Go ahead."

"After your talk with Claude, I tried to reconcile petty cash. Eddie used petty cash for personal expenses from time to time, but never more than 50 to 100 bucks at a time. He always left a note in the box reflecting how much he took, so I could reconcile it easily."

"In the three months before he died, he took out $500, $1,000, and $2,500 on three separate occasions—each time, more than the time before." He leaned across the table and dropped his voice. "He replenished it with checks, reflecting bogus expenses."

"Have you reported this to Claude Brown?"

"No, sir."

"Well, you have to. Anything else?" I asked.

"Still lookin'."

"Thanks for the heads up, Jimmy, but I can't sit on this. You need to tell Brown, so when the police come to question you, it won't be a surprise."

His eyes grew bigger and wider, his brows arching above the rim of his glasses, his face ashen. "Oh, God, Mr. Cole. I never thought about being questioned by the police!"

"Don't worry, Jimmy; you've done nothing wrong. They can't eat you!" I thanked him again and headed back into town.

Deputy Kockritz was at his desk when I stopped in to tell him of my meeting with Jimmy Adams.

"Well, it looks like Triplett *was* being blackmailed." He whistled. "I don't know what we can do about it now. He never reported it, and he's dead."

"Just thought you might want to follow up," I said.

"Thanks, Cole."

CHAPTER 59

I stopped by the office of the state attorney. Haskell Montgomery had practiced law in Henderson for over 30 years in one capacity or another—not overly gregarious, but pleasant enough. Montgomery was nearing 60, about five feet eight, and a good prosecutor—fair, but good.

He invited me back to his private office. "What's on your mind, Hoyt?"

"I got a couple issues nagging at me. Did Detective Brackett inform you of an affair between Selma Weiskopf and Maurice Rednour, the regional vice president of the Coldiron Mining Company?"

"Yeah, he mentioned it in passing. Hard to see how it's relevant, after the fact."

"Whaddaya mean, after the fact?"

Montgomery leaned forward over his ponderous stomach, peering over the tops of his glasses at me. "Well, you might question her morals, starting an affair so soon after her husband's murder, but it's hardly relevant to the outcome of the trial."

"Haskell, the affair's been going on for six months or longer!"

"Holy shit! A trial has been held, a man found guilty, a sentence passed. The case is closed. Why are you just now reporting this?"

"Pretty much, Guinea's response, Haskell! I told him the same day I found out. I'm not saying Clyde Gish didn't do the killing, but if Rednour knew about the plan, doesn't that at least make him an accessory? Perhaps he masterminded the whole thing, using Clyde to get rid of his lover's husband. Or he could be just another gullible pawn in a scenario orchestrated by a conniving woman. Shouldn't these possibilities at least be explored?"

"Hell yes, they should! I'll get Brackett in here right away. Sonofabitch didn't outright lie, but he didn't correct my assumptions. I'll make sure he brings Rednour in for questioning. What else you got?"

"I want to discuss information that I'm not supposed to be privy to, and I can't reveal the source."

He harrumphed. "What else is new? Go ahead, I'll listen."

"I understand a hand-printed note was found in Eddie G.'s car. A note that seemed to indicate suicide. Do you know about that?"

"Yeah, Kockritz showed it to me."

He stared at me for a long moment. "You got another shoe to drop Hoyt?"

"No, just want to make sure you're seeing all the cards in the deck. What are your thoughts?"

"If, in fact, it is a suicide note, that eliminates murder. It also raises the question: Why did he kill himself? If the note is legit, it suggests blackmail."

"Did Kockritz tell you the note was not signed?"

"No, he left off that little piece of information."

"Makes you wonder, doesn't it? Keep me in the loop, Haskell, to the extent you can."

"See you later, Hoyt, and thanks—I guess."

‡

"Haskell Montgomery on the phone for you," Marge reported. It had been a few days since our conversation in his office.

"Put him on." I rolled my chair forward, moved the phone to my left hand, and picked up a pencil with my right.

"Yeah, Haskell?"

"We brought Maurice Rednour in for questioning yesterday."

"And?"

"Why don't you come down to my office. Guinea's here; we'll go over it with you."

"Be right there."

It was a pleasant day, and his office was only a few blocks away, so I walked. The dog days of summer had passed and the bitter winter was weeks away. The four, clearly discernible seasons were part of what made living in Henderson worthwhile.

When I arrived, Haskell's secretary sent me straight back. Haskell sat behind his desk with Brackett across from him.

"Come in, Hoyt, take a seat," he said, motioning to the vacant chair next to Brackett's. "Give him the rundown, Guinea."

"We sent a car around to pick Rednour up. Just to spook him a bit, see how he would react. Well, it worked all right. By the time he got here, he was like a dog shittin' peach seeds.

"I started right in. Told him we knew he'd kept a room at the Gateway Motel under the name of Carl Duncan for the last six months, at least. Told him we knew he was carrying on an affair with Selma Weiskopf and further shocked him when we told him how they performed their secret comings and goings using the attached garage and separate taxis."

" 'With all that,' I said, 'we could arrest you right now and charge you as an accessory in a capital murder.' "

"That's when Haskell asked him, 'You want a lawyer, Mr. Rednour?'

" 'I called our company attorney when Detective Brackett told me he was sending a car. He should be here any minute,' Rednour said.

"Haskell poured Rednour three fingers of bourbon. He took it in shaking hands and drank the entire contents," Guinea continued. "The attorney entered the office only minutes later and took the chair you're setting in now, Hoyt. Haskell recounted everything I'd told Rednour.

" 'You don't have to say another word, Maurice,' the attorney stated.

" 'I know that, but this isn't going away. I may as well address it now as later,' Rednour said.

" 'I had nothing to do with Herman Weiskopf's murder. I had no knowledge of it until the morning after I arrived in town when his body was found.' He sat forward on the edge of his seat, folded his hands in front of him and gazed for a long time at the floor in front of him.

" 'Everything else you outlined is true. I'm not proud of it—God knows, I'm not—but it *is* true.' "

Rednour had been married to the same woman for more than 25 years—a "wonderful woman and a good wife." They had two grown children. She'd been diagnosed with Multiple Sclerosis five years before and had become completely bedridden. Selma had made herself available, and in a weak moment, Rednour had succumbed. "I'm not a young man anymore," he'd said, "but I still have desires and urges." After the initial encounter, it became easier and easier. "Not an excuse," Rednour said. "Just an explanation.

"Gentlemen, you can arrest me. You can charge me, and you can try me. My defense will be just what I've presented to you here today. If you do, it'll ruin my reputation, shame my children, and likely cost me my job—all justifiable, I'm sure."

"I told him we'd be in touch," Guinea concluded.

"Whaddaya think, Hoyt?" Haskell asked.

"If he's telling the truth—and I want to believe he is—it's a damn shame." I related what Carla Broadbent had told me about Selma's ambitions. "It's entirely possible that Maurice Rednour is another hapless victim of Selma's social climbing."

"There's certainly enough suspicion and extenuating circumstances to try Maurice Rednour as an accessory," Haskell said. "There is also enough human compassion not to. Rednour's story rings true."

"If we arrest and charge him," Guinea said, "we'll have to charge Selma."

"I appreciate your including me up to this point, gentlemen," I told them. "I'll leave the legal wrangling and decision-making to the two of you."

CHAPTER 60

Everything in the office was in disarray. Technicians were frantically working on the linotype machine to get it up and running in time for the afternoon edition. I'd covered a terrible accident out by the old north Y: A motorcyclist had been decapitated when he crossed the centerline, clipped the driver's side of a northbound car, and smashed, headfirst, through the windshield. I was trying to write the report in time to make deadline when my phone rang. I snatched up the receiver, hoping to terminate the call quickly. "Yeah?"

"Cole?" a male voice asked.

"Yeah, who is this?"

"The bartender at Pal's. How's the investigation into Glenn Triplett's murder going?"

For God's sake, I don't have time for that right now! "Well enough I suppose." I looked over the pool of typists, still pecking away, and through the front window, where I could see that traffic was still backed up.

"Look Mr. Cole, I wasn't exactly forthcoming the other evening.

Glenn Triplett was a very nice man, well-liked and respected by everyone here. His . . . partner for the last few months . . . not so much."

Intrigued, I picked up a pencil. I realized I might need to take some notes. "You referring to David Howard, the name you left for me.?"

"Yes, sir!"

"Can I ask your name?"

"Henry Gordon. I go by Hank."

"You have anything else to allow, Hank?"

He paused long enough for me to wonder if the connection had been broken. "Hank?" I asked, almost hoping that *was* the case.

"If David Howard was a woman, he'd be called a gold digger," he said. "He targets men like Glenn and milks them for as much as he can. Triplett began to see through Howard sooner than most and was trying to terminate their relationship."

"What are you driving at, Hank?"—trying to conceal my impatience.

"Howard is always the one to end things. He takes rejection personally."

"You seem to have more than a little insight into the dynamic of their relationship, Hank."

"You've been here long as I have, you pick up on stuff," he said. "I know you're a reporter and not a police officer, but if I were investigating Glenn Triplett's murder, I wouldn't be too quick to dismiss David Howard as a suspect."

"As far as I know, he's not a suspect," I said.

"Maybe he should be." The line went dead.

What a time for a call like that!

I needed to clear my head and focus on the unanswered questions. I was easily distracted by them, and there were too many interruptions at work and in town. My mind wouldn't let me merely report the facts. I needed to solve the unresolved. I need a place to think.

‡

Audubon State Park sat on the east side of Highway 41 North, about a mile from the Ohio River bridge. Opened in 1934 on 575 acres, the park was a sanctuary for birds and native wildlife. It had cabins and camp sites, hiking trails, and a lake. It offered six and a half miles of trails, from leisurely strolls to backcountry hiking. It had been one of my favorite places for as long as I could remember. I headed back there.

I strolled one of the leisure trails under a canopy of mature, old-growth trees. The air was cool and fresh smelling, the ideal setting for clearing my mind. But I couldn't erase the unresolved circumstances and wearisome issues nagging at the back edges of my mind.

The mysterious David Howard, supposedly Eddie G.'s "special friend." Carla Broadbent's description of the ambitious Selma Weiskopf.

So damn many loose ends.

Was Clyde Gish the straightforward killer of Herman Weiskopf? Did Selma Weiskopf entice and encourage him with promises of marriage and insurance proceeds? Did Maurice Rednour mastermind the plot to eliminate Herman so he could marry Selma? Did both he and Selma play Clyde for a witless dupe? Was Rednour an innocent target of a heartless woman? Did she use Clyde to eliminate Herman, giving her an unfettered path to work her devious subterfuge on Rednour?

I passed south-facing slopes on one of the most picturesque sections of the trail, where wildflowers bloomed among sugar maples, various species of oak, and tulip popular. Vague, restive notions slipped in and out of my mind, so elusive I couldn't quite form coherent thoughts. They teased at the boundaries of my conscious mind, perplexing me.

Strangely, I wasn't troubled by the unsolved murder of Pearly Martin and didn't ponder it. But the issues surrounding Triplett couldn't be pushed aside. Was Eddie being blackmailed? Could he have taken his own life? Was he murdered? If so, by whom, and for what reason? Was he in fact homosexual? Was he having an affair with David Howard? Did Howard kill him because Eddie ended their relationship?

David Howard troubled me.

Was it because of Hank's call? Perhaps. I couldn't explain Howard crashing Eddie's monthly poker game or his strange behavior that evening. And what about his black eye and the cut above it?

I didn't know what I'd do when I got there, but I was going to Maxim's to confront David Howard.

CHAPTER 61

Maxim's was in the middle of the 300 block of Main Street, in downtown Evansville. Couture fashion designers such as Christian Dior, Cristobal, and Hubert de Givenchy were all represented on mannequins in the large, plate-glass windows on either side of the entrance. Men that shopped there were well groomed and stylish.

I made my way through racks of three-piece suits, sport coats, and slacks. Shelves displayed dress shirts, and neckties were fanned out on tables in attractive arrays. I examined a button-down shirt and a tie with a regimental stripe. Various accessories—belts, hats, socks, and sweaters—were strategically positioned throughout the store.

Eventually, a well-dressed salesman approached.

"I'd like to see David Howard,"

"Do you have an appointment?" he asked rather stiffly, looking down his nose at me with his chin tipped up.

"No, I'm sorry. Do I need one?"

"Mr. Howard is head of our custom-tailoring department upstairs and works only by appointment." His manner was obviously intended to impress the uninitiated.

"If you will indulge me, please call upstairs and tell him a friend of Glenn Triplett is here and would like to see him. My name is Hoyt Cole."

"Very well, Mr. Cole." After cradling the phone, he said, "Please take the elevator to the second floor."

Howard came forward to meet me at the elevator. "Mr. Cole?"

I nodded.

"Please have a seat, I'm just finishing up with Mr. Van Cleve."

Full-length, three-paneled mirrors stood at the ready, with low, carpeted stands in front of them. Four upholstered chairs beckoned from an area rug; complimentary coffee, water, and soft drinks were stationed nearby. When I absent-mindedly picked up a book of fabric swatches on one of the round tables and thumbed through it, a salesman removed it from my hands, as a mother would a small boy. He replaced it on a stand with other books of swatches, turned, and walked back to his cubicle without a word.

Howard returned to his customer, smiling, warm, and gregarious, displaying all the sales charm he could muster. He was almost obsequious. After Van Cleve departed, he returned to me, smiling and friendly. "What can I do for you Mr. Cole?"

"I'd like to speak to you about Glenn Triplett."

His demeanor changed immediately; his smiling welcome disappeared, and his eyes narrowed with suspicion. "What about Glenn? And why should I speak to *you* about him?"—as if the word left a bad taste in his mouth.

"I'm investigating his murder."

Tensing he adjusted his tie and folded his arms across his chest. "Are you a police officer?"

"No, I'm a newspaper reporter. It's my job to ask about it, but he and I had also developed a warm friendship over the past few weeks."

He took the bait. "Step into my office, Mr. Cole."

"I'm told you unexpectedly dropped in on his monthly poker game, the night before his body was found." His hand went nervously to his left pinky, as if to reposition a ring he wasn't wearing.

"Did you know he was being blackmailed? The police found a suicide note above the visor in his car. I understand you two were close?"

He paused a lengthy period of time, perhaps hoping I'd continue and give him time to formulate his thoughts. I did not fill the dead air. I looked him in the eye, unblinking, but he looked past me. He appeared robotic, impersonal. He remained silent, staring vacantly into the middle distance.

After a time, I said, "Mr. Howard—*was* Glenn Triplett being blackmailed?"

He crossed his arms again, lifted his left hand to his chin, then moved it to his nose, pulling on it unconsciously. "Yes." He glanced off to the side. "He told me he was."

"For how long?"

"Six weeks, maybe more."

"Do you have any idea who it might have been?"

Suddenly he straightened himself, lifted his head slightly and marshaled all the arrogance he could muster. "I do not! And frankly, Mr. Cole, I resent your questions. You used Glenn's name to see me without an appointment, leading me to believe that you were a potential customer. I've spent all the time with you I intend to. Good day." With that he turned to face the opening of the cubicle, expecting me to immediately trail out as he directed.

"I'm sorry you feel that way. I apologize for misleading you." He turned back to face me. "How did you get the black eye and the cut above it?"

He did not respond.

"Oh, one last thing," I added. "Since you and he had a *relationship* . . . You may be interested to know that the sheriff's department is bringing in a forensic team from Louisville tomorrow. They intend to do a thorough search of the cabin and the area around it. Often, clues are left behind that normal investigation techniques miss. Everyone is anxious to find Eddie G.'s killer."

CHAPTER 62

Haughty, arrogant, and self-absorbed. I didn't like Howard, and I hoped it showed. I went to see Karl Kockritz, told him about my visit, and revealed the plan I'd devised on the way back, but he wasn't interested. I asked him about Deputy Katterjohn. He considered it, surprised that I knew her.

"I can spare her. For once she'll be good for something." He looked at me, shook his head skeptically, and walked away.

I don't know how long she'd been there, but when I arrived at the Kingdon just after five, Deputy Katterjohn was waiting for me in the lobby. "Give me a minute to change," I told her.

A few minutes later, we walked out the back of the hotel. "Let's go in my truck, if you don't mind. A cruiser might alert Howard."

The smell and taste of dust blew through my open windows. Roadside weeds were turning brown, drooping for lack of moisture. We drove between dry fields, and I told her what I knew about David Howard, as well as the loosely formulated plan I'd fashioned. More than once, we had to pull onto the shoulder to let a rumbling coal truck pass. Occasionally there was a dead cat or opossum, lying flat in the middle of the road.

"I appreciate you asking me along, Mr. Cole."

"I'm glad to have your help."

I drove on past the turnoff for the cabin, on to the ferry crossing. I'd made previous arrangements to leave my truck behind the operator's clapboard house at the top of the grade, where Howard was unlikely to notice it.

We hoofed it back to the Marshall cabin. Dusty dandelions and goldenrods grew tight against the edges of the crumbling blacktop. A hawk circled idly overhead. The odor of cow manure and river debris hung on the evening air. Leaving the paved surface, we continued up the lane and walked the cabin's perimeter, reconnoitering. Katterjohn stifled a gasp as she stumbled over the eviscerated body of a raccoon. Likely killed by a night predator, a fox or coyote. I'd obtained the key from Eddie's uncle, Frank Marshall. We climbed the three steps to the front door and went inside.

The one-room cabin was built of logs harvested on the property. The front entrance was in the middle on the long side, and there was an exit directly across, on the back wall. I surveyed the locations and sightlines of the windows. The cabin had no running water or indoor plumbing. Occupants had to bring in jugs of water for bathing, drinking, and dish washing, along with ice. The furnishings were rustic and sparse: Beside the ice box, the kitchen space had a long table with eight chairs. A large stone fireplace stood opposite, and two southwestern-style area rugs stretched across the floor of the wide, open room. Insect repellent and citronella candles stood at ready on the small kitchen counter.

Katterjohn had brought a shoulder pack containing flashlights, lanterns, metal cups, a thermos of coffee, and some snacks. I had my USMC issued, semiautomatic M 1911 Colt .45 in its holster, tucked under my shirt behind my back. I'd brought along a couple of surplus wool Marine Corps blankets.

"We may be on a wild-goose chase, deputy. My suspicions may be ill-founded. This is a long shot, no doubt, but if Howard decided to come look around, I wanted to be here."

We settled in, and strategically situated ourselves to view the front and side windows; we made small talk to kill time. When we'd exhausted it, Katterjohn said, "The *suicide* note I found? It's probably forged. We sent it to a handwriting expert in Evansville, along with some copies of Mr. Triplett's known writings, and showed it to his wife. She couldn't say for sure, one way or the other."

"I believe he was being blackmailed, regardless," I said. "The comptroller determined Eddie'd taken cash from his company on three separate occasions, unaccounted for. Cash in the amounts of $500, $1,000, and $2,500."

The shadows were lengthening. I slipped out of my chair and sat on the floor.

"If Howard doesn't show tonight, I didn't spook him, or he had no reason to *be* spooked. In that case, I might have to eliminate him from suspicion, leaving me to further deliberate on who might have killed him or to conclude that perhaps he killed himself."

"He could have been blackmailed *and* murdered."

"Why would the person blackmailing him kill him? After all, his scheme was working. He was being paid. Why cross that line?" I asked.

"Maybe he was being blackmailed by one person, and murdered by a different person for separate, but possibly related, reasons, both of which might have to do with homosexuality." She dropped to the floor across from me.

"Damn, Katterjohn . . . You pose a complex and convoluted prospect. Did you share that line of thinking with anyone in the department?"

"No."

"Why share it with me?

"We're here, killing time. You've treated me with respect. You're the only one since I took this job who has treated me as if I had any credibility at all."

Shadows stretched to join irregular dark and light patches spread across the cabin floor. I raised the windows a few inches to let fresh air in, and to allow us to hear better. The earthy smell of decomposing leaves and rotting wood wafted in on the night air. At length, we sat in the dark, speaking in hushed tones when we spoke at all. Katterjohn drew her legs up and hugged them in both arms. She leaned forward and rested her chin on her knees. I began to count the logs from floor to ceiling and examine the pattern of stones in the fireplace.

I could hear the river slapping against its banks. Intermittently, night birds punctuated the steady insect buzzing. Now and again, a screech owl cried in the distance. Moths bumped the window screens. The wind picked up, rustling the leaves. Dead branches fell against the roof. Katterjohn started at each unexpected sound. The deep darkness and the quiet night sounds heightened the sense of isolation. We drank coffee. I smoked a cigarette. Katterjohn ate a packet of cheese crackers. Midnight came and went.

I was beginning to feel beaten. I'd wasted half the night in a desolate cabin on a deserted stretch of Green River bottoms. I was about to pack it in when Katterjohn whispered, "Cole!"

She nodded toward the side window. A narrow beam of light scanned the ground where cars usually parked. We moved toward the window, crouching, she on one side, me the other. The searcher was dressed entirely in black from his shoes to the sock-cap on his head. He'd even gone to the trouble of blacking his face. Dead leaves and debris blew across the beam of his flashlight. He must have parked his car down the road and walked onto the property. I don't know why, but I had assumed that he'd drive onto the property, and we'd have no trouble detecting his arrival—an unrealistic assumption, as it turned out.

We had previously agreed Katterjohn would make the initial confrontation, since she represented law enforcement. She moved toward the front door, drawing her .38 Special service revolver from its holster and gripping a flashlight in her other hand. She silently nodded to me to head out the back. I signaled with thumbs up and quietly crept outside. We emerged from opposite corners of the cabin at the same time. Katterjohn took about five steps into the open space, flashed her light on the man, and aimed her revolver at him.

"Henderson County Sheriff's Department. Put your hands in the air!"

He froze and stood with his back to us for a long, breathless moment—maybe contemplating his options with a lone female.

"Extinguish your light and turn to face me with both hands high in the air, sir!"

Still, he didn't move. He didn't turn to face her.

I stepped forward. "Put your hands in the air, Howard. She's not alone." I stepped out from behind the cabin, remaining slightly behind Katterjohn and nearer the back corner of the cabin.

Night birds called, and a large limb fell into the river with a loud splash. He turned slowly to face us, sweeping his light over the area, illuminating us.

Katterjohn held his face in the beam of her light. "Extinguish your light, sir! That's an order!"

Howard tossed his flashlight onto the ground without turning it off. The beam splayed randomly over the dust.

"Mr. David Howard, you're under arrest on suspicion of murdering Edward Glenn Triplett."

"You can arrest me, but you've got no motive and no evidence."

"That shiner and the cut over your eye are from firing both barrels of that 20-gauge with just one hand. Kicked up pretty good, didn't it?"

"I ran into the corner of an open door in the dark."

Katterjohn edged to the right, closer to me, and handed me her revolver. She pulled an evidence bag from her pocket. "This what you were searching for Mr. Howard?" Using a pen, she took the onyx ring from the bag and held it in the light. She'd caught me completely off guard. I'd had no idea she had it. "It was found under the front seat of Mr. Triplett's car. I bet you lost it when you pulled out the shotgun."

"Should have had it resized, Howard. Wouldn't have slipped off so easily," I said.

Katterjohn replaced the ring in her pocket and extended her hand toward me for her revolver. "Turn around with your hands behind you, Mr. Howard."

He turned slowly and placed his left hand behind him. Still 10 feet away from him, Katterjohn holstered her revolver and removed her cuffs from the back of her belt. Howard pulled a .22 revolver, whirled, and squeezed off two quick pops. One bullet tore a hole in Katterjohn's shoulder; the second caromed off her collarbone, breaking it. The shots spun her to her right, and she dropped to her knees, blood soaking her blouse.

"Drop the gun, Howard!" I pulled my .45 and pointed it at him. He fired two more quick shots in my direction. One splintered the log at the corner of the cabin; the other ricocheted off a nearby tree, whining out over the river. I shot him twice in the center of his chest. The .45 bucked in my hands, and the rounds knocked him backward and slammed him to the ground, some three feet from where he'd stood. Two blood-red blooms rose from the holes in his chest. I knew the holes in his back were much larger. His face was pallid, drained of blood; his eyes were open, staring blankly into eternity. A foot shuddered as his electrical circuitry discharged across the last few synapses.

My heart raced and my limbs shook from the sudden adrenaline rush of killing a human being. My breathing was shallow, and I could see deep into the dark as my pupils dilated. I stood motionless for a brief moment; the smell of cordite roused me. I rushed to Katterjohn on wobbly legs. She was crumpled over on her right side. I sat her up against a tree.

"Sorry, Cole . . . I got careless," she said, sucking air through clenched teeth.

I pulled her two-way radio from her belt. She was able to call in the incident, while I went inside for towels to stem her bleeding and a blanket to cover her shoulders. She was in shock, but she was one tough young lady.

I didn't examine Howard. Didn't have to; I knew he was dead.

An ambulance and a hearse arrived on the scene about 30 minutes later. Still conscious, but in considerable pain, Katterjohn related to Karl Kockritz what had happened. They strapped her to the gurney, gave her a shot of morphine, and took her to the hospital. There was no rush with Howard. He was already dead when he hit the ground.

"Not such a far-fetched scheme after all, huh Karl?"

Kockritz grunted.

"You guys need to pay more attention to Deputy Katterjohn. She's a valuable, resource," I said. "Might make y'all one of the best departments in the state."

CHAPTER 63

The Henderson Circuit Court convened on Monday, September 24. I entered the chambers of the old courthouse and seated myself near the rear. The space smelled stale and moldy. The American flag and the Kentucky state flag stood in opposite corners of the room. There were the usual whisperings and hushed conversations, coughing and throat clearing. People shifted uneasily on creaking wooden seats.

We had everything in place. Walter T., his wife and friend had done a tremendous amount of legwork, gathering all the incriminating evidence. We had the affidavits typed as prescribed. We had the *Evansville Press* primed to break the story. Dahlke had operated by the numbers; up to that moment every aspect of Jeffries's instructions had been meticulously followed. His presentation would be the culmination of hours and hours of work, planning, and execution. All the chips had been shoved to the middle of the table. I allowed myself to believe that our plan was going to work.

Reverend Dahlke, Walter T., his wife, and their friend were seated in the front row. Judge Arnold Davenport entered the courtroom in his black robe and seated himself behind the bench on his elevated stand. Dahlke immediately walked up to him with the folder containing the 57 affidavits.

"Your honor, we wish to present these affidavits concerning gambling in Henderson County for the consideration of the court and the grand jury, and respectfully ask that the grand jury investigate them and the law-enforcement officers working from the sheriff's and county judge's offices. We feel that these statements warrant such an investigation."

Judge Davenport turned away, without acknowledging Dahlke, and spoke to the bailiff, ignoring the stack of affidavits lying on the bench. Finally, he rose and exited the courtroom, back through the door that led to his chambers. Reverend Dahlke remained standing in front of the bench, seemingly dismissed. The entire room fell silent; no one knew how to react to the judge's unexpected behavior. Finally, after what seemed like hours, the judge returned to the bench. He looked at Reverend Dahlke as if he'd only just seen him. "Don't give me anything. Give whatever you've got to Commonwealth Attorney Norsworthy."

What? We weren't prepared for that! Dahlke certainly wasn't prepared for it. He stood open-mouthed, momentarily flummoxed. It looked like the whole plan had disintegrated in one brief moment. Confused, Dahlke looked to Nathan W. Norsworthy. Norsworthy shook his head, almost imperceptibly.

Dahlke looked around dejectedly for some direction from *someone*. He returned to his seat with the folder under his arm. I could only see him from the rear, but his head drooped and his shoulders bent forward around his chest; his whole body slumped.

Could this really be happening? Could all the work, time, and effort be so easily dismissed? I could see only the back of Walter

T.'s head, but I could envision the steam rising from his collar. His face would be red. I feared he might well erupt. Walter T. didn't do subtle. Given his personal investment in acquiring and accumulating the vast incriminating evidence and his personal grudge against L. S. Furlong, I was afraid of what he might do.

For God's sake, what else can a community do? If this doesn't work, the appetite for such a battle will be lost for years to come. Could our legal system be so easily abused? It looked like the gamblers and corrupt politicians might win—again!

Jeffries had not told Dahlke what to do if the judge refused to accept the evidence. None of us had ever considered this possibility.

Had my taking Headley into our confidence and seeking his help torpedoed the entire project? After all, neither he nor his paper had ever spoken out against the gambling and lawlessness in our town. *Damn it! Cole, you've killed the only real chance this community had! Walter T. will have your ass, and who can blame him?*

Everyone held their collective breath. The quiet and the stalled procedure were accentuated by the slow ticking of a large wall clock. People shuffled their feet and moved in their seats with apprehension and uncertainty. The courtroom echoed with nervous coughs and muffled voices. Everyone present knew what was at stake, regardless of the side they were on. The anti-gambling faction could envision their last, best opportunity being dismissed like a leaf in the wind. The pro-gambling group likely breathed a collective sigh of relief, believing their protective mechanisms were firmly in place and functioning properly.

Suddenly the judge, a chain smoker, began a paroxysm of loud coughing, gagging, and gasps. He fumbled under his robe for a handkerchief and held it to his nose and mouth, choking and spluttering. His face was red, and his eyes watered. While this was going on, J. Rhoades Cunningham rose and walked to Reverend Dahlke, largely unnoticed. He cupped his hand to Dahlke's ear and spoke to him very briefly before returning to his seat.

As if suddenly emboldened, Reverend Dahlke rose again, and walked slowly forward, like a man headed toward a firing squad. Without saying a word, he placed the folder on the judge's bench and walked back to his seat.

Finally recovered, his brow sweaty and his eyes bloodshot, the judge rasped, "What am I supposed to do with this?"

Dahlke rose and nodded politely. "That's up to you, sir."

Judge Davenport motioned for Norsworthy to approach the bench and looked directly at Dahlke. "All I can do is give this to the commonwealth attorney."

"That's fine with me, sir," the minister replied, no doubt remembering Cunningham's advice that the judge's acknowledgment of the evidence would constitute its presentation in open court.

Nathan W. Norsworthy smiled broadly. I leaped to my feet and ran straight from the courtroom to the newspaper office, to advise Mr. Headley of what had transpired. It was imperative that these proceedings be reported in the afternoon edition. Every minute was critical.

"Marge, I need to see Mr. Headley immediately!"

"I'm sorry, Hoyt, but he had to go home suddenly. Apparently, some mishap has occurred."

"You gotta get him on the phone! Right now!"

"I can't do that. What's so important? I can't call him at home."

"The hell you can't! You dial the number; I'll talk to him."

How many more stumbling blocks can be thrown in the way!

Mrs. Headley answered. I identified myself and said, "I'm sorry, but I need to speak with your husband right away."

"He's out in the yard, talking to the tree trimmers. We had a limb break and fall onto the garage. Can he call you back?"

"No! This is a desperate circumstance. Please ask him to come to the phone." I couldn't keep the impatience out of my voice. I would regret it later, and apologize, but right then, I couldn't care.

When he finally came to the phone, I explained what had just transpired and how urgent the situation was. True to our agreement, he immediately called his contact at the *Evansville Press* and asked him to get the gambling allegations in the afternoon edition. Headley had me oversee the mechanism necessary to engage the Evansville paper in this critical last step of a plan as complex as a military maneuver. Miraculously, after all the missteps, I was able to effect the day's most important task.

Within two hours after we appeared in court, the *Evansville Press* had its EXTRA edition on the streets of Henderson. In addition to reporting on the presentation of the affidavits to the court, the paper listed more than 30 establishments, citing their locations and the number of gambling devices in use at the time of the visits. The story was picked up by the *Louisville Courier-Journal* and other newspapers across the state. Even my own paper, the *River City News*, reported the "alleged" illegal operations.

These proceedings and the newspaper reports created a serious dilemma for the newly convened grand jury. On the one hand, they had all the data and implied accusation contained in the Dahlke/Browder folder. On the other hand, they had reports from the sheriff's office for the months of May, June, July, and August—the same time period covered by Browder's affidavits. Every monthly report was worded exactly the same: "Each nightclub in the county was visited by me or one of my deputies and no violations noted." Facing such conflicting evidence, the jury voted to recess for two weeks.

‡

Dahlke thought that keeping the pressure on during the recess was critical. He wanted to maintain interest and enhance public awareness. He called a special meeting of the ministerial association.

"Gentlemen, we've got the ball rolling. Louis Jeffries has advised us to form a concerned citizens' group. We need for it to be active and vocal, in full swing, by the time the jury reconvenes.

"I want each one of you to get 10 or 15 church members, men *and* women, to come with you to next week's meeting." They decided to invite Jeffries to speak to the group. He was a real spellbinder when he spoke on good government. I was asked to attend.

Over 150 people showed for the meeting, a real cross section of factory workers, farmers, homemakers, and professional and business people. Likewise, a representative from each of the more than 17 smaller communities in the county came to the meeting.

"Furlong and his counterparts have unlimited funds," Jeffries told the group. "All of you in this room must make up your minds that you're in a fight, and you must continue to fight 365 days out of the year, regardless.

"You've got a cadre of corrupt public servants in Henderson, including your mayor, the sheriff, Judge Davenport, and several other county officials. Every one of them is seriously and criminally derelict in the performance of his duties. If you seriously want to put an end to conditions here, the responsibility is squarely on your shoulders. And you have to get the entire community thinking as you do.

"The situation here could not exist without participation and support of corrupt local politicians. Your elected officials have acquiesced to gambling and liquor interests because they make large financial contributions to their campaign funds. But if the citizens of Henderson demonstrate that they want an end to gambling and lawlessness, they will heed your wishes. If the people of this community have the courage and commitment, my services are available to help you fight for real law enforcement in Henderson County." Frequent bursts of applause and shouted amens were interspersed with Jeffries's words. When he finished and finally sat down the room exploded in thunderous applause. The outcome was the formation of the Henderson County Good Government League. A slate of officers was elected, lending credibility to the endeavor.

I continued to write articles under the Noah Logan byline, doing my part to keep the issue in the limelight. The city and county school boards became vocal in their support of the effort to rid the area of vice. In the second week of the recess, a group of young business and professional men circulated a petition to churches and civic groups, pressuring the judge to commit to calling a special grand jury in the event the current one failed to act on the affidavits before it. The petition gathered thousands of signatures.

‡

The grand jury reconvened in early October. L. S. Furlong, Sheriff Fletcher Agnew, W. T. Browder, his wife and friend, and 10 other witnesses were called. Judge Davenport was presented with a petition containing almost 1,800 signatures. It called on the judge to use the powers of his office to obtain grand jury indictments. And failing that, to replace the current jury with a jury that would.

Feeling like things were progressing, I went by Reverend Dahlke's office to get his assessment.

"We're having an impact, Hoyt. I've been receiving threatening phone calls at the office and at home—some around supper time, but most come late at night, after we've gone to bed. Some callers make extremely vulgar comments, particularly when a female voice answers. We had to tell our daughter stop answering the phone.

"I'm sorry Reverend, but I guess that goes with the territory. It must be quite disturbing to your wife and daughter. Can you get an unlisted number?"

"I suppose I could, but ultimately, they'd acquire that as well. So far, I've only been threatened. The new president of the Good Government League, a local farmer, had a prize hog slaughtered during the night." One member's grade-school child had been approached walking home from school by a man who warned: "Your daddy better be careful who he makes mad."

Dahlke continued. "The Good Government League has notified the Alcoholic Beverage Control Board. We requested they investigate all establishments charged with violations. The grand jury remaining in session for the full term seems to be a good sign. Previous efforts ended when they closed after two to three days."

"You're doing good work, Reverend Dahlke. Keep it up. Thanks for keeping me in the loop. Call me if you need me."

A Noah Logan article covered the opening-day events in both the Evansville and Louisville papers. A second article outlined the contents of the telegram sent to the ABC Board, causing other newspapers across the state to begin reporting on the goings-on here.

Reports on our efforts headlined throughout the commonwealth: "State Board Joins Drive on Gambling," "State ABC Board

May Investigate Henderson Taverns," "Request for Jury Records Studied," "Henderson Gambling Investigators Ask State to Probe over 30 Taverns and Nightclubs."

Logan also published an article entitled "Can the Blight on Henderson Be Eliminated after All These Years?" a week after the grand jury session began, reporting that a group of determined people had formed six weeks earlier with the goal of breaking up commercialized gambling and attendant lawlessness. The group had grown into a county-wide movement, operating under the name of the Henderson Good Government League.

I gave voice to the doubt about the efforts of this group in fact accomplishing its goal, rather than ending in the cemetery of lost causes, like previous endeavors had. I parroted Jeffries's contention that the lion's share of responsibility rested on Henderson's citizenry, for both the gambling and political corruption *and* for the cleanup, if there was to be one.

The conditions in Henderson were a long time in the making; they would not be overcome quickly, or without considerable and concerted effort. Henderson's Good Government League was attracting the attention of communities throughout the state. The league and the increasing membership of intelligent and determined recruits had no intention of stopping, in spite of threats and acts of vandalism. Their efforts had involved the state Alcoholic Beverage Control Board, which had promised action.

I closed with the following: "The Good Government League has a tough fight on its hands, but with the indispensable element of popular awareness and support, the fight can be won, and the blight on Henderson's name can be erased."

CHAPTER 64

"I don't think a damn thing will come of it. It'll be business as usual. There's just too much at stake," said one of the barbers. The local gambling issue had largely replaced talk of sports and weather in the shop.

"The fix is in here, has been for years. I'll be shocked if the grand jury acts at all," another opined.

But one of the customers wasn't as sure. "All the preachers in town are talking about it from the pulpit, and the Henderson Good Government League has brought a lot of pressure to bear, both locally and statewide. It may be different this time."

This kind of back-and-forth could be heard in almost every business I entered downtown.

It was the principal topic at Matt's News Stand. The mood among league members was as mercurial as autumn weather in Kentucky. One day, the sun was shining, the temperature was in the 70s and the sky was clear. The next day the temperature dropped, it started to rain, and the clouds hung low and dark in the sky.

The threatening calls to Reverend Dahlke and other HGGL

members intensified, and a suspected case of arson raised the ante. While ominous and alarming, these events certainly indicated that the league was having an impact.

On October 10, the grand jury returned true bills on 38 people and two corporations, but as the Bottoms and the Cosmopolitan were corporations, L. S. Furlong remained untouched, personally. The sheriff, the county judge, and the mayor were not indicted, either. Perhaps most discouraging: all the indictments were for *misdemeanors*.

It felt as if we had won a minor skirmish in a raging war!

With the November elections looming, Louis Jeffries came back to Henderson to address the Good Government League on October 15. In that meeting he announced plans to file written charges with the governor against Sheriff Agnew. To ensure a response from the governor during his upcoming visit, we sent a telegram urging him to tell Kentucky what he proposed to do to remedy vice in Henderson County, should he be reelected. In a move that shocked me and the rest of the HGGL members, our local paper printed the first ever editorial on the subject on October 17. The piece touted the work of the "strong group of aroused citizens" and pressured the governor to clarify his position before the November election.

During the governor's October 20 visit, he made two statements of significance amid his usual political pontificating and doublespeak. The first: "I feel your problems are local and should be handled locally." Thunderous round of boos and catcalls alerted him to his blunder. He deftly changed gears and segued to a more conciliatory response. "However, as your governor, I won't hesitate to use all the methods and powers of my office to break up organized gambling." Ever the politician!

The second statement of significance concerned the charges

against our sheriff. "The citizens of Henderson County have the full right and authority to file affidavits to prefer charges against any local official," he began. "If the affidavits are presented properly, when I return to Frankfort, I will perform my duties immediately. I won't hesitate to comply with the law."

The Monday following his appearance in town, the governor turned over the affidavit on Sheriff Agnew to his attorney general, asking him to provide an "official opinion." The affidavit was in legal form and acceptable; the governor prepared an order for the ouster of Henderson County Sheriff Fletcher Agnew.

‡

But the gambling and illegal factions in town were not going down without a fight. A new garage under construction by one of the HGGL members burned down under suspicious circumstances. And after the *River City News* editorial, Headley's office window was painted black. No one involved in the anti-gambling efforts was exempt; threats and late-night calls were common, underscoring the lengths to which our adversaries were willing to go. Despite continued threats and at least two suspicious fires, the HGGL kept the pressure on.

The *River City News* weighed in with another editorial:

> Judge Billy Rakestraw painted a condemning picture of Henderson's lawlessness when he sent his January 21 report to the governor. He outlined violation of laws against gambling, while pointing out that law enforcement was virtually nonexistent. He further stated that these conditions have existed here for many years and have continually grown worse.

> All types of gambling schemes are openly operated, from slot machines, roulette, and blackjack to cockfights. It's apparent now that the people of Henderson will no longer tolerate these conditions. Open disregard for the law will no longer be tolerated. Our government is not for sale!

When the HGGL began to devise a plan to replace the mayor and commissioners, two men's names kept coming up. One was an intense, hard-nosed, no-nonsense druggist named Sam Chapman. The other, Ed Moore, was a taciturn, local building contractor with an untidy, somewhat disheveled appearance and an indifferent demeanor. Both men operated successful businesses and had never been involved in politics before.

Chapman was college educated and articulate, although very direct and abrupt. He didn't suffer fools lightly. He became the spokesman for the duo, telling the group that the only way they'd consider running was if a city manager form of government was established, one that would require community approval on a special ballot. "If enacted," he said, "we'll agree to serve one term—only."

Chapman expounded: "That will necessitate hiring a qualified and accredited city manager. We don't expect to find such an individual locally, and he won't be cheap! With that in place, at the end of our two-year term, in addition to the new city manager, the city will then have to elect a new mayor and *four* new commissioners."

Moore's laconic speech and casual nature fooled people into to taking him too lightly. He was just as tough, even stubborn, as his running mate. He was a great judge of people and cared little for flattery or praise. These men wanted nothing and sought no favors. They would not be compromised and could not be bought.

Their plan seemed almost as important as ridding the community of gambling.

The HGGL began to believe their plan was complete. They would remove gambling and corruption and have something of tangible value to offer in their stead.

CHAPTER 65

As the efforts of the Henderson County Good Government League continued to unfold, I continued to report on the progress. I started to feel a strong need to interview Lloyd Furlong. In addition to being the undisputed kingpin of illegal gambling in the area, he'd become one of Henderson County's largest landowners.

It's easy to vilify someone you don't know. Out of loyalty to Stormy Jack, I felt I should hear this man's story. I had retained the phone number John had penciled on the sheet beside his bed. I called the number, and as before, Furlong answered. I stated my name, hoping he'd remember our previous meeting at John's. He did. I asked if he would agree to speak with me. He consented and invited me to his home that same afternoon.

I drove to his estate overlooking the Ohio River, out on Wolf Hills Road. I navigated the snaking drive up the hill to the summit, approaching the residence from the rear, and followed the drive around the house to the river-facing, front elevation. I pulled my truck into one of the eight or ten paved parking spots across from the white brick mansion, a two-story, six-bedroom, dwelling of approximately 10,000 square feet. The roofline of the main house was lined with three-foot balustrades and topped with a cupola. All in all, tastefully presented. As unostentatious as such an extravagant dwelling could be, I suppose. My truck looked forlorn and out of place beyond the immaculately maintained front lawn and the eight-foot Greek statutes bordering the walk to the entry.

I knocked on one of the double entry doors and was almost immediately greeted by what I assumed must be a butler. I told him I was Hoyt Cole, to see Mr. Furlong. He took one long step backward with almost military precision, allowing me to step inside. He kept his chin level above his stiff, wing collar and stared straight ahead, both hands behind his one-button black jacket. "Right this way, sir." I felt I was in a scene from *The Maltese Falcon*.

I followed him across an enormous terrazzo foyer toward a winding stairway farther in. He showed me to a room with large floor-to-ceiling bookcase anchoring one end, and what looked to me like original art strategically placed on other walls. The man invited me to sit, indicating four wingback leather chairs in an open square at the center of the room.

Within minutes, Furlong entered and closed the door. I stood to greet him and extended my hand.

"Thank you for agreeing to meet me, Mr. Furlong."

"Not at all, Mr. Cole, please be seated and call me Lloyd or L. S."

The man was an enigma and a contradiction: a ruthless businessman and a kind philanthropist. Even though he'd built his fortune and made his living on the soiled boundaries of humanity, he had cultivated a credible reputation for generosity and benevolence toward people in need. He provided cash and bought groceries and coal for destitute families. Often, he didn't know them and hadn't met them.

"I'm Hoyt," I said, rather lamely.

He nodded almost imperceptibly. "Now that the formalities are out of the way, what do you want to talk to me about?"

It took real effort to focus. "I'd like to hear your comments on gambling in Henderson and the efforts to stop it currently being made by the Good Government League."

"If you are here representing the media and are seeking an interview for print, I'm sorry you wasted your time driving out here. I have nothing to say on the subject. However, in deference to your kindness to John, I'm willing to talk to you, *off the record,* for your personal insight and understanding. In addition, I will consent for you to use anything I tell you, in any way you wish—after my demise. Hopefully in some other day and time."

That consent caught me off guard and added a degree of credibility to whatever he might say. "Whether you speak to me on the record, or off the record. I want to hear your position, your reasons, your motives, and your defense. If you tell me your comments are personal and off the record, I'll honor that."

"I'll answer your questions, as best I can. I don't know that I'll volunteer anything else. We'll see. But before we begin, will you join me in a drink? I believe in making situations such as this as convivial as possible."

"I'll have whatever you're having," I said.

I couldn't help being impressed by the room's opulence, and I tried with some difficulty not to gawk open-mouthed at the 12-foot ceiling, walnut paneling, oak floors, and large decorative rug. I reckoned it to be a den, library, or drawing room where he perhaps withdrew for privacy. Regardless of the nomenclature, it was a very warm and comfortable space. Furlong moved to a polished cherry armoire, its open doors framing an array of liquor and glasses, and poured two bourbons on the rocks. Handing me my drink, he raised his glass.

"To the memory of John Calhoun Storm, my oldest and very best friend. May he rest in peace."

I tipped my glass to his and nodded.

Returning to his seat, Furlong crossed his legs and adjusted the dark gray, pleated slacks at the knees for comfort. "Please begin."

"By all accounts, you are an intelligent man. I suspect you could have been successful in almost any endeavor. Why did you choose bootlegging and gambling?"

"I don't know how much or how little you know about my childhood and upbringing, but often when choices are limited, you go through the first door opened to you."

"Does it bother you that your wealth and empire have been built outside the law, in illegal activities?"

"No." He leaned back in his chair, uncrossed his legs, and stretched them in front of him; he held his drink casually in his right hand, dangling over the arm of his chair. He was in his element, at home and comfortable.

"But it's illegal!"

"You asked if it bothers me. It does not."

"A pretty terse answer, Mr. Furlong. Care to elaborate?"

The light through the window glowed warmly on the black leather of his Chelsea boots.

"We can discuss my morals and value system at another time, if you'd like. But nothing I might say would satisfy you, I'm sure. Suffice it to say, what is legal and illegal does not necessarily provide a straight path to what is right and what is wrong.

"I have provided this community with a commodity. That commodity, at its basis, is entertainment. Along the way, lots of people have been able to earn a living—people unable to do so for the 10 years prior—as a result of an economic disaster exacerbated and prolonged by failed political policies. Though they were legal, I might ask: Were they right or wrong? What has done more economic damage to this community, those policies or my commodity?"

Leaning forward, he extended the hand that held his drink and gestured in a casual and offhanded manner. "I forced no one to partake of the entertainment I provided. Each individual availed himself of the services offered without coercion.

"I ask you: Who is wrong—me for providing the commodity, or the individual for partaking of it? The technicality currently driving the community is the fact that gaming is illegal here."

"A real fact, and a pretty strong argument," I replied. "To call breaking the law a 'technicality' seems disingenuous, Mr. Furlong. Lawlessness in a community is a serious consideration. Tolerating the breaking of one law—albeit beneficial to the common good—allows for the less beneficial breaking of other laws. You introduce the topic of good and bad laws as a diversion, to justify your lawlessness. It seems to me the issue is not whether a thing is good or bad, but whether it is legal or illegal."

"To the contrary, Hoyt. The Volstead Act was a law, legal by definition. But by all accounts, it was universally bad. That single bad law was responsible for more lawlessness and violence during its 13 years of existence than the *absence of laws* in the period known as the Wild, Wild West."

No matter my arguments, Furlong was never going to see the error of his ways, throw up his hands, fall to his knees, and repent of his past and current sins. *I'm not going to win this chess match!* However, I was certainly gaining insight into the man behind the circumstances here for the previous 20 years.

Attempting to switch gears, I asked, "Do you care to comment on the political corruption here and to what extent you are responsible and implicated?"

He rose and slowly circled his chair, formulating his thoughts in the process. He paced the carpeted area between the chairs. "To what degree the politics here is corrupt is a very subjective evaluation, one I am not willing to make. But to allow the discussion of that topic to continue, let us assume a degree of political corruption does exist. To what extent I am responsible is also a subjective evaluation. In order for corruption to exist, individuals must be corrupt—or at the very least, corruptible. Do corrupt individuals live here? I suppose, yes. Are they in politics, likely. If bribes and payoffs are the rules of the game, one has to play by those rules if he wants to play. Cost of doing business, as it were.

"I'd like to remind you that I'm speaking to you strictly off the record," he said. "To be completely candid, if there is political corruption here, I will admit to being implicated. I refuse to acknowledge responsibility."

I sat forward in my chair and placed both elbows on the arms. "You defend your actions and enterprise as one might defend a fort under siege," I said. "You have been very successful in leading our discussion into the subjective. Being more objective, I'm going to state that while not single-handedly responsible, the existence of your *commodity,* as benign and benevolent as you depict it, has created and allowed for lawlessness and political corruption in Henderson County for more than 20 years. Your enterprises have created an atmosphere that allows for many more unsavory and destructive activities in this community than you may have first intended.

"Our community is rife with prostitution, underage drinking, strong-arm tactics, embezzlement, and corruption of all types.

Those are the obvious results. There are secondary consequences such as physical violence, adulterous affairs, a high divorce rate, and school truancy, to mention just a few. I concede our community has been complicit in these activities for way too long. It appears, however, that we may have reached a tipping point!

"In spite the failures of previous efforts, the Good Government League is making progress. It's conceivable that they could put an end to gambling and political corruption in Henderson. How do you respond to that?"

"Nothing lasts forever!"

"That's it? That's your response? As the impresario of such a prosperous and well-established enterprise, an enterprise currently under siege and facing demise, I can't imagine such a sanguine response."

Furlong stood and walked casually to the window, gazing outside. "A businessman does what he can to protect the longevity of his business. I will continue in those pursuits. At the same time, I pride myself on being realistic. When the battle is lost, I discontinue the fight."

He turned back to face me, "I started this discussion referencing my childhood and early existence. I've managed to extract myself from my circumstances. I'm in no way bragging, just stating facts. I currently own a few thousand acres of Henderson County farmland. I own or hold leases on over 50 oil and gas wells here. Regardless of what happens, I won't have to return to the economic conditions of my youth. At the risk of offending you by evoking the Almighty, I consider myself a blessed man."

"You may be blessed, savvy, shrewd, or lucky. Define it as you choose. But the devastation exacted on this community has been immeasurable." Somehow my words sounded pompous and arrogant, even to my own ears.

"Have we exhausted this topic to your satisfaction, Mr. Cole?" He'd deftly switched from Hoyt to Mr. Cole.

"Yes, sir. I think so. I appreciate your time and your candor. I assure you I will respect your condition that this conversation be kept off the record." Strangely, I didn't want the meeting to end on hostile terms. I rose and extended my hand. "You're a fascinating man, Mr. Furlong. Thank you for your hospitality and your frankness."

He accepted my hand. "I'll see you to the door."

Likely, I will never see Lloyd Stanley Furlong again.

Back in my truck, I stared through the windshield at the river for a long moment. With the political corruption, lawlessness, and attendant violence in the community, Furlong had never been held responsible for using or encouraging violence himself. Locals said he never used strong-arm tactics to establish or perpetuate his empire. He was also reputed to have made large cash donations to local churches and charities. If the rumors were true, more than one church had received a new organ or refurbished pews through his largess, and he used a local funeral-home proprietor to deliver money and other items to people in dire straits. Whether these donations were real generosity or made to quell opposition to his enterprise, I'll leave to anyone's guess.

In spite of all the machinations in which I felt myself embroiled, the Ohio River flowed continuously, effortlessly, and without being perturbed in the least.

CHAPTER 66

For the second time, I was summoned to Haskell Montgomery's office. When I arrived, both Deputy Karl Kockritz and Detective Homer Brackett were present and seated. A third chair had been added to the space.

"Come in, Hoyt. Take a seat," Haskell said, pointing to the vacant chair.

"Looks like a serious gathering, gentlemen. What's the agenda?"

"Just trying to wrap up a few loose ends. We thought you were entitled to a progress report," Haskell continued.

"We've decided not to arrest and charge Maurice Rednour in the murder of Herman Weiskopf. We questioned him, in the presence of counsel, several more times. We even asked the commonwealth attorney to set in on one of the sessions. We concluded the only real thing he's guilty of is an extramarital affair, certainly not a prosecutable offense. Admittedly, his timing was bad and his choice of women was unfortunate, if he in fact chose her. More likely Selma targeted him. We investigated his personal situation, and he's telling the truth about his wife.

"We did some independent investigation on Selma Weiskopf, and no doubt she'll be indicted and tried, likely for being an accessory before the fact. Femme fatal is the perfect epithet for Selma Weiskopf. Dangerous woman!" Haskell paused and looked at me for a response.

"I appreciate the update gentlemen, but if you're looking for a response or a reaction from me, I have none. As I said the last time we met on this subject. The decision on Maurice Rednour is up to you."

"Just wanted you to know Hoyt," Guinea offered.

"The second issue is a little more complicated. Deputy Kockritz, you want to offer your information, thoughts, and conclusions on the Edward G. Triplett case?"

Karl turned to face me and began rather hesitantly. "Well, Hoyt, to put it bluntly, your killing of David Howard left more questions than it supplied answers."

I didn't respond.

"No doubt, you saved Deputy Katterjohn's life. But it would have been better if you'd only wounded him. Did you have to kill him?"

I tried, with some difficulty to suppress the resentment rising in my chest. But there was no way to control the redness in my face. I paused for a time, took a deep breath and said, "I'm not Gene Autry or Roy Rogers, Karl! Katterjohn and I weren't in a Hollywood western. None of my Marine Corps training was on how to *wound* a man. We were taught to kill. You don't pull, aim and squeeze the trigger on your weapon with any other thought in mind. At that moment, I didn't give any consideration to how inconvenient the consequence would be for you!"

He dropped his eyes and looked at the floor.

Sensing my ire and resentment, Haskell spoke up. "We're all

satisfied David Howard killed Eddie G. But as Karl indicated, questions remain. Lots of questions. Did he come to the cabin with the sole purpose of killing Eddie? If so, why not bring his own gun? How did he know the 20-gauge was under the front seat of Eddie's car? What was he looking for?

"Why tie Eddie G. to the tree? Was it to scare him, to intimidate him, to leave him to be shamed and embarrassed? Did he kill him accidentally? You said yourself, he fired both barrels. Did he fire the gun accidentally, causing the weapon to kick up and bust his eye? Eddie almost certainly was being blackmailed. Was Howard the one blackmailing Eddie? If not, who was?"

Haskell paused and looked at me again.

I stood, trying to take all three of them into my gaze, "Legitimate questions all, but I can't provide the answers." I turned to Karl. "You guys have an officer in your department with a degree in forensics and criminal justice. To my knowledge, none of the rest of you do. For the life of me, I don't understand why you wouldn't use such a valuable resource. Is it because she's a woman? That's the only obvious conclusion I can draw."

I walked from the room, leaving them to consider what I'd said.

‡

Selma Weiskopf was charged with being an accessory before the fact and indicted.

When she entered the courtroom, the first day of the trial, she looked nothing like the woman I saw getting into the back seat of a car with Pearly Martin at the Bottoms. Her hair was pulled back in a bun. She wore no makeup beyond a light pink lipstick.

The gallery was full, overflowing into the hallway. The judge took his seat. To his right, the court stenographer was poised to record every moment of the proceedings with pencil and paper, in Gregg shorthand. The jury was also seated to the judge's right, on the left side of the courtroom. The witness stand was on his left, facing the jury box at an angle. Down in front at separate tables, were the prosecutor on one side, and the defendant and her legal counsel on the other. Behind them was a wooden barrier with a swinging gate, separating the proceedings from general seating. The bailiff kept an attentive eye on the gallery.

Selma's defense attorney was the newest and youngest member of the town's most prominent law firm, a nephew of the senior partner. The trial rapidly deteriorated into a highly technical battle between the prosecutor and the defense, which lasted several hours. The prosecution suddenly moved that the indictment be quashed. The motion was granted, but Selma was later reindicted on three separate charges: the original one, a charge of murder, and one of conspiracy to commit murder.

Selma was as good an actor as you could imagine, though she was probably coached. On the witness stand, she displayed all the proper facial expressions, voice inflections, and corresponding body language for each emotion the questions were expected to evoke. She wore dark, horn-rimmed glasses. Her dress was straight and drab, extending well beyond her knees. It appeared she had flattened her ample breasts, as her feminine figure was totally obscured. If she'd walked in carrying a Bible, her transformation would have been complete.

Even though young, her attorney had already cultivated many courtroom mannerisms and theatrics. He escorted Selma to the witness stand, moved to her left and faced the jury. Selma had on black lace-up shoes, akin to those commonly worn by old-maid school teachers. No mascara, no eyeliner, and no rouge, aging her by 10 years. Her attorney walked slowly to the jury box, his Florsheim shoes squeaking with each step. He turned and leaned his backside against the rail.

Clyde Gish was cast in the role of star witness for the state, but they played their hand poorly. They made a production of bringing him from prison to the courthouse under heavily armed guards. In the courtroom he appeared bewildered and befuddled; he looked around quizzically. He testified under the muzzles of machine guns, manned by a National Guard detachment.

"We"—here Selma's attorney tilted his head slightly toward the jury indicating inclusion—"can only imagine how difficult this is, Mrs. Weiskopf, but please do the best you can. Tell the jury about your experience with and attitude toward Clyde Gish."

Selma was brilliant! Her lips trembled and her chin quivered, as she told how menacing he'd been and how she had feared for her husband's life because of his frequent presence in their home. She pressed her elbows into her sides, making her seem small and frail. When she was questioned about the $25,000 life insurance policy, her eyes grew wide, and she made a slow, disbelieving shake of her head. "He did that without my knowledge," she said.

The prosecutor launched a blistering attack on her character, accusing her of entering into a love triangle with Clyde Gish and plotting with him to kill her husband for the insurance proceeds. When the defense cross-examined her, he ignored all the plaintiff's accusations and asked her to relay her feelings when she realized her husband had been murdered.

"We were blissfully happy, and now my world has come to an end," she said in an emotion-choked voice. She clutched a handkerchief in her fist and pressed it to her mouth, her chest hitching as she stifled a sob. Her attorney led her in her story of Gish forcing his attentions on her and how, even though she'd been deathly afraid, she'd tried to resist. She whimpered, alternating between staring intensely at Clyde, as if unable to look away, and recoiling, as if unable to bare his sight. She went through bouts of uncontrollable shivering and trembling. The defense centered its case on the plea that she had protected her husband against Gish even though she was mortally afraid of him.

Clyde's comments and testimony reflected extreme dislike for the defendant. His voice rose at times to a shout. At one time he pointed his finger at Selma and shouted, "She oughta get the same as I got!" His limited emotional range vacillated on a narrow spectrum, from angry to merely loud—no match for Selma's. The fact that he was brought in wearing leg-irons and chains made it difficult for the prosecution to garner any goodwill from the jury members toward their star witness.

Both sides made their final arguments and the judge instructed the jury, which deliberated only six hours before returning a not guilty verdict.

The courtroom erupted in a demonstration said to have never before occurred in a Kentucky courtroom. Jurors wept openly as they leaped to their feet and shook hands with Mrs. Weiskopf. Six months later, Selma married the young attorney who had defended her. Clyde Gish was returned to Eddyville prison. He was released on a governor's pardon, after serving 14 years of a life sentence.

CHAPTER 67

Matt Musgrave was never successful in effecting an intervention for Bob Craig. Through Sally's friend Ginny, I learned that he continued to drink heavily and browbeat Sally when the mood struck him. Sally became withdrawn and reclusive, leaving home only to go to work and church. I didn't see her for weeks at a time, and for a while that worked well for me. She was not mine. I wasn't responsible for her. I didn't want to think about her. It was best if I didn't see her. With my job and involvement in the HGGL, I stayed busy and focused.

Then I had the dream!

Sally and I were together again. It was like we were in high school with all the same warm, wonderful, loving feelings for each other—only this time, we were adults, and it was mature, richer, and real. There were brief interwoven snippets and vignettes, gauzy and laced with feeling and emotion, rather than action and dialogue. The settings were vague, changing, and unclear, insignificant to our being together. When others were present, they were peripheral, but loving and supportive—happy for us, enriched by being in our presence.

As with many dreams, there was no real sense of time. There was no feeling of past or present, no particular starting point. The dream felt infinite. We weren't moving toward any particular goal or through any circumstances or conflict. There was the awareness of mutual love, equal in depth and commitment, deeper than anything I'd felt before. It was everything I wanted, all I'd *ever* wanted.

Long before I was fully awake, I became aware I was in a dream. I struggled to hold on to it, fought to remain asleep, but at the same time, I knew it was fading. That marvelous vision dissolved, leaving me feeling terribly empty and alone. I wanted to go back to sleep, to retrieve it. I didn't want it to end.

I lay awake for a long time, trying to recall every aspect of it. It was like trying to reconstruct a cloud with my hands. Like trying to hold wet tissue paper together. And in time, it became only a feeling of deep longing and emptiness. The dream had awakened an awareness I could no longer ignore.

I arose, determined that I wasn't going to spend the rest of my life without Sally. I was no longer going to be noble and take the high road. I felt my life would have no meaning or purpose without her. Over the next few days, I couldn't focus; I couldn't concentrate. I was at loose ends. I had to find a way to see her, to talk to her, to extract her from her marriage to Bob Craig. How could I facilitate a private meeting in a place where we could be alone, a place where we could talk and plan?

Surely, I would run into her somewhere in town. In the past, I'd seen her more often than I wanted to. Now that when I wanted to, I *never* saw her. I could call her at work, even though that wasn't ideal. She couldn't talk freely there.

A month went by. Two more weeks went by. The feelings imparted by the dream did not fade. Instead, they lingered, filling my every waking moment. Finally, out of desperation, I called for her at the bank.

"May I ask who's calling?" the receptionist inquired.

"Hoyt Cole."

"Hold please."

I held. And I held! I continued to hold, for what seemed like forever! Finally, when I had decided the connection was broken, or worse yet, she didn't want to talk to me, just as I was about the hang up, she came on the line.

"I'm sorry, Hoyt. I was with a customer—I couldn't get away."

"I need to talk with you, Sally. Is there a time or a place where we can meet?"

There was the longest pause.

"You want to talk with me?"

"Yes, Sally! Yes!"

"Oh! I don't know, Hoyt. I . . . I just don't know. I need to think. Can I call you back?"

"Yes, call me at work or at my hotel. Leave a message if I can't answer."

"Bye," she said. The line went dead before I could respond.

Well. That was a less than enthusiastic response. Realistically however, what kind of response should I have expected? Had I expected her to be ebullient . . . giddy even? *You started the ball rolling, Cole. All you can do now is wait.*

Fortunately, I didn't have to wait long. She called me at work the next morning, as soon as the bank opened. "My birthday is tomorrow. Ginny's taking me to dinner at Fuzhen's Steak House in Evansville. She's gonna be over there shopping. I'm supposed to meet her at 5:30. Can you meet me there at 4:30 in the lounge? We can talk there."

"Yes! See you there. Thanks, Sally."

I hurried to Bohn's Ladies' Wear on Main Street and bought a $50 gift certificate for her birthday.

Fuzhen's was a very upscale restaurant on S. E. Fourth Street. While it was a steak house, it was famous for its Cantonese cuisine. It was the first place in the tristate you could order Chinese food. I walked through the doors at exactly 4:30. The place reeked of class: the patrons were in fine attire, men in business suits and ladies in dresses, jewelry, hose, and heels. The bar area consisted of several intimate spaces for two to four, some with sliding rice-paper partitions allowing for private conversation, as if you were the only ones in the entire place. Each table had upholstered chairs and linen tablecloths and napkins. The lighting was indirect and subdued.

I looked around for Sally, but she was nowhere to be seen. I moved past the bar and walked up to the hostess stand, peering into the restaurant. People were seated with scarlet menus the size of a spread newspaper open in front of them. Still no Sally! I began to feel foolish. Was she late? Had she decided not to come? I looked at my watch; perhaps I was early.

I felt the slightest tug on my forearm. "Hoyt," she said quietly. "I'm back over here." She took my hand and led me back into the bar, into a private space. I hadn't seen it on my initial scan of the area. Perfect!

I joined her in the space, and a waitress immediately appeared to take our order. Sally ordered water and I ordered a bourbon highball. I reached into my inside jacket pocket and handed her the gift card. "Happy birthday, Sally!"

"You shouldn't have, but I'm not at all surprised you did. Thank you, Hoyt." She reached across the table, patted my hand, and smiled.

Sally was nervous, uncertain—frightened even. We made

awkward small talk until the waitress delivered our drinks. Not wanting to appear rushed, but not wanting to waste the mere 60 minutes I had before Ginny arrived, I began. No coy back-and-forth. No subtle lead in. "Divorce Bob and marry me, Sally! I'll help you do it. I love you. I want you to be my wife."

Her eyes grew wide and her mouth fell open. She leaned forward and almost whispered, "Oh, my God, Hoyt. Is that what you wanted to talk with me about? I had no idea!" She looked around cautiously, as if her very thoughts might reveal my suggestion to everyone in the place. "You've caught me completely off guard!" I don't think she could have been more shocked if I'd dropped to one knee and presented a diamond engagement ring.

She opened her purse and nervously retrieved her compact. She examined her face in the mirror and self-consciously ran the powder puff over her cheeks, forehead, and chin. Buying time, she made a small production of closing it and replacing it carefully in her purse.

"Why are you surprised? You've always known that I love you. I never stopped loving you. You don't have to stay with someone who hurts you!"

"If it were only that easy, Hoyt!" She clasped her hands tightly, pressing them down in her lap.

"It *is* that easy! Just do it! I want you to *do it*!" I'd taken on a persona I didn't recognize. Was I pleading? Begging?

"You don't know how many times I have regretted marrying Bob Craig instead of you. You are, and always will be, everything you were when we were in high school." She reached across the table and took my hand in hers. "I love you too, Hoyt, and I always will. You will forever be my only true love."

"Then it's settled. Get a divorce. I'll pay for it."

"You've presented me with a very appealing option. One I'd love to choose."

"Then choose it!"

She twisted her wedding ring and fingered her necklace. She rocked in her seat, transferring her weight from one hip to the other, tugging her skirt toward her knees. Then she looked deeply into my eyes, holding my gaze as if trying to convey emotions her words couldn't express. Her eyes welled with tears that overflowed and ran down her cheeks. She left them to dry on her face, making no attempt to wipe them.

"You know Bob and I are both Catholic. In our church, marriage is a covenant, a sacrament, like holy communion and baptism. Inviolate! Divorce is not an option for me."

"Then get an annulment. You don't have any children. Have the marriage annulled."

"Hoyt, in a sacramental marriage, annulment is not an option either."

"We love each other, Sally. We should be together. Man and wife!" I grabbed both her hands in mine, leaned across the small table, and kissed her full on the lips. The table was the only thing preventing us from falling into each other's arms. She held the kiss as long as possible, putting love, warmth, and lust—so much emotion—into it.

Oh God! What are we playing with here? Where is this going to lead?

I was overwhelmed with all sorts of conflicting thoughts, arguments, and justifications. Could I really ask her to go against her religious beliefs and principles? If I coerced her into going against her faith, how long would it be before she became unhappy with me? How long would it be before her husband's abuse robbed her of her innate vibrancy? What if his abuse became physical? What would I do then?

"Oh, damn you, Hoyt Cole! Why have you done this? I never wanted to confront the worst mistake of my life. I deluded myself, one day at a time."

She can't be happy in her marriage. I believe Sally loves me . . . or does she just need me? I know I love her! I need her!

Damn it! What kind of religion demands you remain in a loveless marriage? Does she really know what she wants? I'm not sure she does. Maybe she wants it both ways.

"You coming back here, seeing you from time to time, interacting with you, even briefly, gave me respite from the unhappy elements in my life. Can't we just go on as we have been?"

Perhaps, but I'm satisfied in time, we'd become intimate. We'd become lovers, adding an entirely different dynamic into our relationship. Where would that take us? How long would that last? Do I want her so bad I'd do that? Yes! I want her that bad! I don't know if I can do it. I don't know if I can keep *from doing it.*

"I suppose we could, Sally, but I'm not sure. I don't know how long I can continue to be your emotional life jacket, hanging on a nail in the boathouse until I'm needed. How long before you'd lose respect for me? How long before I'd lose respect for myself?"

She wants me, she turns to me—when things get unbearable. Then after a brief interlude with me, she's able to return to Bob again.

"It's up to you Sally. You have to choose, and it appears to me you've chosen . . . at least for now. I've played all the cards in my hand." I stood to leave.

"Don't do that. Don't leave—please!"

She grabbed my hand and stood with me. She threw both arms around me and pressed her face to my chest. "I love you, Hoyt. You know I do!"

"Yes, I do! Which makes this all the more tragic."

She began to sob audibly into my chest and squeezed me as

hard as she could, oblivious to anyone who might be watching. I reached behind me, unlaced her arms, and bent to kiss her on the forehead. She tilted her head back and kissed me passionately. A kiss full of meaning and longing.

"Don't go, Hoyt," she pleaded. Tears streamed down her face.

"Ginny will be here soon. You need time to compose yourself. I have to go. I love you!"

I left her standing there. I walked out of the restaurant, feeling empty and dreadfully alone. It was more than a routine goodbye. I feared it was my last time to be with her. *Was that our last kiss? What if Bob Craig died . . . or was killed?* Where would I be? How long could I wait?

Back out on the street, it was a warm and sunny early evening. I saw Ginny park in a space across the street. Couples approached the restaurant laughing and talking, holding hands. Their happiness was like a slap in the face, like salt in an open wound.

In defending her position, Sally had left out one critical aspect of marriage. Secularly and civilly, marriage is first and foremost a contract. One of the differences between a contract and a covenant is that the signatories to a contract always have a third party to whom they can appeal. There's always a court lurking in the shadows of every dispute. But parties to a covenant have no recourse for appeal. There's no compensation for the breaking of a covenant, because the covenant wasn't a means to some more useful end. A covenant is an end in itself. If it ends, there is no consolation prize.

If the contract comes first and both parties work toward it, in time it can turn into a covenant. Many Christians and religions start with the assumption that contracts are "worldly" and covenants are "heavenly" and that we should always be wary of the first and aim for the second. That is simplistic and naive, from my perspective. We must recognize that marriage is first and foremost a contract. With both parties working together toward a common goal, they can slowly but surely turn their contract into a covenant. For while contracts can give us security, only covenants can bring us joy and delight in God and our mate.

Starting first and solely with a covenant leaves no escape route when it goes bad. But that's where Sally started, and I knew I had to accept that, like it or not. Starting there gave Bob Craig free rein to violate any commitment he may have originally intended. If I coerced her to my way of thinking and she did divorce Bob, she would grow bitter and resentful, in time. No win in that. I also knew I had to accept the reality of our situation, as painful as it was to acknowledge. The dream must be pushed back into the shadows and allowed to die.

Somehow, that bit of rationale left me feeling as cold and empty as a condemned building waiting for the wrecking ball.

CHAPTER 68

The call came in just as I was preparing to leave work. "Noah Logan?"

I was caught completely off guard. "What? Who *is* this?"

"Don't play games with me! I know who you are."

Day shift employees were straightening their desks, putting personal items in drawers, emptying ashtrays, and turning off their desk lamps.

"There's no one here by that name. You've called the wrong place."

"Quit wasting time. If you and Headley don't want your whole scheme blown completely out of the water, come to the Kain-Tuck Lounge at nine o'clock this evening. We can work this out. Go to the bar and order an Old Fashioned. I'll contact you." The line went dead.

What the hell is going on?

I placed the receiver back on its cradle, sat back down at my desk, and looked to the windows at the front of the news room. Who could possibly know I was Noah Logan? *Only me and Harry Headley know that, and I sure as hell haven't told anyone.* My old doubts and suspicions about my boss resurfaced. *Is he playing both ends against the middle?* I didn't want to believe that. There was too much evidence to the contrary. *He worked with me to get news of the court proceedings out that same afternoon. If he was so inclined, he could have intervened right then.* Was he having pressure applied from outside sources? Perhaps from Grimshaw or Furlong? Have things gotten so desperate they'll resort to anything?

I'd never understood Headley's hesitancy about addressing the lawlessness in the paper. He seemed to *want* to address it. Otherwise, why fashion the subterfuge of Noah Logan? *There must be some compelling reason preventing him from doing so openly in his own paper.* I needed to speak with him, but he'd already left for the day. I placed several calls to his home, but got no answer.

Is there some significance to the name "Noah Logan?" After all, Headley came up with it. Could it be a code name for something?

I walked to the Right Quick Café, went in, and sat down in my usual booth. I ordered the dinner special: two pieces of fried chicken, mashed potatoes and gravy, and green beans. Black coffee. I was so distracted, I hardly tasted it. *I never expected anything like this. Who was the caller? What does he want?*

It was only six when I returned to my hotel room. With the ominous meeting looming over me, time seemed to drag. I showered and changed clothes. Downstairs, I sat in the lobby, and smoked a cigarette. I picked up a magazine and thumbed through it, but I couldn't concentrate. I checked my watch. Only 45 minutes had elapsed. I crossed and uncrossed my legs. I bounced my knee up and down. Unable to sit still, I got up and paced back and forth. Frustrated, I walked outside into the evening air.

With most of the downtown business closed, there was little street traffic and no pedestrian traffic at all. The heat and humidity of the day enveloped me as I walked toward the park on the river.

An elderly street sweeper slowly pushed his big, steel-wheeled, wooden cart up the ramp from the river onto Water Street and headed toward the city garage, his brooms and shovel handles protruding over the back of a cart filled with riverfront detritus. The flood plain smelled of mud and decaying organic matter.

Why the Kain-Tuck Lounge? God knows I had no particular fondness for the place. In addition to the call, it was the site of two previous unpleasant encounters. I'd gotten my head bashed and my ass kicked the first time. The second time I'd challenged Sally's husband and provoked the bouncer. Was there a reason the caller wanted me to go there? *More than a coincidence? Could Bob Craig be behind this charade? Is he planning retaliation?*

I sat on a bench overlooking the river, near the park's western edge. A trail of coal smoke followed a locomotive across the L&N railroad bridge into Indiana, as the sun began its slow daily descent behind the trees on the other side of the river. The smell of soot and ash floated on the evening air.

I ducked reflexively when a car backfired behind me. My mouth was dry and my hands were cold. Since receiving the call, my mind had been churning with questions, speculations, and imagined scenarios. The caller mentioned me *and* Headley. Was Headley under some yet unknown obligation or impediment, preventing him from involving *River City News* until after a certain point? Would exposing Noah Logan now put Headley in danger? Was Headley more deeply involved in the sinister elements here than I knew? *Had he been forced into an uneasy alliance, like my grandfather?*

Perhaps the caller had dropped the Noah Logan name in the ploy most likely to ensure that I'd react as dictated. Could this be directed at me personally? After all, I had alienated more than a few people in the past few weeks and months. Was Furlong's calm, in-control demeanor and professional appearance a carefully crafted stratagem designed to charm and disarm, concealing a more dangerous and sinister personality?

I know Grimshaw's vindictive. He didn't get where he is by being a nice guy.

I sat at the river 'til almost dark. I watched pleasure boaters back their trailers into the river and crank their boats onto transport frames. Finally, I headed back up Second Street toward the Gold Coin. A Greyhound bus was pulling into the station across from Kluckey's, the idling engine spewing pungent exhaust. I watched the passengers climb down from the coach. Two tough-looking guys without luggage emerged, one after the other. Alarms went off in my head. *Was I getting paranoid . . . imagining things . . . reading too much into mundane occurrences?*

I went into the Gold Coin, took the last booth, and sat looking toward the entrance. Strangely, I was the only one there. I nursed a single beer and smoked a few cigarettes, killing time. Only the caller and I knew what I was doing or where I was going. I was alone and on my own. I went to the pay phone and tried Headley one more time—still no answer. *Had they enticed Mr. Headley to a different location? Was he in danger?* The whole thing just didn't feel right. *Suppose I don't go? What would they do then?*

Just past 8:30, I loaded into my truck, behind the hotel. The still of the night was suddenly shattered by a sharp slap and the piercing yelp of a mongrel dog. It raced toward me from around the corner of the building, knocking over a garbage can, tail between its legs, before disappearing into the shadows. I started my truck and headed south down Green Street toward the Kain-Tuck, driving at a speed calculated to put me there a little before nine.

The wind picked up, and the trees cast menacing shadows

against the building's facade. I parked and entered through the front. The dim lighting cast eerie shadows. Employees stood ghost-like at their posts, unmoving, staring blankly into space. The place seemed dead, almost abandoned, reminding me of Hopper's *Nighthawks*. There was less smoke and better visibility than usual: The gambling stations were vacant and most of the slot machines were unoccupied. I walked unimpeded to the bar in the back. Two unremarkable-looking men stood there, motionless in the silent tableau. I walked to an open space, placed one hand on the bar, and waited for the bartender to take my order.

He slowly turned to face me. "What'll it be, pal?"

"Fix me an Old Fashioned."

"What?"

"An Old Fashioned!"

"I don't get many requests for that drink in here. Most *men* just order whiskey. Not sure I know how to make one of them fufu drinks, may have to look it up in the guide."

"Do what you gotta do."

Old Fashioneds are a bit labor intensive. I'd had one before. You have to muddle the sugar and bitters before adding the ice and bourbon. A pharmacist's mortar and pestle work best for the task, but I was satisfied this guy didn't have such. He turned his back, retrieved a book from under the counter, and began flipping through it.

I lost interest in the process and began to look around, trying to guess which of the men in the place had made the call, but I didn't know who or what I was looking for. After a time, the bartender placed the drink on the bar. "Here you go buddy. Let me know if it's not the way you like it."

I took a sip. It was OK—not great, but passable. I nursed it along, waiting. I milked it as long as I could, drinking about half of it over a 10-minute period, but you can only make a short drink last so long. No one approached. I was beginning to think I had been sent on a snipe hunt. When only the dregs of the amber liquid were left, I drank the rest and remained standing at the bar, waiting.

At some point, the man to my left moved closer. "Did you order an Old Fashioned?"

I turned to face him. My movements seemed impeded. His features were blurry; I tried to focus, but couldn't. I rubbed my eyes trying to clear my vision. His image began to break apart into horizontal sections. One section moved to the left; the section above and below that moved to the right, in alternating patterns. My senses were confused. I could smell sounds and hear odors. He began speaking a language I couldn't understand. I felt the floor dropping out from under me, like an elevator that had its cables cut, plummeting down an endless shaft. My last conscious realization was I'd been drugged, chloral hydrate, likely. Slipped a Mickey.

Damn that bartender!

CHAPTER 69

I heard what sounded like someone shaking a large piece of sheet metal the way a housewife shakes a rug. Later on, I realized it was thunder. I had no idea how long I'd been out or where I was. I smelled humus laced with hints of ammonia and phosphorous. I began to feel cold and wet and to shiver. My mouth was dry, and my throat was tight. I couldn't swallow. *Where am I! How did I get here?*

I faded in and out of consciousness and only gradually realized that I was lying face down in mud, soaking wet from rain that had poured on me for what turned out to be most of the night. *How many drinks did I have?* I'd never gotten *that* drunk.

I couldn't move. Was I paralyzed? Had I been in an accident? Who would look for me? No one knew where I was. Hell, I didn't know where I was. I struggled to right myself, but could not. By the time my head began to clear, the sun was just coming up. My hands were bound behind my back, and my legs were tied together.

Two men grabbed me and yanked me to my feet. My legs were so weak, I crumpled to my knees. I smelled manure. A muddy paddock? My vision was beginning to clear when my head was shoved under water. I kicked, strained, and struggled, but to no avail. I was held in the unbreakable grip of two strong men. My mind was still so confused, I didn't know what to do. Full panic set in: Not only was I confused, but I was too weak to resist them. They held me under water so long I didn't think I could hold out any longer. *Oh, my God! I'm going to drown with no idea why.*

Finally, one grabbed me by my hair and yanked my head up out of the water. I was spitting and sputtering, gasping for breath. My hair was plastered to my forehead and water streamed into my eyes and mouth. I couldn't see them. I could only feel their meaty hands on my head and shoulders. I was weak and limp. I was no match for one of them, much less both.

"You've pissed off some very important people, paperboy! You and Headley may have done irreparable damage. He's too prominent to be taken out, but you're dispensable, and he'll get the message! You pay the price!"

I was kneeling in front of a horse trough. Struggling to get my breath, I gasped, "Who are you? Who are you working for?" I was still panting for air when they pushed my head under the water again. I held my breath. My chest burned and I felt as if my lungs would burst. Then I began to let my breath out ever so slowly, hoping and praying they would bring me up before I expelled the last of it. Just when I'd exhausted my air, they jerked my head up and out of the trough.

"Very impressive! That was almost two minutes. We'll have to do it longer next time."

"What do you want? What are you trying to accomplish? What does Noah Logan have to do with this?"

"We don't know Noah Logan from a load of coal. We got no purpose or agenda other than to make you pay. You're gonna wish you'd never returned to Henderson. How many times were you warned to back off? You must be a slow learner. Well, we're here to give you your final exam, and to make sure you don't pass it." With that they shoved my head back under the water.

I realized that the more I struggled, the less oxygen I had to sustain me. I tried to calm myself, to relax and concentrate on controlling my breathing.

I was warned three or four times! Maybe I should have stayed out of it altogether. What have I been trying to prove?

They intended for me to drown. My head and upper body strained against the pressure. Could this really be it? *After all the campaigns in the South Pacific, escaping death daily in real combat, am I going to die face down in a horse trough in remote Henderson County?* My arms and legs began to ache as lactic acid replaced the oxygen in my blood. I was at the end of my endurance and about to surrender to my fate when, miraculously, the grip of the man on my left weakened. Just as I managed to tilt my head in his direction and snatch a breath of air, I heard the report of a shotgun blast. Had to be a 12 gauge. I was struggling to get my feet under me and stand when the man on my right toppled backward, yanking me up and back with him. I fell backward myself, lying flat on my back in the mud and manure, gasping for breath—and heard the second blast.

I looked up directly into the morning sun. I could feel the mud caked on my face. I saw a hawk soar across the cloudless sky and dive for its prey. A shadow passed before my eyes and another face blocked the sun. Was a third assailant going to shove me back in the water? I had never felt so helpless in my life. *Who fired the gun?* Was it the disembodied face blocking the sun? *Death by drowning or shotgun blast.*

Dead is dead!

"Cole! Cole! You OK, Cole?" a trembling voice called to me. I couldn't respond; I was still trying to bring the face into clear focus when I was slapped. "Damn it Cole, it's me, Katterjohn! Gimme a sign, shake your head, nod, blink your eyes. Do something!" She sounded distant, muted.

"Katterjohn?" I rasped.

She stood the 12 gauge against the water trough and pulled a long folding knife from her belt. She cut the cords around my legs. "I'm going to roll you over and cut your hands free."

I was trembling and in shock, too weak to help or resist. Even though I was conscious enough to know what was happening around me, I still wasn't completely clearheaded. With some effort, Katterjohn sat me up against the water trough. Both the assailants were likely dead, but she tied them together and handcuffed one of them to a ring on the trough. She called dispatch to report the incident and request an ambulance to the location.

The broadside of a stable made up one leg of the rectangular pen. A single roan horse's head protruded from one of the stalls. A wooden gate stood open on the side across from the stable, a black four-door car in the opening. The smell of oats, hay, and stable muck floated on the morning air. I saw a barn cat walk stealthily around the corner of the water trough. I heard a rooster crow. A horsefly buzzed my face. Cattle lowed. Traffic passed. The sun shone.

I was alive!

At some point an ambulance arrived. The driver and attendant loaded the bodies of the two men into the back. They handcuffed them together and headed to the hospital. They didn't seem to care if they were alive or dead. When backup arrived, they helped Katterjohn load me into her car. I gave my truck keys to a deputy and asked the driver to drop him off at the Kain-Tuck Lounge, so he could pick up my truck and deliver it to the Kingdon Hotel.

"Leave the keys at the desk."

At the hospital they determined I was suffering from exposure and shock and decided to hold me overnight for observation. During that time, my head began to clear somewhat.

According to Katterjohn's report, when she approached the assailants, she identified herself and instructed them to put both hands in the air. They pulled handguns and fired at her. I didn't hear their shots; my head was underwater. Katterjohn then fired her shotgun at one, jacked another shell into the breech and shot the second man. I had been kidnapped and thrown in a horse lot on 136, near Geneva, and it had rained off and on through the night. My captors had waited in their car for me to wake up.

Later in the week, I asked Katterjohn to join me at the Right Quick Café for supper. I wanted to buy her a meal and hear a complete account of how that evening and morning unfolded.

"I was on midnight to eight, and the call came in a little after one. The caller identified himself as an insect or bug—I don't remember for sure. He said he worked at the Kain-Tuck and when you passed out, two thugs drug you outside."

"Termite, maybe?"

"Yeah, that's it! Termite!"

"When he took out the trash, your truck was still there, but you weren't in it. That's when he made the call. He seemed to know you. He was worried.

"I drove down there to question him. He said he had no idea where they'd taken you. He appeared very apprehensive, scared even. But he had nothing more to offer, so I left and returned to the office.

"About an hour later, Termite went next door to the motel and called again. 'There's a property down state road 136 toward Geneva, where Slade Thornton stables some horses. Maybe check there,' he said."

It was almost 3:30 a.m. by the time Katterjohn checked out a cruiser and headed toward Geneva. Not knowing where she was going and being unfamiliar with the area, she drove back and forth past the location two or three times. Finally, in desperation, she took a dirt lane off the highway, turned off her headlights, and drove toward the back of the property. Lucky for me, she was on the property next to where they held me.

She sat for a long time before catching a glimpse of the flame from a cigarette lighter, almost 200 yards away, on the adjoining property. I was still unconscious, lying in the mud, but she didn't know that. She didn't know whether I was there or not.

"I grabbed my 12 gauge and headed out on foot, beyond the property where I thought they might be holding you, and moved up on the back side of the stable. The moon was full and I could see a car parked at the gate of the corral. All I could do was wait.

"When they started dunking you, I moved forward and announced myself. Both pulled handguns and fired in my direction. Crouching low, I ran forward and shot them both."

Over the ensuing days Katterjohn and Kockritz learned the identity of the two goons. They were professional button men from Cairo, Illinois. No one in the bar knew who they were. While Slade did stable horses at the location where they took me, he only rented the property and disavowed any knowledge of the assault. He claimed he mailed a check twice a year to a post office box. The investigation revealed that the property was held by a corporation in Cairo. The investigation determined that it was a shell corporation with no officers, income, or expenses. As Slade Thornton was less than cooperative about who he leased the lot from and how he knew about it, the matter was dropped.

Termite Hawkins and Deputy Katterjohn saved my life. Obviously, my two attackers were hired by someone in Henderson. Their intent was not to merely scare me off or expose me as Noah Logan. I have no doubt they intended to kill me.

CHAPTER 70

Late that summer, a special election approved the city manager form of government. Sam Chapman and Ed Moore were elected commissioners in the November election. They immediately hired Flem Burlew, a qualified city manager, for an annual salary of $12,000. Mayor Grimshaw and his fiefdom were eliminated.

The hearing to consider the ouster of Sheriff Fletcher Agnew began on Monday, November 19, at 10:00 a.m., in the circuit court room of the Henderson County Courthouse. By law, the sheriff was only required to testify in the presence of the governor, and his attorneys declared that he would not testify in the proceedings. Judge Billy Rakestraw of Paducah was the commissioner hearing the arguments for both sides; his reputation for being honest, fair, and efficient was well-known. At the close of the hearings, Rakestraw was to make a recommendation to the governor that the sheriff be retained in office or impeached.

During a mid-morning recess, I called the office and asked for a typist. I wanted to get everything down as quickly and as accurately as possible without relying on notes or memory more than absolutely necessary.

"Go ahead, Hoyt," she said.

"A real cross section of people testified to the evidence of illegal gambling in Henderson. Reverend Dahlke was called, along with Walter T., his wife, and their friend. The president of the Good Government League also testified."

"Anybody else?"

"Oh yeah, Womack. Max Womack, the reporter from the *Louisville Courier-Journal.* He told of his previous visits to several taverns and nightclubs. He testified that he had personally observed gambling in all the joints he visited."

"What about the sheriff?" she asked.

"Witnesses were steadfast in stating that the sheriff, if not complicit, was certainly well aware of illegal activities. Several witnesses testified to seeing various sheriff's deputies present at the Cosmopolitan Club—and that the sheriff had a designated parking spot there.

"Many witnesses spoke of seeing small children in these establishments. When asked if the children were observed playing the slot machines, one witness replied, 'most of them couldn't reach the machines.'

"Browder's friend testified that in one of the joints, more than a third of the customers were teenagers—likely referring to the Kraver Klub. He also stated that while he saw no bookmakers in the clubs outside the city limits, he did see them at the Gold Coin and Bushrod's Bar, both inside the city."

It took more than two days to hear the testimony of the first group of witnesses, and there were almost 100 more to be called. Halfway through the third day, Judge Rakestraw abruptly ended the hearing, stating that the testimony already presented was sufficient, since conditions had already been well established. While the sheriff had some of the best lawyers in the county representing him, it was obvious he had no defense. At the close of the hearing, Judge Rakestraw said that he would receive briefs from both sides until January 1 and would make his recommendation to the governor by January 15.

In mid-November I got a call from Deputy Kockritz. "Sheriff Agnew has just been rushed to the hospital. They think it's a heart attack."

"Thanks Karl! Let me know the outcome when you know for sure."

Later that day Karl called again. "Massive heart attack. He's in critical condition. Best case, he'll be incapacitated for months. They're not sure he'll recover."

On January 15, almost 30 Henderson County nightclub operators and two corporations pled guilty to gambling charges and were fined a total of $8,650, plus court costs. On the same day, the governor received Judge Rakestraw's preliminary recommendation concerning the ouster of our sheriff. The final decision would have to wait for Sheriff Agnew's personal appearance before the governor, whenever that might be, as he was still in the hospital.

By this time, the FBI was involved. In raids across 17 cities in Kentucky, 3,230 slot machines were seized by federal agents. Over 400 machines were confiscated in Henderson County alone. L. S. Furlong lost more than 100 machines, the largest number impounded in any Kentucky city.

On February 15, the governor extended Sheriff Agnew's deadline until March 1. His doctors were to determine if he would be able to appear before him. A few days later, Sheriff Fletcher Agnew resigned. Deputy Karl Kockritz was appointed to fill out the remainder of Agnew's term, which ended the following November.

In a surprising turn of events favoring the cause of the HGGL, I. W. Napier, chairman of the state Alcoholic Beverage Control Board, had prepared almost 30 gambling citations to be issued against Henderson liquor and beer licensees. Three establishments in the county immediately pled guilty to charges that they had violated state liquor laws. Slade Thornton, owner-operator of the Kain-Tuck Lounge and holder of beer, drink, and package permits, did not contest charges that his place had sold to minors and drunks, permitted loud music, and had dimly lit premises.

The ABC Board began revoking the beer and liquor licenses of the taverns and clubs in town and in the county. They were shut down on various counts, from selling to minors and allowing them to loaf on the premises, to employing women as bartenders. The board eventually cited more than 30 bars, taverns, and nightclubs on gambling charges.

I couldn't help but wonder: *After all the years of illegal gambling and political corruption, and all the previous missteps, fits and starts, it almost seems like things are moving along too smoothly. When's the other shoe going to fall?*

Even though Sheriff Agnew had resigned, on April 1, a reporter for the *Louisville Courier-Journal* leaked Judge Rakestraw's recommendation to the governor. After giving the background on the ouster hearing, the writer printed Rakestraw's full report, which recounted the deplorable conditions in Henderson County and declared that law enforcement had been completely nonexistent for years. The report summarized the unanimous testimony of "a representative cross section of Henderson residents," who had all testified that gambling had been conducted openly on a large scale, with little or no effort to suppress it by local law enforcement. The report recalled that prior efforts to rein in illegal gambling had resulted in not a single indictment from successive grand juries.

Rakestraw's report concluded that removal of a duly elected official was a serious matter, but neglect of duty, especially by a peace officer, was even more serious, and that conditions in Henderson were inviting to gangsters who might want to capitalize on the local scene. "When the chief law-enforcement officer of the county fails or refuses to perform his duties, the general public is all but helpless," the report said. Rakestraw recommended that the sheriff of Henderson County be removed from office.

The following November, the president of the Good Government League, Haywood Goodacre, was elected sheriff. Every candidate the HGGL supported won their respective office.

‡

To my surprise, and independent of my Noah Logan articles, Max Womack of the *Courier-Journal* wrote a lengthy spread outlining the tension in Henderson surrounding the ouster hearing and the ABC Board hearings. He reported on the growth and effectiveness of the Henderson Good Government League, and on the threats, arson, and other violence directed at some of its members—all in all, a comprehensive and in-depth account of local developments.

At almost the same time, the *Evansville Press* published a similar piece, terminating with: "the lights along the strip are beginning to dim."

I was beginning to think the tide just might be turning.

At the courthouse on a research chore, I ran into Commonwealth

Attorney Norsworthy. "Looks like things are going along pretty good, don't you think?"

"I don't know, Hoyt, many of the ABC Board liquor license revocations and suspensions were based on the assumption that gambling in and of itself was disorderly conduct. The state attorney general, in a blatantly political move, has issued a ruling that the ABC Board had no legal right to suspend or revoke the liquor license of an establishment because gambling was the *only* offense."

"Isn't that the basis for the actions of the ABC Board chairman?" I asked.

"Yes. We'll have to wait and see what happens."

The resultant ambiguity threw the progress into disarray and uncertainty. Once again, it appeared that gambling interests had found a loophole that would allow them to continue operating in Henderson County. *How many setbacks are going to be hurled in the path of this endeavor?* I wondered if ours was an insurmountable task. So much work had been done, so many people working toward a common cause. Could it all be undone by another corrupt and vindictive politician?

But in November, a new attorney general was elected. He won on the promise of reform and pledged support for a change in the statute regarding gambling and disorderly conduct. The governor supported it, and the HGGL was confident the new General Assembly would vote to approve the change.

After passage in the House on February 7, the state senate "without debate or dissent" passed the bill 29–0, making gambling on the premises a direct cause for revoking and/or suspending alcohol licenses. The governor signed it immediately. We all breathed a giant sigh of relief: gambling in Henderson County had been effectively outlawed.

Seemingly overnight, all the gambling, prostitution, violence, corruption, and lawlessness came to an abrupt end—not through violent confrontation or in a hail of gunfire, but legally and peacefully, without notice or fanfare. There were no parades, no marching bands, or public celebrations. Henderson transitioned from being "Little Chicago" one day, to a sleepy little Kentucky river town the next—peaceful, quiet, and respectable.

EPILOGUE

At the end of Chapman and Moore's two-year term, a new mayor and four new commissioners were elected. All were handpicked by the Henderson County Good Government League. Chapman and Moore went back to their respective business pursuits, never again to participate in local politics.

By the end of 1952, every one of the 38 gambling and vice enterprises had closed. To this day, not one of them has attempted to reopen.

Having satisfied his sole purpose of bringing down L. S. Furlong, Walter T. faded into anonymity. He continued to operate his one-man garage until his death in 1973.

Rev. David Dahlke left Henderson in 1953 to accept an appointment to serve the Christian Church in Richmond, and later Covington. Following those pastorates, he became a regent at Lexington's College of the Bible. He retired to Buford, North Carolina, where he died peacefully in 1979.

The Henderson County Sheriff's Department finally put Deputy Billie Jean Katterjohn in charge of solving the murder of Edward Glenn Triplett. Almost immediately, she discovered five blackmail notes in a folder in Triplett's desk drawer. Eddie's uncle told Katterjohn that he'd recently purchase a johnboat for fishing and tied a new length of rope to the tree to secure his boat when he was at the cabin, eliminating one mystery. David Howard's reasons for looking through Eddie's car remain unknown. Likely, Howard only meant to threaten and terrorize him with the gun he discovered under the seat, as it appeared that he had no prior experience with firearms. The hand-lettered "suicide" note found over Eddie's visor was determined to be forged, likely by Howard, based on samples of his handwriting. Katterjohn speculated that after Howard killed Triplett, he wrote the note to mislead investigators. The blackmailer was never identified.

In 1956, the Internal Revenue Service charged Furlong with owing more than half a million dollars in back taxes for the years 1944–46. Furlong settled the charges by paying a little over $125,000. Furlong padlocked the Cosmopolitan Club, and it remained a silent testament to a bygone era. The building remained padlocked for nearly 30 years. An entire generation of Henderson residents was born and came of age, driving by the abandoned structure, with only a vague notion of its notorious past. The property was briefly a car dealership, a bowling alley, and a youth recreation center before finally becoming a bingo parlor in 1983—a rather ignoble end to a once-elegant, yet infamous facility. The old Cosmopolitan Club went up in flames on January 7, 1990, when the furnace malfunctioned in the middle of the night.

After closing the Cosmo, Furlong managed and operated his 3,500 acres of farmland and oversaw oil production on land he owned or leased in Henderson County and southern Indiana. He went on to cofound Evansville's Petroleum Club, an upscale supper club catering to those in the oil business and other prominent business and professional men. Lloyd Stanley Furlong died of liver disease in July of 1981. He was 82 years old.

Harry Headley died of throat cancer in 1953. His daughter took over the ownership, publishing, and editing of the *River City News.* I never received a satisfactory explanation regarding why the paper was so timid in reporting on and condemning the gambling and corruption during Henderson's Little Chicago era.

Forest Grimshaw's wife died the same year he was voted out of office. He lived the remainder of his life in virtual obscurity, rarely seen in public. In March of 1956, his tobacco warehouse was set ablaze, bringing the last vestige of Henderson's tobacco economy to an end in one of the largest fires in county history. Grimshaw died of a self-inflicted gunshot wound to the head in 1959. It was five days before his body was discovered by his daughter, after she was unable to reach him by phone.

No one knows what became of Everett Lightfoot. One Friday evening in 1953, after closing his work space, he loaded a few possessions into his car, locked his house, and disappeared into the night. His household furnishings and remaining clothes were left behind. Likewise, the tools and equipment in his garage remained as he had last used them.

Leon Remington also faded from sight, but it was believed that he made a comfortable living building and repairing guitars for musicians, in Nashville.

Tom's Grocery, Inc. sold to a larger regional chain in 1959. In an era before company benefits and pensions, G. L. Butler remained an employee of the family. He was provided a company car and a monthly stipend until his death in 1968.

The Kingdon Hotel, built in 1891, fell into disrepair and was demolished in March of 1973. The Soaper Hotel still stands, empty for the most part, but for a few businesses on the ground floor.

Sally Morgan Craig died of ovarian cancer in 1965. She was 42 years old. Three months after Sally died, Robert B. Craig married the surgical nurse from Evansville he'd conducted an affair with for more than three years. I attended Sally's funeral and return annually to visit her grave on the anniversary of her death.

I took a job with the Bingham family in Louisville, on the *Courier-Journal*. In 1960, I was nominated for a Pulitzer Prize for my reporting on political corruption at the state level. I completed my career as a political columnist and feature writer. I never married.

‡

The murder of Otis Earl "Pearly" Martin was never solved. Leon Remington and Everett Lightfoot possessed the size and strength necessary to deliver the beating that killed Pearly, but Leon eliminated himself from scrutiny by passing the lie-detector test that he himself insisted on taking. Everett Lightfoot was never even suspected. The local consensus was that if there was ever a man who needed killing, it was Otis Martin. In reality, there were too many with strong motives to narrow a list of suspects down at all. Maybe several men acted in concert or hired outsiders to kill Pearly. Maybe it was best for all that his murder was left unsolved.

The Ohio River flows unimpeded, unperturbed and unaffected by the human events playing out along her banks. Henderson has grown to a host a population a little over 25,000 since attracting a couple of national corporations. A few homegrown companies have also thrived here. Henderson remains a peaceful, somewhat provincial, river town, full of warm and friendly people.

My hometown.

ACKNOWLEDGMENTS

I owe a debt of gratitude to local author Marianne Walker and to her husband Ulvester: to Marianne for her review, support, and encouragement, and to Ulvester—whose father was a nightclub owner/operator during the era of the novel—for his perspective, historical recollection, and wealth of photographs, all of which he willingly shared.

Kentucky Justice Bill Cunningham of Princeton, KY, also offered encouragement during this endeavor. His work *On Bended Knee* was an indispensable resource for background and historical perspective on the Black Patch Tobacco Wars.

Another important resource was the late Rev. Charles Dietze's out-of-print book, *The Henderson Crusade.* I relied heavily on its contents, particularly for material relating to the court proceedings as the cleanup came to fruition. His son Bill granted permission to use his father's book.

The Henderson Public Library's archive department provided critical historical perspective and support.

Thanks also to Frank Boyett, David Dixon, and the *Henderson Gleaner* for the historical and nostalgic articles on the era, which provided valuable information and insight. Chuck Stinnett, retired reporter for the *Henderson Gleaner,* offered his insight, perspective, and encouragement.

I consulted Rachel Alexander's honors thesis, "Little Chicago: The Secret History of Henderson, Kentucky," submitted to Eastern Kentucky University, Spring 2005.

I'd be remiss if I didn't acknowledge my high school classmate Jerry Rhoads, a retired attorney and Kentucky state senator. Jerry's father was politically active during the era, and Jerry shared his remembrances and offered encouragement.

In addition, I want to recognize my own personal wordsmith and friend, Johnny Maglinger, who played no active role in this endeavor, but whose love of words, daily writing discipline, and enigmatic perspective on life provided me with an inspiring example.

Finally, I owe a tremendous debt of gratitude to my editor, Dianne Bellis, senior editor for Butler Books of Louisville, KY. Her knowledge, experience, insight, and professionalism guided me through the arduous process of bringing this book to completion.